AIRLIFT

AIRLIFT

STEVE EASTWOOD

Copyright © 2020 Steve Eastwood

The moral right of the author has been asserted.

Apart from any fair dealing for the purposes of research or private study, or criticism or review, as permitted under the Copyright, Designs and Patents Act 1988, this publication may only be reproduced, stored or transmitted, in any form or by any means, with the prior permission in writing of the publishers, or in the case of reprographic reproduction in accordance with the terms of licences issued by the Copyright Licensing Agency. Enquiries concerning reproduction outside those terms should be sent to the publishers.

Matador
9 Priory Business Park,
Wistow Road, Kibworth Beauchamp,
Leicestershire. LE8 0RX
Tel: 0116 279 2299
Email: books@troubador.co.uk
Web: www.troubador.co.uk/matador
Twitter: @matadorbooks

ISBN 978 1838592 400

British Library Cataloguing in Publication Data.
A catalogue record for this book is available from the British Library.

Printed and bound in Great Britain by 4edge Limited
Typeset in 11pt Adobe Garamond Pro by Troubador Publishing Ltd,
Leicester, UK

Matador is an imprint of Troubador Publishing Ltd

1

Berlin

Saturday 7 May 1949

Konrad was woken by the sound of trams outside his bedroom window. He'd had barely a few hours' sleep, having got to bed around 7am after working through the night. It was always the same with night work. He could get off to sleep straight away but it only took some clown to sound his car horn outside in the street and he would be awake for the rest of the day. The alarm clock told him that he'd been reasonably lucky on this occasion as it was now 4.30pm. Konrad was a handsome devil. He was thirty-three years old, he stood six feet two inches in his stockinged feet and at 200lbs he was, in boxing parlance, what one might call a heavyweight with a powerful build. A shock of greased-back blonde hair completed the picture.

Konrad believed that, as far as looks were concerned, he was -"God's gift to women-", but he lacked confidence. As a late developer Konrad had suffered more than his fair share of rejection and this had made him bitter. He had always set his sights too high, aiming to impress and conquer the most attractive girls, but he simply could not sustain the necessary charm and influence and so he fell prey to mockery. Thereafter an element of spite and punishment began to form a part of his psyche and his attitude towards sexual relations with the opposite sex. He finally discovered that women who were less attractive were more likely to submit to his desires. He enjoyed sex with them and the rougher the better. Konrad even found that some were turned on by hard physical treatment and extreme pain. Not all of them responded in that way unfortunately, but he would find their threshold and he would often exceed it. He would, in many cases, leave them devastated. It really was too bad when that happened. But he got over it.

Konrad was due at work for another tour at 11pm. But he stayed in bed for a while longer before showering and shaving. He laid out his clothes for his next shift and then left the building to go out onto Potsdamer Strasse. Catching the eye of barmaids-, Silke and Ute-, as he entered the Gasthof Zehn, he acknowledged them by giving a cheery wave and then took a seat at his regular table. He ordered omelette and poms frits and he was not disappointed. The girls ensured that Konrad received the very best of service. He turned down the stein of beer that was offered to him as he knew that he would later be required to keep a clear head to do his work.

Although they were very flirtatious, he had no intention of trying to snare one of the barmaids, since they wouldn't finish their shift until gone midnight and he needed somebody to satisfy him earlier. Anyway, he didn't want a relationship, and he didn't want to get involved with them. They were too close, and they might learn too much about him. No, he wanted to find someone anonymously.

The sudden discovery of some sexual fascination from a new target. That was exactly what he needed. A predatory conquest. No compromise. He was, after all, an animal. An animal with a strong merciless instinct. He just wanted to take possession of a woman whom he could use in every way possible. Total power. Punishment. He was a man and all-powerful.

One day he would deal with the bitches in his past who had treated him with so much disrespect and disdain. He would make them pay.

Konrad, after eating well, left the Gasthof and continued along Potsdamer Strasse, making his way slowly towards the Tiergarten. This was Berlin's inner-city park which was 210 hectares in size and among the largest of urban gardens in Germany. It had dense shrubbery and was the ideal theatre for fulfilling his needs.

It was now 7pm. He stopped off at a café, found a table overlooking the Tiergarten and drank a few glasses of Coca-Cola. Konrad waited until dusk before he made his move. He left the café, and crossed the main road into the wooded area to get the lie of the land and a closer look at any prey that was on offer.

He saw three young women who were busy strutting their stuff along Tiergarten Strasse. They were openly displaying their breasts to the drivers of cars that were passing. Two of them soon attracted punters and they each moved off in a car to conduct their business. This left one girl. Fortunately for Konrad this girl was the one he had set his sights on. He casually walked across the road and he observed the dance that unfolded before him. She writhed and massaged her breasts, enticing him, as he moved towards the object of his desire. She was barely twenty-two years old. Tall for a woman, she had shoulder-length blonde hair with long legs and an ample bosom. Although, clearly rough trade, she had classic good looks with high cheek bones. She wore flat shoes and a skirt that rode just above the knee. She was gorgeous.

Konrad found himself wondering why this beautiful young woman was offering herself for sex. Surely, if she cleaned herself up, she could do better in life, marry well, maybe, with the right sponsor, even secure a glamorous job as a fashion model or dancer. Konrad was transfixed by her beauty and he moved rapidly towards her, lest someone else get to her first. She acknowledged him with a mercenary stare and a forced smile.

There were no niceties, no introduction.

'Hi baby. Wollen wir mit machen?'(Shall we play?) she said.

'Was meinst du?'(What do you mean?)

'Wollen wir ficken?'(Shall we fuck?)

'Ja. Konnen wir,'(Yes, we can,) said Konrad. 'Was kostet das?' (What will it cost?)

'Zehn mark.'(Ten marks.)

'Nein, zu teuer.'(No, too expensive.)

'Oder, vierzig zigaretten.'(Or forty cigarettes.)

'Ja. Aber wo?'(Yes. But where?)

'Kommen Sie mit.'(Come with me.)Konrad felt in his pockets and produced two packets of twenty Lucky Strike cigarettes which he handed to the girl. She took his hand and led him into the darkness of the wood. She took him to a clearing where there was a nest of grass and it was obvious to him that she had used this spot before. She immediately laid on her back, opened her legs and exposed herself to him.

Even in the darkness he could see that she had no knickers but he was not surprised. Clearly, in her line of business, they were an unnecessary encumbrance.

'Kommen Sie hier baby.'

Konrad, having taken out a condom, lowered his trousers and lay down on top of her. He entered her and started pumping away. This went on for ten minutes or so. It wasn't love making. As far as she was concerned, it was supposed to be just a business transaction and the girl was starting to lose patience with him. She was used to a quick in and out. It was going on for far too long and she had other customers to service. After all, this wasn't love. It was robotic sex. She needed the business and this man was taking up far too much of her time and attention.

'Beeilen sie sich.'(Hurry up.)

He didn't answer her and just kept ploughing away. Losing patience, she tried to wriggle her body out from underneath him. But Konrad was having none of it. He was determined to continue to his own satisfaction and tried to keep her pinned down, but she wriggled even more. He suddenly felt cheated and in order to keep control he moved his hands to her throat and squeezed. He became filled with anger and went into something of trance as he maintained his grip until he could feel that, after a time, the life had left her body.

Konrad paused for a few seconds and then turned his attention to her breasts. He ripped open her blouse. She was without a bra and this gave him easier access to her prominent nipples. He opened his mouth and covered her left areola clamping his teeth around her soft flesh. He bit down hard and as his upper and lower teeth came together her flesh became detached in his mouth. He chewed and swallowed the woman's flesh. He had inflicted his punishment and he felt the power surge through him. *Yes. Another bitch dealt with.*

After relishing the experience for a few minutes Konrad came to his senses and reminded himself that he was vulnerable to discovery. Glancing around the immediate vicinity he satisfied himself that he was alone and unobserved. He got to his feet and stared down at the woman who was lying semi-naked on the ground. She had her back arched, head tilted back and her tongue was protruding from one corner of her mouth. She looked, for all the world, as though she was playing the fool.

After straightening his clothing, he walked casually away through the Tiergarten, emerging on the far side of the park. He was calm and measured in his movement away from the scene, using the trees and bushes as cover to minimise his exposure to the few passers-by who were prepared to venture through the gardens after dark. Skills that he had learned and employed during the war.

It took Konrad just under an hour to get back to his apartment block, having skirted his way through the various adjacent streets. This left him just enough time to change clothes and get off to work. Later, as he sat on the bus bound for Templehof, he began reliving this latest conquest in his mind. He lit up a Lucky Strike and inhaled the smoke with a smile of pleasure breaking across his face.

A young blonde woman, who was sitting a few rows in front of him, caught his eye. She saw him staring and turned away in embarrassment. He sat and considered her.

The taste of his victim's feminine flesh came back to him, he savoured the memory and there was a stirring in his loins. He wondered about his fellow passenger. *She certainly fits the bill. Maybe, she's one for the future.*

Konrad told himself to be patient, as he had seen her before on the bus and he was confident that, when the time was right, he would be able to bend her to his will. Besides, there were plenty of available women in Berlin and he knew from experience that although they came in all shapes and sizes, by and large, they all tasted the same.

2

Berlin

Sunday 8 May 1949

Klaus Walter was the senior detective on duty covering the night shift for the Central Berlin Police District. It had been a busy night and the cells at the police station were almost full to capacity with the usual drunken dross arrested for fighting in the streets and bars. It always amazed him that even though most people had very little money and lived a "hand to mouth" existence, some were still able to find the wherewithal to drink themselves into oblivion. Fortunately, none of the night's incidents amounted to anything serious and minor offences were the province of the uniform patrol officers.

In the absence of anything substantial Walter had settled into some long overdue paperwork. He had been deep in concentration, but was nodding off, when the telephone rang, which caused him to almost leap out of his seat. He grabbed at the handset. 'Walter.'

'Control room here, Herr Hauptkommissar. We have a report of a murder in the Tiergarten. Are you free to attend?'

'Yes. Is there anyone at the scene yet?'

'Gerhard Siegler is there. He requests your attendance.'

'Do you know anything about the victim?'

'Not much sir. It's the body of a young woman and it sounds like one of the local tarts, judging by the description of the way she's dressed.'

'What's so different with this one? Prostitutes are always being murdered. Siegler can deal with it, can't he?'

'I can't help you there, sir. I'm only the messenger.'

'OK. You had better give me the exact location then.'

The control officer complied and having taken down the details, Walter replaced the receiver. *Scheisse! (Shit)*, thought Walter. *That's all I need. Just as I was getting somewhere with the pile of paper on my desk'*

'Jochen!' shouted Walter.

'Yes, Herr Hauptkommissar?' shouted a disembodied voice in reply.

'Bring the car around to the front, will you? We've got another murder to go to in the Tiergarten.'

'Zum befehl!' (As per your order!)

Klaus Walter was a hard-bitten and cynical individual who, having already had experience as a police officer, had been drafted as a reluctant member of the Feldgendarmerie (Military Police) during the war. He had served in Crete and, in the final days of the conflict, he'd found himself back in Berlin, as the Allied forces closed in for the kill. Walter, a Berliner, fearing the arrival of the Russians, had managed to arrange for his parents and sister Kristel to escape to Luneburg, in the British-occupied territory, where, he believed, they would be treated more humanely.

At the war's end many Feldgendarmerie, particularly those who had not fallen into Soviet hands, found themselves assigned to police roles by the Western Allies. As for Walter, he surrendered to the British and after a short period of internment and "Re-education," he was able to join the civilian police force that had been established to help restore some semblance of normality.

Walter searched out his murder bag from the cupboard and made his way to the front door of the station. Inside fifteen minutes he and Jochen were approaching the park. They had no trouble locating the scene, as they were drawn to a group of police vehicles with their blue lights flashing. The way that they had parked the vehicles reminded Walter of a wagon train encirclement, within which stood a redundant ambulance. By now, dawn had broken, but they could still barely see beyond the kerbside shrubbery.

Walter left his vehicle and spoke to a uniformed officer who was holding a clipboard and appeared to be directing operations. The officer immediately recognised him and, although the detective was not in uniform, gave him a perfunctory salute.

'Good morning, Herr Walter. This is a bad one. It's a young woman.'

'Is it? We certainly don't need another one, Karl. We've enough on as it is, and we're short of staff. Is Siegler with the body?'

'Yes, sir.'

'Where is it?'

'The body is about thirty metres into the wood, in that direction.'

The officer indicated the direction that Walter should take, and he saw that there was an avenue of tape indicating a path into the woods. After Walter had cautiously taken a few paces along the path, he called out, 'Gerhard. Where are you?'

'Keep coming, boss. I'm over here.'

Walter continued along the taped walkway, towards the sound of the voice. After fifty metres or so he came to a clearing where he saw Gerhard Siegler and a young ambulance man standing over the body.

'Who found her?'

'An elderly gentleman, boss, who was out walking his dog. He's very traumatised so I got a couple of the men to take him home.'

'Did he see anyone or hear anything?'

'No, he didn't. At least that's what he told me. I have verified his details though. So, we can speak to him again. We got a written statement from him.'

Walter had to ask the inevitable question of the ambulanceman; 'I don't mean to be crass, but are you absolutely sure that she's dead?'

'Yes, sir. I gave her a thorough examination. It looks like she's been strangled by some one using their bare hands, and one other thing which is very unusual, or at least I haven't seen the like of it before; It looks like she's had her left nipple bitten off.'

He indicated the woman's breast. Walter had to lean across the victim to gain a view as she was lying on her left side with her back to him, in a contorted position.

'Yes. I see what you mean. Well, sadly, in my experience, it's not that unusual,' replied the detective.

'Really?'

'Yes really. You're too young to remember, probably, but you should have seen what some of the Russian troops did to our girls when they arrived here at the end of the war.

Bloody animals.' Walter continued, 'Gerhard, we need to get a doctor here to absolutely confirm the death and, when it gets lighter, we'll examine the scene for evidence, which, of course, will include the search for a missing nipple.' Gerhard returned to his vehicle and grabbed the radio handset. He made the necessary call to the force control room. After a wait of some forty minutes the doctor arrived on the scene to examine the body. He quickly confirmed that the young woman was deceased, concurring with the ambulanceman's hypothesis of the cause of death.

Later that morning, and in the light of day, a physical search was made of the scene. It was established that the victim had no purse or any means of identification on her person. Other than an unopened packet of Lucky Strike cigarettes, there was nothing of any significance found at the scene. Not even as much as a nipple. The body was removed to the mortuary.

❖

The apartment was silent, and Inge Bohm was lying in bed awaiting her usual early morning coffee. It was a daily ritual for her daughter Julia to wake her with a coffee around 8am and Inge could usually set her watch by her. Inge was bedridden, and she relied on Julia for food, care and attention to her general needs. But where was she?

This was not like Julia at all. She was a good girl and fastidious as far as her mother's care was concerned. As far as Inge knew, Julia was working lunchtime and evening shifts in a city centre restaurant, but she would always be at home during the morning time.

They had arranged for evening care to be provided by Magda, a good friend who lived across the hall in their apartment block. She had been given her own key to their front door.

It was now 10.35am and Inge had been repeatedly calling out for Julia, but to no avail. She felt completely alone and afraid, both for herself and her daughter. Inge realised that she had two options. She could either; wait it out, or fall from her bed and crawl to the front door, from where she might be able to shout and alert a neighbour.

Inge loosened her bedclothes and slid down onto the floor. She managed to raise herself to her elbows and slowly she began dragging her body across the bedroom. Inge was in her late sixties and she hadn't taken exercise for some time, so to drag herself along required a monumental effort.

She finally reached the front door of the apartment and tried to raise herself up in an effort to reach the letterbox, but she didn't have enough strength and fell short. Inge therefore resolved to listen for movement on the landing by pressing an ear against the door. She maintained this position for what seemed like at least an hour, before she heard footsteps on the stairs. Inge shouted with all the volume she could manage. 'Hilfe! Hilfe!' (Help! Help!)

The footsteps stopped for a few seconds and then continued.

'Hilfe! Hilfe!' The footsteps stopped. A female voice called out. 'Who is it? Who is there?'

'Frau Bohm at number 6.'

'How can I help you, Frau Bohm?'

'I'm disabled, and I can't open the door. Who is this?'

'Annelise Mueller from number 10.'

'Frau Mueller. I have a problem. Can you please knock on the door of number 5 and speak to my friend Magda? She has a key to my apartment.'

'Moment.'

Inge heard footsteps, a knock and a muffled conversation. A few minutes later she heard a key in the lock and felt the pressure against her body as the door started to push against her.

'Inge, what is the matter?'

'Julia hasn't come home and I'm on my own. I'm against the door, Magda. Give me a few seconds and I will move away then you can open it.'

After a brief pause Magda managed to force open the door and she found Inge lying in the hall.

'Julia has left me to myself. I can't imagine where she is. She said nothing to me yesterday, about being away this morning.'

Magda knew of Julia's occupation, having seen her walking her beat on one occasion at the Tiergarten. She knew a prostitute when she saw one, but she had long since decided that she would not tell Inge. The very idea of it would most likely kill her. Although a beautiful young woman, Julia dressed like a tart and clearly, she was a tart. But Magda realised that it was the only way that Julia could support herself and her mother. Unfortunately, it was a case of necessity.

'Where could she be, Magda?'

'I don't know, Inge. But I'll do my best to find out. I will get Jurgen to speak to the police. In the meantime, I will stay with you.'

Magda called her son Jurgen, who helped her to carry Inge back to her bed, after which they retired to the kitchen to discuss what was to be done. Jurgen was firmly of the opinion that insufficient time had elapsed for the police to be interested. It was agreed that Magda would stay the night with Inge and that they would reassess the situation the following morning. Hopefully, Julia would return in the meantime.

3

Monday 9 May 1949

The night passed without incident. Julia did not return home and the situation took on an even grimmer atmosphere. Around 8am, having taken delivery of the *Berliner Morgen Post* newspaper, Jurgen knocked on the front door, which was answered by Magda. He waved the paper under her nose.

'Mother, I think you need to read this article in the paper. The police are asking people to come forward if they think they know the identity of a young woman who was found murdered in the Tiergarten. I'm sorry to have to say it, but I honestly think the description fits Julia.'

'Oh no. I was afraid that something like that might have happened. Stay with Frau Bohm, will you? I had better go to the police station and try to find out more.Magda walked across to the mantelpiece, picked up a picture frame and removed the photograph of Julia which was inside. She was dreading what she might learn, but for Inge's sake, she had to get to the bottom of the situation.

It was twenty minutes before Magda reached the Central Police Station and she was to remain in the front waiting area for another half-hour before she was joined by Gerhard Siegler, who introduced himself and took her to an interview room. Magda explained the reason for her visit, citing the article in the newspaper and her relationship with her disabled friend and neighbour. She produced the photograph and handed it to the officer, who examined it.

'Is this a good likeness, do you think?' asked Siegler.

'Yes, it was taken about a year ago when Julia tried to sign up with a modelling agency.'

'Well, I regret to say that she does look like our murder victim. Do her parents know that you are here?'

'There's only her mother and she can't leave the apartment as she's disabled.'

'Did this young lady sign up with the modelling agency?'

'No. She sent a copy of the photograph and went for an interview, but they didn't take her on. She was a pretty girl, but she didn't quite make the grade.'

'What does Julia do for work?'

'She told her mother that she was working at a restaurant, but I saw her hanging around the Tiergarten, and it looked to me like she was working as a prostitute.'

'I'll do a check to see if we have her on record, but we'll need someone to look at the body to see if they can identify her. Would you be able to carry out that task or would you find it too distressing?'

Magda's heart sank as she sat and thought about the question. She knew that Inge would be incapable of leaving her home, let alone go through such a torturous process.

'I could do that,' answered Magda, with resignation, 'I know her well enough and frankly, there isn't anyone else.'

'No time like the present, then,' said Siegler. 'The body of the deceased is resting at the mortuary, which is only about a ten-minute drive from here. I could take you. Are you available to go there now?' Magda agreed and thirty minutes later she found herself standing over the body of a young woman who was laid out on an examination table in front of her. It was obvious to Magda that the mortuary staff had done their best to make the body more presentable.

'Please take your time, Magda,' said Siegler. 'We have some clothing to show you as well.'

'No. I can tell you straight away that this is Julia Bohm. It's so sad. Her mother will be devastated. Such a waste of a young life.' Magda was reduced to tears and began dabbing her eyes with her handkerchief.

'Where was she found?'

'In the Tiergarten. She was found by a gentleman who was out walking his dog. As you said earlier, she appears to have been working as a street prostitute.' A mortuary assistant appeared with the victim's garments and footwear which were contained in various paper bags. He laid them on a side table and Siegler removed the items individually, inviting Magda to view them. She recognised the blouse and skirt, which were both colourful and distinctive.

'Yes. They are Julia's. She wore them a lot. She didn't have much of a choice in her wardrobe. Can you tell me how she was killed?'

'Why would you need to know that, Magda?' asked Siegler.

'Her mother is bound to ask me.'

'Well, sadly, that is my next duty. I need you to come with me and a colleague to break the news to Frau Bohm. I don't want her to find out the details from anyone else.'

Magda took his point.

'Besides,' said Siegler, 'We will have to hold an autopsy to be absolutely sure of the cause of death, so I don't want to speculate at this stage.'

Magda returned home with Siegler and a female colleague. She let herself into the flat, where she found Jurgen and quickly briefed him out of Inge's hearing. She then showed the officers into Inge's bedroom where they introduced themselves. Inge looked horrified and quickly understood that she was about to be the recipient of distressing news.

'Is this about Julia?'

'Yes, Frau Bohm. It is. I'm sorry to have to tell you that your daughter Julia was found in the Tiergarten. We believe that she was murdered.'

Inge screamed, 'No! No!' rolled herself into a ball and clenched her fists. 'My girl! My beautiful girl!.'It took her some minutes to stop sobbing, before she turned to question the officers, as disbelief started to creep into her mind.

'Are you sure it's her?'The female officer took Inge's hand to comfort her and explained that Julia had been identified by Magda.Inge was again convulsed with grief.

'She was all I had,' stuttered Inge, through her tears. After a few minutes Magda arrived with a mug of coffee laced with schnapps. She remained with Inge while the officers carried out a thorough search of Julia's room. They found nothing of interest other than clothing in the wardrobe. Magda feared for her friend and neighbour as she was now alone and her life would change fundamentally. She resolved to provide as much support as she could, but long-term, Inge's wellbeing would be uncertain.

4

Friday 30 September 1949

Konrad had been feeling restless. He hadn't tasted a woman for days and he needed satisfaction. The demands of his work had prevented him from pursuing any of the women that he had been cultivating over recent weeks. One of the women he had chatted to casually in a bar, and whom he'd had high hopes for, had ridiculed him over the fact that he tended to use too much hair cream. She had told him, quite openly, in answer to his question as to whether she found him handsome or not, that he was too "greasy" for her liking. Rather than show his displeasure, Konrad had passed this off as a joke, but the brazen cheek of the woman, had already whetted his appetite for revenge. Presented with a challenge, Konrad worked on the information that he had managed to elicit from her during their conversation. Her name, job, place of work and general home area. So, he could not believe his luck when, one afternoon, he came across her standing alone at a bus stop, in a neighbouring town. Strangely, she appeared quite pleased to see him and she readily accepted a lift home. In a self-deprecating manner Konrad pointed out that he had taken her advice, had rid himself of the hair cream and had styled his hair naturally. This made her laugh, he lavished his charm on her, and he began to see that with a bit more attention she would be his to command.

Aged mid to late twenties, with shoulder-length blonde hair, exquisite face with full lips and a curvaceous body with prominent breasts, she was beautiful. But like many beautiful women, she was a manipulative bitch. He drove off in the general direction of her home area, but he took the country route. After a few miles of small-talk and general banter, Konrad suddenly declared, 'Anyway. It was my birthday yesterday.'

'Really. How old are you?'

'Guess.'

'Oh. I'd say, about thirty-nine.' She laughed.

'That's not very nice!' he said with mock indignation.

'Go on then. How old are you, tell me?'

'Thirty-four. Anyway, I was working in Piedmont last week and I managed to get my hands on some bottles of top-quality Asti Spumante. Would you like to share some of it with me?' asked Konrad.

'Where is Piedmont?'

'Northern Italy. It's where they make it.'

'I've never had Asti Spumante. What does it taste like?'

'It's special. You'll love it. It's a bit like champagne and it gives you a nice warm buzz inside.'

'Yes. I like the sound of that. I'll try some.'

'We'll have to drink it from the bottle, though. I have no glasses with me.'

'That doesn't bother me.'

Konrad drove off the main road, turning onto a dark lane that led to an old unused airfield, where he knew they would not be disturbed. Everything was going according to his hastily made plan. He brought the vehicle to a halt and reached onto the back seat, retrieving a bottle from a box of twelve.

'Here we go.'

He slowly loosened the cork and fired it away into the bushes.

'Let me just try this first to make sure that it's not corked, as they say.' He took a deep swig from the bottle, swilled the liquid around his mouth and declared it,

'Fantastic!'

Konrad handed the bottle across to her. She took a deep swig, swallowed and then took a second mouthful.

'Hey. Don't drink all of it at once. It's to be savoured,' he laughed.

'Oh, I do like that,' she said. The bottle passed back and forth between them until it was empty.

'Oh no, it's all gone. What'll we do now?' she giggled.

'Don't panic. I've got another one,' he said. Konrad reached into the back of the vehicle and produced a second bottle, which he opened without difficulty and handed across to her. She continued to drink from the bottle.

'Ooh, what a wonderful man you are,' she said in a seductive voice.

Great. It's working, he thought to himself, *but I won't try anything quite yet, I've got to time this right.* He was pleasantly surprised when she suddenly leaned across and kissed him full on the lips. Konrad put his arm around her and cuddled her. He left the bottle in her grasp and she continued imbibing, as if her life depended on it.

Whatever inhibitions she might have had were disappearing rapidly. She made no defensive moves when Konrad undid her blouse and slid his right hand into the cup on the left side of her bra. She continued kissing him passionately and he rolled her nipple between his thumb and forefinger. He couldn't wait to taste it. Knowing that they would be unable to take matters further in the front seats, Konrad left the driver's position and walked around to the front passenger door. He ushered her into the rear of the vehicle and she willingly complied, climbing in first with Konrad taking a seat on her left. They got back into a clinch and he wasted no time in finding her knickers, slipping the fingers of his left hand inside her gusset, She began to writhe with pleasure

'Oh, you're a naughty man.'

'I want to get inside you, baby.'

'I want you inside me, but only if you have a rubber.'

'I haven't got one. But don't worry. I'll pull out at the right time.'

'No. You won't. I can't be getting pregnant.'

Konrad ignored her protestations. He was going to have her, so he pulled at her knickers with both hands. She grabbed hold of the waistband and held on for all she was worth. She then began to panic.

'Konrad, don't! I told you I won't have sex without a rubber. There's no rush. We can do it another time.'

This was not good enough for him. He slapped her face and she gave out a scream. She was momentarily stunned, and Konrad took advantage of her surprise by sliding down her knickers and tearing the flimsy material apart. He forced her legs open and thrust himself inside her. She let out another scream.

He started to move inside her. Konrad told himself that she was obviously enjoying him and having taken control of the situation, he had relieved her of the decision and, therefore, the guilt, when rough sex, was just what the dirty bitch wanted. This was further evidenced by the fact that every time he thrust inside her she squealed. He gathered pace, she wriggled and squealed then she began to shout, 'Stop! Stop!' And then, 'Help me!' which she repeated over and over.

It was clear to him that she was loving every minute of it, but her noise was beginning to grate on his nerves.

Konrad wanted to shut her up, so he placed his hand, tightly, over her mouth. She fought fiercely to free herself and bit his hand. This caused him to fly into a rage and attracted a flurry of punches from him. She continued to scream. He placed his hands around her throat and squeezed the sound from her voice box. She wriggled and twitched and then went limp.

Now was his time to make his mark. He went straight to her left breast without a second thought. At that moment he was an automaton. He pushed up her bra and sank his teeth into her left nipple, bit down, separated the nipple from her breast and he swallowed her flesh.

A few minutes elapsed before the normal pattern of his breathing was restored. He had sated his lust and now he had to dispose of yet another body.

Konrad climbed back into the driver's seat and started the vehicle. Luckily, he knew his way around the immediate area and made his way to an old air raid shelter which was located in a remote corner of the airfield. He took a torch from the glove box and entered the shelter.

On shining the light around the interior he saw that the floor was completely covered in a layer of fallen leaves that were, in places, up to a foot deep. This was ideal for his purposes.

He ran back to the jeep and unceremoniously dragged the dead weight of his victim from the back seat. As her corpse was taken from the vehicle the young woman's head banged on the floor. Konrad winced. His feelings had returned, he suddenly felt sorry for her, but he reminded himself that she would not have felt a thing. He dragged her across the ground and down into the shelter where he placed the body in one of the deeper areas and covered it with leaves.Konrad returned to the vehicle where, with the aid of the torch, he located her handbag which, for a moment, he considered taking back to the shelter and placing alongside the body. He thought better of it. He would dispose of the bag and the Asti bottles elsewhere. Luckily, his vehicle started without a problem and he drove back the way he had come. He was buzzing. He'd never felt so alive.

5

Abberton Reservoir Colchester, Essex
Sunday 2 October 1949

'A good night, Podge. That's six so far,' said Levi. 'Just one more net to do.'

Levi Loveridge and his brother "Podger," were out poaching eels at Abberton Reservoir which was located some six miles from Colchester. This, for them, was a regular activity. They were of gypsy stock, but they no longer travelled or lived in caravans, the interruption of the war having put an end to their itinerant lifestyle. Levi and Podge (Absalom) had both served their country well, and they were back to the life that they were used to, even though they now lived in a council pre-fabricated bungalow (pre-fab).

They were well known to the local constabulary for their activities both before and since the war. Such was their reputation that, nobody would employ them, so they subsisted by poaching eels, stealing sheep and other nefarious activities which enabled them to earn themselves a few quid.

The brothers' *modus operandi*, which on the face of it appeared diverse, was in fact quite systematic and integrated. They sold the sheep to a "friendly" butcher who would slaughter them and pay them for the carcasses, however, he would also provide them with the offal and a healthy portion of the animal's blood which were then used to bait the eel nets. Thus, very little went to waste.

It was a warm, still, summer's night and the brothers went about their business quietly and stealthily until their peace was shattered by the sound of a motor vehicle which was being driven erratically along the dirt track, that led in the general direction of the reservoir car park which was some 200 yards' parallel to their position. Levi was about to disgorge the final net when his attention was drawn to the noise. Podge was standing above him on the embankment, and he was in a better position to observe what was happening.

'Allo. Who's this coming up the lane?'

'Coppers?'

'Don't know. Can't really see from this far. Whatever it is, it's got its fog lights on,' said Podge, providing a commentary. 'Turning around in the car park and it's now facing back the way it came in. Lights are off.'

'Have they seen us, do you think?'

'No. No chance.'

'OK. We'll probably be alright if we keep our heads down. We'll be finished in a minute. Anyway, you lazy bugger, don't just stand up there gawping, come here and hold the bag open, will you?' Podge slid back down to Levi, who was at the water's edge, and unzipped the holdall for Levi to transfer the eels from the net into the bag. They then heard a series of feminine cries coming from the direction of the vehicle. Their prurient attitude to women told them that this was surely a lady having a good time.

'Sounds like they're he-ing and she-ing, boy,' said Podge. 'Dirty lucky sod. I wonder if he needs any help.'

'No. Don't think so, mate. Sounds like he's doing all right on his own. Can't be the law then, can it? Anyway, don't worry about them. Just pay attention to what you're doing and let's get this done, then we can fuck off.'

After another ten minutes, having emptied and re-baited the nets, they both scurried back to the top of the embankment. As they did so, they heard the engine start up again and the vehicle moved off, disappearing back down the lane towards the main road.

'Good,' said Levi, 'That's them out of the way.'

'I wonder who it was,' said Podger, 'dirty, lucky sod.'

'Well, it might not have been the Old Bill, but the engine sounded like an army jeep to me.'

The brothers continued along the bank to the car park where they retrieved their van, which they had earlier hidden from view at the rear of the toilet block. Levi got behind the wheel and after finally managing to get the engine started, reversed the van out onto the dirt track. As he did so, the headlights swept across the lane ahead of them and they noticed what looked like a bundle of rags lying on the grass verge.

'What's that?'

'Bloody hell, Podge. It looks like it could be a body. Let's get closer.'

He moved the van to within ten feet of the bundle, they got out, and walked hesitantly to the front of the van, where they crouched down. On closer inspection of the bundle they realised that it was the body of a young woman, and although she was lying on her side, they saw enough to realise that her face was covered in blood. She was wearing a long black skirt and a white blouse which appeared to have been pushed upwards, exposing her waist and the lower part of her ribcage. Levi took a hold of her shoulder and shook it gently. 'Miss. Are you all right?' There wasn't a glimmer of a response. He tried a second time, but to no avail.

'I think she's dead.'

'Poor girl. What do you think's happened to her?' said Podge.

'I don't know, but she stinks. I think she's shit herself.'

'We've been here, what? An hour? And she wasn't here when we drove down earlier. She must have come from that car,' said Podge.

'When we heard the screams, I didn't think it would be for something like this. Thought it was just sex.'

'Fuckin' rough sex. If you ask me!'

'What we going to do with her? We can't just leave her,' said Levi.

'Why not? It's got nothing to do with us. Somebody will find her sooner or later. We can't afford to get involved.'

'What if a kid was to find her? It'd scare 'em to death. We can't have that.'

'Leave it to luck, Levi. It's not our fault.'

'No. We can't do that. There's just a small chance that she's still alive. Anyway, if we don't report it and somebody sees us, they might think we done it. No. I'll stay with her, you run down to the telephone box and call an ambulance.'

Podge did as he was told and ran off down the lane as quickly as his considerable bulk would allow him. In his absence, Levi gave the woman the occasional shake in the vain hope that she would respond. He was devastated for the poor woman.

About fifteen minutes later the lights of a vehicle came along the lane. Levi realised that they belonged to an ambulance and he had a momentary feeling of relief, but this was dispelled when he saw that it was being closely followed by a police car. The vehicles both came to a halt with their lights trained on the body. He was soon joined by an ambulanceman, who gave the body a quick examination and then turned his attention to Levi.

'Is she with you?'

'No,' said Levi.'I was just driving along the lane and I found her like this.'

'Was it you who called the ambulance?'

'My mate did. He's not back yet.'

The ambulance-man left Levi and approached the police officers who were stood away from the body at the rear of their car.

'Body of a young woman, and from the blood on her face looks like she's got some head injuries. Anyway she's dead, poor kid, so we won't be taking her away. You need to treat this as suspicious, I reckon.'

PC Fred Nicholls, the older and more experienced of the two officers, felt like telling the ambulanceman that he was "stating the bleeding obvious," but he kept his irritation to himself.

'What does matey say about it?' asked Nicholls, nodding towards Levi.

'He said she's not with him and he just found her as he drove down the lane.'

Nicholls told his colleague, PC Tim Jeffs, to get on the radio, to control, to get them to call out the police surgeon, duty sergeant and the CID.

Nicholls had only recently been posted to the Colchester Division but Jeffs knew Levi Loveridge of old and advised his colleague to keep a close eye on him to prevent him running off.

'Levi, isn't it?' said Jeffs.

'Yes, sir.'

'I need you to come away from the body now, Levi. We mustn't disturb things any more than we have to.'

Levi walked across to join the officers who were standing at the rear of the police car.

Nicholls realised that he should grip the situation and question the man about the circumstances of his finding the body.

'So, Levi, suppose you tell us what you were doing here?'

Against his basic instinct Levi knew that he would have to tell the truth. Under the circumstances in which he now found himself, anything less than total frankness would just not do.

'I don't want to tell you who I was with sir, because I'm not a grass, but he was the one who called the ambulance while I stayed with the lady. We was out here poaching for eels.'

Nicholls was confronted by a thief, but he had to be sure that he wasn't also the murderer. His hesitation prompted a further response.

'Look. If you don't believe me, look in the back of me van. There's a bag of eels in there and the nets are still in the water.' Levi pointed in the direction of the reservoir bank.

'Is the van locked?'

'Yeah but look, I'll show you, if you want.' Levi flourished a set of keys from his trouser pocket, walked to the back of the van and unlocked the doors. The officer watched him pull out a holdall which was almost moving of its own free will, the contents still being alive. Nicholls could also see that the van was almost totally full, with old scrap metal, and could not have been used to accommodate a human body.

'OK. Thanks for that, Levi. We'll have to take you in for questioning though. I'm arresting you for larceny.' The officer cautioned him. Levi remained calm. He knew the drill. Nicholls took him back to the police car and placed him in the back under the supervision of PC Jeffs. They were soon joined by Ted Glover, the duty sergeant, who arrived with another couple of officers who immediately did their best to cordon off the scene with a length of rope which was staked into the ground.

Next to arrive were the CID in the person of DI Albert Cooper, who would have the dubious honour of being the Senior Investigating Officer. Also present were Detective Sergeant Brian Pratt and Detective Constable Linda Collins.

Fred Nicholls and Ted Glover gave Cooper and his colleagues a quick briefing on the situation.

Albert Cooper had served with the Colchester Borough Constabulary both before and after the war. He was Colchester born and bred, knew his ground and the people on it, and enjoyed the sobriquet of "Alby" which had been given to him by school friends.

He was thirty-seven years of age, a large man standing at 6 feet 3 inches in his stockinged feet and was of strong lithe build. He had a full head of black hair which was neatly cut in a "short back and sides" and smoothed with Brylcream. Alby was quite a handsome individual with a strong chin, although he did have a boxer's nose, which was a souvenir from his army days. Cooper's "bagman," Brian Pratt, was thirty-six years of age, slightly shorter at 5 feet 11 inches and of thin build. In terms of physical stature, he was a shadow of his boss. Unfortunately for Pratt, he had inherited the balding gene. What was left of his hair was blond, as were his eyebrows and moustache.

Whatever their shortcomings were in the looks department, Cooper and Pratt were regarded by their colleagues as thorough and capable detectives.

Hard on their heels was the police surgeon, Doctor Donald Henshall, and the Scenes of Crime officers.

'What have we got here then, Albert?'

'A young lady apparently, doctor. The ambulance crew reckon that she's been beaten about the head, her clothes are in disarray and it looks like she might have been sexually assaulted as well.'

'Do we have a name for the lady?'

'No. I haven't been near her myself, but I understand that the first officers on the scene couldn't find any handbag or purse.'

'Who found her?'

'Apparently a couple of local didi coys who were out poaching. One of them is here in the car. He's been arrested for the poaching. Don't know about the other one yet. We haven't located him.'

'OK Albert. Let's take a look at her then.'

They both went into the cordoned area. Cooper stood a few yards off and observed from a distance as the doctor approached and crouched over the body. He appeared to carry out a very detailed examination, but he was at pains to disturb the body as little as possible.

Cooper could see that, all the while, Henshall was making copious notes, muttering and talking to the body of the woman, as if she were still alive. After he was satisfied about the victim's condition, he rose and turned to Cooper.

'Albert. I can confirm death, which was most likely caused by strangulation, but, we'll have to wait for the post mortem to confirm that. She's been beaten about the head, which has caused heavy bleeding, and one other thing, which I've heard of, but not seen before, is that she has had her left areola bitten off.'

'Areola?'

'Left nipple to you and me, Albert. A savage act.'

"Christ, doc,' said Cooper. 'What kind of evil bastard would do that?'

'As I said, it's not unheard of. In fact a few months ago I attended a very interesting lecture by Professor Keith Simpson, of Guy's Hospital, who is a leader in the field of forensic odontology. He was the pathologist in a case last year in which he was able to prove an individual was responsible for a murder where the victim had bite marks on her body. Apparently, this was done by comparing the bite marks with the teeth of the suspect.'

'Really? It would be very useful in this case, if we could seek his opinion. I'd be grateful, doc, if you would write his details down and let me have them. A telephone number would be even better.'

'I'll dig that out for you, Albert. The key thing that he was at pains to stress about his case, and the crucial factor, was, that his victim died quickly, before bruising could distort the bite marks on her body. There was little blood around the nipple area on our victim which tells me that our case might be very similar to theirs, in that respect.'

'Thanks for that, doc. That's very helpful. I'll make sure that, when they arrive, the forensic pathologist is made aware,' said Cooper.

'Obviously I'm unable to issue a death certificate. But I'll let you have my report as soon as I can and I'll inform the coroner. Best of luck, Albert. Let me know if I can be of any further assistance.'

'Thanks, doc.'

Doctor Henshall departed.

Cooper called a quick meeting of the troops.

'Ted, I want you and your lads to maintain the security of the scene. No-one is to approach the body other than Scenes of Crime and the pathologist when he arrives. Can you start a log, please?'

'Yes, governor.'

Cooper turned his attention to the patrol car. 'Brian. Let's find out what Mr Loveridge has to say.' They walked across to the vehicle. Cooper opened the rear passenger door and put his head inside, 'Levi.'

'Mr Cooper. How are you, sir?'

'Fine thanks. Family all right? How's Patience?'

'Oh Paish. Yeah. she's all right. Busy with the kids.'

'How many have you got now?'

'Four, and another one on the way.'

'That's good. So Levi, tell us what happened here then.'

'Me and my mate heard a jeep come along the lane while we was sorting out the nets. It was about a hundred yards away, so we couldn't really see it clearly.'

'How did you know it was a jeep?'

'I know the sound of a jeep all right, Mr Cooper. I drove one every day for four years.

Anyway, it drove up to the car park and turned off its lights. We thought it was your lot at first but when we heard a woman crying out we thought it was a couple shagging. So, we finished what we was doing. A little while later the jeep drove off back down the lane to the main road and it went away.'

'Did you see which direction it went in?'

'No. I didn't see. Anyway, when we walked back to the van and turned on the lights we found her lying on the grass.'

'Did you touch her?'

'No. Mr Cooper, why would I do that? I'm a thief. Not a fucking pervert or murderer.' Levi became very incensed and felt insulted.

'No, Levi. Calm down, mate. I didn't mean like that, silly bugger. I meant did you try and see if she was all right.'

'Oh OK. I thought you was accusing me. Well, I shook her a little bit, just to see if she was alive.'

'And did she respond in any way?'

'No. I couldn't get anything out of her. She looked like she was dead already.'

'Did you see anything of the jeep itself?'

'No. I was down on the bank, but my mate was up higher, and he saw the lights. I knew what it was though. I could definitely tell by the engine.'

'OK, thanks Levi. That's helpful. What's going to happen now is, you're going to be taken down to the nick. We need to satisfy ourselves that you're not involved so we'll have to take your clothes for forensic examination. Then you'll be interviewed.'

'What? And I'll have to sit around in me pants and vest, will I?'

'No. They'll give you something to wear. We're going to have to speak to your mate as well. Who was it?'

'You know me, Mr Cooper. I'm not a grass.'

Cooper suspected that the second man was likely to be Podger, since it was well known locally that they came as a pair and were virtually joined at the hip. However, Cooper decided not to push the point at this stage as he sensed that he would be seeking Levi's help as a witness.

'Levi. We've known each other for a long time and you know that I wouldn't chiv you, mate. I need your help. We're investigating a vicious murder and we're really not interested in a few eels.'

'That's what I've been nicked for though, isn't it?'

'Look. Cooperate, and we'll probably forget about the eels, all right?'

'I'll think about it.'

Loveridge was driven away to the police station and Cooper turned his attention to Brian Pratt and Linda Collins. 'Brian. Job for you. I want you to go to the garrison police station and speak to the military police. Tell them about the murder and the fact that the suspect vehicle might have been a jeep. I want them to speak to the sentries at each of the guard rooms, also, the motor pools to find out who has a jeep signed out to them.'

'Yes guv.'

'Linda. You jump in with him and get him to drop you back at the nick. I want you to telephone Superintendent Stockwell at home and inform him of the murder. Then Brian, I want you to speak to Inspector Rice and arrange for the early shift to be briefed on the murder and arrange for some troops to relieve Ted Glover and the night shift officers here at the scene. I also want you to call in Ian Mills and the late turn CID for eight o'clock when you finish that bring the car back, please.'

'Right oh, guv.'

Cooper threw the car keys to Brian and they went on their way.

It was now 10.15pm, and it had taken the Scenes of Crime officers some time to find and erect a tent to cover the body, but fortunately, the weather was warm and dry with little wind. A couple of hours later the forensic pathologist, Professor Graham Westlake, arrived on the scene, having been conveyed from London by a Metropolitan Police vehicle. Alby Cooper made himself known.

'Our victim is a woman, Professor. The police surgeon, Doctor Henshall, has been and gone. He pronounced death and he's going to inform the coroner.'

'Thank you, Inspector.'

Cooper introduced him to Brendan Withers, the senior Scenes of Crime officer, and after a brief discussion Westlake and Withers both entered the tent. Cooper remained with

Sergeant Glover and ensured that the details of their entry were written into the log. It was at least an hour and a half before Westlake re-emerged.

'Well, Inspector. She's dead all right. There's no mistake about that.' He gave a chuckle as he spoke the words.

Don't be bloody flippant, thought Cooper. *This woman was someone's daughter.* Cooper was incensed. How dare this pompous arse make light of the situation. He gave Westlake a withering look that hit home immediately.

'I'm sorry, Inspector. I don't mean to be callous. The deceased is a woman of around thirty-six years old. Blonde hair, slightly plump. She's been beaten around the head which has caused lacerations to her chin and forehead. It looks like her assailant was wearing a ring, which is the thing that was likely to have caused the lacerations. One other thing, though, that I found most disturbing. She has had her left nipple bitten off.'

'Yes, Professor. The police surgeon made me aware of that. But, did that happen before or after death, I wonder?'

'I think that it was after death, but before we draw any firm conclusions on that, let's wait until we've carried out the post mortem. No pun intended.'

Cooper winced but didn't respond to the Professor's forced levity. The remark was enough for him to realise that this was obviously how he suppressed his own emotions.

'Doctor Henshall, the police surgeon, told me earlier about Professor Keith Simpson, of Guy's Hospital, who is a leader in the field of forensic odontology. Apparently, he was the pathologist in a case last year in which he was able to prove that an individual was responsible for a murder where the victim had bite marks on her body. Apparently, this was done by comparing the bite marks with the teeth of the suspect.'

'Yes. I'm aware of that case, Inspector, but before we get too carried away, I must point out that it is something of an inexact science, I'm afraid.'

'Surely, it's worth referring the case to him, isn't it?'

'Possibly,' said the professor.

'Well, professor, I expect the case to be referred to Professor Simpson,' said Cooper, losing patience, 'and I will make a note of the fact in my policy log.'

'If you say so.'

Cooper was not a well-educated man. He didn't have two academic qualifications to rub together. But he was under a duty to leave no stone unturned to catch the animal who had killed and mutilated this poor woman, and left her to perish at the roadside.

The professor dealt with dead bodies on a regular basis and he had become somewhat indifferent to their plight. He would never have to speak to their loved ones or impart tragic news. As far as human emotions were concerned, he performed his role at a safe distance. A very safe distance indeed.

'So, what was the cause of death then, Professor?'

'Asphyxia caused by strangulation. On first blush, it doesn't appear that a ligature was used. Whoever it was, probably killed her just by using their bare hands.'

'Perhaps you will let me know when the post-mortem is to be held.'

'Of course.'

'Are you content for the body to be removed to the mortuary?'

'Yes. But we still haven't found the victim's left nipple, so we need to consider that when the body is lifted. It might be underneath her. I'll help you with the transfer when the undertaker arrives.' Cooper turned to Brendan Withers of Scenes of Crime.

'Brendan, I need you to escort the body to the mortuary so that we can prove continuity.'

'Yes, sir.'

About 2.45am Brian and Linda returned with the Wolseley CID car. The uniform staff would remain on scene providing security until relieved and a search of the area could be carried out in daylight. Cooper returned to the police station where he found that the early turn uniform personnel and the additional detectives were starting to arrive. He would soon brief them accordingly.

6

Town Hall Colchester

Monday 3 October 1949

It was 9.30am and the heads of department were in the divisional commander's office reviewing the actions taken so far.

'What kind of evil bastard would bite off a woman's breast?' exclaimed Stockwell, the divisional superintendent, in total disbelief.

'According to the pathologist it's not unknown, sir,' observed Cooper, 'And, I'm told that it's possible to prove guilt by comparing a suspect's teeth with the wound.'

'First, find your suspect,' said Inspector Arthur Willis, sardonically.

'Well, quite right, Arthur,' added Stockwell. 'Where on earth do we start?'

'If I may, sir. I can tell you where we shouldn't start. We shouldn't start telling the press about our victim having been bitten, on the breast or anywhere else,' said Cooper.

'Surely, we need all the media coverage we can get, don't we?' said Stockwell.

'I agree, sir. Up to a point. But when we interview a suspect, we need to be able to tell whether their admissions are genuine and drawn from their own experience. If we tell all and sundry about the biting, any nutter and attention seeker could turn it around and feed it back to us,' said Cooper. 'It's of paramount importance that we keep that kind of detail under wraps.'

'Sound tactical thinking, Albert. I take your point. Write it into the policy book, please. No disclosure regarding the bite wound. On the same note, only a few key members of staff need to know about it. I don't want one of our staff letting the information slip out, inadvertently or otherwise. Who knows about it up until now?'

'The only officer who approached the body was PC Nicholls. It's likely that he would have seen the extent of her wounds. Also, DC Pratt, WDC Collins and other detectives on the murder team. Oh, and Scenes of Crime, of course.'

'Right. Speak to them all, will you, Albert? Impress upon them the importance of staying silent on this particular issue.'

'Yes, sir.'

'And we'll give the press details of the fact that a young woman's body was found at Abberton reservoir, but no cause of death. The object being to get the victim identified and any witnesses who might have seen or heard anything.'

'I think that would be best, sir.'

'Any news from the military police yet?'

'Yes, sir. Just before the meeting I spoke to Joe Graham, a staff sergeant on the Special Investigation Branch (SIB). No joy from their enquiries on the garrison, I'm sorry to report.'

'What do you make of this man Loveridge's claim that he heard a jeep?' asked Stockwell.

'I believe it to be genuine, sir. He may be of gypsy stock and a well-known thief, but he served with distinction in the war at Anzio and Normandy and would know the sound of a jeep. He's well-intentioned in that regard, I'm sure.'

'What about the search of the scene?'

'Nothing found. No handbag or purse.'

'What about the woman's nipple?' asked Stockwell.

'No, sir. No trace of that.'

'Did you find anything?' asked Stockwell, in ill-disguised frustration.

'Only thing found was an empty beer bottle in the bushes near the body. It's been preserved for fingerprints. I believe, though, that we should extend the search from the end of the lane outwards for half a mile or so in each direction.

'Fine. OK. How far is it before the road changes its course in either direction?' asked Stockwell.

'About three-quarters of a mile towards Layer village and a mile the other way towards Peldon, sir,' said Arthur Willis.

'OK. I think we should cover that. Arthur, see if you can get a half-dozen bods together and let's get on to it.'

'Yes, sir, I think I know where I can find them.'

◈

'Who's for tea then, ladies?' said Enid Johnson, holding up the office kettle.

'Yes, please Ene,' said Mavis and Beryl in unison.

'Nothing for you then, Gladys?' said Enid, turning to a rather large lady who was concentrating on her typing at the back of the office.

'Oh. Go on then. But no sugar for me, thanks.'

'You on a diet then, ducks?'

'You taking the mick? I'm getting as fat as a pig, and you know it,' said Gladys, with a certain amount of resignation.

'I wouldn't say that. You might need to lose a little bit but you're tall and buxom,' said Enid as she poured milk into the cups.

'That's very nice of you, gel, but you know that's a load of balls as much as I do. And, I'm not big-boned either. I don't much fancy having to apply to "Queenie" for any new uniform. Rotten cow wouldn't let me hear the last of it.'

It was 10.35am on a Monday, and "Queenie," otherwise known as Woman Police Sergeant Cecily White, had not been seen in the office so far that morning. She was the officer in charge of the Colchester Women's Police Department who, subject to the exigencies of duty, worked a basic nine to five, Monday to Friday. It was their role to deal with issues relating to women and children while twenty-four-hour uniform beat policing was left to the shifts which were staffed entirely by men.

'I can imagine. Actually, I can't say that I've seen her in the office yet today,' said Enid.

'Has she signed on in the duty book?'

'No,' said Beryl. 'There was a murder over the weekend at Abberton Reservoir and C shift were called in to work early. There's a big meeting of the Heads of department going on. She's probably at that.'

'Who was murdered, then?' asked Enid.

'Some girl was found over at the reservoir. A courting couple had a row, I think, and he did her in,' said Beryl.

The women settled down to their tea and paperwork and around a half hour later they were joined in the office by Inspector Arthur Willis.

'Is Sergeant White about, ladies?'

'No, sir. She's out on an enquiry,' said Gladys defensively, with a lie. Although "Queenie" was unpopular, the women were a tight-knit bunch and they certainly didn't welcome any intrusion.

'Well, I've got a job for you, ladies, to do with the murder that we had at the weekend. Ordinarily, and as a matter of courtesy, I'd wait to consult Sergeant White, but time being of the essence, I need you to get on with the job as soon as possible. I'll just have to catch up with her later.'

The women were intrigued. They seldom got involved in murder enquiries and this was likely to be an interesting departure from the norm.

'So, have you got anything on, workwise, this morning?'

'No, sir.' They answered as one, wishing to get involved before the inspector changed his mind.

'Good. I want you all to report to Sergeant Jacobs in the parade room in fifteen minutes where you will be briefed. Bring a mac with you. You'll be out in the open.'

7

Tuesday 4 October 1949

Alby Cooper was in the superintendent's office bright and early and was apprising Tom Stockwell of the state of the investigation so far.

'We still have no identity for our body then, Albert?'

'No, we haven't, sir.'

'And what about our friend Mr Loveridge?'

'We took his clothing, and we'll have it forensically examined, just to be on the safe side, you understand.'

'Was he involved in the murder, do you think?'

'No. I don't think he was, sir. When he was questioned at the scene, he said that his friend had gone to the telephone box to report the matter and to call for an ambulance, which was in fact true. I don't think that he would have hung about at the scene if he was responsible for killing the woman.'

'Could be bullshit,' suggested Stockwell.

'Well, you might think so, sir, but he's our only witness at present and we'd like his mate to come forward, but he doesn't want to name him.'

'And involve him in the theft of the eels, I suppose,' said Stockwell.

'Quite, sir. I'm sure that's probably the way their minds are working, but I really believe it would help if you were to give them your assurance that, as far as the poaching is concerned, they would be free from prosecution.'

'I don't know about that, Albert. It smacks of us holding them to ransom, don't you think? A bit unethical.'

That's typical of Stockwell, thought Cooper. *Awkward and ponderous. But often, he can be persuaded, and can even be quite courageous, when he has thought the facts of a situation through.*

'Sir, with respect, I do think that we need to put matters into perspective. On the one hand we have a theft of a few eels, that the Essex Waterboard are unlikely to miss. On the other hand, we have the brutal murder of a young woman, by an individual who is likely to strike again. We need some witnesses and all the help we can get. The eels are small beer by comparison, don't you think?'

'I agree, Albert,' said Stockwell thoughtfully, 'I just don't want Loveridge and his mate telling you some "cock and bull," story to get themselves off, and it complicating the murder investigation.'

'No. I do understand that. But, if I may say so sir, I think that you might trust my judgement. You appointed me as the Senior Investigating Officer, and it would be helpful if you allow me to continue treating Loveridge more as a witness than a suspect. If we can identify the other party, we would speak to them separately and what they have to tell us could be thoroughly assessed and tested.'

'And, where is Loveridge now?'

'He's been bailed until Friday, pending further investigation. We couldn't keep him locked up indefinitely.'

'Very well. I will hold off on the poaching. But I want a witness statement from him and one from his friend, if we can identify him.'

'Thank you, sir. Can I have that in writing?'

'No. You can't.'

Cooper was exasperated. He returned to his office and found Brian Pratt, who was at his desk, clearing his "in tray."

'The Women's and Children's team didn't have any joy on the roadside search yesterday, then, Brian?'

'No, governor. I spoke to Arthur Willis this morning. There were about ten of them, on the search, including the entire Women's team.'

'Not their usual line of work but it was a good idea of Arthur's to get them involved. Radical, but I like it.'

'Yeah, and they must have covered about four miles. It took them most of the day. Still, at least that's that done.'

'It's been a couple of days since the body was found. You'd have thought somebody close to our victim would have reported her missing by now.'

Cooper leant back in his chair and tossed a newspaper across the desk to Pratt.

'It's front page news in the *Gazette*. Let's hope we get something from that.'

Brian Pratt laid the paper out across his knees and gave it a scan.

'Nothing about bites?'

'No. Thank Christ.'

'Let's hope it stays that way, guv.'

'Anyway, fancy a cup of tea, Brian?'

'Yes, thanks guv.'

'Good, it's your turn. I noticed Doris a minute ago in the main office with her trolley.'

Brian got to his feet, with a look of resignation on his face. He'd been had again.

Five minutes later he returned with the teas and Cooper gave him a summary of his meeting with Stockwell.

'Another piece of news for you, Brian.'

'What's that, governor?'

'Post-mortem is at three o'clock.'

'And you want me there, do you, governor?'

'Of course. As my deputy.'

Pratt hated attending post-mortems. He'd always managed to remain dispassionate and professional until the day he'd attended his first PM involving an infant. This had come within a year of his wife Pamela losing their first baby, who was stillborn. The experience had totally floored him. As a result, Cooper had decided to deal with any future child cases himself, but he was also trying to rehabilitate his friend and colleague. Once again, Brian Pratt would be tested.

◈

'Women's Police Department, WPC Johnson speaking. Can I help you?'

'Hello, Enid. Trevor Young here at Copford Section. Is Sergeant White in the office, please?'

'No. She's out at present, Trevor. In fact, we haven't seen her all day.'

'Only, we've had her purse handed in at the front counter by a couple of kids.'

'Crikey. Where did they find that, then?'

'Along Fountain Lane on the way to Layer. Anyway, I've got their details in case she wants to thank them herself and I've locked it in the Sergeant's cupboard.'

'OK. Thanks, Trevor. When she turns up, we'll let her know.'

Enid replaced the receiver and sat wondering how "Queenie" could have mislaid her purse. Then a pain visited her in the pit of her stomach. She needed to find Cecily White to dispel her concerns, and quickly. Enid ran upstairs to speak to Linda Collins in the CID office.

※

'I'm not looking forward to this, governor,' said Brian, with a distinctly glum look on his face. They were just pulling into the car park of the Essex County Hospital in Colchester.

'Brian. Just try and take a professional approach and remain calm, will you? If it all gets too much for you, just walk out of the room. You've really got to do your best to overcome this aversion to post-mortems. In adult cases, at the very least. It's an essential part of your role as a detective.'

They left the car, walked into the hospital foyer, and although they knew their way, they found themselves passively following the variously painted lines on the floor leading to the mortuary, where they were met by a member of staff. Cooper and Brian were given their robes and as they pulled them on Cooper couldn't resist a slight dig.

'Blimey Brian. Your face matches the colour of that gown.' Brian muttered something in reply behind his face mask. Fortunately, Cooper couldn't hear what was being said.

The mortician led them into the examination room where they could see a female corpse laid out on the slab in the middle of the room. They were welcomed by the forensic pathologist, Professor Westlake, who was standing by the slab with Brendan Withers, the senior Scenes of Crime officer.

"Good afternoon, gentlemen. We have made a start in so far as cleaning the blood from the lady's face and taking some samples for analysis.'

Brian stared at the corpse intently. He couldn't believe his eyes. She had indeed been cleaned.

'So, tell me, Inspector. Have we discovered a name for the lady yet?'

'Yes. We bloody well have. It's Cecily White!' said Brian.

He tore the mask from his face and stormed out of the examination room.

'Brian!' Cooper called after him, but Brian kept on walking.

'Well. It seems that we have our identification,' said Westlake, coldly.

'This is somebody you both know, is it?'

'Yes, Professor. Unfortunately it is, she was one of our Colchester officers. Sergeant Cecily White.'

Brendan Withers took a note of the name.

'OK. I'm very sorry about that, Inspector.'

'Yes. I'm afraid that this sad revelation is going to cause a lot of upset and heads might roll.'

'Well, I'm going to have to carry out the full examination now, Inspector, but for your information, having seen her today I'm inclined to the view that she was throttled: That is to say that, in my opinion, she was manually strangled.'

Professor Westlake indicated various scratches around the victim's neck.

'Thank you, Professor. What would you say about the bite wound?'

'Well it is fortunate that there is no distortion. We have photographed it. I have taken advice from Professor Simpson, of Guy's Hospital, and I will continue to liaise with him. I will say, though, that the biting does indeed appear to have happened after her death. That could prove useful.'

'The victim obviously soiled herself. Why would that have been? Could she have been punched in the stomach?'

'Yes. It's an unfortunate mess, but she wasn't punched in the stomach as far as I can tell. It was simply caused by shock. It is a common feature of strangulation.'

'Shock?'

'Yes, it's a regular feature. Anyway, I'll get Brendan to take a set of fingerprints from the body and he can have them compared against her set of elimination prints, kept in the fingerprint bureau at police headquarters.'

'Yes. That would be conclusive.'

'And Inspector. If you want to go and check on your colleague, I'll carry on with my examination and give you a report of my findings later.'

'Thank you, Professor.'

Cooper left the room, took off the gown, and walked outside to find Brian, who was sitting on a low wall in the car park, smoking a cigarette. Brian's hands were shaking and tears were streaming down his cheeks.

'I'm so sorry about that, Brian. I had no idea it was

Cecily when I saw her at the reservoir. I didn't get that close to her as I wanted to preserve the scene and I hadn't really looked at her on the table before you recognised her.'

'I'm sorry, Alby. It was a shock, that's all. She was the last person that I would have expected to see on the slab. As you know, I went out with Cecily for quite a while and I would have married the woman. I thought the world of her, and I loved her. We could have married but she was strong on the fact that she didn't want any kids and I did. I'm sorry, boss. I've made a fool of myself.'

'No, no. Not at all, Brian mate. It was a shock for both of us.' He put his arm around Brian's shoulder and led him back to the car, where they sat until Brian had regained his composure.

'What I can't work out is why nobody recognised her at the scene. There were others there. Someone should have recognised her.'

'Not really, Brian. Think about it, PC Nicholls, who was first on the scene, has just, in the last week, been posted from Brentwood and he didn't know her. She was lying on her side with her face covered in blood and the Scenes of Crime officers who attended are based at Chelmsford HQ. They don't know her either. Other than the doctor and the professor, people kept their distance, so as not to contaminate things. I'm just sorry that it had to be you who first recognised her.'

'Before I met Pam, I had a really good relationship with Cecily.'

'I know you did, Brian. I remember.'

'And we saw each other for a couple of years.'

'And you with your aversion to post-mortems. I'm so

sorry that this happened, mate.'

'I'd like to catch the bastard who did for her, Alby.'

'We will, Brian, but I'm not letting you anywhere near them when they're caught. One murder's enough. I suppose I'd better go and break the news to Stockwell. He's going to go off the fucking deep end!'

The two detectives drove back to the police station in silence. Brian was feeling a bit sorry for himself. Cooper, was deep in thought, dreading his meeting with Superintendent Stockwell. He wasn't going to be happy. As they entered the back door of the station they were leapt on by Linda Collins.

'Governor. I think I've got some bad news.'

'If it's about Cecily White, Linda, we've just found out.'

'Poor Cecily. It was her, then?'

'Afraid so,' said Cooper.

'How did you find out that it was her?'

'Brian has just identified her in the mortuary and that happened quite by accident.' Linda shook her head.

'I'm so sorry, Brian.'

'Why? It's not your fault.'

The men ascended the stairs with some purpose. Linda followed on behind. As they reached his office Cooper picked up the phone and dialled Stockwell's secretary.

'Hello Lucy. Is the boss in his office?'

'Not at present. He's downstairs in the hall at a meeting of the Police Committee and he won't be back for a couple of hours or so.'

'I need to speak to him urgently. Can you get someone to pass a message for him to give me a ring as soon as possible, please?'

The call was short and to the point. Cooper replaced the receiver. He was in no mood for pleasantries and he certainly wasn't looking forward to the conversation he was about to have with Stockwell.

'There is one other piece of news, governor,' said Linda.

She went on to explain about the finding of Cecily's purse and how, fearing the worst, Enid Johnson had sought her out to tell her about her concern for Cecily.

'I did try to contact you, governor, but nobody was answering the phone in the mortuary office. But I did get Scenes of Crime to collect the purse from Copford.'

They agreed it was purely bad timing that this had come about after Cooper and Brian had already become heavily engaged at the hospital for the post-mortem, however; they were pleased that Linda had taken the initiative to arrange for the purse to be brought back to Colchester for it to be forensically examined.

'Any early indications of marks on the purse, Linda?'

'Yes, governor. Luckily, it's a patent leather purse with smooth shiny surfaces and they found some good fingermarks.'

'Let's hope they don't all belong to the kids.'

'Scenes of Crime certainly think that they are more likely to be adult prints.'

'Well. That's positive news, anyway. Who is dealing with it at SOCO?'

'Dougie Johnson, governor.'

'OK. That's good. Linda, can you speak to the parents and get the boys to show you where, exactly, they found the purse. I think we should get a team to search the area to see if we can find anything else belonging to Cecily. Also, can you arrange for them to give a set of elimination prints, please?'

'Yes, guv.'

The phone rang. Cooper, with a gut-wrenching feeling of foreboding, picked up the handset.

'Albert. You wanted to speak to me?' said Stockwell.

'Yes, sir. I need to see you urgently about something to do with the murder at Abberton Reservoir.'

'I'm about to go into an important meeting with the police committee, can't it wait until later?' demanded Stockwell.

'No, sir. It can't. Where are you now exactly?'

'I'm at the town hall, using the phone in the town clerk's office.'

'Then, with respect, sir, I think it best that you go back to your own office so that I can speak to you there in private.'

'Whatever it is,' said Stockwell, ' just spit it out man. I'm very busy.'

'With respect, sir, are you sure about that?'

'Yes. Just get on with it, man.'

'We have identified the body of the victim…'

'Yes, and?'

'…and it's that of Sergeant Cecily White.'

'What!'

8

Wednesday 5 October 1949

'This looks bad, Tom. Very bad indeed,' said the chief constable. 'We have a murder in our force area, and then we give out a press release appealing for witnesses to the murder, urging the public to come forward if they have any knowledge of who our victim might be, and all the while the victim is one of our own officers. How, for heaven's sake, does something like that happen?'

'A series of unfortunate circumstances, sir,' replied Stockwell, his own words making him cringe with embarrassment.

'OK, then. Tell me about these circumstances, will you?'

'The inspector in charge of the Women's department is on leave. Miss White should have been in the office on Monday, but she was absent. The women on the team were deployed to carry out a search of the area near the murder site and they assumed that she was otherwise engaged at a meeting.'

'What about the officers who attended the scene. Didn't any of them know her?'

'I spoke to DI Cooper on that point, sir. He tells me that the first officer in attendance was PC Nicholls and he's only been posted to the division in the last week. The Scenes of Crime officers are from headquarters and they didn't know her either and Cooper kept himself at a distance so as not to disturb the integrity of the scene. Scenes of Crime supervised the movement of the body to the mortuary. So, it wasn't until DS Pratt attended the post-mortem that she was recognised by anyone.'

'He couldn't have been mistaken, could he?' said the chief, who was clutching at straws.

'No, sir. Her identity has now been confirmed by fingerprints.'

'OK, Tom. I'll accept that the situation was unfortunate but with hindsight I think you should have had somebody acting for their inspector while he was on leave. Miss White's absence might have been spotted straight away.'

'It wouldn't have prevented her murder though, sir, would it?' said Stockwell, boldly.

'No, Tom. But it might have prevented us looking ridiculous and unprofessional. Anway, I want it stressed, when we break the news to the press, that Miss White was off duty when her body was found.'

'I'll do that myself, sir.'

'Who did she live with?'

'Her father, sir. He's a widower.'

'Have we been to see him to break the news?'

'DI Cooper is performing that sad duty as we speak, sir.

He wanted to wait for the result of the fingerprint check first, just to be sure.'

'Poor chap. When it comes to the time, Tom, I want a funeral with full police honours, unless Mr White says otherwise.'

'Won't that just compound the embarrassment to the force, sir?'

'Well yes. It might indeed, Tom. But we'll just have to live with that. It's the very least we can do.'

◈

Bernard White sat in the living room of his home, a solemn and dignified figure. Alongside him was his sister Beryl, who was holding his hand and doing her best to comfort him. He had just lost his only child, Cecily, in the most disturbing of circumstances. It had been Alby Cooper's unpleasant duty to have to break the news of her death and he was now sitting, listening to Bernard's words of lament as the realisation of his daughter's death gradually dawned on him.

Cecily had been a very experienced officer. She had served with the police throughout the war years, she was involved in many air raid incidents and had dealt with refugees, evacuees, and enemy aliens, yet it had come to this.

Bernard was immensely proud of Cecily and he dearly wished that she had found a man to make her happy and give her the grandchildren that he had always craved. Unfortunately, Cecily had had little desire to be a mother and Bernard put that down to her experiences in the war, witnessing the pain of bereavement that so many families had had to endure. She appeared to have wanted a simple life of work and enjoyment. She had loved to dance and had done so at least twice a week, work permitting. She was never happier than when she was "tripping the light fantastic".

While Bernard was being cared for downstairs, Linda Collins and Jane Stewart, another female detective, were carrying out a slow and painstaking search of Cecily's rooms. She, apparently, had occupied the entire upper floor of the house since her father could no longer manage the stairs. He had taken up residence in what, hitherto, had been the dining room, and he used the downstairs privy and an old tin bath in front of the fire when necessary. He washed and shaved in the kitchen sink. It was an arrangement that had worked well for them. But no longer.

'She had some lovely dresses, did our Cecily,' said Jane, 'and she loved her dancing. I wonder if that was what she was doing on the night she was murdered.'

'She was certainly dressed for the part. Have you found her diary yet, Linda?'

'No. There's not much in the drawers either. A few letters, old tickets and a membership card for the Women's Institute.'

'Oh yes. Which branch?'

'Braintree.'

'We'll have to have a word with them then. See what they can tell us.'

'There's another membership card here,' said Linda, as she held it up to the light. 'For Colchester Hockey Club.'

'Didn't know she played any kind of sport,' observed Jane.

'Well it's for this year.'

Jane and Linda were carrying out a systematic search, one room at a time, starting by taking half the bedroom each and gradually working towards each other. They were intent on gleaning as much information as they could about Cecily White's personal life in the hope that they might learn the identity of any men she was seeing.

Cecily certainly appeared to have kept the details of her love life to herself. Her father had been unable to be of any great assistance in that regard. Linda had earlier attempted to take elimination fingerprints from the old boy and in the process had carefully and obliquely questioned him about Cecily's habits and customary movements. Despite her lightness of touch, he had become distressed, so she resolved to leave it for another time and carry on with the search.

❖

After carrying out their sad duty they made their way back to the police station with Cooper driving.

'Christ. That was bloody awful, Ladies. I felt so sorry for the old boy. Thank God he had his sister on hand to comfort him,' said Cooper. 'I dread to think what might happen if he were left on his own.'

'I suppose there's not very much you can say in a situation like that, all you can do is try and find someone to support them and deliver the bad news,' said Jane.

'Anyway, thanks for coming with me. I couldn't have brought Brian Pratt. Given his history with Cecily, he would probably have become upset and it would have only made matters worse.'

'Glad to be of service, governor,' said Linda. 'Her dad tried to put a brave face on things, but he looked absolutely shattered, didn't he?'

'Yes, he did. We really must catch this evil bastard.'

'Yes. We must.'

But, just how the hell are we going to manage it, with so little to go on, thought Cooper who wanted to stay positive and didn't want to share his thoughts.

'One thing in our favour is that it's an unusual *modus operandi* and I'd lay money on the probability that, whoever killed Cecily, has done it before and bitten their victims in the same way, so Linda, I want you to make enquiries with other forensic science labs to see if they have any similar murders on record. If you speak to me later, I'll give you the number for Professor Keith Simpson, of Guy's Hospital. He's the leader in the field of forensic dentistry. It would be a good place to start.'

'I'll get on to it straight away.'

Linda was pleased and not a little flattered by having such a key part of the investigation entrusted to her.

'You'll have to bear in mind though, Linda, the need for absolute discretion. We can't have details of the biting getting into the public domain, otherwise by sharing the *modus operandi,* of the offender we'll have every nutter this side of London claiming that they did it. We must keep that up our sleeve.'

'You can trust me to do the right thing, governor.'

'I know that.'

Cooper and Linda, as well as being colleagues, were in fact in a relationship, and although Jane had her suspicions, she kept them to herself. However, this was something quite unknown to their other colleagues, particularly Tom Stockwell, her uncle.

Both were aware of the perils of a relationship between a senior and junior officer and they were at pains to ensure that it didn't interfere with their working relationship. But, there was a growing intensity between them, and the time was fast approaching when one of them might have to move to a different department.

⊗

'How are we getting on then, Brian?' said Cooper, as he arrived back in the office.

'We've seen the kids, boss, and they showed us to the ditch where they found the purse, and, finally there's some good news. After a search, we found Cecily's handbag as well. It was in the undergrowth.'

'Where is it now then, Brian?'

'Being fingerprinted as we speak.'

'Good. What about the contents of the bag? Was there anything inside it that links it to Cecily?'

'Yes, governor. There's a letter and a few other bits and pieces inside with her name and address on them.'

'Good. Well done, Brian. That will save us having to go to see her dad and upsetting him further by expecting him to identify it.'

'Absolutely,' said Brian, wincing. 'I'm sure he'd have been devastated if we'd gone down that line.'

'In due course we'll show it to the girls on her team. One of them might recognise it.'

'Yes. Worth a try.'

'One other thing, Brian. Can you get on to Brendan Withers, please? If there are any marks found on the bag and the purse, I want them compared to the marks on the beer bottle we found at the scene.'

'Yes, leave it with me. Oh, and Mr Stockwell wants to see you, boss.'

'Thanks, Brian.'

Shit. What does he want now? Thought Cooper. *I wish to God he'd just let me get on with the job.*

Cooper made his way along the High Street to the town hall where he mounted the steps to the first floor. As he did so he mulled over the state of play within the investigation, trying to anticipate what Stockwell was about to ask him. On entering the management suite, Lucy, the boss's secretary, looked up from her work and, on seeing Cooper, instantly got to her feet.

'Morning Alby, Mr Stockwell needs to see you. He's on his own. So, you can go straight in.' This was said almost brusquely, which made Cooper wary of what was about to come. He knocked on the open door.

'Ah, Albert. Come in and take a seat,' said Stockwell, who had been standing looking out of the window. 'Tell me. How are things going with the murder?' They both took a seat and Cooper told him about the discovery of the handbag.

'Good, good. It sounds as though we're making some progress. I wanted to speak to you about Linda Collins.'

Oh hell. What's coming now? thought Cooper, anticipating

the third degree on their relationship.

'Yes, sir. She's doing well.'

'Gets on well with her colleagues, does she?'

'Yes, sir.'

'It can't be easy for her, bearing in mind that she's my niece.'

'Yes, sir. As you know, the troops are fully aware of that and they get on well with her. She has a nice personality and she works hard.'

'And you get on well with her yourself, don't you?'

'Yes, sir.'

Oh dear. He's getting warmer.

'How long has she been with you on CID? About six months, isn't it?'

'Well, actually it's about five and a half, sir.'

'And she recently passed her sergeant's promotion exam.'

'Yes, sir. We are all pleased for her. I know she studied hard for that.'

'Whereas, none of the staff on the Women's and Children's team are qualified to sergeant. So, I'm going to make her temporary sergeant in place of Cecily White. It would be good experience for her, and I think it would provide the team with a bit of leadership at this difficult time.'

'I'm sure she'll do a fine job, sir. I shall be sorry to lose her though,' said Cooper, trying not to show his relief.

'So be it then. Can you ask her to come and see me?'

'Yes, sir. Would you mind if I tell her what it's about?'

'No, you can tell her, by all means. Although it would probably be a good thing to stay quiet about it as far as the others are concerned. But it would give her a chance to think it over before she sees me.'

'I'm sure she'll be delighted, sir.'

'OK. Thank you, Albert. That'll be all,' said Stockwell, imperiously.

Cooper got up and left the room. He walked back down the High Street. He wondered how Linda would take the news but recognised that her posting would take a significant amount of pressure off their relationship. He had fallen deeply in love with the girl and they were finding it increasingly difficult to hide their relationship from their colleagues. Besides, he was serious about her and wanted them to marry in their own time and not be rushed by the imperatives of the police force. It was none of their business, after all.

On his arrival back at the police station, Cooper called Linda to his office.

'Come in, Linda, shut the door and take a seat.'

'Oh dear,' said Linda, 'This sounds a bit ominous.'

'Not at all, Linda. Quite the opposite, in fact.'

'Pray tell, governor darling.'

'I'll come straight to the point. Mister Stockwell wants to see you. He wants you to take over from Cecily White as temporary sergeant on the Women's department.'

'Really?' Linda was lost in her own thoughts for a few seconds.

'You know what a bunch of nasty cows they are.'

'Yes. But you told me yourself, there were some right horrors who served with you in the Wrens during the war. I'm sure you'll soon sort them out.'

'Sounds as though you're trying to get rid of me,' she

laughed, almost nervously.

'Don't be daft, Linda. It's a great opportunity for you and a feather in your cap. Besides, it's Mister Stockwell's idea, not mine, but I happen to agree with him, and, I imagine it wouldn't be long before we get you back on the CID. I'm very proud of you, darling, and as your boyfriend, I want you to do well and be successful.'

'Thanks, Alby darling. I'd like to think so. Well, I suppose I'd better go up and see him and hear what he has to say. I know that it won't be easy with that load of bitches but I'm sure that I could manage. I've worked with them before.'

'Before you go, how about I make you dinner later this evening? There's something I want to speak to you about.'

'Yes. That would be lovely.'

'Say, seven o'clock at my place?'

'Great. See you then, darling.' She pecked him on the cheek and left the room.

Cooper had recently taken up residence in a terraced house, having moved from digs that were in a house owned and occupied by Pearl, his predatory landlady. The house was three doors down from the Hole in the Wall pub and he had got into the habit of visiting it on almost a daily basis. Cooper resolved to moderate his alcohol intake after this had led to him having a brief drunken fling with Pearl. He immediately regretted it and to escape Pearl's attentions, Cooper had relocated to give him the space to pursue his relationship with Linda.

Not long after Linda had left his office, Cooper left the Station and walked into the town to see Sadie, his aunt, who ran a green-grocer's shop in the High Street. He wasn't the best of cooks and having rashly offered Linda dinner, he knew that he would need all the help that he could get.

◆

'Hello, governer darling.'

Linda was on the doorstep wearing a little black dress, seamed black stockings and high heels. She had a raffia bag over her right shoulder and Cooper saw that it contained two wine bottles. An educated guess told him that it was more of her mother's parsnip wine, and he knew, instantly, that it was going to be a long night. Experience told him that the stuff was lethal as he had fallen foul of it before. Cooper bid her enter the house. He closed the door behind her and swept her up in his arms.

'God, I love you, little lady.'

He gave her the most passionate of kisses and, without breaking the embrace, he guided her into the front room.

'Something smells nice.'

'Thanks. Just a little something I prepared earlier. I'll be dishing up in a minute. You like chicken stew, don't you?'

'Yes, darling. I love it. Was that your Aunt Sadie I saw walking up the street a couple of minutes ago?'

'Yes, it was. She just stopped by to drop off some fruit for us. Anyway, why don't you pick out a record from my collection and stick it on the radiogram? I've got to finish off in the kitchen.'

'Can I help you with anything?'

'No, darling. This is my show. You sort out the records, please,' Cooper said firmly.

Linda took off her high heels and sank to her knees to riffle through the stack of records that were on the bottom row of the bookshelf.

'So, how did you get on with Uncle Tom?' shouted Cooper from the kitchen.

'Fine. He stressed the point that it would be a good move for me as far as my career development is concerned, and as I already know the women on the department, I know how to handle them. I know I'm going to have to get a good grip of them right from the off.'

'Did he mention anything at all about our relationship?'

'No, he didn't. I did wonder whether that was what lay behind the move. But he kept on asking whether any of the girls on the team were close to Cecily and knew who she was seeing. He said that he wants me to keep my ear to the ground in case any of them is holding something back.'

'Yeah. I agree. It would be good to have you in place to pick up on anything of interest. Did you say anything to him about coming back on to the CID as a sergeant?'

'Yes, and he seemed quite supportive of the idea.'

'Good, good. We're going to miss you, you know. You've done bloody well. But it's too good an offer to turn down.'

Linda smiled to herself as she fired up the turntable with an Al Bowly record, "The Very Thought of You," which she put on at low volume.

'There is another bonus to the move, governor darling, the fact that we won't have to hide our relationship and creep around like we have been doing for the past six months.' Linda giggled at her comment like a naughty school-girl.

'Well, I was going to speak to you about that.'

Cooper appeared from the kitchen carrying a bunch of red roses and presented them to Linda, who was already sprawled across the settee. She sat up in surprise.

'Oh Alby, they're lovely.'

'And that's not all,' said Cooper, as he knelt in front of her.

'I know it's only been six months, Linda, but would you do me the honour of being my wife?' He produced a small box which, she told herself, must contain a ring. She didn't give an immediate response, not out of hesitation, but because she was simply overcome with emotion.

'Yes. Of course I will, darling. I love you so much.'

Cooper opened the box and he showed her the ring. She immediately threw her arms around him and they both tumbled to the floor, kissing passionately. After a few minutes they broke their clinch.

'I suppose we'd better see if it fits,' said Cooper, who removed the ring from its box and slid it on her finger.

'It's perfect,' said Linda. 'But how did you know my size?'

'I guessed it, with a little help from Sadie.'

'Oh Alby. I can't wait to tell somebody.'

'I understand that, love, but let's just be a bit careful about how and when we tell people, shall we?' said Cooper, gently and not wishing to dampen her joy.

'I wonder what Uncle Tom will say about it.'

'I'm sure that he'll be delighted,' said Cooper.'

'You sure that he didn't say anything to you about our seeing each other?'

'No, he didn't, but I know he's genuinely happy that we

get on well, and if you are not directly under my supervision, there can't be a problem.'

'No, I suppose not. Anyway, darling. Shall we have dinner?'

9

Thursday 6 October 1949

'You're looking very happy, governor,' said Brian, looking up from his desk as Cooper entered the office wearing a broad grin.

'Yes, Brian. I've had some good news.'

'Really? What's that then, guv?'

'Well, I've just had Brendan Withers on the phone, and they've got a result for us on the fingerprints. Firstly, they have confirmed that the body is that of Cecily. Unfortunately, that's no real surprise, but also, they've compared the marks on the purse with those on the beer bottle found at the scene, and they're sure that they are from the same person.'

'Have they got an owner for the marks on record?' asked Brian.

'No. Obviously they've checked the marks against Cecily's fingerprints and they're not hers. They don't belong to any of the kids either. We've just got to find the owner.'

'Easier said than done. guv.'

'Don't be so negative, Brian. At least, now, with this, we've got some more evidence to work with.'

Nothing was going to dampen his spirits. He was confident and determined that they would get a result and find Cecily's killer.

'Anyway, we've got Levi Loveridge coming back tomorrow to answer his bail. Have we checked him against the marks?'

'Yes, Brian. They did him as well and it was negative. All we need now is to know the identity of his mate. I'm pretty sure that it was Podger Loveridge, but he was checked against the prints and they weren't his either. Mister Stockwell has given us some latitude on the theft of eels charge so I'm hoping that we can persuade Levi to come across with a bit more detail on what he saw.'

'I wouldn't hold my breath, governor.'

'Brian, do cheer up, mate.'

It was indeed good news, and it did give them something to work on, but Brian could tell that there was something else. He probably knew Alby Cooper better than anyone in the force. He was a good friend as well as a colleague, and he could tell, from his demeanour, that he was inordinately happy.

'That's not everything, though, is it, guv?'

'No. It's not, Brian. I'm getting married. Perhaps you'd like to do me the honour of being my best man?'

'Blimey, Alby. You are a dark horse. Who is the lucky lady? Or should I say, the lucky Linda?'

'Yes, it's Linda Collins all right. How did you know?'

'It's been noticeable that you have been studiously

correct with her for some while. Your team think the world of you, Alby, and they notice things. Particularly when you are being extra polite. I'm sure that, to a man and woman, they'll all be chuffed to bits that you've found happiness together.'

10

Friday 7 October 1949

Levi Loveridge arrived at the front counter of the police station at the appointed time and he was met by Brian Pratt, who took him through to the station sergeant to be booked in, after which he took him to an interview room. They were soon joined by Alby Cooper.

'Well, Levi. Have you thought about what we said to you, last time?'

'Yes, I have. What about the poaching charge?'

'I've got authority to be flexible on that. And your friend?'

'I'm not a grass, Mister Cooper, but I'll give you all the help I can.'

'Did you speak to your friend?'

'Yes. I did. But I couldn't 'vince him to come in with me. He didn't want to know 'cos he doesn't trust coppers. Anyway, he had nothing to do with it. He only made a phone call for an ambulance. It's true we're poachers and thieves, our records show that, but we're not murderers.'

'Yes, Levi, but as the boss says, we can be flexible,' said Brian.

Cooper realised that the cooperation of the second man was no longer a major issue. Fingerprint examination of the recovered items had told him that. They would be unable to prove his presence at the scene of the murder without an admission, which would be extremely unlikely and not worth the time or effort. He decided to take a pragmatic approach and not pursue the point.

'Levi, we won't push you on the identity of your friend or do you for the poaching. But we will want one thing in return,' said Cooper.

'What's that?'

'A detailed witness statement about what you saw at the reservoir. You don't have to name your friend and the body you found was that of a woman who we've since been able to identify.'

'What was she doing there?'

'Wouldn't we like to know?' said Pratt, ironically.

Levi sat in silence for a few moments and considered his position. He then drew a deep breath and gave his answer.

'OK, Mister Cooper, I'll make a statement. But that means I'd have to give evidence at court, doesn't it?'

'It does.'

'Well, I suppose it wouldn't make me a grass and whoever did it deserves to have their neck stretched, the bastard!'

'Thank you, Levi. Good man,' said Cooper.

Brian Pratt put pen to paper and later Levi Loveridge was released without charge.

It was about midday when Loveridge was finally released, and Cooper made his way to the town hall where, for now, the divisional commander was still based. Tom Stockwell had been the chief officer of the Colchester Borough Police before it was subsumed into the Essex Constabulary earlier in the year. He now held the rank of superintendent and although he had been effectively reduced in status, he was still regarded as the sheriff; Colchester was still his fiefdom; and he still had a grip on the borough. Stockwell had an extensive network of contacts and nothing much escaped his attention.

He and Albert Cooper enjoyed a cordial working relationship, but it was likely that this would soon be tested by the revelation of Cooper's engagement to his niece. The timing and delivery of this information would be of the utmost importance but first there were more pressing matters to discuss.Lucy, the boss's secretary, showed Cooper into the office.

'Come in, Albert. Tell me, how did it go with Mr Loveridge?'

'He still wouldn't give us the name of his friend, sir, to use the vernacular, he thinks it would make him some kind of "grass".'

'Well, that won't do at all, Albert. He needn't think that he can play games with us. What have you done with him?'

'If I may, sir, things have moved on and it isn't really that much of a problem. We have already established a forensic connection between the beer bottle found at the scene and Cecily's purse, which was found in a ditch near Copford.'

'That's encouraging. Who is it?'

'Scenes of Crime haven't identified anyone yet, sir. Both bear the same fingerprints and they have already been checked against those of Levi Loveridge, his brother and side-kick Podger, Cecily and her father. None of them match. That being the case, we have taken a detailed witness statement from Loveridge about finding Cecily's body and the circumstances surrounding it.'

'OK. Fair enough. I follow your logic on that. And the beer bottle found at the scene. What brand of beer was it?'

'That's the thing, sir. It was a brand called Schlitz.'

'Never heard of that one,' said Stockwell.

'No, neither have I. It's certainly not British. I must say it sounds German, if anything, sir.'

'Good lord. Surely we're not importing German beer already. What is the world coming to? You had better make a few enquiries to find out its origin, Albert.'

Well. Why didn't I think of that? Thought Cooper.

'Anyway, how is my niece getting along?'

'Fine sir. I understand that she's scheduled to start with the Women and Children's team on Monday of next week.'

'Yes. Is that too soon, do you think?'

'No, sir. She's up to date with her workload.'

'Very well. I'm sure it will be good experience for her.'

'Yes, sir, I'm sure it will, and I'm hoping that by working closely with the Women's team she might be able to glean some valuable information about Cecily White and her off-duty interests. The women on that team are quite a tight, defensive bunch and getting information out of them is like pulling teeth, but if anyone can manage it, it's likely to be Linda.'

'Yes. I agree. Perhaps I'm biased, but she is very intelligent. If there is anything to be learned, she'll tease it out of them.'

'Anyway, sir. There is another matter, of a personal nature, that I wish to discuss with you, if you can give me a few minutes of your time.'

At that moment, as if on cue, there was a knock at the door and Lucy entered the room.

'I have the chief constable on the phone, Mister Stockwell. He wants to speak to you.'

'Thank you, Lucy. Put him through, will you, please? Albert, our discussion will have to keep for another time. I will see you at two, for the briefing.'

Cooper withdrew and returned along the High Street towards the police station. On the way back, he called in at his Aunt Sadie's greengrocer's shop. She immediately looked up from the counter as he entered.

'Just a minute, ducks, I'll just serve this lady and I'll be with you.'

She thrust her right hand into the potato skip, filled the brass scale pan and placed it on the scales in one fluid movement. She then poured the contents into the customer's bag.

'There you are' Mrs B.'

The customer paid with a ten-shilling note and received change.

'Is this the nephew that you've been telling me so much about, Sadie?'

'Oh yes. This is him all right. Our Alby,' said Sadie, playfully ruffling his hair .'Isn't he a dish?'

'Oh yes, Sadie, he's a dish all right,' said Mrs B. 'He can turn down my sheets any time he likes!'

The old girl gave a phlegm-ridden laugh followed by a cough. She left the shop smiling.

'I think you've made quite an impression on Mrs B, Alby.'

Cooper shook his head in resignation.

'I'm going to stop coming in here if you keep embarrassing me like that,' said Cooper with mock horror.

'Oh, do stop it, don't be a soppy date,' said Sadie. 'For a detective, you're far too easy to wind up, you know.'

'Anyway, Auntie dearest, I have some good news. But I don't know if I want to tell you now…'

Sadie was intrigued. 'What is it?'

'…what with all your teasing and that.'

'Oh, don't torment me, Alby. Please.'

'I thought you'd like to know that Linda and I are engaged to be married.'

'That's great news, darling.' Sadie was clearly delighted. She grabbed him and gave him a bear hug.

'It was obviously my chicken stew that did it.'

'Yes. That and my charm and a bunch of roses.'

'Have you set a date for the wedding yet?'

'No, not yet, but there's only you and Brian who know about it. I did try to tell her Uncle Tom about it when I saw him earlier, but he was too busy, so I'll save that for later. I'd be grateful if you'd keep it to yourself for now.'

'Don't worry, ducks. I'll be the soul of discretion.'

'Yes, I'm sure you will,' said Cooper with a laugh.

He knew full well that, for the best of reasons, she wouldn't be able to contain herself.

❖

'Right! Listen in, folks!' shouted Pratt.

It was two o'clock and a meeting had been called by Cooper for the team to be brought up to date with the progress of the investigation. The room went silent and officers got to their feet, as a sign of respect, when Cooper and Stockwell entered the room.

Brian Pratt passed around copies of the briefing sheet along with carbon copies of Levi Loveridge's witness statement.

'What's first on the agenda then, Brian?'

'Post-mortem report, governor.' Brian slid him a copy.

This had the potential for being distressing for some members of the team who had known Cecily well, but they were professionals and they were expected to treat the information in a business-like and dispassionate way.

'Yes, ladies and gents, I received this by courier this morning. In short, it confirms that our late colleague Cecily White was manually strangled to death. The shock caused her to soil herself and I imagine that, for this reason, she was not raped, but that's just my speculation. However, she was indecently assaulted after death.'

There was a groan of anger from one or two members of the group.

'How do we know that she was indecently assaulted, governor?' asked Jane.

'For the simple reason, Jane, that she had her left nipple bitten off.'

'Christ! That's evil,' cried Jane.

The room was in uproar. The anger was palpable.

'I know, I know,' said Cooper, in an attempt to calm the situation.

'I was furious when I first learned of this fact. So, we'll have a ten-minute break to calm down. Anybody who wants to use the lavatory, do so now, or if you want to grab a cup of tea from the canteen, I'll have two sugars. We'll reconvene in ten minutes. Don't discuss this with anyone else outside the team. It's vitally important. I can't stress that enough.'

Ten minutes later, they had all returned to the top room, minus Stockwell, who had been called away. Cooper continued:-

'Now this brings me to a very crucial point. And I make no apologies for repeating myself. It is vitally important for the investigation that we keep secret the fact that she had one of her nipples bitten off. This is a fact only known to us, the pathology team and the murderer. We cannot afford to waste time on any nutters who want to seek attention and admit to something that they haven't done, OK? -We've all met them, people who have so little in their lives that, to boost their self-esteem, they'll admit to anything, just to get a few hours of attention.'

'Doesn't Levi Loveridge know about it though, governor?' asked Jane Stewart.

'No. He made no mention of it at all, Jane.'

'Wasn't the nipple found at the scene then, governor?' asked DS Ian Mills, the incident office manager.

'No, Ian. The murderer either took it away or swallowed it. A dreadful thought. One thing which is in our favour, though, is that as the nipple was bitten off after death the wound was not engorged in blood. It means that if we arrest a suspect and can get a mould of their teeth, it could be compared with the wound. It's as good as a fingerprint apparently. But that could only be done if they cooperate.'

'I don't want to be negative, guv, but they are not likely to sit still for that, are they?'

'Yes, Ian. Any villain worth his salt is unlikely to cooperate, but we don't really know who we're dealing with.'

'But that's not all we have to go on, is it, sir,' said Brendan Withers, senior Scenes of Crime officer, 'We have a fingerprint match between the beer bottle found at the scene and Cecily's purse found half a mile away.'

'Good point, we do, Brendan, and that's a real bonus. By the way, the bottle is locked away at the lab, isn't it?' asked Cooper.

'Yes, sir. Safely under lock and key.'

'The make of the beer was "Schlitz" wasn't it?'

'Yes, sir.'

'Doesn't sound very nice, does it? Not with a name like Shits!' laughed Tom Rogers.

'It's Schlitz. For Christ's sake, grow up, Tom!' said Ian.

Cooper shook his head and moved on.

'Did you see from the label where it was brewed?'

'In the USA, sir.'

'Right. Job for you, Ian. I want you to make enquiries into the Schlitz brand and ascertain whether it is imported to the UK and where it is sold,' said Cooper.

'Will do, governor.'

'Oh, and you had better take young Rogers along with you. It might help to complete his education.'

'Yes, governor.'

'We also need to bear in mind the fact that, according to Loveridge, the suspect vehicle was a jeep. As he drove one throughout the war, I have no reason to doubt him on that point. Our murderer could be a squaddie.'

Cooper then turned to Linda Collins.

'Linda, can you tell the team how you got on with the search of Cecily's rooms, please?'

'Yes, governor. Jane and I searched her rooms, but we didn't find much of interest to be honest. She doesn't appear to have kept a diary. She had a nice selection of ball-gowns though, and according to her father, she loved her dancing and it was something of an obsession with her.'

'As you know,' interrupted Cooper, 'she was wearing a nice long skirt and blouse when she was found at the scene and may well have been to a dance that night. We certainly need to find out where she had come from and, of course, who she was with.'

'There were some bits of paperwork in her purse and her handbag, weren't there, Linda?' asked Brian Pratt.

'Yes, sarge. One was just a letter from the pay office at headquarters and the other was a gas bill, so not much interest there. Cecily's warrant card was also in her purse,' Linda continued. 'When we searched the bedside cabinet, we found a current membership card for the Colchester Hockey Club and, apparently, she was also a member of the Women's Institute, Braintree branch. One of her other hobbies was embroidery and there were some nice examples of her work in the bedroom.'

'Well, we need to make enquiries with the Hockey Club and WI. You never know, Cecily may have confided in someone about a date or a regular boyfriend. I suppose now would be a good time to tell you all about the fact that Linda is going to leave the department to take up the post of temporary sergeant in place of Cecily White as of Monday. So, congratulations to you, Linda,' said Cooper.

'Thank you, governor.'

'Yes. Best of luck with that,' said Ian Mills. 'Where's Matthew Hopkins, the witchfinder- general, when you need him?'

'Oh, they're not that bad,' chipped in Jane, with a grin. 'A bit bitchy, perhaps, but they can be quite nice on a good day.'

'Yes, it will be a bit of a challenge for you,' said Cooper.'

'It will, that,' said Linda, smiling ruefully.

'I'm sure you'll manage though, and the added benefit will be that, if you are in day to day contact with the ladies on the team, you might pick up some valuable information. Right. Any other business?'

Cooper looked around the table, but nobody raised any issues.

'Right. Well, having got to the end of today's briefing, there is one personal matter that I wanted to raise on behalf of Linda and myself.'

Linda caught his eye and looked at him coyly, as if to say, are you sure that this is the right time to tell people?Cooper hesitated for a few seconds and then carried on. 'I have asked Linda to marry me and she has accepted.'

The room erupted in cheering and they all took turns to shake Cooper's hand and embrace Linda.

'What took you so long, governor?' said Brian.

'It's only been six months, Brian.'

'Is that why Linda's being promoted?' said Ian.

'She deserves a medal, I should think,' said Brian.

'Cheeky pair of buggers!' Cooper feigned a punch on Brian's chin.

'Only joking, guv. We are all absolutely delighted for the pair of you. In my opinion you suit each other down to the ground.'

'Thanks, Brian. Anyway, Linda and I will have to go and see her Uncle Tom before he finds out from someone else. I'd like to buy you all a drink when we get the chance but, under the present circumstances, that'll have to wait for another day. But all the drinks will be on me.'

'We'll hold you to that, governor,' shouted Brian.

❖

The town hall clock struck five as Alby and Linda climbed the stairs. *"For whom the bell tolls" indeed,* thought Alby. He wasn't at all sure what kind of reception they would receive when they broke the news to Tom Stockwell. As they entered the outer office of the management suite they bumped into Lucy, the boss's secretary, who was just putting on her jacket and apparently leaving for the day.

'Is Mister Stockwell in, Lucy?'

'Yes, he's on the phone,' said Lucy, beaming from ear to ear.

'Who is he speaking to?'

'He's talking to the Mayor about the Oyster Feast, I think. I wonder which stars we'll get this year. It was Tommy Trinder last year.'

'Yes, it was. He went down well, apparently. Let us know if you find out, Lucy. I'll see if we can get an invite this year.'

'What? You and me?' teased Lucy, winking at Linda, knowingly.

Cooper coloured up. 'No. Sorry. Me and somebody else.'

Lucy just grinned at him and went on her way.

Alby and Linda remained in the outer office until they heard the receiver go down on its cradle. Alby took it as his cue and stepped into the open doorway and knocked. Stockwell did not appear to look up at the pair standing in front of him but continued writing at his desk.

'Come in, Albert, Linda, take a seat. Bear with me. I shan't be a minute.'

Stockwell continued with his notes for a few more minutes and this troubled Alby. It was almost as if he was working himself up to deliver a bollocking. He finally put his pen down and gave them his full attention.

'Albert. How are things with the murder? Is there any progress?'

'Yes, sir. We have a couple of good lines of enquiry.' Alby spoke about the origins of the beer bottle, found at the scene, and the belief on the part of Levi Loveridge that the murderer had used a jeep.

'That does sound encouraging. I know that we've spoken to the military police on the garrison but I think it best that we also make a point of speaking to our American friends at RAF Lakenheath.'

'Do we have a point of contact there, sir?'

'Yes, we do, Albert,' said Stockwell. 'Leave it with me. When I can, I'll speak to someone I know at the base. That is, if they're still in post. Nice enough chap, you know, but it seems that American airmen move around so quickly these days, one has a difficult job keeping up with them.'

'There was one other thing I need to speak to you about, sir.'

'Really?' Stockwell was playing dumb. 'What was that Albert?'

'Yes, sir. You might recall I tried to raise it with you earlier, then the chief constable rang.'

'Yes, I remember. Anything to do with marriage, is it?' asked Stockwell.

'Well, as a matter of fact, it is, sir,' said Cooper, the wind having been well and truly taken out of his sails.

'Yes. I understand that congratulations are in order,'said Stockwell, who looked at them sternly. He then broke into a broad smile and laughed. 'Well done you. I couldn't be more delighted. Just wait until I tell your aunt, Linda. She'll be over the moon. When did you pop the question, Albert?'

'A couple of days ago, sir.'

'Well, I'm very pleased for you both.'

Alby felt a surge of relief pass through his body. Uncle Tom Stockwell came to the fore, shook Alby's hand vigorously and kissed Linda on the cheek. He then picked up his phone.

'You can come in now, Lucy.'

The door opened and into the office came Lucy, who was carrying a tray of glasses and the bottle of champagne that Stockwell had had tucked away at home for just such an occasion. Lucy placed the tray on the boss's table and he immediately scooped the bottle up.

'Now folks, shall we have a glass of bubbly?'

'Yes, please,' said Linda.

'I'm not going to shake this. It's not Silverstone and we don't want to waste any of it.' He wrestled with the cork, shot it across the room into the fireplace, and filled each of the four glasses before handing them around.

'Here's a toast to you both, Linda, Albert, wishing you both every happiness.'

They each took a sip of champagne. Murmurs of pleasure went around the group.

'Ooh! Uncle Tom, that's lovely. Thank you.'

'That's OK, Linda. Anything for my best niece.'

'I am, in fact, your only niece.'

Uncle Tom laughed and almost snorted his drink through his nose.

'Yes. I know. But you're still the best.'

'Anyway, how did you know what Alby was going to say?' asked Linda.

'It's a small force and news travels fast. Speaking of which. Have you told your mum and dad yet, Linda?'

'Not yet, no.'

'What about you, Albert?'

'No, sir. I've got to take Linda over to West Mersea to see my parents, at some point.'

'Well, I think it would be best that you two get over there and tell them asap. I would hate for them to find out from someone else. Have either of you got anything urgent on this evening?'

Linda looked at Alby. 'I don't know. Have we, governor?'

'No. Nothing urgent, sir.'

'Well, what about this? Take my car and Trevor my driver and I want you to go and see both sets of parents and do your duty. Just make sure you get him back by, say, nine o'clock.'

'That's very kind of you, sir.'

'My pleasure. To say I'm chuffed would be an understatement.'

Linda's mother and Alby's Aunt Sadie were old school chums and it was their matchmaking that had brought Linda to Alby's attention six months previously. Linda knew that her mum would be delighted. Triumphant even.

11

Saturday 8 October 1949

It was Cooper's turn to cover as the weekend senior officer and he was sitting at his desk thumbing through the pages of an evidence file.

He was suffering a bit of a hangover from last evening's celebrations, but he didn't regret it, as it had been a marvellous evening. Linda's mum had burst into tears when Linda announced that she and Alby were to be married. This rather startled Alby, as, misunderstanding the situation, he had immediately taken this as a negative response to the revelation. He need not have worried. It turned out that they were tears of joy.

After calling at the home of Linda's mother, they made their way, with the aid of Tom Stockwell's driver, to Mersea Island where they visited Alby's parents. They had already met Linda on several occasions and they both adored her. They were beside themselves with glee when they broke the news. Even, Buster, the dog, sensing that something exciting was afoot, seemed to give them extra attention.

Now, after little sleep, he was hoping for a quiet day in the office with no dramas, but his hopes were dashed when in mid-afternoon Brian Pratt put his head around the door and announced, 'Looks like we've got a sudden death, governor, with strange and suspicious circumstances.'

'Oh bollocks! Whereabouts?'

'Out at Layer. I've got the car ready.'

On arrival at the scene they were met by a uniform constable who led them to the rear garden of the cottage, where they were shown the body of a man, who had been laid under a red ambulance blanket on the lawn. The constable explained that he had requested that the CID attend the scene as, in his opinion, the cause of death was "suspicious", and the circumstances were somewhat unusual. The deceased, a Mr Tom Munson, who lived alone in the cottage, had apparently drowned in the well.

Mr Munson was about fifty years old and a large man of about sixteen stones in weight. He was wearing white shirt and grey trousers which had clip-on braces attached to them. His body and clothing were saturated with water.

'When I first arrived on scene, I was met by Mrs Alsop who lives next door. She was the one who made the nine call. She showed me around here to the back garden and I saw that Mr Munson was down the well.'

The constable showed them to the bottom of the garden where the well was located. As they approached, Cooper could see that there was a large round wooden cover that was laid on the grass at its side.

'There was no way I was going to be able to get him out of the well on my own, governor, so I called out the fire brigade. They were here quite quickly. I showed them where

Mister Munson was and left them to it while I went back to the car to call control on the radio. After a few minutes I returned to the back garden and I saw that the firemen had managed to get him out of the well and up onto the lawn. They said that they had immediately tried "mouth to mouth" but that it was too late, they couldn't revive him.

The ambulance crew who arrived soon afterwards said the same, but they and the fire-officers have since gone.'

'So, what is it that you find suspicious?' asked Cooper.

'I can't quite put my finger on it, governor. But something's not right,' said the constable. Cooper was not just going to dismiss the officer's concerns without making some enquiries of his own. He started by going next door to Mrs Alsop, the neighbour who had made the initial report. Mrs Alsop answered the door. Cooper and Pratt introduced themselves.

She was a middle-aged woman, plump, with straight greasy hair, green uneven teeth and a stubbly beard that Cooper found it difficult not to stare at. Cooper marvelled at her countenance. *Everyone is entitled to be ugly,* he thought to himself, *but this woman abuses the privilege.*

'Mrs Alsop, I believe.'

'Yes, officer. It was me who telephoned the police.'

'Can you please tell me what happened here?'

'Earlier this afternoon, about an hour ago, I suppose, I was sitting outside in the yard when I became aware of someone moving about in Tom's garden. My view was a bit restricted by the fence, but I recognised the sound of the wooden cover being dragged from the top of the well; it made a sort of clunking noise. Then I heard a shout followed by the sound of splashing water and this made me look over the fence. I couldn't see anyone in the garden, but I could see that the wooden lid of the well had been removed and that it was laid on the grass. I was frightened that Tom had fallen so I rushed next door and I found him submerged in the well and he wasn't moving. I tried to reach him, but the water level was too low. I just couldn't manage it. So, I ran back indoors and called the police.'

'Did you see or hear anyone else in the garden?'

'No, I didn't. Well, not until Constable Hicks arrived, anyway.'

'How well did you know Tom, madam?'

'Well, we've been here three years and he was here when we arrived. Tom's wife sadly died not long before we came to live here. We had a good relationship with him, and we socialised quite a lot. But, in recent months, he's suffered from mental health problems and he's become somewhat erratic in his behaviour. It's very sad. It's totally changed his personality. I blame it on the war, you know.'

'Really? Why is that?'

'During the war Tom was captured at Dunkirk and he was a prisoner of the Germans. It left him with a mental condition where he suffered depression. He would have good days and then you would hardly see him at all. He just shut himself away.'

Cooper nodded. He understood fully as he himself had been incarcerated by the Germans in a prisoner of war camp for three years. As far as his mental health was concerned, he had survived relatively intact. He counted himself lucky.

Mrs Alsop continued, 'Recently he has taken to shouting and swearing at aircraft as they are passing overhead. I know he couldn't help it but the language was atrocious. He was convinced that it's still wartime and that they were all Germans.'

'I see. Do you think that he could have been suicidal?'

'I've never known him attempt to kill himself. But he wasn't right in the head. That's for sure.'

'Would you be prepared to let us take a written statement from you along the lines of what you have just told us, Mrs Alsop?'

'Yes, of course. If it helps.'

Brian Pratt took a statement from her covering the circumstances, which would be presented later at the coroner's inquest. While this was going on Cooper returned next door and he rejoined PC Hicks, who was standing over the body chatting to Inspector Bill Marshall, who had just arrived.

'Before we think about getting the undertakers to take Mr Munson to the mortuary, I think, to be on the safe-side, that we had better have the body examined by a police surgeon,' said Cooper.

Inspector Marshall went off to make the necessary phone call and within half-an-hour they were joined by Doctor Grahame Stevenson. After greetings, the doctor went about his examination.

Cooper removed the blanket and they saw that Tom was laid on his back. The doctor then examined the victim's head and the front of his torso after which, together, they rolled Tom over onto his front. What they saw made them gasp.

There were two holes through the shirt and further inspection revealed that, correspondingly, there were two deep holes in his body, each of about one inch in diameter.

These had pierced the rib cage. However, curiously, there was a complete absence of blood.

'Bloody hell, governor, He's been stabbed!' said Hicks. 'Good job we found that before the body went to the mortuary, otherwise, we would have been in deep shit.'

'Well, if he was stabbed,' said the doctor, 'it happened after death.' He didn't seem the least bit perturbed.

'As for the cause of death, I would say that it is most likely due to drowning. Of course, we won't know for certain until after the post-mortem examination.'

At this point Inspector Marshall asked the constable, 'How did the fire brigade get the body out of the well then, boy?'

'They told me that they pulled him out by his braces, sir, but I didn't see them do it because I was on the radio at the time.'

'No lad, that's bollocks!' said Inspector Marshall. 'You can't get them bloody things to stay on at the best of times.'

'Yes, Bill, he's certainly a big bloke and the water would have made him even heavier,' said Cooper.

'You know what, Alby,' said the inspector, 'I reckon the fire brigade gaffed him and dragged him out that way.'

'What do you mean when you say they gaffed him?' asked Cooper.

'They gaffed him like a fish. I've seen them do it before when I was on the Diving Unit, callous sods. They use a bloody great pike staff with a hook on it to fish bodies out of the water.' They considered the facts as they saw them, including the absence of blood around the wound. This indicated that the body had been stabbed after death and added total credence to the inspector's hypothesis. On that basis Cooper took the decision to have the body taken to the mortuary.

Brian was dispatched immediately to the fire station to speak to the station officer and to try and recover the offending implement. Luckily the relevant fire engine had since returned to base and Brian was able to make enquiries with the crew and seize the pike staff without too much trouble. This would later be compared to the wounds by the pathologist. For now, there was nothing else to be done.

12

Sunday 9 October 1949

Rest Day

13

Monday 10 October 1949

It was day one of Linda's attachment to the Women's Police Department as temporary sergeant and she made a point of being first to arrive in the office. She made herself a cup of tea, and settled at Cecily White's desk. As she did so she looked around the office and across to the desk that she, herself, had occupied only five months earlier. Nothing much appeared to have changed. There was the usual vase of flowers on the window and general female paraphernalia, powder compact on Enid Johnson's desk and biscuit tin poised in fat Gladys's in-tray ready to satisfy her sudden cravings. Linda found a bunch of keys in Cecily's tray and she started to experiment with the locks on her desk drawers. Two of them fitted and she was about to start rifling through the drawers when she was joined in the office by the first team member to arrive, Mavis Carey, who greeted her with a smile.

'Morning, Linda, or should I say sarge?'

'Linda will do, Mavis.'

'Having a look through Cecily's desk?' asked Mavis.

'Yes,' said Linda. 'I thought I'd better check to see what's in here.'

'only Inspector Wallis did her desk and lockers last week.'

'I need to, if I'm going to occupy it for a while, Mavis. Not only that, there might just be some helpful information.'

'I'm going to make some tea, Linda. Do you want another one?'

'No thanks. Could you show me which ones are Cecily's lockers?'

Mavis put the kettle on the gas ring and took Linda next door to the locker room. She pointed out two lockers.

'I wonder why she had two lockers?'

'Well, she had uniform in one and civilian clothes in the other. She often used to go out straight after work.'

'Really? Where did she go? Any idea?'

'She was very secretive about her private life and she didn't tell us anything about where she was going, but she would dress herself up to the nines. That's why she got the nickname "Queenie."'

'What about boyfriends?'

'She didn't speak of any. But then, she wouldn't have.'

'So, how often would she go out after work?'

'A couple of times a week, maybe. Judging by the style of dresses that she wore, we all agreed that she was probably going dancing.'

'I don't remember her having two lockers when I was on the team,' said Linda.

'I know. It was about six months ago when you left to go on the CID, we had a bit of a reorganisation of the lockers, that was when she claimed yours.'

'I see. Didn't waste much time, did she?'

'No. She seemed to change. She was always out and about.'

'Did she drink much alcohol?'

'Yes. As you say, it was almost as if she was making up for lost time. She always did like a beer and the odd glass of scotch. That seemed to increase, as well, but she didn't go out with the girls much, other than on special occasions. She did have a drink with us last Christmas, If you remember, we went to the George Hotel for dinner.'

'Yes, I remember,' said Linda. 'Right. Shall we open up and have a look?'

Linda produced the keys and found one that fitted the padlock. On opening the door, she saw that the locker contained items of uniform, tunics, greatcoat, shoes and a peaked cap. There were shoes and a briefcase which was the only item in the locker that was not standard issue. She took it out and locked the door. Linda attempted to open the case but found that it was locked. She put it aside for later.

'Right. Let's have a look at the other one. Shall we?'

Linda found the key and opened the door of the locker. She saw that it was stuffed full of various garments that were a riot of colour; also, two pairs of stilettos, dancing pumps and various items of make-up and toiletries. However, there was nothing else of interest to the investigation and so Linda locked the door.

On returning to the main office she saw that other members of the team had arrived for work, Enid Johnson, Beryl Hayes and Gladys Evison. She knew them well, their strengths, foibles and personal circumstances. She realised that she faced a challenge and would have to take control from the outset.

Linda called a meeting for later that morning, but for

now she carried on with the search of the desk and briefcase. The desk drawers held no surprises but what of the briefcase? She pulled a pair of tweezers from her handbag and fiddled with the lock of the case until she gave up in frustration, so she took it down to the basement to see the station caretaker, who made short work of the problem with a hammer and chisel. She took it back to the office where she examined the contents.

Linda found that it contained various items including a photograph of a young man and a 1949 diary. She thumbed through the pages eagerly and noticed that the name Johann appeared consistently. Cecily was obviously seeing this Johann on a regular basis and, given the name, Linda was beginning to understand why Cecily was so secretive. There were also several love letters written in broken English and signed by him. It was clear, from the text, that the author was an ex-prisoner of war now employed locally as a farm hand. The letters provided the address of the farm, which was clearly the best place to begin enquiries. The diary entry for the night of the murder showed "WI".

Linda took the briefcase upstairs to see Cooper. As she reached his door she peeked in and saw that he was alone.

'Got a minute, governor?'

'Yes, of course. Come in and shut the door, Linda. What have you got there?'

Linda held up the briefcase. 'I've just found this in Cecily's locker, and it contains some interesting items.'

'Well done. What have we got?'

'Her diary for this year and there are some love letters. It looks like she's been seeing a German on the quiet.'

'Christ! No wonder she wanted to stay schtum about

the man in her life. The women on her team would have made her life a misery.'

'Yes, I imagine they would. Apparently, he works at Folly-foots farm in Tiptree. To be fair the letters seem to be quite sincere. They give the impression that they were deeply in love and in quite a serious relationship.'

'OK. I think we should go and speak to the farmer discreetly and find out about young Johann. I'll need you out of uniform.'

'Oh, governor darling, you are awful,' Linda laughed.

'You've got a wickedly naughty sense of humour, sergeant.' Said Cooper, smiling and shaking his head. 'Just wait till I make an honest woman of you.'

Cooper took a deep breath and got back on track.

'Is there anything in the diary about the night she was murdered?'

'The only thing were the initials "WI."'

'Well, we need to speak to them as a matter of urgency. Is there a telephone number on the membership card?'

'Yes. The secretary is a lady called Constance Farrow. She has a Braintree telephone number.'

'Please give her a ring then, Linda. Let's find out what they were up to that night.'

'What about the enquiries with Professor Simpson, at Guy's Hospital. Have you been able to speak to him yet?'

'No. I thought that as I am now on the Women's department you would have given that enquiry to someone else on the team.'

'No. Sorry for not making myself clear. But I still want you to do it.'

'OK, darling. I'll get on with it right away.'

'Tell me, how are you getting on with girls?'

'They're all right so far. I've got an office meeting later. I was shown Cecily's lockers earlier, that's how I came to find this.'

'She had more than one locker, then?'

'Yes, one for her uniform and one for her evening attire.'

'Evening attire?'

'Yes. Ballgowns, stiletto's and such. Apparently, she often went out straight from work and got ready in the locker room.'

'Presumably, she didn't want her father finding out that she was seeing a German ex-POW.'

'Yes. I suppose that's probably it,' said Linda.

'Right. We need to speak to this young man as soon as possible. Have a discreet word with the farmer and get his details, then we'll speak to the military to try and find out more about his background.'

'I'll get onto it.'

The door was shut so Cooper rose from his chair, walked around the desk and took Linda in his arms. He gave her a long lingering kiss.

'Well done, darling. Keep me posted.'

Linda left the briefcase with Cooper, so that he could examine the letters at his convenience, and she returned to her office.

❖

Linda called the meeting to order.

'Ladies. As you know, I have been placed in temporary charge of the team following the murder of Cecily White. Apparently, this is merely on the basis that I am the only female officer on the division qualified to sergeant, having passed the exam in recent weeks.'

'Are you sure it's not a reward for agreeing to marry DI Cooper?' teased Enid Johnson.

The girls laughed.

'Quite sure,' said Linda, smiling. 'On a serious note, we need to clear up this tragic case and we need your help to solve it. There may be information to your knowledge that might be of great benefit. Things that you know about Cecily White, or Queenie, as you so lovingly called her, that could make all the difference to the investigation. So, I want you to rack your brains, ladies, and let's see if we can come up with some detail that can take us forward. Beyond that, I'm here, not just to supervise the team, but to help and care for you following her murder.'

The women said nothing for a few seconds, but sat and reflected.

'Her best friend was a woman called Maggie. I believe that she was a nurse, but that's all I really know about her,' said Mavis.

'She was obviously seeing someone,' said Gladys. 'Nobody takes that much care of their appearance unless they are in love.'

'Obviously, you're not in love then, Glad,' said Enid.

Gladys smiled and gave Enid two fingers.

'Come on now, girls. Play nicely,' said Linda.

'Yes. She used to go out dancing at least twice a week,' said Beryl,' but she didn't confide in anyone here?'

'No. She played her cards very close to her chest,' said Gladys. 'But, she was devoted to her father, I know that.'

'That reminds me,' said Linda.'On the subject of keeping

things close to our chest, the press know nothing of the fact that Cecily has been identified as the murder victim and, it is absolutely vital. I repeat, vital, that they are told nothing at this stage. Be very careful not to discuss it outside of this room.'

The team all nodded gravely.

'OK, ladies. If you think of anything, then please let me know.'

The meeting continued with a discussion about current cases with individual officers taking their turn to explain their progress.

At the end of the meeting Linda returned to her desk. One thing troubled her. The letters indicated a strong bond between Cecily and Johann, although their relationship was based on secret liaisons, and it was a fact that the press had not yet been told that Cecily was the murder victim. But, having not heard from her for a week, she wondered why he hadn't, at least come to the police station. Hopefully all would be revealed in due course.

For now, Linda had to make a call to Professor Keith Simpson, at Guy's Hospital, who was the leading authority in the field of forensic dentistry. She didn't feel comfortable making such a telephone call from her desk, surrounded by the rest of her team, so she made her way to the collator's office, where decorum reigned.

All larger police stations had a collator and at Colchester the post was occupied by Sergeant Reg West, aided by his assistant Eve Samuels. It was the collator's job to act as the local intelligence officer and what Reg didn't know about his ground, was not worth knowing. He was also the local police liaison officer for Berechurch Hall Prisoner of War Camp, which was located to the south of Colchester.

Linda told him about the latest information concerning Cecily and Johann and the fact that they were intending to visit the farmer at Folly-foots farm in Tiptree. Reg agreed to make enquiries to ascertain the details of the owner. Whilst he did so, Linda settled into a quiet corner and dialled the number for Guy's Hospital in London. As luck would have it, and after being redirected a couple of times, she found her man.

'Professor Simpson.'

'Professor. I am Sergeant Linda Collins of the Essex Constabulary, based at Colchester Police Station.'

'Good morning, Sergeant. How can I help you?'

'We had the murder of a young woman, a week ago, who apparently was strangled and after death she had her left nipple bitten off. The pathologist in the case was Professor Westlake and I understand that he liaised with you in relation to the bite wound. Is that correct, sir?'

'Yes Sergeant. He did.'

'I have been asked by Detective Inspector Cooper, the senior investigator, to contact you to find out whether you are aware of any other cases in this country that have had the same *modus operandi,* that is, where any biting has taken place.'

'Not lately, no. As you may know, I have made a study of forensic odontology, and these types of offences do happen from time to time. Normally, you get them in a series. The last one was about three years ago in Bradford, and they caught the chap who was responsible.'

'I dare say, he went to the gallows.'

'He did. Of course. I would put a caveat on my being

informed about cases in so far as I don't necessarily get to hear about all of them.'

'I see. So, how would you normally be informed about cases of this type?'

'By telex message from either the police or forensic pathologists.'

Linda was silent for a moment, trying to think of any other relevant questions.

'Of course, if I do hear of another case, I will be in touch with you straight away. I do have a list of forensic pathologists in the UK. If you would like, I will get my secretary to retype the list and send it to you. That way you would be able to get letters off to them yourself.'

'That would be very helpful Professor. Thank you.'

Linda provided the professor with her contact details.

'If there is anything else that I can help you with, do not hesitate to contact me. Although, I must just say that as of Monday next week I shall be attending a two-day conference in the Hague, but I shall be back on Wednesday. If there is anything more urgent, then my secretary, Phyllis, will know how to get in contact with me.'

'Thank you, Professor.'

'My pleasure.' Simpson ended the call.

'Get what you needed, Linda?'

'Yes, up to a point, Reg. Nice chap. I'm pretty confident that if he does learn anything, he'll pass it on.'

'I've just spoken to my contact at the local branch of the National Farmers Union. She gave me the farmer's name, Norman Smith, and a contact telephone number.'

'Brilliant. Thanks for that, Reg.'

Reg West handed over the note with the details.

'What mystifies me is, why does a POW want to work on a farm in the UK. Why don't they just go home?'

'Well, to start with, this country is still desperately short of agricultural workers, and some German POW's just don't want to go home, particularly if they are in a relationship with a British woman. Some have their original home in the Soviet zone or maybe they are so horrified, after having learned of Nazi atrocities, that they don't want to go home. That being the case the government created a scheme under which men could be discharged from their POW camp and apply to become civilian workers. I would imagine that that's probably what happened here.'

Linda thanked Reg and went back to her office.

❖

Later that afternoon, Linda returned to the collator's office, where she found it even quieter, the occupants having left for the day. She dialled the telephone number that had been provided by Reg West earlier. A woman's voice came on the line. 'Folly-foots farm, Mrs Smith speaking. Can I help you?'

'Yes, Mrs Smith, this is Sergeant Linda Collins, speaking from Colchester Police Station. Can I speak to Mr Norman Smith, please?'

'My husband, yes. I think, maybe, he's out in the yard. Bear with me, I'll try and find him for you.' The phone went quiet for a few minutes, then a booming male voice came on the line.

'Hello. If this is about the theft of my sheep, I'm not a happy man. Not happy at all. I reported it three bloody weeks ago and I've heard bugger all about it from Tiptree Police since.'

'Please, let me stop you there, Mr Smith. This has nothing to do with the theft of your sheep. It's about an investigation into the murder of a young woman at Abberton Reservoir. Shall we start again?'

'Yes, indeed,' said Smith. 'I do apologise, only the theft case has got me very exercised of late. I was thinking about making a complaint to my old school chum, Tom Stockwell, who is the chief constable, I believe. Do you know him?'

'Yes, sir. He's my uncle.'

'Well, well. He's your uncle, is he? Bless my soul. What a small world it is. How can I help you, officer?'

'We understand that you have a young ex-prisoner of war working for you on the farm, called Johann. Is that correct?'

'Yes, we do. Please don't tell me that he's responsible for it.'

'No, Mr Smith, I'm not suggesting that at all. We do know that he and the deceased, whose name was Cecily, were very fond of each other.'

'Yes, we know of Cecily. She's a police officer. So she's been murdered, has she?'

'Yes. I'm sorry to say that she has. Although the press are unaware of it and we wish to keep it that way for now.'

'That's very sad. Johann will be devastated. He thought a lot of the girl. One might say he was besotted. And judging by the amount of telephone calls we received from her, she was very keen on him too.'

'We would like to speak to him about their relationship and when the last time was that he saw her. It would be a great help to know whether he could shed any light on her movements during the final few days of her life.'

'Well, I'm pretty sure that he would do his utmost to help you. I am surprised though. He has said nothing to us about Cecily being murdered. However, to my knowledge he hasn't been off the farm for several days. I doubt that he even knows about it.'

'How has he been in recent days?'

'He has been in reasonably good spirits lately. He is generally quite an earnest young man but I'm pretty sure he would have said something to us about it.'

'Tell me, how have you found his attitude to work and his colleagues?'

'I have been impressed by his attitude and willingness to roll up his sleeves and work hard.'

'How does he get on with his colleagues?'

'He's on reasonable terms with the other workers, all of whom are British. He gets his leg pulled occasionally but he takes it in good part.'

'So, they tease him, do they?'

'Yes, but not in a vindictive way. They say that Germans have no sense of humour, but I have seen at first hand that that is not true. The others have taken to him. He's an asset. And I'm pleased to have him working for us.'

'What is Johann's surname?'

'According to his discharge papers it's Weber. He comes from Hamburg and served in the Luftwaffe. He was shot down on the Kent coast.'

'He came to you from Berechurch Hall camp, didn't he?'

'Yes. That was about eighteen months ago.'

'Where does he actually sleep?'

'He has a large room above the stables, here on the farm.

It has all the necessary amenities, a small kitchen, bathroom etcetera. He seems quite content there.'

'Does Johann have access to any motor vehicles?'

'Only the tractor, which he uses for ploughing and such. Other than that, he uses his pushbike.'

'OK. We need to come and see him and ask him for his help. I do stress that, just because he's German, it makes no difference. He's not a suspect.'

'Well, that's good to know.'

'We will need to take some elimination fingerprints from him, though, and I would be grateful if you didn't tell him about Cecily's death. That will be our unpleasant duty.'

'You can rely on that, I can assure you.'

'Is it possible for us to see him tomorrow?'

'Yes. That would be convenient. Could we say about 4pm?' said Smith.

'Thank you, Mr Smith. That would be fine. See you then.'

14

Tuesday 11 October 1949

It was the second day of Linda's temporary attachment to the Women's department, and those members of the team, who were on duty, were out of the office pursuing their own cases. She had apprised Cooper of the call made to Norman Smith and had arranged to meet him around 3.30pm for their visit. Farmer Smith had obviously been true to his word as she had received no distressing telephone calls from Johann Weber.

Reg West had contacted the POW camp at Berechurch Hall and he had learned a few more details about Johann.

Johann Weber was born in St Pauli, Hamburg on the 21st of November 1917, which made him thirty-one years of age. He joined the Luftwaffe in 1939 and became an air gunner on bombers. He was on a bombing raid in September 1940 when his aircraft was shot down by an anti-aircraft battery over the Isle of Sheppey. He managed to parachute to safety and was captured. Weber's conduct in Berechurch Hall Camp was said to be exemplary. There was little general information about his background, but she knew that that was the way of these things. Name, rank and number.

Linda, who was now sitting at her desk, was examining Cecily's papers in more detail. She looked at Johann's photograph. *Yes. I can see why you had a thing for him. You, naughty girl ,*she mused.

As she read the various pages, one fact that stood out was that although Cecily loved to dance, there was no suggestion, in any of the letters, that she had ever danced with Johann. *Maybe*, she thought, *he just couldn't dance or, maybe he didn't like to dance.*

But after due consideration, Linda felt it more likely that Cecily and/or Johann realised that they would not have been accepted as a couple in polite society due to his status and the quite recent ravages of the war. Perhaps they were biding their time before dipping their toes in the water more deeply. Linda recognized that it was a brave path that Cecily had been following, although knowing that the ticking of her biological clock was not an issue, she probably thought that she could take things slowly.

❖

DC Tom Rogers was sitting in his office which was located at the top of a tower up a flight of stairs, above the top floor of the police station. This was affectionately known as "the Crowsnest". There was only room for four officers, who were rarely there at the same time, but in the office with him was DC Jane Stewart. He was twenty-five and had only been on the CID a matter of months, but he had gained useful experience in that time. Jane was a lot older and although they got on well as colleagues, she was not his type. If anything, they were mates. No, he was more interested in Enid Johnson from the Women's team. He definitely had the hots for young Enid and he had made it known. Tom liked the top office because it was quiet, out of the way, and the sergeants were on the floor below, which meant that he could relax and work at his own pace. Tom was bright and keen enough, but he was mischievous, easily distracted and regarded by some as the office clown. The office gave a commanding view of Queen Street and particularly the telephone kiosks on the far side of the road, and for reasons best known to himself he had obtained the telephone numbers.

'There she goes,' said Tom, leaning towards the window.

'There who goes?' said Jane

'That hot little minx, Enid Johnson. I think I'll give her a call.'

'Oh Tom. Do behave,' said Jane, rolling her eyes.

Tom dialled the operator and after informing her that it was a police call she put him through to the number for one of the call boxes.

He heard it begin to ring, and Tom gave a commentary.

'She's nearly at the kiosk. Now she's looking at it. I bet you anything you like, that she won't be able to resist picking up the phone.'

Jane joined him at the window and she saw Enid Johnson enter the call box and pick up the receiver.

'Hello. Can I help you?' said a disembodied female voice.

Tom affected a strange accent.

'Hello. My name is Thomas. Is that the call box opposite Colchester police station?'

'Yes, it is.'

'Is it outside Arthur Wenn's the butchers?'

'Yes, it is.'

'Are you a Christian?'

'Yes. As a matter of fact I am.'

'Would you do me and my mum a great kindness?'

'Of course. If I can.'

'Well, my mum, she's disabled, and I'm partially-sighted. I've done my leg in and I can't get into town. I fell down the coal hole and broke it in three places.'

'Oh, that sounds nasty. I'm sorry to hear that. I'd be glad to help you if I can.'

'Could you kindly go into the butchers and ask them whether they can tell you which part of the animal they get their pigs' trotters from. The thing is, my mum won't have them from the back end because she thinks they'd be dirty.'

There was a slight pause before the answer came.

'Yes, if it makes her happy. I will, of course, dear. Just a minute. I'll go and ask.'

Tom and Jane both watched Enid leave the telephone box and walk into the butchers shop. They could see her through the window of the shop chatting to the two butchers, who appeared calm one minute and then suddenly they became convulsed with laughter.

Jane put her hands up to her cheeks and broke into fits of giggles.

'Oh Tom. You're wicked. I can't believe that she's actually gone into the shop to ask that question!' They watched Enid leave the shop and stroll back to the telephone box, where she picked up the phone.

'Thomas? Are you there?'

'Yes. I'm here.'

'I spoke to the butchers.'

'Yes.'

'And they told me that they only use the front trotters and throw away the back ones for the very same reason your mum thinks. They think they're unhygienic too.'

'Oh good. Mum will be pleased. Thank you for that.'

'My pleasure.'

'Can I ask you a question?'

'Ask away.'

'Are you a police lady?'

'Yes. As a matter of fact, I am. How did you know?'

'It's in the voice. Kindness mixed with authority.'

'That's very perceptive of you, Thomas.'

'Yes. When your eyesight goes you get almost a sixth sense to compensate for it. For instance, your voice tells me that you are a very attractive redhead.'

'Really?'

'And I'm thinking that you've got quite a short Christian name. Something like Ella or Eva.'

'Well, actually, it's Enid. That's brilliant!'

'Can I ask you just one more thing before I put the phone down?'

'Go ahead.'

'What colour knickers have you got on under that uniform, Enid?'

'What? Who is this?'

'I can see you. Look up and give us a wave. Top office at the police station.'

They watched her step out of the kiosk. She looked up at their window and pointed, shook her head and smiled.

She returned to the box. Tom put down the phone in its cradle. Jane sat back down and nearly fell out of her chair with laughter.

'Ooh! You are a silly bugger, Tom! You're really going to get your backside kicked one of these days.'

A few seconds later their office phone rang.

'Blimey, she's come back to us already. Can you answer it, Jane? Perhaps you can pretend to be Mum.'

Jane snatched up the phone and put on her best old lady's voice.

'Hello dearie.'

'Hello Jane, front office here. Are you all right?'

'Yes, fine.' She feigned a cough. 'Sorry. Just had a frog in my throat.'

'You sure you're all right, Jane?'

'Yes, yes,' said Jane, stifling laughter.

'You got anyone up there available to attend a burglary?'

15

Wednesday 12 October 1949

Cooper, Collins and Brendan Withers arrived at Folly-foots farm at the appointed time and they were greeted at the front door by Mrs Smith, who showed them into the house. She took them through to the large kitchen at the rear of the farmhouse, where they found Norman Smith sitting at the kitchen table with Johann Weber. Both were nursing a mug of tea. On seeing their visitors, they stood up and shook hands. Cooper and Collins introduced themselves.

'Herr Weber, thank you for seeing us. It is nice to meet you,' said Cooper.'

'I am sorry gentlemen, but I have no idea what you want to see me about. I am a bit worried to be honest.'

'All of that will be explained. But I want you to know that we're not here to give you trouble, we just want your help.'

'I will try.'

The officers were offered a seat at the table and they were soon supplied with mugs of tea by Mrs Smith.

'Let's make a start, Johann. Do you mind if we call you Johann?'

'Yes. No problem, call me Johann, please.'

'Johann. Do you know a lady called Cecily White?'

'Yes. She is my girlfriend.'

'How long have you been seeing her?'

'About four months I think it is. I met her when I was helping in the farm shop and she came in to buy some vegetables.'

'Do you know her job?'

'Yes, sir. She is with the police.'

'When did you last see her, Johann?'

'About a week ago. It was on a Friday. We met for a drink in Colchester at a pub called the Leather Bottle.'

'How did you get to Colchester?'

'By bus.'

'And you didn't see her after that?'

'No, sir.'

'Didn't you wonder why she has not been in contact with you since then, Johann?'

'I thought that she must have been busy with her work. Why are you asking me this? What has happened to her?'

'There is no easy way of saying this, Johann, but we have some bad news. Cecily was murdered a week ago.'

'Mein Gott. Nein!' Johann broke down in tears. He was sobbing. Mrs Smith supplied him with a glass of whiskey. After a short time, he had composed himself enough to carry on speaking to the two detectives. He seemed angry but eager to help.

'Where did this happen? Was it to do with work?'

'It happened at Abberton Reservoir, which is about nine miles away. She was not working. It was a Sunday evening.'

'The day of the Lord.'

'Unfortunately, it was, yes. She was found lying on the ground in the car park. She had been strangled.'

'Could it have been because I am German?'

'No, Johann. We have no reason to believe that that had anything to do with it.'

'Oh my God. Poor Cecily. Who would hurt her? She was such a lovely lady.'

Johann shook his head and fought back more tears. Again, he took some time to regain composure, taking several swigs of his whisky.

'Where were you on that day, Johann?'

'I was here, painting my rooms.'

'Yes, that's right, he was with me,' said Farmer Smith, 'I was given some paint as a part payment for some bales of hay. We decided to give Johann's rooms the once-over and make use of it. He was with me throughout. I'll show you, if you like.'

'Thank you, but that won't be necessary, Mr Smith. What time did you finish the work?'

'About half nine. Then we left it overnight to dry off and Johann slept in our spare room because of the smell of the fresh paint, which was quite overwhelming.'

'Johann. Did you know that Cecily was going out that night?'

'No. I did not know about that, but she did not need to tell me everything.'

'How did you and Cecily contact each other?'

'I did not telephone her at her home because her father would not have liked that, with me being a German, so she would telephone me here about six o'clock on some evening's or if I was out on the farm, she would leave a message.'

Farmer Smith chipped in, 'Yes, that's true. My wife and I would often take messages from Cecily.'

'Final thing then, Johann. We found her handbag and purse, that had both been thrown away. They have fingerprints on them. So, we are taking fingerprints from the people that were close to her to be checked against them.'

'Do I have to come with you to the police station?'

'No, you don't,' said Cooper, 'Brendan here has a portable fingerprint kit and he will set it up and do the job here.' Cooper turned to Farmer Smith. 'Unless, of course, you have any objections, Mr Smith?'

'That would be fine, Inspector. By all means, use the kitchen table if you like. The sink is over there if you need to wash your hands.'

Brendan Withers opened the small portable fingerprint stand, spread the legs and stood it on the table. He placed a rectangular onyx tablet on top, onto which he squirted several dots of ink from a tube. He then took a hand roller and smoothed the ink out, so it was evenly spread across the surface.

'Will you stand up next to me please, Johann?'

Johann rose from his chair and stood to Brendan's left.

'Just relax and let your hands go limp. Let me do the work, Johann.'

He took Johann's right hand and pulled it gently towards him by the thumb, offering it to the tablet. He rolled the thumb across the ink on the tablet, then transferred it to the page of the fingerprint form, where he rolled the thumb again, creating a print. Brendan continued the process with all other digits until completion.

'Right. Thank you, Johann,' said Brendan, 'If you would like to wash your hands? Then I need you to sign the form.'

Johann walked across to the kitchen sink and gave his hands a scrub with carbolic soap. The ink took some time to dissipate.

Brendan turned to Cooper.

'While we are here, I think that it would be a good idea to obtain a mould of Johann's teeth, governor.'

'I agree. I'll speak to him when he's finished at the sink.'

Johann returned to the table.

'Johann, there is just one other thing we need your help with. There was something else to do with this case that I cannot tell you about. But we need to take a mould of your teeth. I'll tell you again, we want your help and are not treating you as a suspect, but if we do this, we can be sure and move on.'

'That is no problem, sir. I want to help you in any way I can, if we can catch the swine who did this to my lovely Cecily.'

'Good. Thank you, Johann. Brendan will tell you what he wants you to do.'

'Yes. I just need to go out to my van to get something.'

Brendan left the room for a few minutes and returned carrying an attache case, which he placed on the table and opened. He took out two small wooden boxes and a tea towel.

'Now, Johann. Can you please go to your room and brush your teeth? When you come back, we will take the samples from you. Don't worry. It will be quick, and it will not hurt.'

Johann looked relieved. 'So, you are not going to take away any of my teeth?'

Brendan suppressed a laugh.

'No, Johann. That's not the idea at all. I'm going to ask you to bite into some blocks of cheese and that will give me a mould.'

Brendan washed his hands and set about obtaining a sample mould of Johann's upper and lower teeth. He then carefully transferred each sample to one of the two wooden boxes to preserve their integrity for analysis in the laboratory. While this was happening, Linda took a written witness statement from Norman Smith, who had effectively given Johann an alibi. At the end of this activity Cooper thanked them both.

'Johann, thank you for your help. Please do not talk to anybody else about this, particularly the people from the newspapers. We will keep in touch with you. If you think of anything else that you think may help us, please let us know. Mister Smith has our telephone number so that you can contact us.'

'I will, sir. Can you tell me when Cecily will be buried?'

'It will not be soon, Johann. But we will certainly let you know when they have been able to arrange a date.'

'Thank you, sir.'

Cooper bid Johann and Mr Smith farewell and the officers went on their way. On their return journey back to the station, Collins posed the question.

'Do you think that Johann could have killed Cecily?'

'No. I don't think he did. He is well alibied by farmer Smith, who I think is genuine and obviously quite fond of the lad. He doesn't have access to a jeep, apparently. Anyway, we can check his prints and teeth samples and the results should come back quite quickly. Or at least the fingerprints will.'

It was 6.10pm when Cooper and Collins arrived back in the rear yard of Colchester police station. As Cooper went to speak to the control room sergeant, Linda ascended the stairs to the CID office, where she was met by Jane Stewart.'

'Hiya, sarge. How did you get on with Cecily's fella?'

'Fine. He was helpful, but we've taken his fingerprints and a mould of his teeth, so we can check those samples to be sure.'

'Could he have done it, do you think?'

'It's looking unlikely. He's alibied by the farmer.'

'Oh. There was a call for you earlier. A lady from the Women's Institute. I've left a note on your desk.'

16

Thursday 13 October 1949

Just before 9.30-am Alby Cooper arrived at the town hall for the weekly senior officers' meeting, in which Superintendent Tom Stockwell attempted to catch up on the performance (or otherwise) of the various sections of the division. He entered the outer office, where he was met with the sight of various uniformed wallahs chatting over tea. Young Lucy, his secretary, was seated at her desk, trying hard to concentrate on her work and doing her best to ignore the din that had enveloped her. Tom Stockwell's door was shut, and Cooper wondered what was going on within. After another ten minutes or so the door opened, and Stockwell appeared in the doorway.

'Come on in and take a seat, gentlemen. I'm sorry to keep you waiting, only I had the chief constable on the phone. He wanted an update on the Cecily White murder investigation, which I did my best to give him. It's fair to say that he's more than a little frustrated, as we all are. So, I'll make that our first subject on today's agenda. Perhaps you can update us, Albert.'

'Yes, sir. Cecily White's body was found ten days ago, late at night, in the car park of Abberton Reservoir, by Levi Loveridge, one of our local "didicoys", and another, who is yet to be identified. She had been manually strangled and indecently assaulted.'

'How do we know that she had been indecently assaulted?' asked Chief Inspector Julian Sproat, Stockwell's deputy, a man deeply unpopular with the troops.

'Forensics,' said Cooper.

'Explain,' demanded Sproat.

'Sir, with the greatest respect, it's a matter of "need to know." A policy decision has been taken and as you have no role to play in the investigation, you do not need to know. It's better that way, believe me.'

Sproat took this remark personally and became indignant.

'I beg your pardon, Inspector. Are you inferring that I'm not to be trusted? Is that what you're saying?' Sproat stood up.

'Sit down please, Julian,' said Stockwell. 'A policy decision was made, and not with you in mind specifically, it's just that there are certain facts that we cannot afford to let into the public domain which relate to the *modus operandi*. The more people who know, the more difficult it will be to keep those facts secret. If the public knew, it could seriously compromise our investigation. It is simply, that you have no operational role in the investigation, therefore, you do not "need to know."'

Sproat sat down with a grunt.

'Please continue, Albert.'

'Loveridge insists that he and his friend had been poaching for eels, which is confirmed, by the way, when earlier they heard the sound of a jeep come up the drive into the car park. Then they heard a female screeching and they put this down to a courting couple having sex. They carried on emptying their nets, during which-time they heard the jeep return down the drive and leave the area. Soon after, they walked back to their van, which was hidden behind the toilet block, and when they turned on the lights of their vehicle and went to pull away, they saw the body of Cecily in the grass at the side of the car park. When they went to investigate, they found her dead. Levi Loveridge sent his friend away to telephone for an ambulance while he remained with the body. An ambulance attended with the Colchester area car within fifteen minutes, and I attended with some of my officers soon afterwards.'

'And you arrested Levi Loveridge?' asked Sproat.

'Yes sir, for larceny of eels.'

'Carry on, Albert. What happened after that?' asked Stockwell.

'The doctor came and certified death, the area was cordoned off and Scenes of Crime preserved the scene until Professor Westlake, the forensic pathologist, came to examine the body. It is true to say that none of the officers or medical professionals realised that the victim was Cecily White until DS Pratt saw her at the post-mortem.'

'Why didn't you recognise her?' asked Sproat.

'Several other officers had been in attendance and at that stage I didn't need to get close to the body. If too many enter the area it would contaminate the scene. Besides her face was covered in blood.'

'OK, Albert. What did you do next?' said Stockwell.

'I instructed officers to speak to the Military Police and get them to speak to the guardrooms at the various barracks, on the garrison, to ascertain who had a military jeep, off camp, at that time. They came up with no information.'

'And what has happened to Loveridge?' asked Sproat.

'We are treating him as a witness.'

'And you have recovered a few items, haven't you?' asked Stockwell.

'Yes, sir. On the same day as the post-mortem a couple of young lads handed in Cecily's purse at Copford section and later, after a search of the area where they had found it, we located her handbag. There were some good finger-marks that we are yet to identify the owner of; however, they are identical to marks found on a Schlitz beer bottle found at the scene of the murder. It's a beer brewed in the United States. We have yet to follow that line of enquiry.'

'In fairness to you, Albert, I've still to get in contact with my man at Lakenheath in relation to that,' said Stockwell, 'I understand that you have been to see Cecily's German friend.'

'Yes, sir. We went to see him and his boss on the farm in Tiptree, where he lives. Cecily had a relationship with Johann Weber, an ex-prisoner of war who works on the farm.

They apparently kept their relationship very low key and they would have trysts in local pubs. Cecily would order the drinks herself so that he didn't need to speak openly.'

'Disgraceful,' said Sproat.

The group did their best to ignore Sproat and Cooper continued.

'Johann was very helpful and willingly gave us his fingerprints. They are yet to be checked against our suspect prints. But he has no access to vehicles other than the farm tractor and he was alibied by the farmer who was with him on the night of the murder.'

'So, what do you have planned for the next stage, Albert?'

'We establish whether Johann Weber's prints and those on the bottle and purse are the same; if he is eliminated, we will get him in and completely drain him of everything he knows. We'll use an interpreter for that. We still need to speak to the Women's Institute to ascertain what kind of event she was attending. We have WI written in her diary for the day of the murder.'

'It sounds as though you are making some progress, Albert. Please keep me posted. I'm sure that you have plenty to be getting on with, so you don't need to stay for the rest of the meeting.'

'Thank you, sir.'

He took his leave.

Cooper wasted no time and marched straight back to the police station. He had been disturbed by Sproat's outbursts and resolved to take defensive action.

Once he was back in the CID office, he called a meeting with his two sergeants, Brian Pratt and Ian Mills.

'Gents, I've just been to the senior management meeting and I've had my ears well and truly bent. It seems that the chief constable is far from happy about the progress of the investigation so far. We need to crack on, so Brian, I want you to concentrate on the enquiry with the WI and find out as much as you can about the night in question. Take Tom with you. Ian, I want you to concentrate on the Schlitz beer bottle. Who supplies it in the UK? My guess is it's only available on US airbases. Start with the MPs at RAF Lakenheath and take Jane with you.'

'While we're at it, governor, we'll speak to them about staff access to jeeps, shall we?' said Ian Mills.

'Good thinking, Ian. Anyway, one other thing and I want this to stay between the three of us. I've just had an exchange of words with Julian Sproat, who has not been taken into our confidence in relation to the biting. He tried to make an issue of it but Mr Stockwell told him quite plainly, that he has no need to know. But he's not a happy man. He obviously thinks that to be excluded is beneath his dignity. Anyway, I wouldn't be surprised if he starts creeping around our offices, out of hours, so I want the team to relocate to the top office.

Ian, I want you to get some money out of petty cash and get the lock on the door changed. Make sure each member of the team gets a copy of the key. You can keep your usual desks in the main office with the others but everything relating to this case must be kept in the top office. Is that clear?'

'Clear!'

❖

Brian Pratt hadn't been looking forward to it at all but at Cooper's insistence he attended the post-mortem of Tom Munson. It was held at the Essex County Hospital and the examination was conducted by Professor Westlake. Brian's aversion to PMs had continued to dog him and this had not been helped by his sudden identification of Cecily White as she lay upon the mortuary slab. Cooper, whilst sympathetic to his friend's plight, wanted him to put it behind him and, in an effort to dull his senses, he arranged for him to attend as many adult post-mortem's as he could.

In the event, the examination of Tom Munson presented no kind of emotional challenge for him and Brian was able to take a dispassionate and professional interest in proceedings.

During the process Professor Westlake offered the blades of the fire brigade pike staff to the wounds on the body and he was satisfied that it was that instrument that had caused the puncture wounds to the rib cage after death. The pathologist also concluded that the death of Tom Munson had been caused by drowning.

Earlier, Cooper and Brian Pratt had been able to obtain supporting witness statements from the fire officers to account for the wounds to the body. These, of course, were taken in the presence of a Fire Brigades Union representative. The fire officers had, under the circumstances, made a judgement that Mr Munson was beyond help and with the best of intentions they had taken a pragmatic approach to the problem of retrieving him from the well. Thus, the "murder" of Tom Munson was solved.

◈

Brian Pratt and Tom Rogers approached the front door of the village hall with a certain amount of trepidation. They were about to enter a woman's world.

'Are you going in first then, sarge?'

'No, I'm not. I won the toss. You can go in first.'

'You're the sergeant. You get paid more than me.'

'OK, you tart. I'll go in first.'

Brian walked in the front door, through the foyer, and then he opened the connecting door to the main hall. He could see that the room was packed with ladies of all ages, shapes and sizes. To a woman, their eyes were on him as soon as he entered the room. He felt as though he was facing a firing squad.

'Excuse me. I'm sorry to disturb you, ladies,' he stuttered. 'We are police officers and I'm looking for Mrs Constance Farrow.'

A shrill "'oooh "'went up in the room. A lady on the top table stood up and waved. She left the table, walked up to him and thrust out a hand.

'How do you do,? I'm Constance Farrow, secretary of the Braintree branch of the WI. Are you the chap who I spoke to on the telephone?'

'Yes, madam. I'm Detective Sergeant Brian Pratt of Colchester CID. You also spoke to Sergeant Linda Collins, I believe.'

'Yes, I did.'

'Sergeant Collins has been reassigned to other duties, so the enquiry has been passed to me to continue.'

'Very well, if you'll follow me Sergeant Pratt, we'll go to my office where it'll be a bit quieter.'

After they had reached the refuge of the office Brian introduced Tom Rogers to Miss Farrow.

'This is my colleague, DC Tom Rogers.' She acknowledged Tom with a nod.

'How can I help you, gentlemen?'

'I understand that one of your members is Cecily White. Is that correct?'

'Yes, Cecily is one of our members, although, unusually, I haven't seen her for a couple of weeks.'

'Well, Mrs Farrow, I'm very sorry to have to tell you this, but Cecily was recently found murdered.'

Constance Farrow appeared stunned and although she tried to fight back the tears she began to quietly sob into her handkerchief.

'I can't believe it. Poor Cecily. Where did this happen?' she sniffed.

'Cecily's body was found at Abberton Reservoir which is located to the south of Colchester.'

'Yes. I know where it is. When was this?'

'Last Sunday, week. The second of October. According to her diary she was due to attend the WI. Can you tell us what kind of event you had on that night?'

Constance sat quietly and considered the question for a few seconds and then the answer came.

'Yes, that's right. We were due to have a meeting, but I had to postpone it as so many members said that they would be unable to attend.'

'When did you cancel it?' asked Rogers.

'On the Friday before.'

'How did you get the message to Cecily?'

'I telephoned her during the day at Colchester police station. In fact, that was my usual method of contact and she would call me a couple of times a week from work. She was a very committed member, was our Cecily.'

'Do you have any idea where she went on that Sunday?'

'I have no idea, I'm afraid. Although I'm pretty sure that she wouldn't have gone to church. She was a good, kind woman and she would do anything to help those less fortunate that herself. But, one thing that I do know about Cecily was, that she had no time for religion of any stripe.'

'How long was she a member of the WI?'

'Certainly since 1940. I remember when she joined us. I'm pretty sure that she was the first police lady that we have ever had as a member, well at the Braintree branch any way and she made herself busy almost immediately.'

'In what way?' asked Brian.

'Well, most people tend to think of the WI as being all Jam and Jerusalem and there's a good reason for that. Making jam and knitting were two of our main activities, especially during the war years, but when she joined, Cecily took it to another level by using her contacts.'

'In what way was she able to do that?'

'She had contacts at RAF Wethersfield with the American airforce. That's about six miles from here. I seem to remember she used to go to dances there with her best friend, Maggie McGee. Anyway, she got wind of the fact that the American Federation of Business and Professional Women were about to donate six mobile canning vans to the Women's Institute in the UK. She spoke to someone on the base and we managed to secure one of the six vans. Jolly useful they were too.'

'Canning vans?'

'Yes, for the jam.'

'I see. Well, this friend, Maggie McGee. Have you any idea where we might find her? Does she live locally?'

'I don't know personally, but there's bound to be someone who does. I'll make some enquiries. She isn't one of our members. I know that.'

'Do you still have the van?'

'No. The Americans came to repossess it at the end of the war.'

'Do you know who her contacts were on the base?'

'No. But I could make some enquiries among the members. There are a few of them who went to dances on the base and some of them had American boyfriends. In fact, there's one local woman I know whose sister actually married an airman and now she lives in the US.'

'Can you tell us your friend's name and address please, madam? I think it would be a good idea for us to speak to her ourselves. You never know, she might have some useful background information.'

'Yes, of course, and I'm happy for you to tell her that I gave you her details. She won't mind, particularly since your investigation relates to the murder of a police officer. Her name is Angela Dickson. She is single and lives with her mother at Ruaton Cottage in The Street, Bocking.'

'By the way, did she know Cecily herself?'

'Yes, I believe she probably did.'

'Thank you for your help, madam. We will be in touch again. Meantime if you do manage to glean any information from your members, we can be contacted at Colchester Police Station.'

Brian handed her a card on which he had written his own details and those of Alby Cooper.

They left the village hall and returned to their vehicle.

'Right, young Tom. Let's go and call on Angela Dickson and see if she has anything to tell us about the Yanks.'

On their arrival at the address in Bocking, they found that the house was in darkness, but since it was only just gone 8pm they knocked on the front door. They got no response. It was a job for another day.

17

Friday 14 October 1949

Ian Mills and Jane Stewart arrived at the front gate of RAF Lakenheath around 9.45-am. Jane, who was the driver, pulled up just short of the barrier and wound down the window of the driver's door. They were quickly joined by two Military Police officers resplendent in dress uniform, topped with white helmets. Both of the MPs carried side-arms. One of them walked to the far side of the police car, presumably to provide cover, whilst the other approached the driver's window.

'How can I help you, ma'am?'

'We are police officers from the Colchester Police Criminal Investigation Department. We have an appointment to see Master Sergeant Wilson Rudrow.'

Jane Stewart showed the officer her warrant card. He examined it carefully and mouthed the words to himself as though he was committing them to memory and would be tested on them at some later date.

'Ma'am. If you would park your vehicle in the car park over there and come back to us in the gatehouse. I will call

Mr Rudrow's office.'

He pointed to a car park that was about fifty yards from the gate and outside the perimeter- fence. They moved the CID car across to the car park, locked it and walked back to the barrier. By the time that Ian and Jane had returned the guard had made his phone call.

'The Master Sergeant is expecting you, folks. If you'll follow my colleague, he will take you to the office.'

They were led to the first substantial building, nearest to the gate, and soon learned that it was effectively the police station for the Lakenheath base. They were offered a seat in the reception area and their escort disappeared along a corridor. Soon afterwards, they became aware of a giant of a man walking towards them. He was dressed immaculately in a uniform that had been ironed and starched to an extreme.

'Good morning, folks. I am Wilson Rudrow and I am second-in-command of the police unit here at Lakenheath. How can I help you?'

Ian Mills showed Rudrow his credentials and both officers introduced themselves.

'We are based at Colchester Police Station and we are part of a team investigating the murder of one of our female colleagues, which happened during the late evening of Sunday 2nd of this month at Abberton Reservoir, which is just south of the town. We have reason to believe that the murderer drove our victim to the reservoir in a jeep, and found near the body was a Schlitz beer bottle.'

'And those two factors have brought you to our door?' said Rudrow.

'It was the beer, mainly. It's our understanding that

it is only available for sale on US military bases and we wanted to establish whether that is the case. As for the jeep, I realise that it's just as likely for it to have come from the Colchester Garrison but we have been in touch with the various regiments with no success. The bottle is forensically linked to other items belonging to the victim, so this is an important line of enquiry.'

'I see, folks. Well, let's see what we can do to help,' said Rudrow. 'The beer, as you say, is only available on US bases on sale at the Base Exchange (BX). I'll take you across to ours and show you the layout. I'll also make an enquiry for you Stateside to make sure that Schlitz haven't started exporting to England independently to civilian outlets. As for the jeeps, as you probably know, they are the workhorse of the US and British military and there are hundreds of them in England alone.'

'Do you book vehicles in and out at the gate?' asked Jane.

'No ma'am, we don't go to those lengths as a rule. The sentries on the gate just check the ID card of the driver and any passengers.'

'Tell me, sir,' said Jane, 'do you hold any social events on the base where British civilian women might be invited?'

'Occasionally we do, at the club next to the BX, but nowhere near as many now as they held during the war. Even now, they must be a named guest of a serviceman or woman on the base, and then the rule is that they can invite no more than two guests per person. It's a strange fact of life that we are now more security conscious than we were then. It was more about keeping the guy's morale high in the past. Now we're more worried about the Russians infiltrating us.'

'Would your social secretary, or whoever organised the last function, have kept a list of attendees and guests?'

'Yes. But I can do better than that, ma'am. The rule is that they must submit a copy of the list to us. I'll have someone dig it out for you while we go across to the BX. Oh, and please call me Wilson.'

'Wilson, do you have any knowledge of RAF Wethersfield?'

'Yeah, Wethersfield. I'm aware of it. Our Bomber Groups were there until 1944, then it was taken back by the RAF. Last I heard, the RAF had left the base, and recently, a circus has billeted its elephants in one of the hangers. I can safely say that it's not ours anymore. Excuse me just one minute, folks.'

Rudrow got up from his desk and walked along the corridor. He returned a few minutes later.

'My gal's going to search out the guest list for the last function.'

'One other thing, Wilson,' said Ian 'We have been making enquiries with the Braintree Women's Institute, who are based near RAF Wethersfield. Our victim, Cecily White, was a member. They told us that Cecily had good contacts with some of the US personnel on that base. Apparently, the American Federation of Business and Professional Women were about to donate six mobile canning vans to the Women's Institute in the UK and Cecily became aware of it. She arranged for one of them to be supplied to the Braintree branch. Do you have any knowledge of that?'

'No,' laughed Rudrow, 'I'm sorry, I don't. I've only been

here for the last year. You've gotta realise that personnel are coming and going from this place all the time. For instance, we've had quite an influx in recent months of guys who were on other operations abroad. There's not much of what you might call continuity. It's a vast organisation and that fact alone can cause us major headaches.'

Rudrow got to his feet. 'OK. Let's go and see the BX, folks.'

Rudrow drove them in a Jeep to a large building which was situated some 200 yards away at the far side of the parade square. As they entered the front door and walked into the foyer, they were faced with a long corridor stretching away in front of them. The BX was essentially the hub for two centres of activity.

Rudrow led them off to the right and in through the doors of a large hanger type building. Ian and Jane followed him as he gave them a quick tour of the store, which was packed to the rafters and appeared to cater for every type of commodity for the consumer. Ian and Jane were in awe. Although it was four years since the war in Europe had ended, many foodstuffs were still subject to rationing in the UK. In this place rationing clearly did not apply and there were things on display that Ian and Jane had not seen for many a long day. The store was busy with what Jane took to be off-duty service personnel, some of whom were with their wives or girlfriends.

'OK, that's the store. Let me show you the club.'

They walked into a vast bar area which was furnished at one end with easy chairs, sofas and coffee tables. At the other end were tables and chairs with a dance floor in the space between. The bar counter itself was long and put Jane in mind of a wild west saloon. At the back of the bar was an area containing several pool tables and a ten-pin bowling alley.

'Can I get you folks a drink?' offered Rudrow. 'The bar isn't serving alcohol at this time of day, but I could get you a Coca-Cola or a coffee.'

Ian and Jane both settled for a coffee. Rudrow called the manager across so that the detectives could pick his brains.

'Hi, Wilson. How's tricks?'

'Hi, Leon. Everything's fine, thanks. I want you to meet two colleagues from the Colchester police who are making enquiries into the murder of a female police officer in their area.'

Leon shook hands with Ian and Jane.

'I'm sorry to hear that,' said Leon. 'You are from Colchester, are you? We had your ladies hockey team here a couple of weeks ago.'

'Really?' said Jane. 'That's interesting.'

'Yes. They stayed for the dance.'

'They're particularly interested in the availability of Schlitz beer because a bottle was found near the body,' said Rudrow.

'I see,' said the manager, 'if there's anything I can do to help.'

Leon was obviously of Hispanic heritage and he spoke with a heavy accent that Jane and Ian found hard to understand.

'You sell Schlitz beer, Leon?'

'Yes, on draught and in bottles.'

He walked to a shelf, selected a pint bottle of Schlitz and placed it on the bar in front of them.

'Where does it come from?'

'It is flown in from the States, with all the other supplies, by air-force transport, to the base here at Lakenheath.'

'Do you know if it's sold off-base, by that I mean in shops or pubs in England?'

'No. I'm sure that it is only sold in BXs.'

'But Leon,' said Rudrow, 'we do know, don't we, that a lot of the guys buy bottles from the store cheap on their discount and sell them to the Brits off-base.'

'Yeah. They shouldn't do that, but how can we stop it from happening?'

'To be fair, it's not our biggest problem, but a lot of them do it to boost their income and impress the local ladies.'

They chatted for a while longer, finished their coffee, and returned to the police post where on entering the office Rudrow picked up an envelope from his desk and examined the contents.

'Looks like Rhianna has been busy. She's typed you a copy of the guest list.' He handed the envelope across the desk to Ian, who examined the list with Jane for a few minutes or so.

'This is for a function at the club on Saturday 24th September this year,' said Ian.

'There is no Cecily White listed but there is a Maggie McGee. Cecily was close friends with a woman of that name. According to this, Maggie McGee was a guest of Airman Ryan Noble. I think, with your permission, we should speak to him, while we are here. Is Airman Noble still on base, Wilson?'

'I can find out for you, Ian. Theo!' shouted Rudrow.

They were joined by a young airman. 'Sir.'

'Theo, I want you to go into the personnel records and find out whether we still have an Airman Ryan Noble on base.'

'Yes, sir.' The airman turned on his heel and left the room. After a few minutes he was back holding a sheet of paper.

'Sir. Noble is still with us. I rang his unit and they said that he's currently working in one of the hangers.'

'Right, Theo. Take a vehicle, go to his unit and bring him back here.'

'Yes, sir.' Theo left the room.

In his absence Rudrow, spoke about his previous deployments in Texas and Frankfurt. He also marvelled at the massive undertaking that was the night and day bombing of Germany which was carried out jointly by the US Air Force and the RAF. He was clearly an anglophile.

Ian, for good measure, spoke about his time in the Essex Regiment during the war. But, as he spoke, he realised that it paled into insignificance. Mercifully, it was only a short while before Theo returned to the office.

'I have Airman Noble sitting in reception, sir.'

'Right,' said Rudrow. 'Bring him in.'

Noble was marched into the office where he came to attention and saluted Rudrow.

'Airman Noble, sir.'

'OK, Noble. At ease. I have here two police detectives from Colchester who are investigating the murder of one of their colleagues and want to ask you some questions. You are not in trouble. They want your help.'

Noble was visibly relieved.

'So, take a seat, young man. I will leave you with them. I shall be in the office next door, if I'm needed.' Rudrow left the room.

'Ok, Ryan. I am Detective Sergeant Ian Mills, and this is my colleague Detective Constable Jane Stewart. Do you mind if we call you Ryan?'

'No sir. Go right ahead.'

'Good. Well, as Mr Rudrow said, we are from Colchester CID, and we are investigating the murder of Woman Police Sergeant Cecily White. We have been given a list of people who attended a function at the club on the base on Saturday 24th September of this year. Your name is on the list and it indicates that you signed in a guest named Maggie McGee.'

'God, she hasn't been murdered, has she?'

'No, Ryan, she hasn't been murdered,' said Jane.

'Tell us about Maggie McGee. How do you know her?'

'I met her a few weeks ago on the afternoon of the dance when she and her hockey team came to play our gals' team on the base.'

'Which team was she playing for?'

'Colchester. She wasn't one of ours,' laughed Noble. 'None of them look like her, unfortunately.

'Did you speak to any of the other Colchester women?'

'Yeah. They were in a group with our gals, at a table, outside the bar on the terrace and I just got talking to them.'

'Can you remember any other names?'

'No, sorry. I can't remember any other names, and I spoke to most of them, but it was Maggie who caught my eye. She is absolutely gorgeous. And I wanted to get to know her.'

'So, you invited her to the dance, on the base, which was held later that day?'

'Yes, sir. I didn't want to pass up a chance like that.'

'How long did they stay for?'

'They all stayed for a few hours. There were about ten or twelve of them. The guys signed them in.'

'Why didn't their opposite numbers on your hockey team sign them in?'

'I suppose we must have beaten them to it. Our gals weren't quite as interested in them as we were. Well, not in the same way, anyway.'

'Sorry, I'm not quite with you,' said Ian.

'Most of our women are a bit butch. They're more like men, really.'

'How did you get on with Maggie?'

'Well, she really was a beautiful gal and Maggie could certainly Lindy Hop. She was a great little mover.'

'Did you see her again?'

'No, I didn't, but she gave me the phone number of her nurses' home where she stays in Colchester.'

'Why didn't you see her again?'

'I wanted to. I did ask her out for a drink and she said that she would meet up with me, but not for a couple of weeks, because she was going to be away at her folks' place and that for a few days she'd be on night duty. That suited me because I knew that I wouldn't be able to see her for a couple of weeks anyway.'

'Why would that be?'

'We've got a big military operation going on and it meant that I had to stay on base. But I'm not really supposed to talk about that.'

'Can you tell me what you do?'

'Yes, sir. I can tell you that. I'm an aircraft technician.'

'Did Maggie introduce you to or mention anyone called Cecily?'

'Sicily?'

'No, Cecily.' Jane spelt out the name for him.

'Not that I can recall, no.'

'Ryan. Can you give us Maggie's contact telephone number, for the nurses home please?'

'Certainly, I can.' Ryan took his wallet from his back trouser pocket and rifled through the contents. He handed a slip of paper to Jane, who examined and copied down the number in her pocket note-book. She then handed it back to him.

'That will be all for now, thank you, Ryan.' said Ian.'We need to contact Maggie and speak to her afresh without her having any pre-concieved ideas.So we would ask you not to try and contact her for a few days. Also, please don't discuss our visit with anyone other than Master Sergeant Rudrow.'

'Yes, sir. Thank you, sir.'

For some reason Noble saluted the officers, carried out a smart right turn, and left the room. Jane found this particularly impressive.

They were rejoined by Wilson Rudrow.

'Did you get what you needed, folks?' asked Rudrow.

'Yes. Pretty much,' said Ian.

'So, young Noble was helpful, was he?'

'Yes. He was. It's interesting that Maggie McGee, our victim's best friend, has been on the base socially and that she played hockey here, representing a club of which Cecily is also a member. We now have a contact telephone number for her nurses' home and we're hoping that Maggie can fill in a few blanks.'

'So, Noble is not implicated in any way.'

'No, not at all. He was helpful. But, just to be on the safe-side we've told him not to speak to anyone else about our visit other than yourself.'

'Good. Let's hope he sticks to it.'

'Tell me,' said Jane, 'do you fingerprint air force personnel as a matter of routine, when they join perhaps?'

'No' ma'am. That would be a mammoth task. We only take prints if somebody is charged with a crime.'

'OK. Thank you for all your help, Wilson. We'll take our leave now, but we'll be in touch.'

Rudrow escorted them to the front gate.

18

Saturday 15 October 1949

Tom Rogers was sitting in the top office with his feet up on the desk when Brian Pratt walked into the room. He removed them and sat up in his chair. They exchanged greetings.

'You're in early, boy. Did you wet the bed?'

'No, sarge. Just woke up about six and I couldn't get back to sleep again, so I thought it best to get up and get on.'

'We've got the team meeting at half nine. Have you got the doughnuts?' asked Brian. 'It's your turn, isn't it?'

'Shit! I knew there was something I'd forgotten, sarge,' said Tom.

'Best you nip out and get them, then, boy. You've still got time.' Tom needed no more encouragement. He dashed out of the office and down the stairs. Brian called after him.

'Take it easy. Don't break your neck.'

By the time that Tom had returned to the office the whole team had arrived for the day. This was apart from Cooper, who was still in his office fielding a phone call from Superintendent Stockwell.

There were six of them in an office that had been designed for four and it was cosy, to say the least.

'Are you sure we couldn't have found somewhere else, sarge?' said Jane, addressing her remark to Brian Pratt. 'There's not enough room in here to swing a cat.'

'Well then, don't bring a cat in here, Jane, and you'll be all right, won't you?'

'You know what I mean, silly.'

'Look. It's all done for a reason, Jane. The security of our information is of primary importance. I'm sure that the governor will explain it all when he arrives.'

'OK. So, what's the governor going to explain, Brian?' said Cooper, as he appeared in the doorway.

'I was just saying to Jane that we're occupying the top office for security reasons, governor, and that you're going to explain why.'

Cooper entered the room and shut the door.

'Quite right. Listen in then. I was going to mention it later, but we might as well deal with it now and get it out of the way. You know what I said to you all a few days ago about us keeping the fact of Cecily being bitten to ourselves so that it doesn't get out and into the public domain?' The team all nodded.

'Oh no, it hasn't slipped out already, has it, governor?' exclaimed Jane.

'No, I'm pretty sure it hasn't, Jane. But I was at a meeting in Mister Stockwell's office on Wednesday when we were discussing the murder and the fact that Cecily was indecently assaulted. The only senior officers who knew about the biting were Mister Stockwell and Inspector Wallis.

One of our number wanted to know how it was that we knew that Cecily had been indecently assaulted. I certainly wasn't about to explain that she was indecently assaulted by biting. Mister Stockwell told him unequivocally that, as he was not involved operationally, he didn't have a need to know about the specifics. Unfortunately, the individual concerned was rather put out by that, and went into a bit of a paddy.'

'Sounds like Mister Sproat,' said Jane.

'You might say that, Jane, but I couldn't possibly comment. Anyway, this person's reaction led me to think more deeply about the security of our information. Hence our moving into this office. Now I know it's not the biggest but the occasions when it will contain all of us will be few and far between. Those of you who have desks elsewhere can continue to use them, but I want anything to do with the murder to stay in here. Is that understood?'

'Yes, governor,' replied the troops, almost in unison.

'OK. Lot's to talk about. Keeping it in chronological order, Linda, would you like to start off with our visit on Tuesday to Johann Weber, and by the way, this is something else I'd like us to be discreet about. Not many would approve of the fact that Cecily had a secret German boyfriend, particularly her father, so this is information that I don't want to be disseminated.'

'Yes. On Tuesday we went to Folly-foots farm in Tiptree to see Johann Weber, an ex-prisoner of war with whom Cecily was having a relationship, on the quiet.' One or two members of the team muttered their disapproval.

Linda continued, 'As the governor was saying, that is a fact that Cecily didn't want her father to know about, as he wouldn't have approved of her going out with a German.

He's unaware and it certainly wouldn't help him in his grief were he to find out. As for Johann Weber, we saw him in the company of his boss, the farmer, Norman Smith, who obviously holds him in high regard. When we told Johann about Cecily's murder, he was visibly shocked and upset. I was convinced that his reaction was genuine, weren't you, govenor?'

'Yes, I was. He seemed a genuinely, polite young man.'

'And very handsome. I can see what she saw in him,' said Linda.

Tom Rogers groaned.

Linda continued, 'Anyway, he told us that they would meet for drinks in pubs and he would usually go by bus or pushbike. He has no access to a car and the only vehicle that he drives on a regular basis is a tractor. He lives on the farm above the stables and during the afternoon and evening of the day of Cecily's murder, he was with farmer Smith.

They were both painting Johann's rooms. Not only that, Johann, slept the night in the farmer's spare room because of the overwhelming smell of new paint. So, he has an alibi.'

'What did you make of farmer Smith?' asked Brian.

'Honest and decent, I'd say,' chipped in Cooper.

'How did Cecily and Johann contact each other?' asked Jane.

'It seems that Cecily would phone the farm early evening and, if he was available, she would speak to Johann, or she would leave a message with the farmer or his wife.

He hadn't spoken to Cecily for a few days, so he was starting to wonder why she hadn't called.'

'Do they have a jeep on the farm,' asked Tom Rogers.

'No. I did make a point of asking the farmer that,' said Cooper, 'and he assured me that they never have.'

'What about the forensic side of things ? Did we take Johann Weber's fingerprints?' asked Brian.

'Yes, Brian we did. They are still being checked against the bottle and purse. Not only that though. Brendan Withers took sample moulds from his teeth to check against the bite mark.'

'So, he was pretty cooperative, then?' said Jane.

'Very,' said Cooper.

'I don't want to show my ignorance,' said Tom.

'Makes a change,' said Ian.

'But, how do you take tooth samples?'

'No, to be fair Ian, it's a good question,' said Cooper, who went on to explain the use of cheese blocks.

'Thing is,' continued Cooper, 'You won't be expected to take samples yourself, Tom. We would get them taken by Scenes of Crime. Anyway, Johann's samples are still being compared. Anything else, Linda?'

'No, that about covers it, I think, governor.'

'Good. Thank you. Brian, Tom, can you tell us about your visit to the Women's Institute, please.'

'Yes, boss. A couple of evenings ago Tom and I went to see Constance Farrow, who is the secretary of the Braintree branch, at their base, which is an old village hall on the outskirts of town. She told us that Cecily was a very committed member of the WI and had been so since the early forties. Apparently, she had good contacts at RAF Wethersfield when the Yanks were in occupation and she negotiated, on the WI's behalf, the donation of a mobile canning van.'

'What on earth's a mobile canning van, when it's at home?' asked Jane.

'Well, Jane think of jam and Jerusalem. It's a van equipped with the necessarie's for making jam.'

'OK. Thank you, sarge. Silly question really.'

Brian continued, 'Apparantly Cecily heard that the Women's Institute in the UK were going to get six mobile canning vans from the American Federation of Business Women. She spoke to someone on the base and she managed to get one of them donated to the Braintree branch.'

'Does this Constance Farrow, know who Cecily spoke to at RAF Wethersfield?' asked Cooper.

'No, governor. She just let Cecily get on with it.'

'It would be good to know what Cecily's connection was to Wethersfield and who she liaised with, said Cooper. 'But unfortunately the Yanks are no longer there, and things have moved on.'

'Well, according to Mrs Farrow, during the war, Cecily used to go to dances there with her friend Maggie McGee.'

'That's interesting,' said Jane, 'Our guy at Lakenheath had her on a list of attendees for a function at their club. She was on the base during that afternoon with other members of Colchester Hockey Club. Some of the guys chatted them up after the game and got them to stay for the dance for a couple of hours. They had to sign them in and a copy of the list automatically gets passed to the Military Police. You'll recall that when we searched Cecily's rooms, we found a current membership card for Colchester Hockey Club. She wasn't listed in the book for the dance that night though.'

'What do we know about Maggie McGee?' asked Cooper.

'They said that she's a staff nurse based at the Essex County Hospital.'

'We need to speak to her then. Job for you, Jane.'

'Yes, governor.'

'Just one other thing, governor,' said Ian, 'Brian told me about the canning van and we asked about it when we went to Lakenheath. Master Sergeant Rudrow at the MP post knew nothing about it. But Constance Farrow told Brian that at the end of the war the Yanks came and took the van back. It might help if we found out who that was and whether they had a connection with Cecily.'

'That's a very good point, Ian. Brian, can you get back to Mrs Farrow and find out if they were given any kind of receipt for the van? It might give us something. Also, find out from them what the registration number was of the van. I don't imagine that it was taken back to the US. It's probably been sold on. The county council should be able to help us with that. Once we find the present keeper of the vehicle, we should be able to work it back to the people who took it back from the WI.'

'Will do, governor.'

'Anything else on Lakenheath, Ian?'

'Master Sergeant Rudrow took us across to the BX, which, by the way, stands for Base Exchange, to see the manager about Schlitz beer. It's a very impressive place. You'd be amazed. The building is huge and split into two halves. On one side it's got a store where you can buy virtually anything. Obviously, rationing doesn't apply to them. On the other side is a large bar with small snooker tables, they call it pool apparently. There was a dance floor and even a ten-pin bowling alley.'

'What about the beer, Ian?'

'Yes. Sorry, governor. There's me rambling on. We met the manager. He seemed a straight-up sort of guy. He's convinced that Schlitz beer is only available in the UK on US military bases but Rudrow is going to phone the States for us to check on that point.

One thing that Rudrow did say though, was that a lot of the Yanks buy bottles of the stuff in the store on their discount and sell it to civilians for a nice profit.'

'Christ almighty. That's not helpful,' said Cooper. 'Not helpful, at all.'

19

Sunday 16 October 1949

Jane and Brian were standing on the doorstep of a large detached house in Oxford Road, Lexden, the monied area of central Colchester. Although Jane had pushed the doorbell there was no sign of life other than the sound of a pair of small dogs, which she could hear yapping in the hall on the other side of the front door. Given the fact that it was a Sunday morning, they had waited until around 11am before they visited the house. After waiting a few minutes, they gave up, walked back down the pebbled drive to the front gate, and out onto the pavement. Brian was unlocking the driver's door of the Wolsey but before he could climb back into the vehicle, a female voice called after them.

'Can I help you?'

Jane, who was nearest to the voice, turned and saw a middle-aged woman, standing in the drive. She was, by Jane's estimation, a woman in her early forties, not-unattractive, but sporting an androgynous pixie-style haircut. She was dressed in gardening attire and might have been mistaken for a young man.

'Good morning, madam. Are you Miss Jessica Guest?'

'Yes, I am.'

'Miss Guest, we are police officers. I am Detective Constable Jane Stewart, and this is my colleague, Detective Sergeant Brian Pratt.' Before Jane was able to show the lady her credentials she collapsed in a fit of laughter. After a few seconds of giggling she took out a handkerchief from the pocket of her dungarees and wiped her eyes.

'Oh, I do beg your pardon. I think you must be the first person I have ever met called Prat. You, poor man.'

'Yes,' said Brian, 'not the name I would have chosen myself. But even if I were to have it changed, what would I change it to? Preat or Parrott, perhaps.'

'I'm so sorry,' said Miss Guest, 'I didn't mean to be rude. No offence intended.'

'None taken. Anyway, madam, shall we tell you why we're here?'

'Yes. Please do.'

'We have been given to understand that you are the secretary of Colchester Hockey Club, is that correct?'

'Yes. What have the girls been up to now?'

'Sorry,' said Brian, 'I'm not with you.'

'Well, they are a lively bunch, always up to hijinks and practical jokes of one kind or another. I thought they might have excelled themselves.'

'I think it best, Miss Guest, that I put our visit into its proper perspective before I go any further. My colleague and I are investigating the murder of Cecily White, who we believe, was a member of the hockey club.'

'Oh no,' said Miss Guest, with a sudden change of tone, 'poor girl. What happened to her?'

'She was strangled.'

'Please come into the kitchen, where we can talk more easily.' Brian and Jane followed Miss Guest around the side of the house, through the rear garden and into the kitchen.

'I thought I'd bring you in this way, then you won't have to worry about the dogs. They're a bit of a nuisance but I inherited them from my father, along with the house and the car. Small dogs. I can't stand them. Do you know anyone who wants a pair of chihuahua's?'

'No, sorry Miss Guest, can't say that I do,' said Brian.

Jane just smiled and shook her head.

'I do beg your pardon, I'm forgetting my manners. Would you like tea?'

'That would be lovely,' said Jane.

'This is so sad,' said Miss Guest, calmly. 'When was Cecily murdered?'

'Two weeks ago. When was the last time you saw her?'

'That would have been about three weeks ago, I suppose. When we played up at RAF Lakenheath. That was the last game of the season.'

'Tell us about that, Miss Guest. For instance, how did you get to Lakenheath?'

'Please call me Jessie. I don't like formality and, like you, Mister Pratt, I don't even like my surname much.'

'Oh really? Why is that then, Jessie?'

'It's a family thing. I won't go into it. But, to answer your question, there were about fifteen of us that day. All women. The majority went by coach and we met in the High Street at one 'o'clock. I went separately with my friend Daphne, in my car, as we had a function to attend later in the day. The girls sometimes like to stay on, you see.'

'So, you started at three 'o'clock, did you?'

'Yes. That's right.'

'Did Cecily play?'

'Yes, the second half. She wasn't one of our regular players and tended to be a substitute or she helped out and played when we were short.'

'I see. Did you win?'

'Yes. Quite convincingly. It's not a natural sport for the Americans, you see.'

'So, what happened after the game?'

'We had drinks on the veranda at their club. They were very good hosts as a matter of fact, and the drinks are certainly cheaper than in an ordinary pub. Some of the chaps invited our girls to a dance in the club afterwards. It was a shame that Daphne and I had to go, really. The others stayed for a couple of hours, though, and had a lovely time, apparently. They had to have a whip round for the coach driver to cover his extra hours. I understand they got back to Colchester about ten.'

'Did Cecily stay behind?'

'No. Her friend Maggie did. But Cecily came back in the car with us. She had to get back for her father. In fact, we dropped her off at home.'

'Did you see Cecily talking to any of the Americans?'

'We all spoke to them as a group, generally. I didn't see her speak to anybody on a one to one basis. Not like Maggie. She took a shine to one particular chap. Very handsome he was, too.'

'What is Maggie's surname?'

'McGee.'

'And she was Cecily's best friend, was she?'

'Yes. She was. Isn't it terrible having to refer to Cecily in the past tense?'

'It does take some getting used to,' said Jane. 'She was one of our close colleagues, after all, and a lovely woman.'

'Where was Cecily murdered? Can you tell me?'

'Yes. She was found at Abberton. Next to the reservoir,' said Brian.

'Were you aware of Cecily having any boyfriends?' asked Jane.

'No, none that I can recall. She was a nice lady but very private. Almost shy, in a way. Which was unusual for a police woman.'

'What about her friend, Maggie McGee? What can you tell us about her?'

'A good hockey player. She plays in goal. Very attractive. She's about twenty-nine years old. A staff nurse at the Essex County Hospital. She lives in the nurses' home and during the war she served in the Queen Alexandra's as a military nurse.'

'And, have you spoken to Maggie lately?'

'No, I haven't seen or heard from her. But, it's no real surprise. As I said, that was the last fixture of the season and we're all done until next year. So, I've had no reason to be in touch with her.'

'Thank you for the tea, Miss Guest. We have other enquiries to make. We will no doubt speak to you again.'

Brian and Jane took their leave and drove the short distance to the Essex County Hospital where they entered the nurses' home and approached reception. Behind the counter was a "security man", who was in his sixties with white hair and a white handlebar moustache. He was wearing a blue serge uniform which was not unlike that of a police officer. Apart from his age, the only thing that gave him away was the beige cardigan worn underneath the open tunic.

'And what can I do for you, folks?' he said with an attitude.

'We are police officers,' said Brian, showing his warrant card, 'and we would like to see a resident by the name of Maggie McGee.'

'You can't, I'm afraid. She isn't here.'

'Where is she then?' asked Jane.

'I don't think that I'm at liberty to tell you that,' said the security man, with an air of self-importance.

'We are investigating the murder of Miss McGee's best friend. If you want to obstruct us in the lawful execution of our duty, go right ahead, but it will mean that we would have to arrest you and take you down to Colchester Police Station. I imagine that would do little to enhance your job prospects. Shall we start again?' said Brian.

This was enough to shake the man into submission.

'OK, then. Well, she's away at her parent's place in Weymouth for a couple of weeks for her sister's wedding. Strange thing is I got a phone call from her mother the other day asking for her to call them. I haven't seen her to pass it on, so I assumed that they must have caught up with her. I've had a couple of letters for her as well since then. Both were postmarked Weymouth.'

'When was the last time that you saw her?'

'It was about two weeks ago, around seven in the morning, she had just come off duty, having finished a week of nights.'

'We need to check on her wellbeing. Can you let me have the message and the two letters, please? We will have to contact Maggie's parents. And before we go, my colleague and I want to look around her room.'

'Oh, I don't know whether I can do that,' said the security man.

'What is your name?'

'Bill Osborne.'

'Well, Bill, I want you to understand that this could be a matter of life or death. As I said, this is a murder enquiry. You can accompany us if you wish, that way you can make sure that everything is above board.'

'OK, then. But on your own head be it.'

Bill walked behind the counter and took a set of keys from the peg board on the wall and the two letters from a pigeonhole. He handed the letters to Brian then escorted the two officers up to the first floor to room sixteen. The security man unlocked the door. It was a modest single room containing the bare essentials: a single bed: small wardrobe: armchair: wash basin and mirror. It didn't take them long to search the room. They found a couple of nurse's uniforms on hangers in the wardrobe with sensible shoes and a few old undergarments. Jane took out a folder, from the bottom of the wardrobe, which contained various documents.

'I've got her birth certificate and passport here, sarge.'

'Good. We'll take them in case we need to circulate her as missing.'

Jane handed Brian the passport. He opened the cover and looked at the photograph.

'Yes. She's a cracking--looking girl all right.'

'Sarge. Do behave.'

'Just saying. Anyway, Bill, I'll give you a receipt for these two items. If you hear from Miss McGee, can you please let us know as soon as possible. We need to speak to her, quite urgently?'

'Certainly,' said Bill.

'And before we go, can you let us have the name and phone number of your personnel officer?'

On their return to the police station, Brian wasted no time in opening the two letters. He saw, on checking the postmarks, that they had been sent from Weymouth a week apart. The first was written by Maggie's mother and it alluded to her having failed to arrive at the family home, as planned, and referred to a spat between Maggie and her sister. It was clear that her mother was attempting to heal the rift and was asking her to get in contact.

The second letter, written by her father, re-iterated the points made by his wife, but also referred to the distress that the row between their two daughters was causing her. Brian had met Maggie's parents on a couple of occasions when he and Cecily were courting and they had got on well. But he did not wish to complicate matters, and opting for a softer female voice to take a subtler approach to the situation, he delegated the task of telephoning Maggie's parents to Jane.

'Hello. Weymouth 435. Can I help you?'

'Yes, hello. My name is Jane. Can I speak to Maggie, please?'

'No. I'm afraid you can't. She's not here.'

'I see. Can you tell me when she's likely to be back?'

'No. I can't.'

'Is this Mrs McGee?'

'Yes, it is.'

'Mrs McGee, I am Detective Constable Jane Stewart of Colchester Police I wanted to speak to Maggie about a case that we are investigating which involves a lady called Cecily White, who is one of her friends. Can you tell me when you last saw her?'

'Maggie, you mean?'

'Yes.'

'It was a couple of months ago. Her sister Marjorie is getting married soon and we were expecting Maggie two weeks ago to come and stay with us so that she could help her sister take care of the arrangements for the wedding. But she didn't arrive. I know that the girls had a bit of a falling out over the guest list. We thought that she had changed her mind about coming down because of that.'

'Don't your daughters get on?'

'Yes, of course they do. They were always squabbling as children, but they do love each other really. My husband left a couple of messages at the nurses' home for Maggie, and we even wrote a couple of letters, but she hasn't replied. But that's Maggie. She's a lovely girl really, but she can be a stubborn little minx when she wants to be.'

'Mrs McGee, I'm going to make some more enquiries at the Essex County Hospital to see if we can locate Maggie. I will call you later, when I manage to find her.'

'Thank you, officer.'

Jane gave Mrs McGee a contact telephone number, then rang off.

'You heard all of that, did you, Brian?'

'Yes. Sounds ominous. But we'd better just check with the hospital first to make sure that she's not just doing some extra shifts or gone off with a boyfriend or something. We don't want to alarm her parents unnecessarily.'

Brian and Jane drove back to the hospital. Being a Sunday, the personnel officer was unlikely to be there, so they toured the various wards, speaking to those members of staff that they could find. They drew a blank.

20

Monday 17 October 1949

Alby Cooper was sitting in his office with the door shut. He had arrived early for work determined to deal with the burgeoning pile of paperwork on his desk. He hadn't touched it for the past week and the routine paper flow was threatening to get out of control. Cooper would have delegated the task but most of the reports required a decision at detective inspector level. That was the established protocol and there was no way around it. After an hour or so, Cooper was making reasonable progress. The phone rang.

'Cooper.'

'Good morning, governor, Sergeant Glover here, sorry to disturb you, I have Richard Timmins of the *Argus* at the front counter. He wants to speak to you about the murder.'

'OK, Ted. I'll be right down.'

Bollocks. It was only a matter of time, I suppose. I'd better go down and try and head him off at the pass. Cooper reached the foot of the stairs and opened the connecting door to the foyer. Richard Timmins was leaning against the front counter. Cooper saw that he had a bottle of scotch poking out of his coat pocket. He and Richard Timmins had known each other for several years and they were old sparring partners.

'Good morning, Richard. Do want to come up?'

'Morning, Alby.'

Timmins followed Cooper through the door and back up the stairs to the office.

'Take a seat, Richard. Would you like tea?'

'Yes, please. White. No sugar.'

Cooper picked up the phone and spoke to Tom Rogers. They made small talk until Rogers had delivered the teas and shut the door behind him.

'You want to speak about a murder?'

'Yes, Alby. A source tells me that the woman found at Abberton Reservoir was a policewoman.'

Cooper was taken aback, but he knew that there was no point in denying the facts, now that Timmins had brought them into the open. In the face of the circumstances, containment was what was required and a subtle appeal to the reporter's conscience was the attitude to adopt.

'To be frank, we were hoping, for important operational reasons, to keep quiet about that fact, Richard.'

'Why? What benefit is there to keeping it quiet?'

'You'll have to trust me on that one, but we need the identity of the victim to stay out of the public domain for now. If you can do that for us, Richard, I will apply for permission to get the *Argus* an exclusive for when we catch our suspect.'

'Do you have a suspect, then, Alby?'

'Unfortunately, no. But, believe me, we're working hard on a few leads.'

'What sort of leads?'

'I can't tell you that either, Richard. Not at the moment. It's too delicate.'

'OK. We'll leave it like that for now. Hopefully we can get our exclusive.'

'You've known me for a few years now, Richard, and you must know I'll do my level best for you. Now I appreciate that you're under no obligation to name your source, but do you think that they will talk to the *Gazette* or any of the others?'

'No. They will only talk to me, I'm confident of that.'

'Let's hope so.'

Timmins downed his tea in one. He reached into his pocket and took out the bottle of Scotch.

'Little libation for your Alby, to get the grey cells working,' said Timmins.

'Thanks Richard, but you didn't have to come bearing gifts.'

'Hopefully, we'll have a celebratory swig in due course.'

'That we will,' said Cooper.

'Right, Alby. I'm off to cover the Magistrates Court. Thanks for the tea. I'll look forward to hearing from you.'

Cooper escorted Timmins off the premises and after having done so ascended the stairs to return to his office. He had a nagging pain in his stomach which stemmed from the worry that someone in the station was telling tales out of school. He would keep this to himself for now.

On returning to the office, Cooper abandoned the paperwork and called Brian and Ian into his office for an update.

'Morning, chaps. How are we doing?'

'There are a few things to tell you, governor,' said Brian. 'Yesterday, Jane and I went to speak to Miss Guest, the secretary of Colchester Hockey Club. It seems that Cecily did go with them to Lakenheath on the 24th of September, although because she had to get back for her father, she didn't stay for the dance. Apparently, Miss Guest gave Cecily a lift in her car and dropped her off at home.'

'Did she speak to any men while she was there?'

'The team had a drink on the veranda outside the club after the game, and this attracted some attention from the Yanks. Miss Guest said that Cecily was part of the group but she didn't engage with any individual. The rest of the girls stayed on for the dance, including her friend Maggie McGee, who, incidentally, we still haven't managed to locate yet.'

'Have they been back since?'

'No, governor. Apparently, that was their last fixture of the season.'

'How many of them were there in the group?'

'Oh, about fifteen I believe.'

'We need to see all of them. I want the names of the Yanks they spoke to, including the members of the other team. Hopefully, some might have swapped details like Ryan Noble and Maggie McGee or, at least, they might be able to recall some of the names. That will give us something to go back to Ryan Noble with.'

'What about getting Miss Guest to call a team meeting?' said Brian.

'Yes, Brian. That sounds like a good idea. And if any of the girls don't turn up, we can visit them later.'

'And, it would enable us to break the news of Cecily's death in a more controlled way, don't you think?'

'I imagine, Brian, that Miss Guest will have already done that for us.'

'True enough. Shall we get them to come to the nick?'

'I think that would be best, Brian. That way, if any of them throw a wobbly, we can deal with it and provide a bit of care. I'll speak to Linda and arrange for a couple of her girls to be standing by throughout the meeting. Better still, if Miss Guest gives us a list of names and contact details, I can get Linda to organise the meeting. How does two 'o'clock, Wednesday afternoon, sound?'

'That's good for me, governor.'

'Right. Anything else, Ian?'

'Yes boss. Brian touched on this earlier. Jane and I went to the nurses' home to speak to Cecily's friend Maggie. She wasn't there, and she was supposed to be at her parent's place in Weymouth for a couple of weeks. We rang her parents, and apparently, she didn't turn up. We made enquiries with the staff to try and find her but, we got no joy. It seems that she may have gone missing. Jane is at the hospital as we speak. She's going to have a word with the personnel officer.'

'Let me know how she gets on, please, Ian. If we don't find her, we'll have to go to Weymouth to see her parents. Christ, I hope to God we don't have another body on our hands.'

'One other piece of news, governor,' said Ian, 'Brendan Withers called this morning. Johann Weber's fingerprints have been compared with the bottle and the purse and they don't match.'

'What about the teeth impressions, any news?'

'No, governor. That's going to take a bit longer, apparently.'

'Is that it?'

'For now, governor.'

'Good. Keep me posted on the Maggie McGee situation. I'm off to Mr Stockwell's office for morning prayers.'

◈

Jane Stewart was sitting alone in the top office when she took a call from the switchboard operator.

'CID. DC Stewart speaking.'

'Hello, Jane. It's Mary on the switchboard. Can you take a call for the DI? I can't get an answer from him or any of the sergeants.'

'Yes, Mary. Put it through.'

'Hello. CID, DC Stewart. Can I help you?'

'Yes, thank you. My name is Phyllis. I am the secretary for Professor Keith Simpson of Guy's Hospital. I wanted to speak to DI Albert Cooper or Sergeant Linda Collins concerning the murder of Cecily White. Are they available?'

'Not at present, Phyllis, but I can take a message and get one of them to call you back. Can you please give me your number?'

Phyllis provided the details of their telephone number and address.

'Can I tell them a bit more about your reason for calling?'

'Yes. I wanted to pass on a message from the Professor, who is at a conference in the Hague. He has spoken to a German forensic scientist who dealt with two cases that are very similar to the Cecily White case. He will get as much detail as he can about the cases and the contact details of the scientist. Apparently, in both cases they photographed some marks and they are convinced that the murders were committed by the same person.'

'Where did the murders happen?'

'Berlin.'

Berlin? Thought Jane. *I doubt that they have anything to do with our job.*

'Do they have a suspect?'

'No. I don't think they do, but the Professor will no doubt have more detail when he gets back to the office.'

'OK. Thank you very much, Phyllis. I'll make sure that DI Cooper and Sergeant Collins get the message and I'm sure they'll come back to you.'

※

The senior officers' meeting lasted for an hour and a half, with Cooper providing an update on the Cecily White murder and speaking about the possible missing person's enquiry relating to Maggie McGee, friend of the murder victim. The more that they discussed the situation, the more they were convinced by the notion that both sets of circumstances were inextricably linked. Stockwell, in recognising that the murder team were under strain, placed the Women's and Children's team at Cooper's disposal, to assist with the missing persons' enquiry. As if Cooper's workload was not heavy enough, Chief Inspector Sproat requested that Cooper take on an internal investigation. By the time that Cooper had left the town hall and walked back down the High Street his head was swimming and he fancied a drink.

What a morning. A double scotch would do nicely.

Unfortunately, it was too early, and he had too much to do. On his return to the station he found Brian Pratt and Ian Mills sitting in the sergeants' office. He shut the door and flopped in a chair.

'How did morning prayers go, governor?' asked Ian.

'Good and bad, Ian. Mr Stockwell's given us the Women's team to work on the Maggie McGee enquiry.'

'That's good. And the bad?'

'Sproat. He's doing my blasted head in.'

'What's he done now, governor?'

'Well, you know that Morris car of his?'

'Oh yes. That's his pride and joy. He must spend half his life polishing and fiddling with the bloody thing.'

'Yes. I think he loves his motor more than his old woman.'

'What's happened to it, then?'

'Apparently, he came into the office on Saturday afternoon to collect something he'd forgotten to take with him when he left work the day before. When he drove out of the yard to go home, he had a collision with a fire bucket.'

'Didn't he see it then, governor?'

'No he didn't. Not until it smashed his rear windscreen. It was tied to his back bumper at the time.'

Brian and Ian laughed, heartily.

'Bloody hell, governor that's terrible,' said Brian sarcastically.

'Anyway. He wants me to investigate it. But I'm not going to lose any sleep over it. I'll ask around and speak to the shift who were on duty at the time. But it could have been anybody, couldn't it?'

'There are some wicked people about,' laughed Brian.

'Yes. Who'd do such a terrible thing?' said Ian, grinning broadly.

※

Jane got back to the office after having made a further visit to the hospital. The outcome had been disappointing. The personnel officer had made great efforts to facilitate Jane's enquiries, but they had yielded nothing of any value. No-one could shed any light on Maggie's movements since her return from Lakenheath. She decided to telephone Maggie's parents again. She tried, but there was no answer.

It was becoming a frustrating day for Jane, so she went downstairs to invite Linda Collins to the canteen for a cup of tea. After settling at a table, and following a brief exchange on the subject of Linda's engagement to Alby, they got back to business.

'Linda, I understand that Mr Stockwell has decided to treat the Maggie McGee situation as a missing person enquiry and he's assigned the Women's department to assist with it. Is that right?'

'Yes. I think it's a good idea. It will certainly give them something to get stuck into as a Team and cut down their bitching.'

'Has the DI spoken to you about holding a meeting with the hockey team girls on Wednesday?'

'Yes,' said Linda, 'he's spoken to me about it. I phoned Miss Guest, this morning and she volunteered to contact the team members for us. She was fine about the meeting being held Wednesday afternoon, and if any of the girls can't attend, hopefully, we can catch up with them later.'

'Did she say anything about whether she has told any of her girls about Cecily being murdered?'

'Yes. She's told them all right. To be fair she had to tell them something to get them to the meeting. I expect it's gone around like wildfire by now.'

'So, have you had any thoughts on where we could hold the meeting?' asked Jane.

'Well, the boss has arranged for it to be held in the bar.'

'What? Get them all sozzled and loosen them up, you mean?' laughed Jane.

'Good thinking Jane,' said Linda. 'And I'm pretty sure it would work, but Uncle Tom would, no doubt, take a dim view of it. I suppose we'd better keep the bar shut and just utilise the space.'

'How many of your girls are you going to use?'

'I was thinking that I'd use all of them. We want witness statements from the whole team and it would be best if, after the initial briefing, we interview them individually; that way they won't influence each other. Besides, it would be good experience for them.'

'What do we need to ask them, do you think?' said Jane.

'We need to know who they spoke to at Lakenheath, any exchange of details with the airmen, whether they have any names and contact numbers for the lads on the base and whether they have seen any of them since.'

'And of course, we need to confirm whether Maggie came back with them, to Colchester, on the coach. I tried to contact her parents, in Weymouth, earlier, but nobody would answer the phone.'

'I do hope she turns up,' said Linda, 'but, I have to

admit, it's not looking very good at the moment.'

'Oh. That reminds me Linda. I took a message for you earlier from a lady called Phyllis, who is the secretary for a Professor Simpson. She wants you to give her a call.

Apparently, the Professor has details of a couple of very similar cases, that were committed in Berlin.'

'Berlin?' said Linda. 'What has Berlin got to do with Cecily's case? Oh well. I'd better give her a call and find out.'

When Linda finally got back to her office, she dialled the number on the note that Jane had handed to her. It was now 4.45pm. There was no reply. She was intrigued but, frustratingly, she knew that she would have to wait until the morning to try again.

21

Tuesday 18 October 1949

Linda Collins couldn't wait to telephone Professor Simpson's secretary and she had considered coming into the office early to make the call, but stopped herself, knowing that she probably wouldn't have been at work at that time anyway. She held off until 10am, just to be on the safe side. The phone was answered by Phyllis.

'Professor Simpson's office. Can I help you?'

'Yes. Good morning. My name is Collins. Sergeant Linda Collins. I was given a message yesterday to give you a call. But it was late in the day and you were not answering. Is the Professor in the office?'

'Yes. One moment, I will put you through, Sergeant.'

'Simpson speaking.'

'Professor. Sergeant Linda Collins here.'

'Good morning sergeant . Thank you for calling.'

'How was the trip?'

'Very good, thank you, and I have some information for you that I think could be of some value to your investigation.'

'Sounds intriguing. Do tell.'

'Yes, with me at the conference was Professor Hugo Schreiber of the University of Berlin who gave a lecture on two connected murders. He is a forensic pathologist and he examined two bodies that were found a week apart in Berlin. In both cases the left nipple was bitten off and taken away from the scene and they happened within a mile of each other. Not only that, they have compared the photographs of each bite and they believe them to have been made by the same assailant.'

'Do they have any fingerprint link between the two scenes?'

'I'm not sure about that but I do have the contact details of the detective investigating both cases, a man called Klaus Walter, who is based in central Berlin.'

Professor Simpson spelt out the details and Linda noted them down carefully.

'Thank you for that Professor. Did Professor Schreiber say whether these types of case are very prevalent in Berlin?'

'Professor Schreiber, who like me is a specialist in forensic dentistry, says that they have not had any such cases since the Russians arrived in 1945. It is a well-known fact that when the Russians reached Berlin some of them made it their business to rape and pillage in retaliation for the atrocities committed by the Germans during their invasion.

The Western Allies, apart from a few, behaved more humanely.'

'Are there any Russians in his area now?'

'No, there aren't. Professor Schreiber covers the western half of the city, which is occupied by the British, Americans and French. As I'm sure you will know, they have had a lot of recent activity with the Berlin Airlift.'

'Yes, of course, Professor. I've heard a lot about that,' lied Linda.

'Anyway, Sergeant, I must press on. I'm in the middle of something at the moment. I will send you what I have by courier later today and hopefully, when you and Inspector Cooper have given it a good read through, you can call me again for another chat.

Goodbye for now.'

'Thank you, Professor, Goodbye.'

Linda didn't read the papers much these days. She had heard of the Berlin Airlift but really didn't know much about it. She didn't want to show the professor her ignorance, so she resolved to look it up. No, she would do better than that. She had to tell Alby about her call to the professor, and she expected that he'd know all about the airlift, so she went upstairs, knocked on his door and put her head in.

'I've just had a very interesting telephone conversation with Professor Simpson, governor. Got a minute?'

'Yes, Linda. Come in and shut the door.'

She entered and sat down.

'Apparently the professor's been at a conference in the Hague this week where he listened to a very interesting lecture from a German forensic dentist. Apparently, during the last year or so they had two connected murders very similar to ours, where the victim's left nipple was bitten off. They were both in central Berlin. The professor is sending us more detail by courier this afternoon.'

'Sounds very interesting, Linda. Carry on.'

'Anyway. He said that the Berlin Police haven't had anything like it since 1945. They are convinced that the murders are by the same person, although they have no suspect at the present.'

'Any fingerprints found at the scene?'

'The professor wasn't sure about that, but he gave me the contact details of the officer who is dealing with the two Berlin cases, so that we might give him a ring and find out more. I can't speak German. Can you?'

'No. I can't. But I ought to be able to. Lord knows, I spent enough time with them during the war.'

'Yes, said Linda. 'I was forgetting.'

'What half of Berlin did the murders happen in. Not the Russian zone, I hope?'

'No, the western half, but the professor made the point that recently there has been a lot of activity due to the Berlin Airlift.'

'Yes, I'm sure there has. It involved hundreds of aircraft and airmen. Quite a magnificent achievement by the Allies.'

'I must confess, I don't know much about it.'

'Well, Linda, my dear. You have come to the right man, because I can bore for England on the subject. I followed the Berlin Airlift in the newspapers and I have to say I was fascinated by it.'

'OK governor. Please educate me.'

'It started in June last year, when the Russians put a block on all rail traffic going into West Berlin from the western zones of Germany. Berlin became besieged like an island cut off from the rest of the world. Official access was only permitted by air through three corridors between Berlin and airfields in West Germany like Hamburg and Frankfurt.'

'What was the point of the airlift?'

'It was set up to deliver food and other supplies, like coal, to the people of West Berlin. It was a joint operation by the RAF and the United States Air Force, although they were assisted by crew from other air-forces like the Australians, Canadians and New Zealand.

It was a massive undertaking and a major achievement, but it needed a heck of a lot of manpower.'

'None of whom were necessarily involved in murder,' said Linda. 'But, it's a possibility, wouldn't you say.'

'Yes, of course. But I can't help thinking about the Schlitz bottle, the jeep and the fact that we have airbases not far away from us. Still, let's keep an open mind, see what our enquiries at Lakenheath bring us. In fact, we need to mark Ian's card before he and Jane make any further enquiries with the Yanks.'

'Leave it with me, governor. I'll nip upstairs in a minute and have a word with him, if you like.'

Cooper told her about the senior officers, meeting and his concerns about Sproat which prompted the relocation to the top office.

'Not ideal and not particularly spacious. One or two are moaning about it, but it will be secure and sufficient for our purposes. Anyway, shall I meet you in the Abbey Arms at six for a drink?'

'Yes please, governor darling. That would be lovely.'

◈

Janine Du Fries resided at Greythorpe Manor and had done since she was a child. The estate had been the family home since the eighteenth century, the Du Fries family having been prominent in the world of banking and finance. She was now in her mid-forties and she was already a widow. Attractive, in terms of classic beauty, she had received attention from potential suitors, but she had not managed to find any one man who measured up to her late husband.

The house was remote, being a few miles from the nearest village of Boxted, and living alone she had developed something of a siege mentality. So, she felt a sense of intrusion when, one afternoon, she heard a cacophony of young voices coming from the orchard at the rear of the Manor. Janine was upstairs in the back bedroom of the house, when her spaniel, Colin, first drew the noise to her attention, and her position near the upstairs windows, gave her a commanding view of the garden. She soon spotted who the culprits were and recognised some of them immediately as being boys from the village. There were four of them, all around ten or eleven years old. She knew the names of two of them, and she knew their parents. Janine opened the window.

'Thomas Price, Liam Aldridge. I know it's you. Get out of my garden. I shall be speaking to your parents and if I see you in here again, I shall speak to the constable.'

Eager to do his duty, Colin, the spaniel, raced down to the back door and barked furiously, desperate to be let out. When Janine caught up with him, she unbolted the back door, and he raced out into the garden.

After hearing the dog barking inside the house, Tom Price had anticipated that the hound would soon be among them, so he jumped down from the apple tree and followed the others back through the gap in the hedge that had been their point of entry. The lads each grabbed their bikes and sped off down the lane, lest Colin should reach them and nip at their ankles. Pedalling for all they were worth, the lads managed to put enough distance between themselves and the dog and soon they were free and clear. Colin, defeated, had given up the chase and was patrolling the road just a few yards from his garden, growling and giving out the occasional plaintive bark.

'Shit, that was close Liam,' said Tom. 'I hope she doesn't tell me mum and dad. I'd be grounded for a week.'

'Its Constable Pitts I'm more worried about,' said Liam.

'Nah. She probably won't bother. It's not as though we nicked anything, is it? We didn't get the chance.' The others, being younger, said nothing. They were just happy to be a part of the "gang" and they followed on behind.

It was nearly five o'clock and the lads were still a couple of miles away from the village when the heavens opened, and it began to pelt down with rain. Tom was in the lead and he directed them just off the road to an air-raid shelter that had been part of the old Boxted airfield. The others followed on, with Liam protesting.

'Tom. I haven't got time to hang around in there. I'm late for me tea as it is. My mum'll go mad if I'm not back home soon.'

'Well Liam, she'll go mad if you turn up with your clothes all sopping wet, anyway, won't she?'

'Yeah, she probably will, but I'm going home anyway. I'll see you later.' Liam carried on towards the village.

'See ya,' The others shouted after him. They hurriedly wheeled their bikes to the shelter and parked them beneath an adjacent tree. Tom grabbed the lamp from the front handle-bars of his bike and led the way inside the shelter.

They hadn't got much further than the entrance steps when an all-enveloping stench of decay met their nostrils.

'Blimey! What the hell is that smell?' shouted Tom.

He shone the torch around the room and they saw that it contained old metal bed frames and that the floor was strewn with a thick layer of leaves. Tom's attention was drawn to something in the far corner, where, he could see that, the level of leaves appeared to be higher than elsewhere.

'What's that over there?'

He moved closer to get a better look and was stunned when he suddenly recognised a human arm and hand that appeared to be reaching through the leaves and almost pointing in his direction.

'It's a dead body!'

He turned and fled in terror.

The others, totally spooked, followed him, grabbing their bikes, and after running out onto the road, they sped off towards the village. The rain was forgotten.

'What are we going to do about the body, Tom?' asked Joe, one of the younger lads, who had tears running down his cheeks.

'Tell the police, Joe.'

'Do you think that it could have been a body that's left over from the war?' asked Sam, naïvely.

'Nah. Can't be. Not if it stinks like that.'

As they reached the village, they stopped outside the police house. Tom dismounted, threw his bike to the ground and ran up the garden path. He knocked on the door. After a few minutes it was answered by PC Dick Pitts, who was dressed in his uniform shirt with trousers, braces and carpet slippers. He was holding a mug of tea.

'Hello, young Tom. What can I do for you?'

'We found a body, Mister Pitts,' said Tom, nervously.

'Really?' said the constable. 'Where was this?'

'In an air-raid shelter on the airfield.'

'What were you doing on there then, boy? You weren't scrumping, were you?' said the constable, teasingly.

'No, sir. We were sheltering out of the rain.'

'The person, you saw, couldn't have been just injured and still alive, could they Tom?'

'No, sir. There was a horrible smell.'

'OK. You had all better come in then. We'll get the area car to take us up there to have a look.

You boys want a cup of tea?'

'Yes please, they replied, in unison.

'And maybe, Mrs Pitts can rustle up a few biscuits.'

He sat them down in the office, disappeared off into the kitchen to speak to his wife, and he returned to use the phone. A short time later, Ivy Pitts arrived with the tea and biscuits, and the boys tucked in.

When the area car arrived, PC Pitts grabbed his coat and prepared to get into the vehicle with Tom.

'We only need Tom for this job,' he said to the boys. 'I want you, Sam and Joe, to stay with Ivy until we get back. She will try to get in contact with your parents. We won't be long.'

The police car reached the airfield in a few minutes and parked near the shelter. Tom and PC Pitts were seated in the back.

'Now Tom. I want you to show us to where you found the body. But we don't need you to come in with us. You've had enough frightening experiences for one day.'

Tom directed the officers to the entrance of the shelter which was covered with a dense growth of foliage.

'It's at the back of the room in the left corner, buried under the leaves. The arm is sticking out.'

'OK Tom. Thank you. You have done all you need to. Stay here by the car, will you, please. We'll go in and have a look.'

Pitts entered the shelter with one of the other officers. Tom could hear their comments from his position outside.

'Gordon Bennett! He was right. Something does smell bad in here.'

Tom heard the leaves rustle as the officers made their way to the back of the shelter.

'There it is,' said Pitts.

There was a short pause as the officers carried out a closer examination.

'Yes, it's a body, all right. We had better cordon the area off and call out the CID.'

Pitts and his colleague reappeared in the entrance and both took several deep breaths to clear the stench from their nostrils. Pitts returned to the vehicle.

'Well done, Tom. Good lad. You were right. I'll get the driver to take us back to the office and we'll get in touch with your mum and dad. We need to get a short statement from you about finding the body and the detectives might want to speak to you about it later.'

Leaving the area car observer to guard the scene, they took the lad back to the police office and Pitts was straight on the phone to the control room at headquarters.

Ian Mills and Jane Stewart were the first CID officers on scene and they were soon joined by Alby Cooper, who had been called out from home, having just arrived back after a couple of pints with Linda in the Abbey Arms.

On their arrival, Ian and Jane had found that the area and the shelter had been cordoned off with rope and they were told that the room had not been entered since Dick Pitts and his colleague had made their initial check. Brendan Withers and a colleague from Scenes of Crime were the next to arrive, followed by Doctor Grahame Stevenson, the police surgeon. Alby Cooper remained standing at the entrance to the shelter as Brendan entered. Cooper carefully passed him various items of equipment, including lamps, with which he lit the room. The doctor then joined Brendan, who set about slowly and gradually removing and bagging the leaves, revealing the body of a young woman.

The doctor carried out an examination of the body and gave a running commentary as he did so. Cooper listened, and the facts became all too familiar.

'Judging by the level of decay, I would say that this lady has been dead for over a week. There are signs that she may have had sexual intercourse. She is without her knickers. Her bra has been pushed up and her left nipple has been removed. Probably by biting. On first sight I would say that she appears to have been strangled. A post-mortem will no doubt be required to give us more precision on all these factors. Given the state of the victim and the nature of the scene, I believe that we would benefit from the attendance of a forensic pathologist.'

'Doctor, I have already requested the attendance of the forensic pathologist, Professor Graham Westlake,' said Cooper.

'That's good,' said the doctor. 'I will go back home for now, but I want to speak to him when he arrives, if somebody can let me know.'

'We'll let you know, the minute he arrives, doctor,' said Cooper.

'One thing is in our favour and that is the location of the body. We can keep it away from public gaze and it's under cover.'

It was another couple of hours before Professor Westlake arrived at the scene in a Metropolitan Police vehicle. After having the doctor informed of the professor's arrival and his return to the scene, Alby Cooper made the introductions between Westlake and Stevenson.

So as not to impose his own opinion and unduly influence matters, he left the two medical professionals to discuss victim and scene, after which they accompanied Brendan Withers into the room. Cooper, again, remained outside the shelter. It was over an hour before they re-emerged and shared their findings.

'This, Albert, is very similar to the murder of Cecily White. Probable manual strangulation, sexual interference, one of the victim's nipples, the left one, bitten off after death.'

'Yes, Professor. I rather thought you might say that,' said Cooper.

'As for other personal effects, none have been found yet, but Brendan and his colleague are working in there as we speak.'

'Well, with any luck, they'll find something that contains her details.'

'Let's hope so. But I would also suggest Albert, that for your own peace of mind, when Brendan's finished, you look at the body for yourself.'

'Yes, I will. Thank you,' said Cooper, who appreciated the thought.

'Sad for the victim, but if we can connect the two murders and find some additional evidence it might take us a significant step forward. Anyway, I'm off. If I don't speak to you in the interim, I will see you at the post-mortem.'

'Thank you, Professor.'

It was another two and a half hours before Brendan and his colleague emerged from the shelter. They had carefully swept and bagged all the dried leaves and closely examined the exposed floor of the room. Other than the body itself, they found nothing of any evidential value.

'Unless you require us to do something else, I think that we've done nearly all we can, for now, governor.'

'No. There's nothing else. Thank you, Brendan,' said Cooper.

'You know, there's still the strong probability that we're dealing with Maggie McGee, governor,' said Ian Mills.

'Maggie McGee,' said Cooper, nodding his head in recognition. 'Yes, unfortunately, that's very probable. She was a good friend of Cecily White and she's still a missing person. It's the biting that convinces me.'

'OK, sir. If you agree, we'll deal with the body now.'

'Yes. As soon as you can please, Brendan. I'm starting to wonder who was killed first. Whether it was Cecily or this poor woman.'

'Maybe the post-mortem will give us an idea about that, governor. Are you content for us to get the body to the mortuary now?' said Brendan.

'Yes. If you'll make the necessary arrangements, please. I'll get Ian to travel with the body to the mortuary for continuity.'

'We can do that, if you like, governor. It's on our way and young Evan here can ride with her, in the van.' Brendan's young assistant nodded.

'Yes, I can do that, governor.'

'Good. OK, Brendan. I'll leave it with you. But first, even though we think that we may have a name, I want to view the body.'

Cooper walked into the shelter and crouched down next to body that, in all likelyhood, was all that remained of Maggie McGee. He imagined that who-ever she was, in life, she had been a beautiful young lady. She had now been reduced to a distorted corpse. He didn't recognise her, and now he was sure that she had not been a colleague and they wouldn't have any repetition of the unfortunate circumstances that led to the identification of Cecily White by Brian Pratt. He turned to Brendan Withers.

'One thing you might not be aware of, Brendan, is that Miss McGee is a former member of the nursing staff at the Essex County Hospital. I want young Evan to impress upon the mortuary staff that the circumstances of this case are to be kept confidential and away from her colleagues. Not only that, there is still just an outside chance that the body isn't that of Maggie McGee at all. Somehow, we've got to establish the victim's identity.'

'I'll go in with Evan and make sure, governor.'
'Good man.'

It was 1.20am and there were still things to be done at the scene. Cooper arranged for Ian Mills and Tom Rogers to supervise a search of the area around the shelter at 8am the next morning. There was still the possibility that some item of evidential value might have been dropped or discarded by the perpetrator. For now, the cordon would remain in place and under guard until completion of the search.

Cooper would have to tell Linda that as far as the Maggie McGee, missing person enquiry was concerned, the case may have been solved. As for the members of the hockey team, in the fullness of time, the tragic news would be confirmed.

22

Wednesday 19 October 1949

It had been a long night for Alby Cooper. He had got to bed around 3am and had barely managed four hours' sleep before getting back to the station about 8.15am. The first job, after visiting the canteen, was to telephone the boss, Tom Stockwell, and update him about the fact that the dead body, he had notified him about the previous evening, was likely to be Maggie McGee. Stockwell was grateful for being "kept in the loop".

'Who is the pathologist?'

'Professor Westlake, sir.'

'I see, Professor Westlake, is it? He examined Cecily White, I believe. Did he find anything common to both scenes?'

'Yes, sir. The *modus operandi*. He believed, on first examination, that this young woman had been strangled, that she had had sexual intercourse, and her left nipple was bitten off after death. It's quite obvious that the perpetrator is the same person who murdered both victims.'

'Which means, of course, that we continue with our policy decision of not disclosing the fact of the biting,' said Stockwell.

'Quite.'

'The other thing we need to decide upon is, what are we going to tell the press?'

'Well, obviously we shouldn't disclose the *modus operandi,* but it probably won't take them long to make a connection with Cecily's murder,' said Cooper.

'No. I'm sure you're right.'

'Sir. One thing I need to tell you is that I had Richard Timmins, the crime reporter from the *Argus*, at the front counter on Monday. He had got wind of the fact that the body at the reservoir was that of a police-woman.'

'Did he tell you the source of his information?'

'No, sir. He wouldn't tell me the source of the information and, to be fair, he's under no legal obligation to do so.'

'Unfortunate and rather disturbing, Albert. I hope that it's not somebody within this division'

'Yes, sir. I had to ask him to keep quiet about that, for operational reasons. I think I have persuaded him to keep us out of the paper, for now.'

'Good. Well done.'

'Thing is, I sort of half alluded to the possibility that if he cooperated, the *Argus* might have an exclusive in due course.'

'Albert.' There was a pause, in which Stockwell was obviously considering the revelation.'I wish you'd spoken to me about that first.'

'Sorry, sir. But I was suddenly faced with a difficult

situation and I had to do a bit of fire-fighting.'

'Oh well. What's done is done. I think that the best thing to do for now, is to stay quiet about this latest victim, as far as the press are concerned, anyway, and we'll have to try and impress upon the hockey team that they should not talk to anyone else about it. Although, I'm not optimistic that that approach is going to be successful. But, under the circumstances, it's all we can do.'

'Yes, sir. It might just give us a few more precious days.'

'You have your meeting with the hockey team this afternoon at, what time?'

'Two o'clock, sir, and I have to say that I'm not particularly looking forward to it,' said Cooper.

'No, I don't suppose you are. But you will have Linda's team there to help comfort the girls. Although, if they get too upset, you might have to postpone any statement taking for another day.'

'We'll see how we get on. I think that the news of this latest death will most likely spur them on to give as much help as they can.'

'I hope you're right. Well, let me know if you need anything, Albert.'

❖

Cooper was sitting in the office getting on with the contents of his in-tray, which had been left untouched for the best part of a week. When the phone rang, he felt like picking it up and throwing it across the office. There were just not enough hours in a day.

'DI Cooper.'

'Morning, governor, it's Sergeant Glover in the control room.'

'Morning, Ted.'

'We've just received a radio message from Ian Mills, he wanted us to let you know that they have found a handbag near the scene over at Boxted.'

'Good. Any name inside it?'

'Yes, governor, there is. But, he only wanted to give a Christian name over the radio for security reasons.'

'Go on then Ted. Don't keep me in suspenders.'

'He gave the name of Maggie and he said that you would know who he meant.'

'Yes, I do. Good. Did he say whereabouts he found the bag?'

'Yes, guv. It was in a ditch, about 150 yards along the lane from the shelter. He also wanted us to tell you that they also found a couple of empty wine bottles nearby. Scenes of Crime are on the scene and they are taking possession of the items.'

'Thanks, Ted.'

Cooper sat and thought about what Ted had just told him. That was it. The name of Maggie McGee was confirmed. It was positive news, of a kind.'

◈

It was 1.15pm and Cooper was standing at the bar with Linda Collins. But this was by no means a social event or an adjunct to their courtship. No, this was business, and it was going to be one of the most challenging sets of circumstances that they were ever likely to come across in their career.

In the room were officers of the murder team, supplemented by the entire Women's and Children's team. Cooper began.

'Good afternoon, ladies and gents. For those of you who may not have heard already, we now have two murders that we and the forensic pathologist believe are connected.

The first victim being our much-respected colleague, Cecily White, and now a second, who we believe to be Cecily's friend Maggie McGee. The police in Dorset will, as I speak, be visiting Maggie's parents to break the tragic news. I need now to stress three things. Firstly, the hospital staff, other than those working in the mortuary, have not yet been told of Maggie's death. And secondly, Maggie McGee has yet to be formally identified but we are confident that it is her, as during our search of the area we found her nurses ID card in a handbag about 150 yards, further along the road from the body.'

'Where was she found, governor?' asked Enid.

'In an old air-raid shelter at Boxted airfield. She was found by a group of kids.'

'Can't have been nice for them.'

'No Enid, I suppose it can't have been. Anyway, last and by no means least, we have not said anything to the press on either case about the *modus operandi* or the fact that the two are connected. In fact they know nothing of a second victim and I want us to keep that detail to ourselves, for now. I can't stress this enough. We speak to nobody about this, not even members of your family when you get home.

As for the press, it will be me who speaks to them, and me alone. The fact is, we have a duty to warn members of the public, particularly young women, that we have a very dangerous individual in our area, but if we are ever going to catch this animal, we must be very measured on our disclosure of information. We can't afford for the details to be aired in public.'

'Governor,' said Jane Stewart, putting a hand in the air.

'Yes, Jane.'

'Are you going to enquire whether the members of the hockey team know anything about who the victims are?'

'That's a very good point, Jane. We suspect, but we are not sure, that they will have been told about Cecily by Miss Guest. As you and Brian interviewed her, I want you both to take her to one-side when she arrives and put the question to her formally. But, only as far as Cecily's murder is concerned. She knows nothing about Maggie McGee's murder, as yet.'

'Do you want us to cover that point, about Cecily, in a witness statement, governor?' asked Brian.

'Yes, please, Brian.'

Cooper continued, 'Now, this brings me to an ethical issue and a policy decision that will have to go in the book. We need to question these women and drain them of every scrap of information they have relating to their visit to Lakenheath, the parameters of which I will deal with later. But the fundamental point is this; we need them to have a clear head, untrammelled by emotion. If they already know about Cecily, then perhaps, they will have had some time to get over the initial shock. Here is the crunch. We can't afford to set them off again by telling them about Maggie at this stage. We can do that after we've interviewed them and got their statements.'

'How are we going to break the news to them, guv?' asked Ian Mills.

'Right, well, I've discussed this with Mr Stockwell and we've agreed that the best way is to set up something of a conveyor-belt system. In the cold light of day, some might say that our method was rather callous. Be that as it may, we have too much at stake to do otherwise, but I want us to interview them, take their statement and before they leave the interview room, we tell them about Maggie. The interviewing officer will then take them down the backstairs to the canteen where they will be met by Linda. We have arranged exclusive use of the canteen until five o'clock.'

'Blimey, governor, that is callous,' said Brian. 'But, I follow your logic. We don't want them all reduced to tears before we've got anything out of them.'

'Quite right, Brian,' said Cooper, 'and let's turn the situation on it's head. Any defence barrister worth their salt would make great play of the fact that the witnesses made their statements in a state of heightened emotion, and, that being the case, they could be very suggestable to untruths and be likely to sign anything. We can't have that, can we?'

'Good point, governor,' said Brian. 'Do you want us to take a set of elimination fingerprints from them as well?'

'Yes. But you had best do that before you break the news to them.'

'Anyway, governor. How are we going to kick off this afternoon?' asked Jane.

First, we'll bring them up to the bar and I will give them a welcome and an introduction to what it is that we are seeking to achieve. After that we'll take the first five to the various designated interview rooms. What do we want from them? Well, to start with, the basic sequence of events: Who welcomed them when they arrived on the base, any relevant details about the match, did they notice any male spectators? What went on when they had drinks after the game on the veranda and whether they were approached by any of the Americans, including any of the women.'

'Do you mean if the women are a bit the other way, governor?' asked Tom Rogers, in deadly earnest. Several members of the group rolled their eyes.

'No, I don't mean that specifically Tom.'

'Just a thought, governor.'

'Anyway, to continue, and you would do well to make a note of this: we need names, descriptions, rank, conversations, any detail that they can recall. Did any of the Americans allude to any relationships with persons off-base? What were they and the airforce people drinking? Did they see any civilians that they knew? Dancing, was there a band?

If so, who were they? Have any of the girls been on dates with the Americans since the day of the match? Any vehicles used? Conversations about any previous postings? Abroad? Wethersfield? Boxted?'

'Governor, how will we explain Maggie McGee's absence?' asked Jane.

'We'll fall back on the idea that she is away in Weymouth with her parents. Oh, and another thing. We need to find out if there was ever a previous match against the Yanks with them coming to play in Colchester? Any relationship's forged there? OK. That's all from me. Any questions?'

There was a pause, silence.

'OK. Good luck. Any problems, speak to me.'

'Thank you, boss. Folks, if you'll gather around me,' said Linda. 'We've got about ten minutes before our visitors arrive. I have created a schedule of names and allocated each of them to an interviewing officer and a list of points to be covered.'

Cooper left them to it, nipped to the gents and then walked down to the front counter to speak to Ted Glover, the station sergeant. After five minutes, a group of women entered the station foyer, led by Miss Guest, who introduced herself to the front counter officer. On hearing this, Cooper joined him at the counter.

'Good afternoon, ladies. Thank you for coming. I am Detective Inspector Albert Cooper. Miss Guest, are you all present and correct?'

'Not quite. The only one missing is Maggie McGee. I couldn't get in touch with her, I'm afraid.' Cooper left the counter and let them through the connecting door to the stairwell.

'OK, if you would like to follow me, ladies. We are going to hold our meeting in the bar. It won't be open though, I'm sorry to say.'

'That's a shame,' said Guest. 'I could do with one.'

Cooper led them through the lower corridor to the back stairs, which provided access to the bar on the first floor.

'If you would like to make yourselves comfortable, ladies, my colleagues will serve tea and take your names. We just need to speak to you before we make a start, Miss Guest. If you would like to follow my colleagues, Brian and Jane, whom, I believe, you have already met.'

The three of them left the room and Cooper remained. Brian led the way into an empty office just along the corridor. He shut the office door behind them.

'Jessica,' said Brian, 'we wanted to speak to you, before we interview the members of the team, about what they know of Cecily's death. Did you tell them about it?'

'Yes. I'm sorry but I felt I had to. I didn't want them to find out about it by accident, that would have just been too cruel and would have made matters worse. I contacted them all individually, except Maggie McGee. I know she does all sorts of shifts, so I intended to tell her today. But I simply haven't managed to reach her.'

'How did they take the news?'

'Some were immediately very tearful. Others took it more calmly. One or two of the girls didn't really know her that well.'

'How do you think that the ladies will react when we interview them about their knowledge of Cecily today?'

'I'm pretty sure that they'll want to help you as much as they can. They have had a little time to think about it. One or two of them are very angry about it, as they knew Cecily really well.'

'Jessica, you don't think this process is going to be too much of an ordeal for them, do you?' asked Brian.

'No. They're made of sturdy stuff, my girls.'

'Good. Because what they have to tell us could be quite crucial to our investigation. Jane and I will carry on with our interview shortly, Jessica. But first we need to go back to the bar and have a word with Mr Cooper,' said Brian.

Cooper stood at the end of the room ready to make a start. He had taken off his jacket and had rolled up his sleeves. A subliminal indication that he meant business.

'Good afternoon, ladies. Thank you for coming and agreeing to help us. I understand that you are all aware of the fact that your team-mate, Cecily White, was murdered a couple of weeks ago. As you may know, she was a police sergeant, based here at this station.

However, Cecily was murdered while she was off duty. None of the information has appeared in the press and it is vital to our investigation that it stays that way. In the fullness of time you will, no doubt, under- stand why this is necessary. Given the fact that the last time that any of you were likely to have seen Cecily was on the day of the match at Lakenheath, I want you to cast your minds back and give us as much information as you can recall about your visit. What you did while you were there. Who you might have met. Any detail at all could help us a great deal. My colleagues, here, will take what you have to tell them down in a written statement, if it is relevant. Finally, we need to take a set of elimination fingerprints from each of you. They will not stay on record, and you can apply to witness their destruction after the case has been concluded, if you so wish. Once again, a heartfelt thanks to you all for coming to help us. Now my colleague, Sergeant Linda Collins, will call out your names and an officer will approach you.'

◈

Later, and after fully debriefing the troops in the bar, Cooper had gathered his team to assess the product from the various interviews held with the hockey team. They were now seated in the top office.

'Thank God that's over,' said Linda, to nobody in particular.

'Wasn't nice, was it?' said Jane. 'First having them take us into their confidence, giving us a statement and fingerprints, then hitting them with the bad news about Maggie McGee. It felt like we were playing a dirty trick on them.'

'I agree,' said Cooper, 'but, under the circumstances, it was totally necessary. So, how did they take it?'

'Not too badly. I don't think. With our two ladies we explained why we had to keep the information back until last and they appeared to understand our dilemma. But they were both upset because they had known her for a few years and because she was a very popular member of the team. They both said that they would like to help us as much as they can,' said Jane.

'Yes. My two were much the same,' said Linda.

'OK then. Let's see what we've got. Linda, you read half of the statements and go first, please, and then Jane you can do the rest.'

'OK, governor. It seems that there was no male interest in the match. Probably because during the afternoon all the guys are at work.'

'Were there any spectators?'

'The only people watching were members of the two teams. The managers, the reserves and hangers-on.'

'Did they use the changing facilities?'

'Yes. They used the changing rooms and showers afterwards and then they accepted an invitation from the other team for drinks and sandwiches on the veranda at the club. It was around five 'o'clock, when a lot of the men had finished work, that they started to get some attention.'

'Did they come up with any names?'

'Yes, governor. One of the first to get involved was a young airman called "Ryan," who was known to some of the American team, and he got chatting to the Colchester lot on the back of that. I spoke to Jane about the description given and she says that it sounds like Ryan Noble, who, I'm told, is a bit of a dish. He apparently focussed much of his chat on Maggie, as she was by far the prettiest of the group.'

'Didn't any of the other women get attention?'

'Most of the others are quite plain, "jolly-hockey-sticks," types, I would say.'

'He was the main man, was he?'

'Apparently, he was the one who suggested that they might like to stay behind for the dance and when they agreed he went back to his billet to change. He returned about twenty minutes later, by which time some of the other American guys had also got involved and Ryan arranged for the girls to be signed in to the club.'

'Any other names,?' asked Cooper.

'Yes. They remembered two. A man called "Max," he was a corporal, and a sergeant called Conor, who told some of the girls that his family were originally from Ireland. There were other men, but my lot didn't recall any other names.'

'Any dancing?'

'It seems that the only one who really got involved with the men was Maggie. She had several dances with Ryan and a couple with Conor, too. The other girls had a drink, but they mostly danced with each other. They didn't particularly appreciate the American's brash attitude, but even so, when they wanted to go, they had a hell of a job to get Maggie to go with them.'

'And did she go with them?' asked Cooper.

'Yes. She was a bit tiddly, but they managed to get her on the coach. Apparently, one of the girls got quite drunk, and, on the way back, they had to stop the coach, so she could be sick at the side of the road.'

'Where did they drop Maggie off?'

'At the nurses' home in Colchester.'

'I take it that none of the Yanks got on the coach with them?'

'No. Only the Colchester lot.'

'Was Cecily seen talking to any of them?'

'Not on a one to one basis. Only as part of the group when they were on the veranda. Of course, she went back to Colchester with Jessica Guest in the car, before the others went into the club.'

'Have any of the other girls seen Cecily or Maggie since that day?'

'None of my lot have.'

'Anything else, Linda?'

'No. That's about it, governor. Oh no, just one other thing. The men were all drinking beer from glasses, some of which were filled from bottles. But none of the girls could be specific about who was drinking what.'

'Thanks, Linda. Now Jane, what have you got for us?'

'Much the same, governor.'

'Have any of the girls met any of the Yanks off-base since that day?'

'No, they haven't.'

'Has the Colchester Hockey Club played the Yanks in

any other fixture at all this season or last?'

'No, that was the only game. It was a bit of a one-off apparently.'

'Did any of the girls see anyone they know in the club? By that I mean any other British civilians?'

'No, governor.'

'Did they have any conversations with the Yanks about the vehicles at their disposal?'

'No.'

'Specific jobs?'

'Yes. This guy, Conor, was a bit of a braggart apparently. He was trying to impress the Girls with bullshit. He claimed that as well as being a sergeant he's a test pilot. At least that's what he told them.'

Cooper looked at the list of attendees supplied by Wilson Rudrow.

'There's a bloke called Conor Lucan on the list along with Ryan Noble and a guy called Max Goodchild.'

'Are you going to interview them, then, governor?' asked Brian.

'As you know, we've already spoken to Ryan Noble.'

'What was he like?'

'He was helpful and polite,' said Ian, 'quite a nice lad. He and Maggie had obviously hit it off and she gave him the phone number of her nurses' home in Colchester. They were the only ones who did hit it off.'

'Did they see each other after that?'

'He did ask her out and she said that she'd meet up with him but that it couldn't be for a couple of weeks because she was going to be on night duty and after that she would be away at her parent's place.'

'Or at least, that's what he told us,' said Cooper, 'and of course, when you interviewed him, we knew nothing of the fact that Maggie had also been murdered. We need to get back to him and try and get his fingerprints. My worry is this. And you can call me cynical if you like, but I think we need to tread very carefully with the Yanks.'

'Sorry, governor,' said Ian, 'I'm not with you.'

'We need to approach them in the right way and not just focus on Ryan Noble. If they get precious about the pride of the squadron and take umbrage about us laying the blame at their door on minimal evidence, they could ship Noble and the others back to the States.'

'That would knacker things totally,' said Brian.

'Exactly,' said Cooper.

23

Thursday 20 October 1949

Linda Collins was the first to arrive in the office and although she was in the early days of her secondment, this was starting to become the norm. One or two of the girls were habitually late. Whether they were testing her, she couldn't tell, but the day was fast approaching when she would have to have serious words.

On checking the in-tray on her desk, Linda was delighted to find a courier package that had been delivered to the front counter. On opening it she found a series of scene photographs that had been taken of two separate victims from various angles, including close shots of their breasts showing them denuded of each left nipple. Linda felt a pang of sadness, as this was all too familiar. Accompanying the photographs was a two-page letter, addressed to Professor Simpson and signed by Professor Schreiber. It had been typed in German and although she could not translate or understand it, she could make out the name of Herr Klaus Walter and a Berlin telephone number. She was eager to learn whether any fingerprints had been found at either scene and whether the Berlin police had a suspect.

Linda walked through to the Collator's office to see Reg West. He was busy in one corner of the office making himself a brew.

'Morning, Reg.'

'Morning, Linda. Fancy a tea?'

'Yes please, Reg. White with two sugars.'

Reg brought the mugs across to his desk.

'Reg, you remember that you were telling me about your liaison work with Berechurch Hall Camp?'

'Yes.'

'Do many of the staff there speak German?'

'Yes. Several of them do. They have to conduct a lot of interviews and not many of the inmates speak English.'

'Only, I've had details of two murders committed this year in Berlin that are strikingly similar to that of Cecily. There's a two-page letter accompanying it but it's in German and I can't make head nor tail of it.'

'I could certainly give them a call and arrange for you to go down there. I'm sure they'd be happy to give it the once-over for you.'

'Would you do that?'

'Yes, of course. That's what I'm here for. Leave it with me, I'll give them a ring and come back to you shortly.'

Linda mounted the stairs to the CID office in order to apprise Alby Cooper. He wasn't in his office, then she remembered that he was due to attend a meeting. She would catch him when he returned.

◆

Later that afternoon the staff at the headquarters fingerprint bureau had forged something of a breakthrough. Brendan Withers couldn't wait to pass the news on to Alby Cooper.

They had managed to establish that the fingerprints lifted from both murder scenes had been left by the same person. Unfortunately, the owner of the fingerprints was still not on any police record. He dialled the telephone number for Cooper, who picked up straight away.

'Cooper.'

'Governor. It's Brendan Withers. I've got some good news for you.'

'Fire away, then, Brendan.'

'We have checked the fingerprints on Cecily's purse and those on Maggie's handbag and they are a match.'

'Sounds good Brendan, but could they have both been left by Maggie? They were mates, after all?'

'No, governor. We have eliminated her and have compared all the other sets of elimination prints on the case.'

'Well done, Brendan. Any joy on the teeth marks?'

'Not yet. That'll take a bit longer, I'm afraid. But I can say though, that they were not made by Johann Weber.'

'OK. Thanks, mate.'

'I'll send you over a report with a statement in the next couple of days, governor.'

Cooper walked into the sergeants' office, where he found Brian Pratt, who was sitting at his desk, using the phone. On seeing Cooper's arrival in the office, Brian finished his call and gave him his full attention.

'Is Ian about, Brian?'

'He's downstairs, governor.'

'OK. Can you go down and fetch him? Also, speak to Linda, we need a meeting in my office in twenty minutes.'

A short time later, the four of them were assembled in the DI's office.

'Right folks,' said Cooper. 'I thought that you'd like to know that we have a definite fingerprint match between Cecily's purse and the handbag found near the air-raid shelter.'

'Great news,' said Brian. 'Wasn't there anything on the wine bottles?'

'Brendan said nothing about them. I'm sure he would have done if anything had been found on them. Anyway, the fact of the fingerprint link, taken together with the sound of a jeep at the reservoir and the Schlitz beer bottle, provides us with reasonable suspicion that our perpetrator is likely to be one of the American airmen.'

'Yes, governor. But which one? There are hundreds of the buggers,' said Ian.

'The most obvious suspect is young Ryan Noble. I think we need to know his movements throughout the relevant period. Ian, I want you to call Wilson Rudrow and ask him if he would come to Colchester for a meeting. But say nothing about the fingerprint link for now, please.'

'Right oh, governor.'

'As I said before, we need to tread carefully with the Yanks, but we have no alternative but to trust Mr Rudrow. At the end of the day, RAF Lakenheath is US sovereign territory, so we can't just go onto the base and do what we want.'

'One other thing, governor,' said Linda. 'I received the package by courier from Professor Simpson and the Berlin murders have some very interesting similarities to our own.'

She handed the contents of the pack to Cooper, who examined each of the photographs and handed them around.

'Anyone here speak German?' said Cooper.

They each shook their head.

'How are these murders related to our jobs, exactly?' asked Ian.

'These were drawn to our attention by Professor Simpson, who is a pathologist who specialises in forensic dentistry. The method in each case is very similar to ours,' said Cooper. 'The US Air Force were heavily engaged in Berlin until recently with the "airlift." It's definitely something to bear in mind.'

'There's a two-page letter with the photos which is in German. If you're happy for me to make the enquiry, governor, Reg West has arranged for me to go to Berechurch Hall Camp at four o'clock today to see a Captain Harrington. He could translate it for me, apparently.'

'Good idea, Linda. I'll come with you,' said Cooper.

Ian and Brian both sniggered.

'OK, gents. What's so funny?'

'Sorry, governor,' said Brian. 'It's just that most blokes take their fiancée to the pictures. Not to a military prison.'

Cooper laughed and nodded. 'Fair comment. I see what you mean.'

Ian and Brian left the room, still laughing as they went.

'Cheeky pair of buggers,' said Cooper.

'You have to admit they've got a point,' said Linda.

'Yes, I suppose so.'

'I mean, I know that it was my idea but you could always take me somewhere nicer,' said Linda, teasingly.

'That I will,' said Cooper, 'Anyway, that reminds me, Linda, have you got any plans for Saturday? Only I want to take you down to see Mum and Dad. They've got something for us, apparently.'

'That'll be nice. I haven't made any plans. I was rather hoping that you'd take me out somewhere. What have they got for us?'

'I don't know. They wouldn't tell me. It's a surprise, apparently.'

'Sounds mysterious.'

'One of their friends in the village has got a Labrador bitch and she has just had a litter of pups fathered by Buster. I've got a sneaking suspicion that they might have got one for us,' said Cooper.

'You don't sound very pleased, darling. You like dogs, don't you?'

'Yes. But what would we do with a dog? They're a bit of tie and we're both out all day. Anyway, we're getting ahead of ourselves. Maybe it's not that at all. So, I'll call for you at ten on Saturday morning, if that's OK.'

◈

Cooper and Linda arrived at Berechurch Hall Camp in the CID Wolsey ten minutes before the appointed time. After signing the visitor's book in the guard-room, they were escorted to the adjutant's office, where they were met by Captain Gerald Harrington of the Royal Military Police. After introductions Cooper and Linda were offered a seat.

'Inspector, I understand from Reg West that you have a

letter, in German, that you would like me to look at,' said Harrington.

'Yes,' said Cooper, 'We are investigating a series of murders that have a particular *modus operandi* and, we have been made aware of two murders in Berlin that are very similar. Our forensic scientist, Professor Simpson, drew them to our attention and he has been liaising with his counterpart in Berlin. This is a letter from him. Unfortunately, I have no German and neither does Linda.'

Cooper handed the letter to the Captain for his perusal and he sat reading it in silence.

'I can tell you, in summary, that it is addressed to Professor Simpson and it refers to he and the author having both recently attended a conference in the Hague where he mentioned the Berlin murders to Simpson. The investigating detective is one Herr Klaus Walter of the Central Berlin Police. The offences were committed two weeks apart in May of this year. In each case the woman had her left nipple bitten off and it was taken from the scene.'

Captain Harrington winced. 'My God. How ghastly!'

'Yes, Captain,' said Cooper. 'That happened in our cases also. Although, it is a fact that we are desperate to keep to ourselves for operational reasons.'

'Yes. Understood, old boy. You can rely on me not to spill the beans. Anyway, the letter goes on to say that although, at the time of writing, they have no suspect, they do have fingerprints on a packet of Lucky Strike cigarettes found with the body of Julia Bohm.'

'Really?' said Linda. 'That's brilliant. And Lucky Strike. They're an American brand, aren't they?'

'Yes, I believe they are. That could provide us with a

major leap forward,' said Cooper.

'I wonder if we can get photographic evidence of their fingerprint lift sent over to compare against ours?

'Well, I'm pleased to be the bearer of good tidings. I have the telephone number of Herr Walter here in the letter. Shall we give him a call?'

'Can you do that from here?' asked Linda.

'Yes, we certainly can. If we go across to our communications centre they could set it up for us quite quickly. We call Germany all the time. It's an essential tool of our job.'

Harrington rose from his seat and he led the two officers across the square to the Communications Centre. They were met by a young signals officer at the front desk, and Harrington, after explaining what was required, was ushered through, with Linda and Cooper, into what appeared to be a studio that had several separate call boxes along one side of the room.

'Inspector, if you and Miss Collins would like to take a seat for a moment, my colleague will telephone the number for Herr Walter and when we have established contact, I will take over.'

Cooper and Linda sat and waited for about ten minutes, after which they were rejoined by Harrington.

'I got through to the correct office, but, unfortunately, Herr Walter is not in the office today. I spoke to his deputy, a man called Siegler, a helpfiul chap. He actually attended the scene of the first murder where they got the fingerprints from the packet of Lucky Strike cigarettes found under the body. He will speak to Herr Walter about obtaining photographs of the fingerprint lifts? If that's the correct term?…'

'Yes, that's right,' said Cooper.

'And, he said that they'll get them sent over to you via Professor Schreiber.'

'Good. Thank you, captain. We appreciate your help. We'll let Professor Simpson know what to expect' said Cooper.

'Oh, and one other thing Inspector. As it said in the letter. They still have no suspect. But they are convinced that the same person must have been responsible for both of their murders'

'So he sounded helpful?'

'Yes. They think that they may have a serial killer on their hands and they are expecting a third murder at any time. He said they'd be grateful for all the help that they can get.'

'Of course,I said that I was calling on behalf of the Colchester Police, certainly not from a prisoner of war camp.'

'Well done, captain' said Cooper, 'shrewd thinking.'

'I could make a follow-up call for you on Monday, if you would like me to, Inspector,' said Harrington.

'Yes, if you could. I think I'll send along one of my team for that, if I may. Probably Linda, here, if she's free. Just in case there are any questions raised during the call that only an investigator could answer.'

'Yes, good idea. That makes sense.'

Cooper and Linda both thanked Harrington for his valuable assistance, as he saw them off at the gate. They then made their way back to their vehicle to return to the police station.

'What did you think of that then, governor darling?'

'Very helpful, Linda. Tell you one thing, and I'm not just plucking this out of the sky, no pun intended, I'd lay money on the probability that our murders and theirs are connected and that our man is an American airman. First, we have a jeep and a Schlitz beer bottle. Our second victim's body is dumped on an old US airbase and now the Germans find Lucky Strike cigarettes at one of their scenes.'

'Wouldn't it be great if their fingerprints match ours,' said Linda.

'Christ, that, would be fantastic, wouldn't it?'

'How are we going to find our man, though?'

'I've got a bit of an idea.'

'Do tell,' said Linda.

'Well Linda. It seems to me, that a good place to start would be to get Rudrow to make a list of the airmen who were at both Lakenheath at the time of our murders and in Berlin during May. Any names that crop up could be compared to the guest book for the club.'

24

Friday 21 October 1949

It was 10.55am and Ian Mills had just brought Wilson Rudrow from the front counter up to Cooper's office. Ian made the introductions.

'Good morning, Mr Rudrow. Thank you for coming,' said Cooper.

'I'm happy to help. By the way, please call me Wilson.'

'Well, that being the case, please call me Alby.'

'Alby?' asked Rudrow in surprise.

'Yes, Wilson. It's short for Albert. Bloody awful name. I don't know what my parents were thinking about when they chose it.' They both laughed.

'Is it OK if my driver stays in your rear yard?'

'Fine. We'll speak to the station sergeant and let him know. He could sit in the canteen, if he wants to.'

Cooper called in one of the lads and told him to deal with it.

'Anyway, how can I help you?' said Rudrow.

'Since Ian Mills and Jane Stewart spoke to you, we've had the discovery of a second body. We believe that it's that of Maggie McGee, another member of the Colchester hockey team who visited Lakenheath. She was found in an air-raid shelter at the old RAF Boxted.'

'That was one of ours, wasn't it?'

'Yes. It was used by the US Air Force until they decommissioned it at the end of the war.'

'So, the facts are that we have two dead women connected to the hockey club visit. The use of a jeep and the discovery of the Schlitz bottle at the first murder. On that basis you believe there to be an American connection,' said Rudrow.

'Not an unreasonable line of enquiry, under the circumstances, wouldn't you think?' said Cooper.

'No Alby, I agree,' said Rudrow. 'So, how do you want to play this?'

'We have interviewed the hockey team individually and it seems there were a few of the airmen at the base that were interested. Maggie McGee apparently danced with two of them. Ryan Noble, whom we've already spoken to, and a man called Conor. There was also mention of a man called Max. We have looked at the guest list that you gave us, and they are all on there.'

'Any mention of rank?'

'We're not sure about the one called Max and, of course, Noble we know about. The one called Conor was apparently a sergeant and he told the girls that his ancestors originally came from Ireland. Apparently, he told them that he was a test pilot.'

'That's baloney,' said Rudrow ' He was obviously shooting them a line, to try to impress them. We haven't got any test pilots at Lakenheath and even if we did, they would be an officer, not a sergeant.'

'Yes, I thought it unlikely.'

'Do you want me to interview them?'

'No thanks, Wilson. I don't need you to do that at this stage, but a good place to start would be, if you could find out their whereabouts over the relevant period. Did they leave the base? and did they have access to a jeep?'

'I can certainly do that for you, Alby, and I'm pretty sure I could get my hands on that kind of detail without arousing suspicion.'

'Would be good, if you could. I want to keep this low key.'

'Yeah, I understand where you're coming from, but what I would say is that these guys are moving around all the time. I need to find out if anyone on the list is due for posting. We need to move quickly. Before you know it, they could be sent stateside.'

'What about taking their fingerprints?'

'We couldn't do it without their consent, and we couldn't force them on the evidence that we have. It doesn't point to any particular individual.'

'OK,' said Cooper. 'What if we did something covertly?'

'Sorry Alby. I'm not with you.'

'What if we could get their fingerprints without them realising it?'

'Well, it would give you a place to go if you could get the right guy. But I really don't think the general would authorise it. I couldn't just act on my own. Holy shit! I'd end up in Alcatraz.'

'I have a reason for asking this question that I have to keep to myself for the moment, it relates to the *modus operandi,* but can you tell me if any of the guys on the list, that you gave us, have recently spent any time in Berlin to do with the airlift?'

'Yes Alby, I'm pretty sure that I could give you that information.'

'How quickly could you do that?'

'Tomorrow. No problem. I'll get one of my guys on it.'

'I'd be grateful if you could provide me with details of your personnel who spent May in Berlin, not just the ones on that guest list. The Berlin police had two murders in May that are connected. Both are strikingly similar to ours, and at one of them they found a packet of Lucky Strike cigarettes underneath the body. They lifted fingerprints off the packet and they are going to send a copy of the fingerprint lift to us.'

'Sounds encouraging,' said Rudrow.

'Do you think that there are many of your men who fall into that category?'

'Yeah, quite a few. Women too.'

※

On his return to Lakenheath, Rudrow wasted no time in initiating his enquiries. He called his office manager, Corporal Rhianna Tully, into his office.

'Shut the door, Rhianna, and take a seat. I've got a very important job for you.' Rhianna, an attractive and statuesque brunette, complied.

'Remember that guest list you typed for me when the Colchester detectives came to see me a few days ago?'

'Yes, sir.'

'They needed that because they are investigating the

murder of a police-woman who was part of the hockey team that were signed into the BX club.'

'I see. I did wonder what they needed it for, sir.'

'Well it seems that now another member of the hockey team has also been found dead and the British police have reason to suspect that she was murdered and that one of our people is responsible.'

'Who is it, sir?' asked Rhianna, intrigued.

'They don't know who, exactly, but they have forged a connection to two murders that were committed in Berlin, in May. So, I want you to make some discreet enquiries for me and I need a list of those personnel who are with us now who were working on Operation Vittles. Go back as far as April first.'

'Operation Vittles, sir?'

'The Berlin Airlift.'

'Yes, sir. When do you need this by?'

'As soon as possible.'

'I'll get on it right away, sir.'

'Oh, and Rhianna?'

'Yes, sir.'

'Take care.'

25

Saturday 22 October 1949

Alby was running late. He had arranged to call for Linda at 10am but here he was, in the town centre, having only just managed to stop a taxi that didn't already have a fare onboard. It was now 10.15am. He had no patience with others who were lacking when it came to punctuality, but today, having overslept, he was behind schedule and was potentially treading on Linda's feelings. Alby finally got to her home some twenty-five minutes late and, having asked the taxi driver to wait, walked to her front door and knocked. She was at the door in an instant.

'Hello, darling. Are you OK? I was starting to get worried about you.'

'I'm sorry I'm late, Linda. To be honest I overslept.'

Linda stepped forward and gave him a long lingering kiss, after which she disappeared off into the house and returned with her jacket over her arm.

Well she didn't seem to be put out by my being late, thought Alby.

'Just you wait until we're married, you sexy hunk, I won't

allow that to happen. I've got plans for you.' She laughed knowingly.

I can hardly wait, thought Alby.

They hadn't yet had sex, and, with all due respect, he wasn't going to try anything on. He was prepared to wait. But, at times she made it damned difficult for him. Saucy little minx.

It took about twenty minutes for the taxi to reach Oyster House, the Cooper family home, where they were met by Alby's parents, George and Joyce, who were both busy in the garden. Joyce was the first to spot them as they pulled up on the drive.

'Hello, my lovely,' said Joyce as she gave Linda a hug, 'I hope he's being a good boy and looking after you.'

'Yes, Joyce. He's a perfect gentleman.'

'I wouldn't say he's perfect, dear,' said Joyce.

'Oh, thanks very much Mum.'

'No, he's all right, Linda. He's like his dad. You just have to keep them on their toes, that's all.'

'Don't worry, son,' said George. 'As you know, she's been saying that about me for years. Anyway, we've got a surprise for you two.'

'Shall we have a cup of tea first, before you show them, George?'

'That can wait, dear, but I don't think Alby and Linda can.'

'No, Mum. The suspense is killing us,' said Alby.

'I think you'd better follow me before you explode then, boy.'

George led them towards the garage.

'You know the motor bike and sidecar…'

'Yes. You're going to give it to us?' speculated Alby.

'Not quite, I've sold it.'

'Why?'

'Well, open the doors of the garage and you'll see.'

Alby pulled open both doors of the garage and was met with the sight of a gleaming Austin Seven saloon car with maroon and black livery.

'Think of it as an engagement present, boy,' said George.

'Blimey, Dad. That must have cost you a pretty penny. Are you sure?'

'Yes, of course. Anyway, it's not a brand new one. It's four years old, but it's a good runner. It should do you and Linda for now.'

'Well, that's really good of you, Dad.'

Linda approached George and hugged him. She then turned her attention to Joyce.

'Thank you both so much. It's so kind of you.'

'Why don't you take Linda out in it for a spin?' said George.

'I can't, Dad. I have no insurance.'

'It's registered in my name, and you could drive it on my insurance.'

'Fancy a drive around the island, Linda?'

'I'd love to, darling.'

'Come on then, and we'll take Mum and Dad out for a drink while we're at it.'

◆

Rhianna was on duty over the weekend, when the base tended to be quieter, so it was the ideal time for her to undertake the task set for her by Master Sergeant Rudrow. The guest book page for the signing in of the hockey team seemed, to her, to be a good place to start. Rudrow had managed to secure unlimited access to the personnel department, which was devoid of staff on weekends, so that Rhianna could carry out a search of the records without hindrance or the need for explanation. In order to achieve this, Rudrow had taken the head of personnel into his confidence, and having researched the archive, she had left a sealed envelope for Rhianna which contained a list of names of those airmen and women who had served on Operation Vittles. It was for Rhianna to search the records further to determine the dates of service and posting to and from Berlin.

Rhianna began by examining the list. There were twelve names, which included Max Goodchild, Ryan Noble and two women. There was no record of a Conor Lucan. She found this puzzling. She searched out the file for Max Goodchild and she found that until June 1949 he had been stationed at the US Airbase Templehof, Berlin. He operated as a load master, which had entailed supervising the loading and unloading process of military transport aircraft. He was a single man living in barracks on the base at Lakenheath.

The next file belonged to Ryan Noble. He had been serving at the Lakenheath airbase since August 1948, with only a brief involvement listed in relation to Operation Vittles for the month of March 1949, and no posting to Berlin since that period. Noble's only other absence had been, during December 1948, when he had taken two weeks' compassionate leave stateside, due to the death of his mother. The third and final name on the guest list had been that of Sergeant Conor Lucan. Rhianna carried out a search of the records and found no serving airman with that name. In order to be certain, she carried out a further search of all records, from A through to Z, to be sure that a record for Conor Lucan had not been misfiled. She found no such record. Rhianna walked across to the BX and examined the original guest book. She wondered whether the name had been read wrongly, but there it was, clearly written, the name Conor Lucan.

Rhianna knew that she had been sworn to secrecy by Rudrow and that he was not due back at his desk before Monday morning. She was not at liberty to confide in anybody else, so, for now, she kept her findings to herself. The two ladies from the Colchester hockey team were dead and would not be coming back. So she decided that the matter could wait.

Rhianna's next port of call was the Motor Transport (MT) section, where she sought out the fleet manager, Sergeant Ivan Devaux, whom she knew to be a fastidious individual as far as the vehicles under his control were concerned. She also regarded him as something of a "prince among men." The MT section was housed in a large aircraft hanger and had a cabinstyle office at the back. She could see, through the glass, that Devaux was in the cabin, using the phone. She waited outside the door until he had finished his call and entered the room.

'Hi, little lady. How are you doing?'

'Hi,Ivan. Mr Rudrow wants me to examine your Day Book to do with one of our ongoing investigations. Have you got it to hand?'

'Sure thing, honey.'

Devaux felt under his desk and produced a green hardback diary which he handed over to Rhianna. She could see, from the grease stains, that it was a working record and had been well thumbed.

'Do you mind if I just sit here and go through it?'

'No problem. Take your time. Would you like a coffee?'

'That would be nice. Thanks.'

What a lovely guy. He has no rings on his fingers, but he might just take them off for work. I wonder if he's married, thought Rhianna with a smile.

Devaux stepped into a small room at one end of the cabin and he returned a few minutes later with a mug of instant coffee, which he placed on the desk before her.

'Thanks, Ivan.' She took a sip.

'Lovely. Plenty of milk with one sugar, and hot.'

'Yeah, I remembered how you like it from last time.'

If only you did, thought Rhianna. She was totally smitten.

'How does your wife take it?'

'What makes you think that I'm married? I'm not married, Rhianna' said Devaux, almost indignantly. In fact I was thinking of asking you if you'd like to go out for a drink some time.'

'That would be nice. Why don't you ask me?'

'Would you like to go out for a drink sometime, Rhianna?'

'Yes, I would. When?'

'How about tonight?'

'Yes. OK then, it's a deal.'

'Shall I meet you at the BX about seven and then we could go into Thetford?'

'Great. Have you got a car?'

'You're asking the MT fleet manager whether he's got a car? Of course I have, baby.'

'I'll look forward to it.'

Their eyes locked and she noticed Ivan's look penetrating her. She put on a coy visage.

'Anyway, I suppose I had better get on with looking through the book.'

'OK, I'll leave you to it.'

He left the office and she watched him as he walked across the hanger to the inspection pits to speak to the two mechanics who were working underneath a one-ton truck. *Nice ass.*

Rhianna had to have a serious word with herself in order to get on with the job at hand. She took her time sifting through the pages of the Day Book, some of which were stuck together with various unknown substances. She found no reference to any of the persons subject to the enquiry.

26

Sunday 23 October 1949

Rest Day

27

Monday 24 October 1949

Wilson Rudrow was at his desk, having returned from weekend leave, and his first job was to catch up on any incidents that may have taken place on the base in his absence. After satisfying himself that all was as it should be, he called Rhianna into his office.

'Did you get to search the records in Personnel at the weekend, Rhianna?'

'Yes, sir. Lieutenant Cody left me a list of twelve personnel which included two women.

Also, on the list were Ryan Noble and an Alex Goodchild. Goodchild was stationed at Templehof in May but Noble was here at Lakenheath. He's been here since August last year.'

'What about Conor Lucan?'

'That's the thing. I couldn't find any Conor Lucan on record and he's not on Lieutenant Cody's list.'

'That's interesting.'

'I suppose so, sir, but there's always a possibility that a guest has signed their name in the wrong space.'

'No, Rhianna, it can't have been that. Albert Cooper, the investigator at Colchester, told me that this guy was an airman and that he danced with one of the murder victims.'

'How does he know that?'

'They interviewed all of the girls in the hockey team and the name Conor came from them.'

'He bragged about being a sergeant and, of all things, a test pilot.'

'That's ridiculous. We don't have any, do we?'

'No, we don't.'

'Well, I found no record of him in the Day Book at the MT section either.'

'What about the others?'

'No, sir. None of the names came up as having taken out a vehicle.'

'Who did you speak to?'

'Ivan Devaux, the sergeant in charge of fleet management.'

'Ivan, is it?' said Rudrow teasingly.

Rhianna coloured up. 'Yes. A nice guy.'

'Did you mention the name Conor Lucan to him?'

'No, sir,' said Rhianna, lying.

'I can't help thinking about what we're going to say to the Brits.'

'Sorry, sir. What do you mean?'

'Do we admit that we have a guy on base who obviously feels free to go under a false name?'

'See what you mean, sir.'

'Yes. So before we speak to Mr Cooper, I want us to interview Airmen Noble and Goodchild to see if they can recall anything about this Conor Lucan. Is he still on base? Have they seen him on the base since that night? Have they learned his real name since? Don't under-estimate this, the honour of the USAF is at stake and, at some point, I'm going to have to speak to the base commander to brief him about the situation. I have to admit, I'm not looking forward to it.'

'Do you want me to get a couple of the guys to go and bring them in, sir?'

'Yes, do that, Rhianna, please.'

Within the hour Airmen Goodchild and Noble were sitting in separate interview rooms at the police post. Rudrow took Noble to interview first.

'As you already know, I am Master Sergeant Wilson Rudrow of the US Air Force police. For the record, what is your name, son?'

'Airman Ryan Noble, sir.'

'And your unit?'

'56th Fighter Group, sir.'

'I'll call you Ryan, if that's OK.'

'Fine, sir.'

'A few days ago, you were interviewed by the British police about the night that the Colchester ladies hockey team came to Lakenheath, weren't you?'

'Yes, sir.'

'I want to ask you some more questions about that.'

'I'll do my best to help, sir.'

'You told them that you danced a few times that evening with a young woman called Maggie. Is that right?'

'Yes, sir. She's beautiful. I'm hoping to meet her and take her out some day.'

'You got on well with her, did you?'

'Yes, sir. I'd say we hit it off.'

'You definitely haven't seen her since then?'

'No, sir.'

'Have you telephoned her?'

'No. sir. I haven't. She gave me her number at the nurses home, but she told me that she was going to be away for a couple of weeks. Also, that, at some point, she would be doing night duty. So, we agreed that I would call her after three weeks and then we'd arrange to meet up.'

'That won't be possible, I'm sorry to say, Ryan.'

'Why is that, sir?'

'I'm sorry to have to tell you that, she was found murdered recently.'

Noble was stunned. He sat in silence, staring ahead.

After a few minutes he asked, 'Do you know who did it, sir?'

'No, I don't. But the police in Colchester are working very hard on the case.'

'Where did it happen?'

'I'm gonna have to keep that detail to myself for now, son.'

'It wasn't me, sir,' said Noble with a tone of panic.

'Now, let's get one thing straight. We're not accusing you of the murder, but possibly, you know something that could help us catch the person who did it.'

'I see. Has it got anything to do with the murder that the Colchester police spoke to me about?'

'Could well be. Apparently the two victims did know each other.' Ryan shook his head and sat in silence.

'As I understand it, you signed the girl Maggie into the club. Is that right?'

'Yes, sir.'

'Who else signed the ladies into the club?'

'There was only the one other guy who I saw sign them in. He's called Max. He's a corporal, but I don't know his surname.'

'Did anyone else dance with Maggie?'

'Yes, sir. A guy called Conor. I don't know him. I went back to the block to get changed and when I returned to the club, he was with her, trying to muscle in. I don't think she liked him. He was bullshitting her about his job. She saw through that and tried to shake him off. She asked me to dance with her.'

'So, were you with her all of the time after that?'

'Yes, sir. Pretty much, until I saw her onto the bus with the others, at the end of the evening.'

'Have you seen this guy, Conor, since that night?'

'Only once in the BX shop, sir.'

'When was this?'

'About two weeks ago, sir.'

'Was he in uniform?'

'No, sir.'

'Do you know which unit he's with?'

'No, sir. I don't.'

'So, he's not with the 56th?'

'No. Definitely not, sir,' said Ryan shaking his head, 'I know all of the guys and gals on my unit.'

'Did he have any other people with him?'

'No, he was definitely on his own. He appeared very confident and comfortable in his surroundings. He seemed to know his way around the place as if he's been on base for some time.'

'How would you describe this guy?'

'He's about thirty-five, tall, about six feet, well-built,

athletic even. Blond hair which was greased back. He was clean-shaven, and I think, judging by his accent, that he's probably a Texan.'

'Do you know any of the Air Force girls' team?'

'Yes, sir, I know all of them.'

'So, could you give me all their names?'

'Yes, sir.'

Noble quickly reeled off a series of women's names and their units. And Rudrow created a list.

'How is it that you know all of these gals?'

'I've been here for a while now. About two years, and you get to know the guys and gals in the club.'

'Did this guy Conor appear to know any of them?'

'I don't think so, sir. Although he had quite a fresh attitude to them.'

'What do you mean by, fresh?'

'Trying to get involved with them.'

'And did he have a positive response from any of them?'

'No he didn't, sir. Quite the opposite. They thought he was too familiar and creepy. They didn't appear to like him at all.'

'OK. Well. I have no other questions for the moment, son. Don't discuss our conversation with anybody else.'

'I won't, sir.'

'And if you should see this guy on base, let us know straight away.'

'Yes, I will, sir.'

'And, whatever you do, don't approach him.'

'No.sir. But if he turns out to be the guy who killed Maggie, I don't think I could trust myself.'

'Be careful, son. We don't know, for sure, if this guy is

responsible. And we don't want people taking matters into their own hands.'

'Understood, sir.'

'OK. Dismissed.'

Ryan Noble got up, stood briefly to attention, made a smart left turn and left the room.

After Rudrow had finished his notes he had Alex Goodchild marched in. Goodchild stood to attention before him with his cap under his arm.

'I am Master Sergeant Wilson Rudrow of the US Air Force police. What is your name, son?'

'Airman Alexander Maximillian Goodchild, sir. I'm known as Max.'

'And your unit?'

'The 56th Fighter Group, sir.'

'Do you know why you're here?'

'No, sir.'

'Do you remember a British ladies hockey team coming to the base a few weeks ago to play against our women?'

'Yes, I do, sir.'

'Well, according to the guest book at the BX club, you signed a couple of the young British ladies in to the club for the dance that was taking place that evening. Is that correct?'

'Yes, sir. I did. But I thought that the club rules allow for us to sign in two guests at a time.'

'That's not the problem, son.'

'I'm sorry, sir, but I don't understand.'

'I'll explain, what this is about, in a minute. But, first of all, I want to ask you some questions. Some of the other guys signed in women from the British hockey team that night, didn't they?'

'Yes, they did.'

'Who was that?'

'The only one I know is Airman Ryan Noble.'

'So, you and Noble were at the club together?'

'Yes, sir.'

'Where did you meet the women?'

'After work we called in at the BX for a quick drink. They were already outside on the terrace drinking with the gals from our team, so we joined them. There were one or two hot chicks in the group and one of them took a shine to Ryan. He went back to the block to get changed and he got back in double quick time. He was pretty interested in a chick called Maggie.'

'Were any other guys interested in this Maggie?'

'One guy from another unit was there. He tried to muscle in and steal her from under Ryan's nose.'

'Do you know who that was?'

'No, sir. But I overheard him telling one of the girls that his family came to the States from Ireland. Her eyes seemed to glaze over. I think he was boring the ass off her. Then he moved on and I think he tried it on with all the girls.'

'How do you know that he was from another unit?'

'Sir, I know all of the guys in the 56th, even the new ones.'

'OK. You seen this guy since?'

'No, sir. But he had sergeant's stripes up.'

'I take it you'd recognise him again, if you saw him.'

'Yes, sir, I would.'

'Right. I'm gonna tell you now, what all this is about. Since the day that the Colchester hockey team were here, two members of that team have been murdered.'

'Murdered?' said Goodchild, with alarm.

'Yes, murdered. At different places, and at different times. The detective department at Colchester are dealing with it. The first one happened to be one of their own people, an off-duty woman police sergeant.'

'Was that Maggie?'

'No, son. She was the other one.'

'Who did it? Do they know?'

'They have a few lines of enquiry, but they don't know for sure. We are helping the Colchester Police with the case. Now I expect you to keep this name to yourself. Do you know the name Conor Lucan?'

'No, sir, I don't.'

'On the night in question, some of the other hockey girls were signed into the club by someone using that name.'

'I can't remember seeing that name in the book when I signed it, sir.'

'Well, it's in there. Perhaps he did it after you.'

'Yeah, perhaps he did. Do you think that this guy Conor Lucan is responsible for the murders, sir?'

'Maybe, maybe not, but we certainly need to trace him.'

'Don't we have anyone on the base with that name, sir?'

'No. I've had the records checked and we don't. I think that for whatever reason the guy was using a false name. Right, I need you to give us a detailed description of this guy, who told the British girls that he was from an Irish family. I think he must be this "Conor Lucan." Can you do that?'

'Yes, sir.'

'I'm also gonna arrange for someone to sit down with you and Noble to do an artist's impression of this guy. Anyway, I want you to speak to nobody about this case, not even Noble, clear?'

'Yes, sir.'

'And if you see this "Conor Lucan," again, you let us know straight away, and don't approach him yourself. Is that understood?'

'Yes, sir. Understood.'

'OK. Thank you. Dismissed.'

Goodchild stood to attention. Turned smartly, and marched out of the room.

28

Tuesday 25 October 1949

After all the other business of recent days Brian Pratt and Tom Rogers were finally able to follow up their enquiry with Angela Dickson, the lady mentioned by Constance Farrow, whose sister was married to an American airman. After their visit to the Braintree WI they had called at Miss Dickson's house in The Street, Bocking, and although it was around 8pm they had received no reply at the door. On this second visit they had resolved to call at the house in daylight, in order to increase their chances of a response.

On their arrival, Brian knocked at the front door, which was quickly answered by an attractive blonde woman of around twenty-eight years. She was slim and beautiful with a very prominent bust.

'Can I help you?'

'Yes, madam. We are police officers. Are you Miss Angela Dickson?'

'Yes, I am. Are you the officers who spoke to Constance Farrow at the WI?'

'Yes Miss Dickson, we are.' They both showed their credentials and introduced themselves.

'It's terrible about Cecily White, isn't it?' said Miss Dickson.

'Yes, it is. Actually, that's what we have called to speak to you about.'

Miss Dickson bid them enter the house and they followed her through to the kitchen, where she offered them tea.

'How can I help you?'

'We were told by Constance Farrow that your sister married an American airman. It is a general background enquiry, really, and we're hoping that you might know something of the culture between the Americans and the people locally.'

'Oh, I see. Well, I think that I can definitely help you there. Do you suspect that Cecily was murdered by an American, then?'

'It is a genuine line of enquiry,' said Brian.

'I see. Well, I'll help you if I can.'

'What is your sister's name, Miss Dickson?'

'Please call me Angela.'

'OK, Angela. I'm Brian Pratt and my colleague's name is Tom Rogers.'

'I see. My sister's name is Daisy.'

'Who do you live with?'

'It's just my mother Ruth and myself here nowadays. She's elderly and infirm and I have to care for her.'

'What sort of relationship do you have with the Americans, Angela?'

'I used to go out with an American airman myself, but Johnny was posted back to the States a few months ago. He was a perfectly decent chap and he was very handsome.

Unfortunately, I didn't love him enough to want to take the plunge and marry him and anyway, who would have looked after Mum?'

'Indeed. Well, the fact is, miss, we do have good reason to believe that the person who murdered Cecily is an American, and that's why we thought we'd come to see you to find out if you could give us some background information.'

'I'll certainly do my best. I liked Cecily, she was a nice person. Quite shy though, which was surprising given what she did for a living.'

'Yes, she was a nice woman. We got on well,' said Brian.

'Why do you suspect that the murderer was an American?'

'Well, Cecily was a member of a Colchester ladies hockey team that played against the Americans not long before she was killed. Since then a second member of the team has been found murdered on an old American airbase. There are certain pieces of evidence that are common to both cases and which indicate an American connection. I am not at liberty to divulge the specifics of the evidence, I'm afraid.'

'I see. But, I must say, I'm at a loss as to how I might be able to help you.'

They then realised that they had been joined by an elderly lady who had silently shuffled into the kitchen from the hallway. Although she was bent over and appeared to be frail, there was clearly nothing wrong with her lungs. In a shrill voice she demanded to know who the male visitors were.

'Who are these men, Angela?'

'They are policemen from Colchester, Mum. They're making some enquiries about the Americans at the airbase.'

'That's good. They want to start by locking up that arsehole who married your sister Daisy. Then he won't be able to hurt anybody else.'

'Mum! Mind your language, please! We have visitors.'

'Just saying. That's all,' said the old girl.

She then shuffled out of the kitchen and wandered off, back down the hall towards the front room, apparently ignoring her daughter's entreaties by swearing under her breath.

'I'm sorry about that gentlemen,' said Angela, 'My mother is a bit demented. She never used to use bad language and she was quite prim and proper. She seems to get worse as she gets older and now she's swears like a trooper.'

'That's OK, miss. We are used to that kind of language,' said Tom.

'Who is it that's married to your sister Daisy, miss?'

'Konrad Lukas. He's a sergeant in the US Air Force, and presently stationed on the base at Lakenheath.'

'How did she get involved with him?'

'He met my sister Daisy during the war, when he was stationed at RAF Wethersfield. I can't remember where they met exactly, but he charmed her, and they got married after a whirlwind romance. A few months later he was posted back to the US, to Arizona, and she went with him. Now he's back here and Daisy is stranded over there with two small kids.'

'Why doesn't your mother like him?'

'He used to knock Daisy about. It started when they got to the US. Apparently, he's charm itself until he's had too much to drink, then he gets nasty. Daisy used to tell us about it in her letters. She wanted to leave him, but she couldn't get the money together to fly back with the kids. At least, now that he's over here he can't hit her and cause her any more suffering.'

'Couldn't she have spoken to the Air Force and got some help from the authorities?'

'Maybe. But, it seems, she didn't have the confidence to go to them.'

'How long has he been at Lakenheath?'

'Only for a few months, I believe. He was in Berlin for a while before that, something to do with the airlift.'

'What does he do exactly?'

'He's a fully qualified aircraft technician. He's a very clever man academically. He is a very handsome man, but he's very manipulative. A nasty piece of work.'

'Is there anything else that you can tell us about him?'

'Yes. According to Daisy, he had a very strange relationship with his mother. She was always interfering in the marriage and he would always do what she said. He was a real mummy's boy, apparently.'

'I notice, Miss Dickson, that you are speaking in the past tense about his mother. Is she no longer alive?'

'No. She died about a year ago of breast cancer.'

'You called him Konrad Lukas. Can you spell that for us, please?' Miss Dickson complied.

'The name doesn't sound very American to me,' said Tom.

'No. It doesn't. Apparently Konrad's father was originally from Poland and his mother originated from the German-speaking part of Czechoslovakia. The Sudetenland,

I think it's called. He finds the German family connection particularly embarrassing and likes to keep it quiet.'

'Is his father still alive?'

'We don't know. He told us that he never actually saw much of his father. His parents broke up when he was young and his mother brought him up alone.'

'Does Konrad live on the base?'

'I believe so.'

'When was the last time you saw him?'

'He's been to see us only the once, since he came back. That was about two weeks ago. Mother didn't want him in the house, but I insisted. Anyway, I made him something to eat and then he tried it on with me. He'd had a bit to drink.'

'With your mother in the house?'

'Yes. She's not very mobile, bless her, and once she's settled in the sitting room she can't go anywhere very quickly. He knows that.'

'It didn't stop her surprising us a minute ago,' said Brian.

'I know, but she's as deaf as a post, that's why she shouts so much.'

'So, how did you manage to resist his advances?'

'I just don't fancy him, and he's married to my sister.'

'No, I mean physically.'

'Oh, I see. I kneed him in the groin. I was in the ATS during the war. I know how to look after myself, don't you worry.'

'And he left, did he?'

'Straight away.'

'Good for you,' said Tom.

'Yes, I was quite pleased with myself. I think I embarrassed him. His masculinity couldn't take it, I suppose.'

'Has he been back since?'

'No. I'm definitely off his Christmas list and he knows what kind of a welcome he'd get from Mum. I don't think we'll see him again.'

'Did he touch anything while he was here?'

'Apart from me, you mean?'

'Yes.'

Angela went quiet for a minute. Then she became quite animated.

'Do you suspect him, then?'

'Well, not just him, there are others, but we are keeping an open mind about it,' said Brian. 'We suspect that the murderer could be an American airman based at Lakenheath.'

'So, he's a suspect, then,' said Angela, thoughtfully and with a smile.

'Yes, miss. Just consider it for a minute. You have already told us that he has a propensity for hitting women and that he's a "nasty piece of work." He's definitely worth checking out, don't you think?'

'Yes, I would say so,' said Angela.

'So, did he touch anything around the house?'

'Yes. Now you ask, I remember that while Konrad was here, he saw the framed picture of Daisy and the two children which sits on the mantelpiece in the other room. He took it down from the shelf and kissed it before putting it back up there.'

'Did he indeed?'

'That was of course before he tried it on with me.'

'Tell me, who does the cleaning in your house? Is it you or your mother, or do you have a cleaner who comes in to do for you?'

'Only me. I'm sorry about that. I must confess that it's a bit of a mess and I haven't done any dusting for a while.'

'It wasn't a criticism, Angela, I was just trying to assess the viability of us getting the picture and mantelpiece fingerprinted,' said Brian.

'Oh, I see. That's no problem. Go right ahead, if you think that it would help. I have to admit that I'm rather hoping that it is him. If you're successful, we'll be able to get rid of the evil swine once and for all.'

'Of course, Angela, you realise that if he were to be convicted, we would definitely be talking about the noose.'

'No more than he would deserve,' said Angela.

'Well, that's the law,' said Brian.

'Absolutely. If he's a murderer.'

'When he came to see you, did you see what he was driving?'

'Yes. It was a jeep from the base.'

'A jeep?'

'Yes. He parked it in the drive.'

'Did he have anyone with him?'

'No, I think he drove himself. I didn't see a driver, anyway.'

'Do you have a photograph of him?'

'No, I don't.'

'Can you describe him?'

'Oh yes, he's a handsome chap all right, blonde hair, strong and upright.'

'Any facial hair?'

'No. Well, he was clean-shaven when he came here a

couple of weeks ago and I've never known him to have a moustache or anything.'

'We can always speak to the people at Lakenheath and get a photo, if needs be.'

'What happens now, then?'

'I take it that you have no phone in the house,' said Brian.

'That's right. The nearest telephone box is on the Braintree road next to the Red Lion. When it's working, that is.'

There being no telephone in the house, Tom stayed with Angela while Brian drove down to the telephone box to phone Cooper. Within the hour they were joined by Brendan Withers and a colleague from Scenes of Crime, who dealt with the picture and took elimination prints from Angela and her bewildered mother.

After checking with Angela that there were no other obvious places that should be examined for fingerprints, Brian spoke to Brendan to ascertain whether he'd found any finger-marks.

'Did you find anything, Brendan?'

'I've got some good news and some bad news for you,' said Brendan. 'What shall I give you first, Brian?'

'The bad news, I think.'

'We found nothing on the mantelpiece. It's got a thick covering of dust. No chance of finding anything there, I'm afraid.'

'And the good news?'

'On the glass at the front of the picture are two lovely thumb prints.'

'How quickly can you get them checked against the

other marks in the case?'

'Next day or so.'

'Pardon the pun,' said Tom, 'but fingers crossed.'

❖

Due to the unavailability of Linda Collins, Alby Cooper had arranged for Brian Pratt to attend Berechurch Hall Camp in order to assist Captain Harrington with the follow-up call to Berlin. This time Harrington had managed to get through to Klaus Walter, who had been made aware of the original call by his colleague, Siegler.

Prior to the call, and with Cooper's consent, Brian had briefed Harrington with more detail about the Colchester investigation and this he had imparted to the German investigator, Klaus Walter.

Herr Walter was now even more convinced that there was a connection between his case and the Essex murders and he was anxious to cooperate in any way that he could, offering to send copies of their fingerprint evidence. Brian had also provided details of the address for Brendan Withers at Chelmsford police headquarters so that the evidence could be forwarded that much quicker. Both sides were deeply concerned about the possibility of a third murder on their territory. They knew that there was no time to lose.

It was agreed that, should the German fingerprint evidence be found to be a match for marks found in Essex, Brian would arrange for Brendan Withers to dispatch copies of their own marks to Berlin in order for them to make their own comparison.

29

Wednesday 26 October 1949

Sergeant Konrad Lukas left his room in the sergeants' mess and locked the door behind him. He had a busy schedule ahead and a hearty breakfast was the first order of the day. He descended the stairs to the ground floor where he entered the mess canteen and saw that it was busy, with several other NCOs, some on and some off duty.

Konrad selected a tray from the pile and joined the queue waiting to be served. Daphne and Christine, two local girls, who were civilian employees, were serving behind the counter. Both were in their twenties and one aspect of their presence meant that, due to the dearth of single women on the base, they were in great demand as far as the younger servicemen were concerned. As Konrad reached the head of the queue Daphne nudged her friend.

'And what can we do for you, ducks?' said Christine.

'Give me your address and I'll see what I can arrange, honey.'

'Saucy.'

Konrad gave them a devastating wink and smile which

secured an enhanced meal. Daphne was a tall red-head with an ample bosom, though she feigned an innocent countenance.

She's just my type. I'd love to liberate those tits, thought Konrad.

Konrad, having been served, peeled away to find a table in the far corner which was unoccupied. He was soon joined by Ivan Devaux who was a long-time friend and colleague.

'How are you doing, buddy?'

'Never better. How's your sex life?' asked Konrad.

'Slow. But I'm working on a little babe who works at the Provost unit. Foxy lady and a nice ass. What about you?'

'Ah. Had a few dates but limey chicks are hard work.'

'You were on Operation Vittles, weren't you?'

'Yeah. Until June, anyway.'

'Did you get laid in Berlin?'

'Nah. Too busy for that kind of thing, unfortunately. It was pretty full-on.'

'Yeah. Couldn't have been easy,' said Devaux.

'No, It wasn't easy at all. It was just constant work, eat, sleep and drink. But I think we did a good job.'

'Saved a lot of lives.'

'Yeah, I suppose we did. I was proud to be a part of it.'

'Yeah, so, you should be. I saw the way that the two girls behind the counter reacted to you. Have you laid either of them yet?'

'Not yet, but they're showing a bit of interest and I might give it a whirl at some point. Thing is, I don't know which one to try first.'

'OK, if you pick one, let me know and I'll try the other

one,' said Ivan, 'and perhaps we could go out on a double-date.'

'Yeah, I'll go with that. Good idea.'

Konrad left his table and walked up to the kitchen counter. There was nobody in the queue as the service of breakfast was coming to an end.

'Hello, ladies,' said Konrad.

'Hello, my lovely,' said Christine.

'My friend Ivan and I thought that it would be nice if we could take you ladies out for a drink and maybe a meal, some time soon. What do you think?'

Christine looked at Daphne. Daphne looked at Christine. They smiled.

'Yes, that would be lovely. Just don't promise it unless you mean it. We get a lot of time wasters who come on strong, but then chicken out.'

'We wouldn't do that to you, honey.'

'Well, we are always here to be surprised. Let us know when and we'll come out with you.'

'I'll come back to you on that,' said Konrad. He returned to the table.

'What did they say?' asked Ivan.

'It looks like we're on, buddy. We just have to tell them when. And by the way, I'll have Christine.'

'Sure thing.'

'What about your little babe on the Provost unit?'

'Well, I won't tell her if you don't.'

'I should be very careful. She might find out and then your card will be marked. How did you get involved with a military police woman anyway?' asked Konrad.

'She not exactly a proper policewoman. She works in

the office mostly. If any of our vehicles get into a scrape off-base and the cops get involved, she handles things and I have to liaise with her.'

'Liaise with her? That sounds good.'

'Yeah. In fact, she came to see me yesterday. She wanted to go through the Day Book in the office to see who has had our jeeps out.'

'Why did she want to know that?'

'She told me that it was something to do with the murder of a woman, the limey cops are working on. Apparently, it was an off-duty policewoman in Colchester. She was strangled and her body dumped.'

'Did she find anything?'

'I don't think so. But she asked me about some guy who works on base called Conor Lucan. Does the name mean anything to you?'

'No, I can't say it does.'

'Well, I've been here, at Lakenheath, for a few years now and even I can't say that I know everybody on the base because there's so many. People come and go all the time. But I've never heard of the guy. The name does sound like an Irish version of yours, though.'

'Nah. Nothing like it,' said Konrad, feigning laughter.

Konrad was shaken to the core. He had to gather every ounce of his acting ability to prevent himself from reacting in a way that would show his concern.

Fuck. They're on my case.

'Yeah, I suppose it does sound a bit Irish. Did she mention what section he's supposed to be working in?'

'She told me he said he was a sergeant and that he was some kind of test pilot.' Ivan laughed heartily.

'Yeah, the guy was obviously, shooting a line.'

'Yeah, it certainly seems that way.'said Ivan. 'What is it they say? Bullshit baffles brains.'

'Where was the murder?' asked Konrad.

'Near Colchester. A few weeks ago.'

'Is that near here?' asked Konrad, feigning ignorance of the area.

'About forty miles away.'

'Have we got a base there?'

'No, no base.'

'What would one of our guys be doing over there?'

'No idea. Who knows what goes on in the criminal mind.'

'Let's hope they catch the guy, Ivan.'

'Yeah. I expect the personnel department should be able to trace him.'

'I wonder who would deal with him in a case like that,' said Konrad.

'I suppose it would be the British civilian authorities, if the murder was committed on their own territory.'

'What would happen to him?'

'If they did finally manage to catch the right guy, and he was found guilty of murdering a female cop, they'd hang him, for certain.'

Konrad's throat tightened. He knew that he would have to stay away from the club and keep a low profile. He was just about able to present something of a smile although that, in itself, was strenuous. Luckily, Ivan didn't appear to notice his discomfort.

◆

Lukas was lying in bed thinking. It was almost time to get up for work, though he'd managed hardly any sleep at all. Following Ivan Devaux's revelation about the murder suspect "Conor Lucan" and his speculation that, if caught, he would face the hangman's noose, he was a very worried man. He had continually agonised over it and he had convinced himself that the police were gradually closing in on him. Furthermore, he believed that it was only a matter of time before one of the other guys, who were present at the club during the hockey club visit, would come across him on the base and identify him as "the man".

He was feeling hopeless and exposed and had been loath to even close his eyes lest someone should come for him during the night. He knew that he had to get a grip on the situation, take control and develop a contingency plan. But what to do?

If, at this stage, Konrad was to go absent without leave, he would only draw attention to himself. He resolved to sit tight for now, in the hope that it might all blow over. If, in time, he was to gain some prior knowledge of mounting police interest in him, then, faced with no other option, he would make his move.

Konrad doubted that anyone on the base knew of his connection to Angela Dickson. He was certain that it wasn't on record and he felt it unlikely that, if he were to abscond, the military police would bother to contact his wife in the US. So, he decided that that was exactly where he would head should the need arise. It would at the very least give him time to plan his next move. No, the police wouldn't find him at Angela's place and besides, he could have some fun into the bargain.

30

Thursday 27 October 1949

Cooper was in the office early, as today held the possibility of being a seminal stage of the investigation. Late the previous afternoon, the Fingerprint Bureau at police headquarters had confirmed receipt of the German fingerprint evidence and Brendan Withers had assured Cooper that he would have the results of comparison the next day. Alby Cooper was eagerly awaiting the results with anticipation.

The day had already started well, as, having finally managed to gain comprehensive insurance for his new car, he had driven to work, picking Linda up on the way. He had also spoken to Superintendent Stockwell, who had authorised a parking space in the rear yard which now displayed a sign marked "Reserved / Detective Inspector". Things were definitely on the up.

'Is that your new motor in the yard, governor?' said Brian Pratt, as he entered the office bearing tea.

'Yes Brian. It was an engagement present from my parents. They called me and Linda over to Mersea at the weekend and surprised us with it.'

'Lucky you.'

'Yes, it was a nice surprise. I can't use it on duty, though. Apart from private use, I shall just use it to go backwards and forwards to work.'

'Wouldn't mind a little ride in it at some point, governor.'

'Yes. I'll drop you off home after work, when we have a quiet day. Anyway, have we got anybody in the cells?'

'Just the one, governor. Arthur Dadds.'

'Bloody hell. Not again. What's he been nicked for this time?'

'Malicious damage.'

'Are uniform dealing with it?'

'No. Young Rogers, governor.'

'Not a CID matter is it, malicious damage?'

'This one was part of a domestic dispute, though.'

'That's not necessarily a CID matter either, Brian.'

'With respect. There is a bit more to it than that, governor, the damage comes to a nice few bob.'

'But Maisie Green and Arthur Dadds are always rowing and, anyway, they haven't got two ha'pennies to rub together, have they?'

'Well, she chucked him out a couple of days ago. She told him she wants him to leave because she was fed up with his drinking.'

'She's a fine one to talk. They're as bad as each other.'

'Not only that, she's found somebody else. He told her that she could have her freedom, particularly since she lived in that house before they met, but because they've both been together so long, he wants fifty percent of everything in the house. She wasn't having that at all, so he went and stayed with his mum in Rowhedge.'

'So where does the domestic come into it?'

'Yesterday she went to work and when she came back, she found the fire brigade outside the house. They'd just put out a large bonfire on the front lawn. When she went inside, she saw that every stick of furniture had been sawn in half and one half of everything had been put on the fire.'

'Where is the crime in that though, Brian? It's jointly owned property and they've been co-habiting in that house for years.'

'Well, that's true enough, governor, as far as it goes, but he cut all of the doors in half, as well, and now it looks like a stable block.'

'I know she had it originally but it's their house now, isn't it?'

'No. That's the thing, see. They rent it from the council. They weren't best pleased, when they found out about the damage.'

'Ah, I see what you mean now,' said Cooper, laughing through his tears. 'Keep me posted, on that will you Brian?'

Brian took his tea through to the sergeants' office and Cooper got on with some paperwork.

Around midday the telephone rang, and Cooper picked up the receiver.

'CID, DI Cooper.'

'Good morning, sir. This is Roger Hardcastle, ringing from the Fingerprint Bureau at HQ.

Brendan Withers wanted me to let you know that he is on his way up to see you with a result on your murder case.'

'OK, Roger, I'm all ears. What's the result?'

'I'm sorry, I'm afraid I can't tell you the result, sir, because he didn't tell me. He left the office about five minutes ago so he should be with you shortly.'

'Thank you for letting me know, Roger. I shall just have to sit here in eager anticipation, won't I.' He replaced the receiver.

'Brian,' shouted Cooper.

Brian appeared in the doorway. 'Yes, guv.'

'Brendan Withers is on his way up from headquarters with a result on our German finger-print evidence.'

'Let's hope its positive.'

'Yes. I shall be bloody disappointed, if it isn't.'

'Yes, we deserve a bit of luck on this one.'

'Do us a favour,' said Cooper, handing Brian a shilling. 'Nip down to the canteen and get us both another brew, will you?'

'Yes, guv.'

Brian disappeared downstairs, returning a few minutes later with two mugs. They sat and waited for their visitor. After a frustrating fifteen minutes, Brendan Withers appeared in the doorway.

'Good morning, sir.'

'Morning, Brendan. Got some news for us, I hear.'

'Yes. I have indeed.'

Brendan sat down, opened his briefcase and removed a sheaf of papers.

'Yes. As you know we received the fingerprint analysis from the Berlin police and we have carried out a comparison against our two murders. I can tell you that there is no doubt that the same person left marks at both of their murder scenes…'

'And?'

'Some are the same as the marks left at our scenes.'

This information was delivered by Brendan in such a calm and dispassionate way, that at first, it failed to register with Cooper or Brian.

'Brendan. Are you telling me that the same person who committed the Berlin murders committed our murders?'

'Yes, sir. That is exactly what I'm saying.' Cooper rose from his chair and punched the air. 'Bloody hell! Yes!'

'Well done, Brendan. That's brilliant work.' Cooper rushed around the desk and he shook Brendan by the hand vigorously. Brendan was embarrassed. Brian was beaming from ear to ear.

'Oh, but that's not all, sir.'

'Do you mean there's more?'

'Yes, sir. That's only part of it. I haven't finished yet.' Cooper sat down again.

'Really Brendan? Let's have it then.'

'Do you remember that you sent me out to a house in Bocking the other day to meet Ian Mills and we fingerprinted Miss Dickson's fireplace and the picture?'

'Yes.'

'And we found nothing on the fireplace?'

'Yes.'

'But we did find two nice thumb prints on the picture?'

'Yes, and?' said Cooper, fit to burst. *Spit it out, Brendan, for heaven's sake.*

'The thumb prints match. One of them matches a thumb print lifted from the Lucky Strike packet found at the first Berlin murder and the other matches that found on Cecily White's purse.'

Cooper was stunned.

'Christ, Brendan, that's brilliant!' said Brian.

'I thought you'd be pleased, sir,' said Brendan.

'Pleased Brendan! Pleased! I'm fucking delirious!'

'That's fantastic,' said Brian.

Cooper shook his head and regained his composure.

'Bloody hell, Brendan. When can you let me have that in report form?'

'I've already done my report, sir.'

Brendan handed over a copy.

'Efficiency plus,' said Cooper. He reached into his drawer and retrieved the bottle of Scotch (donated by Richard Timmins) and three glasses. He poured each of them a double and handed them around. They wasted no time in taking a sip.

'So, Brendan. This means our murderer is Angela Dickson's brother-in-law. What's his name…?' Cooper quickly examined the paperwork on his desk.

'Konrad Lukas.'

'Konrad Lukas,' said Brian. 'It's not a million miles away from Conor Lucan, is it, governor?'

'I know, Brian, and this is conclusive evidence.' Cooper waved the report.

Brendan stood up.

'I'm afraid I must go, sir. I'm at court at two o'clock.'

'Many thanks, Brendan. I'll speak to you soon.'

Brendan took his leave.

'Well, what do you think of that then, Brian?'

'Deserves another drink, I think governor.'

'Absolutely.' Cooper reached for the bottle.

'What happens now, then?'

'We're not going to do anything hasty. We can't arrest him on the base ourselves. We haven't got the power. We'll have to speak to Wilson Rudrow and ask him to have Lukas lifted on the base and brought here.'

'What if he does a runner, governor?'

'We have to trust the Yanks. There's no alternative.'

'True, I suppose.'

'We'll certainly need them to provide evidence of his service here in the UK.'

'And in Berlin.'

'We'll have first "dibs" on him. The Germans would have to apply for extradition unless the US Air Force give him up. And I can't see that happening. Still, if he's facing the noose over here, he can only die once.'

'Still. It's a shame he's not a British national. We could have dealt with the UK and Berlin murders at the same time.'

'And we would have to go to Berlin to get the evidence, I suppose,' said Cooper. 'You do realise that it's not the ideal holiday destination?'

'Yes, governor. Still I wouldn't mind going there, all the same.'

'Once I've spoken to Mr Stockwell, I'll call Wilson Rudrow and try and arrange for him to come here for a meeting tomorrow. Then we can explain the evidence trail to him and formulate a plan of action. When this bloke Lukas is off the base, he's in play. It would be great if Rudrow and his colleagues could arrange that for us.'

'Yes, it would.'

'Yes. Unfortunately, though, Brian, given your former relationship with Cecily White, you can't get involved directly with the prisoner. You'll have to take a back seat. We don't want you giving the bloke a good hiding, however much he may deserve it.' Cooper reached for the phone and spoke to Stockwell's secretary, Lucy. Having ascertained that the boss was in his office, Cooper set out on foot, bound for the town hall.

Cooper was fortunate to be able to see Stockwell immediately.

'You wanted to see me, Albert?'

'Yes, sir. I have some good news.'

'And, what is it about?'

'The murders.'

'Yes?'

'We have conclusive forensic evidence against an American Air Force sergeant, putting him at both our scenes…'

'Brilliant!' shouted Stockwell.

'…and not only that, sir, at two strikingly similar murders in Berlin that were committed when he was deployed on the airlift earlier in the year.'

'And the man's name?'

'Konrad Lukas, sir.'

'Where is he now?'

'At RAF Lakenheath. We've been liaising with the US Air Force Police on the base. Particularly, their Master Sergeant, Wilson Rudrow.'

'And what do they say about it?'

'I haven't told them yet, sir.'

'Hopefully, they'll cooperate.'

'Of course, there is the question of jurisdiction, sir. RAF Lakenheath is US sovereign territory and it's not in our gift to just enter the base, when we feel like it, and carry out an arrest.'

'No, that's true. I think I had better speak to the chief constable and have him contact their commanding officer. We need to reach an agreement with them as to the possibility of taking some joint action. Hopefully, they'll give us their full support.'

'Thank you, sir.'

'And Albert. Well done. Excellent work.'

31

Friday 28 October 1949

'Rhianna. Could you come into my office, please?' shouted Wilson Rudrow.

'I'll be with you in a minute, sir, I'm just on the phone.'

On completion of her call Rhianna walked through to Rudrow's office.

'Shut the door and take a seat.'

Rudrow had a very earnest look on his face.

'It appears the Brits have identified their murderer.'

'Is it one of ours, sir?'

'Yeah, apparently so.'

'Have they said, who it is?'

'No. They want me to go and see them, for a tactical meeting, tomorrow. I want you to come with me and work on the case.'

'Yes, sir.'

'Only thing is, now I'm going to have to speak to the major to inform him of the situation. Then he'll want to refer it to the general to get a decision on what we're gonna do with this asshole. Whoever he is.'

It had already been a stressful day for Wilson Rudrow. Now he had been called to the headquarters, Strategic Air Command at RAF Mildenhall to see Major General Howard Westley, who had given him the third degree about his knowledge of the murders and his actions in supporting the CID investigation. So thorough was the general's inquisition that Rudrow was convinced that he had exceeded his authority and that he was likely to be the subject of some disciplinary proceedings. Rudrow was mentally shattered and felt that he was being hung out to dry.

He need not have worried; this was just the general's intense way of getting to the bottom of things. Rudrow was forced to wait for an hour, outside the general's office, while he made a series of telephone calls.

The general finally came to a tactical decision and he had his adjutant call Rudrow back into the office.

Rudrow stood to attention before him.

'OK, Sergeant Rudrow,' said Westley. 'I have had discussions with some key individuals, including the ambassador, and it comes to this. The United States Air Force is no place for a serial killer. If this man is guilty, and the evidence is as strong as the chief of police says it is, then we need to arrest the man and hand him over for the civilian authority to deal with him. I will sign a copy of the decision document and you can take it with you. Speak to the adjutant when you get outside.'

'Thank you, sir.'

'This doesn't show us in a good light at all, Rudrow, but the fact is that this is one rogue among a fine body of men and women. We'll have to bite the bullet and cooperate to the best of our ability. Keep me posted?'

'I will, sir. Thank you.'

'Dismissed.' Rudrow saluted, turned and left the room.

❖

'Hi baby,' said Konrad, as he approached Christine at the breakfast counter. 'How do you fancy coming out for a drink with me tonight?'

'I might.'

'We'd have fun.'

'You're not married, then?'

'No, I'm free as a bird.'

Konrad put his hands in the air, showing that they were devoid of any rings, and he flapped his arms like a pair of wings, which made Christine laugh.

'OK, fine. Where would you like to take me?'

'That's a very good question. As a gentleman, I don't know whether I should answer that. It would be somewhere nice, I can promise you that.'

'Oh, you are a one,' said Christine. 'What time do you want to meet?'

'Depends where.'

'I live about five minutes from the Plough Inn, in the village. Do you know it?'

'Yeah. Shall I meet you outside the Plough at seven?'

'Yes. You going to be in uniform or casual clothes?'

'I'll be in civilian clothes, of course. You can't romance a lady in uniform.'

'I see. Lady, is it?'

'Oh, yes. You're a lady all right.'

'See you at seven then, baby,' said Christine.

She couldn't wait to tell her friend Daphne.

Konrad took his tray to the table where Ivan Devaux was already seated.

'Hi, Konrad.'

'Hi, Ivan. I think I've just cracked it.'

'Yeah? Cracked what?'

'Christine. I'm gonna meet her tonight.'

'Congratulations buddy. So, what about her friend, Daphne? Did you put a word in for me?'

'Nah, sorry about that, buddy. Clean forgot. But I'll tell her about you when I see her, then we'll go out in a foursome.'

'Thanks a bunch,' said Ivan, with a hint of sarcasm.

'Anyway, how's tricks?'

'Good, good. I saw my little lady Rhianna last night. You know, the girl from the Provost unit, I was telling you about.'

'Oh yeah. Did you make out with her yet?'

'Nah. But it's early days.'

'What does she look like?'

'Oh, she's about medium height, slim body, dark brown hair to her shoulders. Pretty face and a nice pair of breasts.'

'She sounds good to me.'

'And she looks good. In fact she's sexy and gorgeous and, I have to say, she'd be quite a conquest.'

'What does she do at the Provost unit, again?'

'She works mainly in the office on the admin support team but she does do some outside enquiries.'

'What rank did you say she is?'

'She's only a corporal but she takes her job pretty seriously and worries a lot. I spend half my time trying to cheer her up. I told her that she could always get a posting to another Group, but she says even though it's stressful, she enjoys it.'

'What's she worrying about now?'

'This mysterious guy, Conor Lucan, they're trying to trace. It seems that the British police have now identified him as their murderer and they're fixing to arrest him in the next day or so.' This revelation chilled Konrad to the bone. Once again, he had to work hard not to display his feelings openly and react with alarm.

'Do they know who the guy is?'

'Yeah. Apparently, they know exactly who he is. They've been pulling out all the stops and it seems that they got lucky.'

'It'll be interesting to see who it is,' said Konrad.

'Yeah. Probably somebody we least expect.'

'Probably.'

'So, where you gonna take this chick?'

'Oh, just for a drink, so we can get to know each other. We've arranged to meet at the Plough pub. Do you know it?'

'Yeah, a nice bar. I've been there.'

'She lives close by.'

'Sounds good. I've got some rubbers, if you want to borrow some.'

'Borrow? You mean you want them back when I've finished with them?'

'No, you klutz.' Ivan laughed.

'Anyway, no thanks. It's probably a bit early in the relationship. I need to see how the land lies on that score, if you know what I mean?'

'You sure? She might surprise you.'

'I'll take my chances, Ivan, thanks.'

Konrad wanted the conversation to end. He wasn't good at feigned congeniality and needed space and time to think.

'Listen,' said Ivan, 'I'm gonna go up and speak to Daphne. See if we can't make tonight a foursome.'

'Don't cramp my fuckin' style, Ivan,' said Konrad with indignation.

'It's no problem, bro. She'll be cool with it.'

'No, that's not what I meant. I don't want you there on the first night, all right? I want my space. And, stop calling me fuckin' bro. I'm not your brother.'

Konrad got to his feet and left the table. He was finding it hard not to give way to the feeling of panic that was beginning to overtake him. He walked back upstairs to his room. It was 8am. He was due at work at 8.30am. He couldn't have cared less about that.

Konrad was not prepared to just wait for the police to come and collect him. If they did he would just deny everything, but, they obviously had a good reason for suspecting him and his denials might not prove to be enough to keep the law at bay. He didn't want to hang. He just knew that he had to get away.

Konrad made a bold decision. He changed out of his uniform and into some civilian clothes, packed a bag with a few essentials and left the block. He marched to the front gate, out and away along the main road. The sentries on the gate didn't give him a second glance and he told himself that, as far as he could tell, he wasn't known to either of them.

He made his way to the village on foot where, after a nervous twenty-minute wait, he boarded a bus to Braintree.

◈

The journey had taken about an hour, due to the many stops at villages en-route. Konrad left the bus when it stopped on the outskirts of Bocking village and, after its departure, finding the bus shelter empty he quickly took a few items of clothing from the bag. He was now dressed in civilian clothes consisting of an old grey overcoat, pullover, dark brown corduroy trousers and work boots, garments that were not typically American in style. He looked, for all the world, like a farm worker making his way to his place of employment. However, there was one item in his possession that was not a typical item of equipment for a farm worker; a Walther P38 semi-automatic pistol with nine parabellum cartridges, which was a souvenir from his time in Berlin.

He knew that, if confronted, he would be equipped to resist any attempt to arrest him. It was a fact that Konrad was experiencing feelings of intense desperation and he was in no doubt that, at some point, he might have to use the weapon to enable him to make good his escape.

Konrad already knew his way through the village and that, if he stuck to the road, he would have to pass the police station, so he took a shortcut across the fields toward the Dickson house, which stood in isolation some two hundred yards from its nearest neighbour. It was a large country house set in two acres of ground with five bedrooms, sitting room, dining room and a study. It had been the Dickson family home for three generations.

As he came within sight of the house, Konrad crept forward and took up a position among some bushes on the opposite side of the lane to the front garden. He was not intending to knock on the door without first learning who was in occupation, so he settled down to keep the house under observation. It was relatively warm and dry for the time of year and Konrad, after camouflaging his "observation post," made himself reasonably comfortable. Provided he kept himself hidden, time was on his side, which was just as well, since it would prove to be some hours before he saw any activity.

32

Saturday 29 October 1949

It had been an uneventful night for Konrad, who had remained undisturbed in his hiding place. Luckily, he had covered himself in leaves and other foliage, so he was untroubled by the downpour that had visited him in the early hours. But he was now hungry and was considering the possibility of calling at the house, come what may.

It was around 9.15am when Konrad saw the front door open and Angela appear on the doorstep. She was wearing a blue gaberdine raincoat and carrying a shopping bag. Angela's hair flowed down to her shoulders and it was moving seductively in the wind.

By any objective assessment, she was a younger and prettier version of his wife, Daisy, and he looked forward to later being able to compare their sexual prowess. He knew in his heart that, when the time came, she would be unable to resist him.

As she stood on the step Angela hesitated briefly while she checked the contents of her shopping bag, then, apparently satisfied, she leaned back into the doorway and shouted aloud,

'I'm off to the shop now, Mum. Won't be long.'

Very helpful, thought Konrad. *There's obviously nobody at home other than the old girl.*

I'll see you when you get back, Angie baby.

He watched Angela leave the house and walk down the lane, gently swinging her shopping bag as she went. He gave it a few minutes before he left the cover of the bushes and crossed the road to the front gate, first making sure that there were no witnesses. Konrad scurried around the side of the house to the kitchen door, where he stopped and carefully tried the handle. The door came open. He walked into the kitchen, stood stockstill, waited and listened. There was silence.

After a few minutes he walked slowly out of the kitchen and along the hallway towards the sitting room, which was at the front of the house. He could see that the door was ajar, so he slowly moved up to it, then stood and waited. After a few seconds his hearing tuned in to the sound of light snoring. This tickled Konrad and he had to prevent himself from laughing aloud. He put his head around the door to investigate the noise and he was met with the sight of his mother-in-law slumped in the armchair on the far side of the room. So, he quietly entered the room, took a seat and waited.

After twenty minutes or so she woke with a start.

'What the bloody hell are you doing here?'

'I've come to pay you a visit. The back door was open.'

'You can piss off. I don't want you here.'

'Don't be like that, Ruth. I'm family. Remember?'

'Yes, I know you are. How could I forget?'

'Why would you want to? I've done nothing to you.'

'No, it's Daisy I'm sorry for.'

'Why?'

'You know damned well, why. And don't call me Ruth. It's Mrs Dickson to you. Anyway, where's Angela?'

'Gone to the shop, I believe.'

'Well, I don't want you here. Go!'

'I'm not going anywhere, Ruth.'

'I don't know what my Daisy was thinking of when she married you. You've treated her like dirt, beating her up.'

'I've never hit her in my life.'

'Says you.'

'No, it's the truth.'

Ruth then flipped her lid, continuously screaming, 'Get out!' 'Get out!' at the top of her voice. This outburst alarmed Konrad and he knew that he just had to shut her up. Even he couldn't punch a woman of her age, so he grabbed her and put his hands around her nose and mouth. She continued to expel muffled shouts through his hands, and even with her light frame she made a valiant attempt to wrestle herself free. He squeezed her tightly, and not in a loving way. She fell into his arms and went limp. Konrad gently laid her on the floor, returned to his seat and waited for some considerable time, expecting her to regain consciousness. She never did. But at least the silence had been restored.Konrad knew that if he was to remain in the house for a few days, he couldn't leave Ruth laying on the floor. He told himself that he had to move her before Angela returned home, otherwise the impending sex would have to be less than consensual. Then he remembered that the house had a large cellar. He leapt to his feet and quickly walked back into the hall, where he located the cellar door, which was beneath the stairs. Konrad found the light, switched it on and descended to the cellar, which he found to be cold and dank. It consisted of three rooms, all of which contained various packing cases and old items of furniture, including a settee, which would be ideal for his purposes.

He could lay down Ruth's body in relative comfort and the temperature should slow down her decomposition, which, in turn, ought to minimise the smell. It was a shame about Ruth. He truly felt sorry, but she was becoming a nuisance and under the circumstances her death was a necessity. He had to lie low for a couple of days and besides, he wanted sex with Angela into the bargain. Ruth would only have got in the way, which would have spoiled it, for them both.

Konrad returned to the sitting room and lifted Ruth from the floor. He carefully carried her downstairs and laid her on the settee, tucked her in with a pillow and blanket, to make her comfortable and went back to the kitchen, where he put the kettle on for tea. He settled down and waited.

About half an hour had elapsed before he heard the key being inserted in the lock and the front door opening. 'It's only me, Mum.' Konrad remained in his seat, expecting Angela to enter the room, but she continued making her way along the hall to the kitchen.

'Couldn't get your humbugs, Mum, so I got you some sherbet lemons instead. Still, I managed to get most of what I wanted.'

Having received no response from her mother Angela returned along the hall.

'You mustn't have too many hours sleeping in the chair, Mum. You won't be able to sleep tonight.' As she completed the sentence, she walked through the sitting room door and was startled to see Konrad in the chair instead of her mother.

'What the hell are you doing here?' And where is my mother?'

'Hey, calm down, baby. I've only come to see how you are.'

'My mother. Where is she?'

'She's down the cellar.'

'Down the cellar?' cried Angela.

'Yeah.'

'What is she doing down the cellar? She never goes down there. She can hardly walk at the best of times.'

'I don't know. She just said that she was going down the cellar.' Angela left the room and went to open the cellar door. Konrad followed on behind.

'Mum, you all right, down there?' shouted Angela into the darkness. There was no reply.

'Well, she can't be down there. The light isn't on.'

'Perhaps she's gone out into the garden,' said Konrad.

Angela pushed past him and went out of the back door to the garden.

'Mum!' No reply came.

'Well, where can she have got to?' mused Konrad.

'She can't have got far. Not with her legs.'

Angela rushed to the bottom of the garden, looked in the shed and searched the various nooks and crannies. She returned to Konrad, passed him and re-entered the kitchen.

'I'm going to look around the house.'

He followed her along the hall and up the stairs. She first entered her mother's bedroom and found it empty, moved on to the bathroom and then on to her own bedroom, where she looked out of the window.

Konrad knew that the time for explanation was fast approaching. He would try to break the news to her gently but realised that he might not have that luxury. After she had entered her room, he walked in behind her and closed the door.

'I have something to tell you,' said Konrad.

'What have you done with my mother?'

'Nothing. She told me that she was going down the cellar for something and then I heard a crash. I went to see what had happened and I found her at the bottom of the stairs. She was dead.'

'Dead? Dead! What do you mean, dead? Are you sure?' said Angela, with distress in her voice.

'Yeah, quite sure. I checked her thoroughly.'

'Well, why come out with all that shit about her being in the garden? Why didn't you just tell me what had happened?'

'I'm sorry, Angela. I didn't know how to break the news to you. I've no experience of that kind of thing,' said Konrad pathetically.

Angela sat on the bed and put her head in her hands. She was devastated. She began to sob, and this went on for some minutes. When Angela had finally regained her composure, she wanted to know more.

'Couldn't you have just gone for some help, Konrad?'

'No, I didn't need to. I did the right thing. I picked her up and carefully put her on the sofa. I tried hard to revive her, and I gave her the kiss of life, but she didn't regain consciousness. She had already passed on.'

'Where is Mum now?'

'In the cellar. I covered her up.'

'We need to call a doctor and the police.'

'I can't let you do that.'

'What do you mean, you can't let me do that?' Angela screwed up her eyes in an accusatory manner.

'You killed her, didn't you? You bastard.'

'No, I didn't kill her. Why would I do a thing like that?'

'Well, call the doctor and the police, then.'

'I can't do that. I'm absent without leave.'

'What has that got to do with it. My mother's life is at stake here!'

'She's gone Angela. Please trust me on that.'

'Trust you? Trust you! You bastard. I want to see her!' Konrad took hold of her by both wrists, partly in sympathy, partly to control her. She fell back onto the bed and sobbed. He put an arm around her shoulders and embraced her. Angela was devastated and she realised that she was not going to be allowed out of the bedroom. They both remained on the bed in this position for some time until she had regained some composure.

'Why are you absent without leave?'

'I've had enough of the Air Force, and all that bullshit. I want a life, but they are on my back all the time.'

'Take me downstairs to see Mum. I want to see my mum,' demanded Angela.

'OK, babe.'

Angela didn't rise to Konrad's use of the word "babe". It was inappropriate at the best of times and this was the worst. She wondered about his motivation. She feared for the lives of herself and her mother.

Konrad led the way along the hall to the cellar.

Angela's mind was working overtime. She faced a dilemma. Should she enter the cellar to see her mother or make good her escape and run to the nearest telephone kiosk to call the police? As they reached the cellar door, Konrad, rather stupidly, led the way down the stairs.

Angela's mind was made up and she used all her weight to force Konrad down the steps. He almost fell to the bottom but just managed to grab the rail and steady himself. Angela slammed the cellar door shut and bolted it. She ran into the kitchen, but was delayed for a moment at the back door when she had to unlock it. Konrad was able, with sheer brute strength, to barge open the cellar door with his shoulder, and he almost caught her, but she just managed to evade his grasp and ran out into the garden. He followed, hot on her heels, and was able to pull her down onto the front lawn before she reached the gate. Luckily for Konrad, there was nobody in the lane and therefore, no witnesses. He fell on top of her and grabbed her fiercely by the very same hair that he had so admired earlier that morning. He pulled her to her feet.

'Come on, you little bitch. We're going back inside and we're going to have some fun.'

◈

Wilson Rudrow and Rhianna Barnes arrived in the foyer of Colchester Police Station. The front counter constable, having been briefed in anticipation of their arrival, showed them to the canteen, where they were supplied with tea. They were soon joined by Cooper and Brian Pratt. After refreshments they retired to Cooper's office and shut the door.

'Thank you for coming today, Wilson. There have been some very significant developments on our murder case.'

'Yeah, so I understand. Can I first introduce my colleague, Corporal Rhianna Barnes, who has been carrying out some research for me.'

They all shook hands and Cooper introduced Brian.

'So, what have we got, Alby? The last thing we heard was about the guys signing the guest book including one called Conor Lucan. I had Rhianna search the personnel records, but she drew a blank on the name.'

'That's interesting. Our enquiries now lead us to believe that the murderer is one of your sergeants by the name of Konrad Lukas.'

'Really? Konrad Lukas. I suppose, that's not too different from Conor Lucan. But how do we now arrive at the name Konrad Lukas?'

'Lukas has a sister-in-law living a few miles from the base and, from what she told us, he has visited her on one occasion since he was posted back from Berlin. During the visit he picked up a photograph of his family in the living room. According to the sister-in-law, he has been very violent towards his wife, who is still in the States, so we thought we should treat him as a suspect and we fingerprinted the picture. Marks were lifted and compared to those found at our first murder scene. They match. He's our man.'

'Holy shit. That's good work,' said Rudrow.

'Yes. But it doesn't end there. We've been liaising with the German police in Berlin about two similar murders over there. They have sent us fingerprint lifts from their two scenes, and we have compared them to ours. They also match. This means that Konrad Lukas is linked to four murders.'

'Holy shit! We need to grab this guy, and quick.'

'Absolutely,' said Cooper. 'The problem we have is that we have no jurisdiction on the base, as it's technically US territory. This man is very dangerous, Wilson. We need to take him out of circulation before he kills again.'

'I couldn't agree more,' said Rudrow.

'The thing is, how do we go about it?'

'Simple, Alby. We arrest him and hand him over to you.'

'Can you do that?'

'Yeah. At the very least he can be arrested under military law and placed in a cell ready to be handed over to the civil authority.'

'Under military law?' asked Cooper.

'Yes, Alby. It covers a multitude of sins. In any case, in view of what you told me before, I have obtained authority from on high to arrest the suspect and hand him over to you.'

'Excellent.'

'So, as you Brits would say, we are singing from the same hymn sheet.'

'It would be good if, at some point, when we have him in custody, we could hold an ID parade to see if the other guys can identify him as having been there with them on the night of the hockey club visit.'

'We could certainly help with that.'

'Do you think you could let us have a photograph of the man?'

'Better than that, we can give you the man himself. Can I use your phone?'

'Be my guest, Wilson.'

Cooper pushed the phone across the desk, lifted the receiver and offered it to Rudrow.

'Wilson, Brian and I will just go next door into the main office to give you some space. Come and find us when you are ready.'

Cooper and his sergeant withdrew to the next office. After going through the operator Rudrow reached his deputy, Sergeant John Jensen.

'Hi, boss. How are things going in Colchester?'

'Very interesting, John. As a matter of fact, I've got an urgent job for you.'

Rudrow explained the matter in hand.

'So, you want me to arrest Sergeant Konrad Lukas for conduct prejudicial to good order and discipline?'

'Yeah. Get him in on that, then we'll take him to the gate and hand him over to the Colchester police.'

'OK, boss. It's radical but effective.'

'I'll see you when we get back.'

Rudrow and Rhianna walked through to the main office and found Cooper.

'Alby, I've got the team on it. They're going out as we speak.'

'Good. Thanks for that, Wilson.'

'So, we had better get back to the ranch and see what's happening. I'll be in touch when we have something to tell you.'

They all shook hands. Rudrow and Rhianna took their leave.

◆

Cooper was beside himself with expectation. It was now several hours since the Americans had left the station and he was starting to worry. He couldn't wait to have Konrad Lukas locked up in the cells of Colchester Police Station. This animal, who had devoured the flesh of four women, including that of Cecily White, a much-respected colleague and former girlfriend of his side-kick Brian Pratt. He knew that, when the time came, it would be wise to interview Lukas with Ian Mills, and once the man's arrest was confirmed, he would send Brian home to minimise the possibility of any future allegations by the defence team of mistreatment of the prisoner. The telephone rang in Cooper's office at 12.10pm and he hastily picked up the receiver.

'CID, DI Cooper.'

'Alby, it's Wilson Rudrow.'

'Hello, Wilson. Have you any news for me?'

'Yes, and I'm sorry it's taken so long to get back to you, but it's not good.'

'Fire away.'

'We can't find our man, Lukas. I spoke to his section commander, who told me that he didn't turn up for work yesterday morning. He was due to start at eight thirty. We've checked his billet and he's not there. According to the canteen staff, he was last seen at breakfast yesterday and was supposed to be meeting one of the girls last evening on a first date. He didn't turn up for that either.'

'Did he report in, sick?'

'No, he didn't, and we've checked with the medical officer, but he hasn't been to the MI Room at all.'

'Do you think he knows that we're after him?'

'I don't think so. How could he?'

'So, what to do?'

'I've got some of my people in plain clothes in and around the BX and club to see if he turns up and we've left some of the team keeping his room under observation.'

'What about the sentries on the gate?'

'We've spoken to the sentries on the gate, but they can't recall having seen anyone like Lukas leaving the base.'

'Is there another gate on the base, say, at the rear?'

'No. Just the one. Security is pretty tight.'

Rudrow realised that that was a stupid remark as soon as the words had passed his lips.

'You'll let me know if he turns up?'

'Yes, of course. Rest assured, we'll keep looking.' Cooper replaced the receiver and walked through to the sergeants' office, where he found Brian and Ian.

'Any news, governor?'

'Yes. It's all gone to rat shit.'

'How?'

'They can't find the bugger. He didn't turn up for work this morning or report in sick and he's not in his billet.'

'Surely he couldn't have got wind of the fact that we're looking to arrest him?'

'How could he?' said Cooper.

'Unless somebody tipped him the wink at the base,' said Brian.

'Why would they want to do that?' said Cooper.

'Or, maybe someone making enquiries on the base just opened their mouth too wide,' said Ian.

'Anyway. For now, we'll just have to hope he'll turn up,' said Cooper.

33

Sunday 30 October 1949

Unusually for Wilson Rudrow, and his normal schedule, he was seated in his office on a Sunday morning, having worked, continuously, all the weekend. He was now pondering over the action he might take to locate Lukas. He had arranged for an observation team to cover certain points on the base at Lakenheath but up until now they had seen no sign of the man. He was therefore going to have to declare him as AWOL (Absent without leave). Even so, Rudrow decided that the true reason for their interest in Lukas should remain undisclosed for the present. He had to tread carefully.

The situation was likely to cause the USAF great embarrassment, in the short term, if it were not handled discreetly, so he decided to keep it from headquarters, Strategic Air Command and Major General Westley. He would take it upon himself to achieve a positive outcome, but he knew that it would not be long before the general would require a progress report. In the absence of a positive outcome, the recriminations would start. The Foreign Legion was beginning to look like an attractive option.

Rudrow wondered how it was that Lukas had felt the need to disappear, particularly since very few people on the base had knowledge of the enquiry. Surely it could not have been a coincidence. No, he had his suspicions, but he was not prepared to disclose them at this stage. He resolved to have enquiries carried out with Lukas's immediate friends and colleagues, though these would be purely on the question of his being absent.

Rudrow was acutely aware that their reputation was at stake and he did not want to miss any opportunity of finding Lukas and handing him over to the civilian authority himself. The game was not yet lost.

❖

'Breakfast is served,' announced Konrad, as he entered Angela's bedroom carrying a tray.

He was dressed in T shirt and underpants.

'You like Eggs Benedict, don't you, baby?' Angela gave no answer and, as soon as she was aware of Konrad's presence, drew her knees up to her chest and adopted a foetal position. She was naked and handcuffed to the bedstead. The cuffs were another souvenir from Berlin.

'I think you'll enjoy this. I made the hollandaise sauce myself.' He laid the tray on the bed.

'I am afraid you'll have to stay handcuffed and I'll feed you myself. We don't want you doing anything silly now, do we?'

Angela maintained her silence. She had had the night from hell with hours of relentless rape and deviance that only ceased when Konrad finally ran out of steam. Angela's sexual organs were stinging, she stank, the bed stank as Konrad would not let her use the lavatory and she had to urinate where she lay. She fully anticipated that the onslaught would continue after breakfast.

The thought of her mother lying dead in the cellar overrode her own despair and she tried to block this from her mind, but to no avail. She was desperate to find out what had become of her.

Angela found herself trying to counter the mental torture of Konrad's sexual attentions by imagining that she was being taken by an ex-boyfriend or a film star. There really was no point in screaming as it was extremely unlikely that she would be heard. No, she had to endure Konrad's attentions until she thought of a means to thwart him.

'Here we are, baby. Open wide.'

The first fork-load of breakfast was gently inserted in her mouth by Konrad. She chewed for a moment and then swallowed. *Surprisingly good,* she thought.

'That's lovely,' said Angela, trying to pander to his ego.

'Glad you like it, baby. I sometimes cook this for Daisy.'

'Lucky girl. I've often wondered, Konrad, why you went for my sister and not for me.'

'Well, if you remember, little lady, you were still at school when I was in England the last time. Your sister is five years older than you, after all.'

'I know. Mum and I miss her, you know,' said Angela.

'So do I.'

'So, why are you having sex with me?' said Angela, bravely.

'You and Daisy are very alike. I'm lonely. You're lonely. We all have our needs, baby, it just seems to me to be the obvious way of meeting them.'

Konrad continued to feed her, but Angela could detect the anger that had started to well up inside him, as a result of her questioning. She decided to stop testing him and return to passive mode. As he got up from the bed and moved the tray, Konrad backed into the bedside chair and brushed against his coat, which was folded over the armrest. There was a thud on the floor that drew Angela's attention. She saw a handgun laying on the carpet beneath the chair. Her pulse suddenly quickened but she said nothing. Up until that point, she had had no idea that Konrad was armed. She wondered why he needed a gun. What was he afraid of?

Konrad made no verbal acknowledgement of the presence of the gun. He just scooped up the weapon and placed it back inside the coat. He then left the room with the tray, to return it to the kitchen.

◈

Cooper was frustrated. He hated having to be dependent on the goodwill and actions of another force. It was his investigation and he wanted to control it, but he had no other option than to observe protocol. In order to save resources, he had stood half the team down and given them a rest day on the proviso that they remain contactable and ready to report for duty at a moment's notice. Cooper was sitting with the residual members of the team, namely Ian Mills, Tom Rogers and Jane Stewart, discussing outstanding actions and lines of enquiry and waiting for the all-important call.

'Governor, Tom and I were discussing the fact that we ought to visit our man's sister-in-law to make her and her mother aware of the situation,' said Ian.

'Yes. A good idea. They may well have seen him since our visit and I don't suppose for one minute that the fact that he is unwelcome would stop him calling on them again.'

'No, he wouldn't care about that, governor,' said Ian.

'Not only that, governor,' said Tom, 'but Angela is a very attractive woman, they are isolated and vulnerable. I think there's a good chance that he'll go there.'

'Good thinking, Tom,' said Cooper, 'He can't have that many local connections, and if he wanted somewhere to run to, that would be ideal. We'll make a decent detective of you yet.'

Cooper chewed the possibilities over in his mind for a few minutes and then left the room to return to his office to make a phone call to DI Arthur Brown, his counterpart at Braintree. After making the call he returned to the main office.

'Right. This is what we are going to do. Not only do we need to call on Miss Dickson and her mother, I want us to sit on the address until Lukas is arrested. As you so rightly said, Tom, they're vulnerable.'

'You going to get uniform to sit a car outside the house then, governor?' asked Ian.

'No. We'll do it covertly, and put the house under observation. We want to arrest this animal, not frighten him off. I've just had a word with Arthur Brown, the DI at Braintree. The house is on their ground so he's going to let us have a couple of his blokes, so we'll be able to give it twenty-four-hour cover. Ian, I want you to liaise with Braintree and call in DC Potter and DC Cuthbert to work, so that one can cover the office and the other can go in the OP.'

'Will do governor.'

'Oh, and call in Brian Pratt, he can also man the office. Bear in mind that he knows that he shouldn't go anywhere near Lukas, should he turn up.'

'Who do you want to go to the house?'

'When we do, it'll be you and me, Tom. We'll aim to get to Braintree for three o'clock and carry out a briefing there. Arthur Brown is going to arrange for a recce to be carried out on the address in advance of the briefing, and they'll sort out the OP. Right, let's get to it. We'll leave here at half two.'

Cooper returned to his office, took the car keys from his desk and went down to the rear yard. He drove to his house, where Linda was preparing Sunday lunch for them both. He let himself in the front door.

'Hi, darling. How's it going?'

'Not quite ready yet, love,' shouted Linda from the kitchen,' 'How are things at work?'

'The Yanks still haven't found our man,' said Cooper, as he threw his car keys onto the settee. 'We're going across to Bocking this afternoon to see if his mother-in-law and sister-in-law have seen him.'

He walked up behind Linda and gave her a hug and a kiss.

'Something smells nice. What are we having?'

'Toad in the hole. How long have you got?'

'About three-quarters of an hour. Sorry to rush you, darling.'

'That's all right. Lunch should be ready in about twenty minutes.'

'Right. I've just got time for a wash and a change of clothes into something warmer. It could be a late one tonight.'

'OK. Do you want me to stay over?'

'Yes, that would be nice.'

Cooper disappeared upstairs and returned after a quarter of an hour dressed in a woollen sweater, dark corduroy trousers and boots. He was carrying an old duffel coat.

Linda served lunch and Cooper wasted no time. He devoured it as if he had been on a starvation diet.

'Steady on, Alby,' said Linda, 'plenty of time.'

'Sorry, darling, but I can't afford to be late.'

Cooper duly finished his meal and rose from the table.

'That was lovely. I'll see you later. Hopefully, I won't be too late.'

He bent over and gave her a passionate kiss.

'Take care, darling,' she called after him, as he shut the front door.

❖

Later that afternoon Cooper and Arthur Brown were holding a briefing in the CID office at Braintree. Cooper gave the troops the background to the case.

'What we have here, ladies and gents, is a dangerous, psychopathic serial killer, who has murdered four women to our knowledge. One of the victim's was Cecily White, one of our sergeants.'

'And the man's name is Konrad Lukas, governor?' said Patrick Walsh, one of the Braintree officers, 'How are we spelling that?'

'Yes, Pat. It is. L-U-K-A-S.'

'Sounds German to me.'

'Yes, well, he's an American airman, with Polish and German ancestry. He's a sergeant, based at Lakenheath. Lukas is married to an English girl called Daisy. She's originally from Bocking but now lives with their kids in the States. The address we're going to sit on is the home of her mother and sister Angela. The family name is Dickson. We know that Lukas has been to the address recently although he's not welcome.'

'Why is that?'

'The Dickson family have got wind of the fact that, in the past, he has knocked Daisy about. However, that probably wouldn't stop him from going to the house because he's thick-skinned, to say the very least.'

'Have we got a photograph of him?' asked Arthur Brown.

'No. not yet, Arthur, because the Yanks told us that they could give us the man, but it seems now he's gone AWOL and he's been missing for a day or two. They still haven't come up with a photo.'

'Description?'

'Yes. A good-looking bugger apparently. Thirty-three years of age, about six feet two inches in height and about 200lbs. Powerful build. Blonde hair and clean-shaven. We have no idea what he was wearing when he did a runner.'

'Why do we think he's going to call at the Dickson house?'

'We have no specific intelligence that tells us that he will, but it's an inspired guess. He's got nowhere else to go. It seems that the US Air Force know nothing of his connection to Bocking and for tactical reasons we've kept that address from them. In the same way that we have no jurisdiction on the air-base, they have no jurisdiction off-base. Arthur, do you want to talk about the OP?'

'Yes. We carried out a careful recce around the area surrounding the house and to the right of the house, as you look at the front, is an old barn about 150 yards away. It has an unrestricted view of the front and rear doors. I spoke to the farmer and told him that we had information about burglars operating in the area. He was happy to let us use it. The farmhouse is about fifty yards behind the barn and the bonus is, that he's got a phone in the office, and he's happy for us to use it. We can enter the barn from the farmyard, which is on the blindside from the target address.'

'Thanks, Arthur. That's just the job. Any questions, folks, before I go into the plan of campaign?'

'Only one, governor,' said Walsh. 'Does this bloke carry a knife or anything?'

'Not to our knowledge. No weapon was used during the murders but take care. We can't assume anything or take anything for granted.'

'No chance of us getting an authority for firearms to be issued then, governor?' said Walsh.

'No. Not on this information, unfortunately.'

'It's a good point, Patrick,' said Arthur Brown. 'If we get any indication of a weapon from what we observe in the OP, let me, or DI Cooper, know, then we'll have to talk about a quick application for firearms, but as it stands, we can't justify it.'

'So, the plan. DS Mills and DC Walsh will take the first eight hours in the OP. I want us to assess the situation first before we consider knocking on the door. For all we know, Lukas could be in there already and we don't want to panic him into doing anything drastic. If we see that the Dickson's are moving about freely then we'll think about carrying out a direct approach. There aren't too many hours of daylight left so we need to get our skates on. DC Rogers and I will go to the village police office and liaise with you from there. Any other questions?'

There was no reply, so the team deployed.

On their arrival at Bocking police office Cooper and Tom Rogers were met by PC Clive Birchfield, who had already been briefed by Arthur Brown. PC Birchfield showed them into the office.

'Been stationed here long, Clive?'

'About three years now, governor. I was posted here from Chelmsford. It's a two-man beat, manned by myself and PC Jim Guthrie. We both live in the police houses attached to the office. The misses likes it here because she's originally from the village and her mum and dad are just up the road. Very handy for baby-sitting.'

'Sounds ideal,' said Cooper.

'There's plenty of milk in the fridge and tea in the caddy by the sink, gentlemen. Please feel free to help yourselves.'

Birchfield pointed out the entrance to the kitchen.

'Do you know the Dickson family?' asked Tom.

'Only the daughter, Angela. She was at school with my misses, but I don't really know her mother. I think she's very much house-bound, as I understand it.'

'Yes, I think so,' said Tom.

'Did DI Brown tell you that we are trying to arrest an American serviceman for the murder of one of our colleagues?'

'Yes, governor.'

'And that he's married to the other Dickson daughter, Daisy?'

'Yes.'

'So, Clive, we need you to stay well away from the house unless we call you.'

'Understood, sir.'

'We've set up an OP in the barn at Peartree Farm. Do you know it?'

'Yes. The farmer is Barry Holmes. He's also a parish councillor. Good bloke.'

'Well, at the moment, the OP is manned by our DS Ian Mills and DC Walsh, from Braintree. Their only means of communication is by use of the phone in the farm office. They will stay in contact with us here and give us an update every half hour or so. Braintree and headquarters control room know what's happening.'

'OK, governor.'

'When does PC Guthrie come on duty?'

'He's on leave until next Friday. I finish at 10pm and I'm back on duty at 8am tomorrow morning. I shall be in the house, if you need me, governor.'

'OK, Clive. Thanks for that. And PC Guthrie hasn't got anyone filling in for him?'

'No, governor. There should be nobody else working this beat.'

'Good. Well, thanks for your help, Clive.'

PC Birchfield withdrew.

'Right, Tom. I want you to start a log of calls and incidents relating to this job.'

Cooper reached into his briefcase and retrieved an exercise book, which he handed across to Rogers.

'Yes, governor.'

'As much relevant detail as related by the blokes manning the OP.'

'Yes, guv.'

'I'll take the calls and dictate the content to you.'

At 3.40 pm the telephone rang. It was answered by Cooper. Ian Mills was the caller.

'On plot at three-fifteen, governor. Clear view of the front and back doors. No movement in or around the house. No lights on in the building. No vehicles parked near or by.'

At 3.55pm, Ian Mills telephoned again.

'A post office van has pulled up outside the target address. The driver is walking along the path to the front door. He has a parcel in his hands. The driver is using the knocker.

He is waiting at the door.' Twenty seconds or so elapsed. 'Nobody appears to be answering. He's knocked again. Still no answer. The postman is returning along the path to the van, taking the parcel back with him. Van moving off.'

At 4.30pm, Ian Mills telephoned again. 'No change.'

At 5pm, Ian Mills telephoned again. 'No change.'

At 5.20pm, Ian Mills telephoned again. 'There is now a light on in the kitchen. Even though we are using binoculars, nobody seen.'

At 5.35pm, Patrick Walsh telephoned from the OP. 'The kitchen light is still on. Still can't see anyone on the premises.' Cooper informed Walsh that he would make his way to the target address.

'I'm going to creep up to the kitchen window to see if I can get sight of the occupants from the garden. Stay on the phone, Tom, and maintain contact with the OP, and let them know what I'm doing. I'll be back shortly, then we'll put a call into the office and get Jane Stewart to come and join us here.'

'Yes, governor.'

Cooper walked outside to the Wolsey and drove it to the end of the lane leading to the Dickson house. He parked up and continued his way on foot. As he reached the boundary fence, he crossed a ditch and carefully made his way through the copse abutting the garden. As he got to a point adjacent to the rear of the house he climbed over the fence and moved slowly through the garden, making the most of the shrubbery and shadows to keep himself concealed. He managed to reach the outer wall of the house at a point next to the kitchen window. He stood and listened, but heard nothing, so he moved slowly sideways to the bottom corner of the window, where with one eye he took a view. He saw a man who was sitting at the kitchen table with his back to the window. In front of him was a plate of food and a bottle of scotch. Cooper stayed in this position for a few minutes. He observed the man, who appeared to be downing the scotch at quite a rate. The man was sitting, talking to himself. Although Cooper could not make out all that was being said, he heard enough to realise that he had an American accent. This was enough for Cooper to satisfy himself that Konrad Lukas was in residence. But where were the women?

Cooper withdrew, slowly and carefully, and made his way back to the lane. He collected the car, drove back to the police office and joined Tom Rogers.

'How did you get on, governor?'

'It looks as though our man Lukas is in the house, Tom. At least, I saw a man fitting his description sitting on his own in the kitchen. I heard him talking to himself. He's got an American accent.'

'What if it's another Yank, entirely?'

'What are the odds of that, Tom? Too much of a coincidence in my book.'

'Did you see the Dickson ladies, governor?'

'No sign of either of them.'

'Doesn't look good, does it?'

'It doesn't. Not only that, why did nobody answer the door to the postman when he called? We need to let the lads in the OP know about our man. Get them on the blower for me, please, Tom, and you need to make an entry on the log about my going to the house.'

'Yes, guv.' Rogers picked up the phone and dialled. There was no answer.

'No reply, governor, but they're not in the same room as the phone. I'll keep trying but we might have to wait for them to ring us.'

'Right, let's ring Colchester and get Jane over here. Then keep trying the OP.'

Despite Rogers' attempts to contact the OP his prediction came true and it was another ten minutes before Ian Mills made contact. Cooper picked up the phone.

'Been trying to get hold of you, Ian.'

'Sorry guv, but we can't hear the phone where we are.'

'OK. Anyway, it looks as though our man is at the address. I saw him sitting in the kitchen wrapping himself around a bottle of scotch. At least I'm pretty sure it's him. Same description and I heard an American accent when he was talking to himself. He seemed quite calm. I didn't see the women, though.'

'What do you propose to do, governor?'

'At some point we're going to have to go in, but I'd rather do it in daylight with more troops and control the situation. We don't know whether he has any weapons, but we can be sure that he would have access to kitchen knives at the very least. It's important to know where the women are. Did you see me in the garden?'

'No, not from our position. We didn't see you at all.'

'Good. I'll come back to you. One of you stay by the phone, please.'

Cooper replaced the receiver.

'Right, young Tom. Job for you. Can you knock on PC Birchfield's door and ask him to come in to see me. I want to pick his brains.'

'Right you are, guv.'

Rogers left the office and returned ten minutes later with Clive Birchfield, who was in his track-suit.

'Sorry to keep you waiting, governor. I was helping the missus bath the baby, only she's got her arm in a sling.'

'No problem, Clive. I wanted to pick your brains. Who do you know locally who would know the layout of the Dickson house?'

Clive considered the question for a few moments.

'The only person I can think of who would know is Nelson Parker. He lives in Braintree.'

'Why would he know about the Dickson house?'

'He delivers coal there. He'd certainly know how to access the cellar through the coal-chute. He wouldn't know much about the inside of the house, though. Only thing is, he's a bit of a rogue himself. You might not want to confide in him, sir.'

'Under the circumstances, I think we'll have to, Clive. Lives could be at stake, and once we manage to arrest this man it will be in the public domain anyway. No, if what he's able to tell us can get us in quietly that could be a life saver.'

'Do you want me to go to his place and ask him, sir?'

'Isn't he on the phone?'

'Not at home, which is where he'll probably be at this time.'

'OK. Tom here will run you up there in the Wolsey.'

'Right you are, governor,' said Tom.

'It's only a couple of miles,' said Clive. 'Shouldn't take us long.'

The two officers left the station and Cooper sat, and considered the risks involved in the few tactical alternatives that were available to him.

At 6.15pm, Ian Mills telephoned. 'No change.'

At 6.55pm Tom and Clive returned to the office. They were both smiling.

'Good news, governor,' said Tom. 'Mr Parker drew a map and described where the coal-chute is situated and he sketched a rough layout of the house. Apparently, he helped the Dicksons move some furniture from the spare bedroom upstairs down to one of the rooms in the cellar.'

'Well done, chaps.'

'It gets better than that, governor,' said Tom. He's given us the key to the padlock on the coal-chute. The Dickson's gave him a spare one in case he came to deliver when they were out.'

'Good work. That should give us the edge. Thanks very much for your help, Clive. Right, I'm going to try and get hold of Mr Stockwell and seek his opinion on the next stage of this operation. No doubt he will want to speak to your boss, Mr Nugent.'

◈

Konrad was seated in the kitchen, working hard to finish the bottle of Scotch that he'd managed to find in the pantry. He knew that there was a half-bottle of whisky with which he could continue should his thirst remain unquenched. He felt safe and in control of his own destiny. The US Air Force could go and fuck themselves as far as he was concerned. They had no idea where he was and, judging by the contents of the pantry, and the hens in the garden, he believed that he had enough food to stay at the Dickson house for several days. After that, the authorities' interest in him might have waned. At least, that's what he told himself.

Konrad began to feel tired and once again he had the urge to jump into bed with Angela, but this time he would settle for the warmth of her body and a cuddle. He felt that she was starting to enjoy his attention and that they might even have a future together. He made his way up to the bedroom, where Angela was still lying in bed with her wrist chained to the bedhead. Konrad walked across the room and sat on the side of the bed. He stroked her hair and saw by the tear stains running down her face that she had obviously been crying.

'I want my mum.'

'Don't worry yourself, honey. She wasn't a well woman, was she, and she's gone to a better place now.' Angela curled up in a foetal position, once again. Konrad offered her the Scotch bottle.

'Have some of this. It'll make you feel better.'

Angela was hit by the overwhelming smell of Konrad's whisky-laden breath. He offered the bottle to her lips and, before she could shake her head away, managed to pour some of the liquid into her mouth. This caused her to cough and wretch.

'What are you doing to me, Konrad? Choke me like you did my mum?'

'I told you it wasn't my fault. She fell down the stairs.'

'I hope you are not lying to me, Konrad. I know she would never have gone down there on her own,' said Angela, pathetically.

Konrad raised his arm as if to strike her but just managed to stop himself from doing so. Angela saw his facial expression change from a grimace to a smile. He stroked her hair gently and kissed her on the forehead.

'Calm down now, baby. I'm here to look after you. Not hurt you.'

'Oh yes. That's why you've got me chained up like some kind of animal.'

'It's for your own good, baby. You're grieving for your mother. People can do silly things when they are grieving. I'm saving you from yourself until you calm down.'

Konrad undressed and slipped into bed next to her. He placed an arm around her shoulders and lay on his left side facing her, resting his head on the pillow. He wanted to talk.

'Tell me. What would make you happy, baby?'

Angela knew that she had to be careful what she said

in reply to Konrad's question if she was to survive and get to make good her escape when the opportunity presented itself. She certainly didn't want to end her life in the cellar.

'I would be happy if we could get to know each other better. You're a sexy man and good in bed. Who knows what the future might hold for us as a couple?'

To get the words out in convincing fashion took every bit of control and acting ability that she possessed, but she realised that Konrad would believe what he wanted to believe.

'That's nice to hear, baby. I'm truly sorry about your mum. But I promise you it wasn't me. I wouldn't do such a thing.'

He reached across to the bedside table and grabbed the Scotch bottle. He took another swig and lay with it resting on his chest.

'Oh, I'm forgetting my manners. Do you want some, baby?'

He offered her the bottle, again.

'No thanks. I don't like whisky. I'll tell you what I would like, Konrad.'

'Go on.'

'Undo me from the handcuffs, please. It's giving me cramp in my shoulder and I need to use the toilet.'

He got out of bed and walked across to the dressing table to retrieve the key, returned to the bed and released Angela's right wrist from the cuffs. She rubbed her wrist and stretched her arm and shoulders.

'Thanks for that, honey.'

Konrad escorted Angela to the bathroom. He opened the door and removed the key from the lock, on the inside of the door.

'Baby. I'm gonna shut the door so that you can have some privacy. But I'll be right outside. I don't want you hurting yourself by trying to climb out of the window. I'll hear you if you try.'

Angela entered the bathroom and shut the door. She sat on the toilet and put her head in her hands. *Mum, oh Mum, I hope you didn't suffer. What am I going to do?* Angela wept for a few minutes. But she imagined her mother stoically telling her to fight Konrad with whatever guile and cunning she could muster. She knew what made him tick. Angela felt a surge of adrenalin pass through her body.

'Angela. Hurry up, please.'

She shouted through the door.

'I'm just going to brush my teeth and have a quick wash.'

Angela carried on with her ablutions and when she had finished she left the bathroom. Konrad was immediately outside, leaning against the wall. He was swaying.

'If you're OK now, we'll go back to bed.'

She walked back along the hall to the bedroom and Konrad trailed along behind her. Angela knew what was coming next so rather than upset him she lay back and opened her legs. To her relief, he didn't last long. The Scotch was getting the better of him. She spoke soothingly and played the game by cuddling and caressing him. Just as she started to believe that she was getting somewhere he turned to her.

'I'm going to turn you over now, baby, give me your hand.'

Angela knew that there was no point in struggling so she adopted the position, he placed the cuff around her wrist and the ratchet clicked into position.

She saw Konrad lean across to the bedside table, and even though she was "on all fours," she could see him take another deep swig from the bottle. He then grabbed her by the hair and forced himself into her from behind. The Scotch appeared to give him extra vigour and he continued to thrust himself inside her for, what seemed like, several minutes. After a while, he slowed and, clearly unable to bring his efforts to fruition, he withdrew from her and flopped onto his side of the bed. He lay there with his eyes closed. He was soon asleep and snoring loudly.Angela moved onto her back and tried to make herself comfortable. Her vagina was sore and stinging and after checking with her spare hand she realised that her anus was bleeding. Before Konrad had laid his hands on her, Angela had not been a virgin. She had enjoyed sex with a former fiancée although, after four years, nothing had come of the relationship. But after the brutal treatment at the hands of her sister's husband, she wondered whether she would ever enjoy sex again. She also feared for Daisy. What would happen to her in the future, being married to such an animal? No, Angela had to deal with this man who had murdered her mother, raped her and had beaten her sister. She resolved that at the first clear opportunity she would kill him, using whatever means was available.

◈

It was 11.30pm. The OP had reported that the lights were now off in the Dickson household and all was quiet.

As far as the Bocking police office was concerned, it seemed that half of the force had arrived, including Tom

Stockwell and Grahame Nugent, the superintendent for Braintree. They were supplemented by firearms trained officers (or "shots" to use police vernacular) replete with Smith and Wesson revolvers and a Thompson submachine gun. A cordon had been put in place consisting of officers on foot and in vehicles covering a 400-yard circumference of the house and blocking both ends of the lane leading to the target address. Nugent was about to chair an operational briefing attended by Tom Stockwell, Cooper, Brown, PC Birchfield and Inspector Ivor Montgomery, the tactical firearms commander. After introductions were made around the table, Nugent spoke first.

'Gentlemen, I will be brief, since we have the potential for a dangerous and fast-moving scenario. The target address belongs to the Dickson's, who are an elderly mother and a daughter in her late twenties. Their son-in-law and brother-in-law is an American service-man named Konrad Lukas, who is usually stationed at RAF Lakenheath. He is wanted for the murders of two women in this force area which were committed in recent weeks.

The investigating officer is DI Cooper. It is his belief that Lukas is present in the house.

Over to you, Albert.'

'Thank you, sir. We have good reason to suspect Lukas of the murders due to strong forensic evidence found at both scenes. As you probably all know, the first of the two victims was Cecily White, a sergeant serving at Colchester. We have been liaising with Master Sergeant Wilson Rudrow, who is the deputy commander of the US Air Force police at Lakenheath. When we were told of the compelling forensic evidence, we informed Mr Rudrow, who sent out a team to arrest Lukas on the base. It seems that he got wind of the police activity and absconded. He is officially designated as being AWOL. That is to say, absent without leave.'

'What brought you to this address?' asked Montgomery.

'Our enquiries revealed that he had married the Dickson's other daughter, Daisy, who is now in the US with their two children. DS Mills and DC Rogers here, called on them to make enquiries, which proved very useful. When Lukas went AWOL, DC Rogers suggested that since he had no known destination, he might make his way to hide out at the Dickson house. I crept the house this evening and I saw him through the kitchen window. But, I didn't see the ladies and that is a bit ominous, to say the least. I was trying to locate all parties in the house with a view to us making a forced entry at the appropriate time. Now, we had no intelligence about him possessing any firearms and there were none deployed by him during the murders.Strangulation was the method employed, although we were obviously wary of his access to kitchen knives in the house.

The situation has changed. Since then Wilson Rudrow has been in contact with Mr Stockwell.'

'Yes,' said Stockwell.' Rudrow rang the office around 7.30 and spoke to DS Pratt, initially. DS Pratt called me at home, and I rang Rudrow back. It seems that one of Lukas's colleagues, who lives in the same block and served with him in Berlin, was aware that our man had brought back a handgun, as a souvenir. Apparently,Lukas also has ammunition to go with it. Rudrow's team searched his room in the sergeants'block, but no weapon was found. On the basis of that information Mr Nugent has obtained authority from the chief constable for the issue of firearms for this operation.'

'Thanks, Tom,' said Nugent. 'So, gentlemen. Where do we go from here? We don't know whether the Dickson ladies are in the house or even alive. Do we go into the house or wait it out? What is your view on the situation, Ivor?'

'In a perfect scenario we would know where the ladies are in the house, but that isn't the case, so I wouldn't advocate forcing the door and rushing in. In my opinion we'd be best to enter by stealth. Albert has already told me that we have the key to the coal-chute, which would allow us access to the cellar. If we can enter quietly, listen and get up to the ground floor, we can try to clear the rooms on the ground level slowly. If we can achieve that, we can gradually make our way upstairs and challenge him in his bed. That way we should be able to locate the women. If we enter at first light, which will be in about six hours time, we should have an advantage.'

'One thing to mention, Ivor,' said Cooper. 'When I saw him in the kitchen, he was drinking Scotch from the bottle. Now that might make him violent and unstable or it might just knock him out.'

'Which leads me to wonder what the ladies have been doing all this time. Has he tied them up? Locked them in one of the bedrooms or even killed them?' said Nugent.'

'Well, I think there's really only one way to find out, sir,' said Montgomery. 'I would advise two armed officers in the undergrowth covering the front door. Myself, and one other to cross the lawn to the coal-chute in darkness. We can then enter at first light.

Two covering the rear door from distance. The two of

us will clear the building alone; that way we won't have any blue on blue situations.'

'Blue on blue?' asked Stockwell.

'Means, we won't get shot by members of our own team.'

'Christ! Heaven forbid,' said Nugent. 'I'd be writing reports from now until Christmas!'

They all laughed.

'OK with that, Tom?' asked Nugent.

'Sounds good to me,' said Stockwell.

'Right. That's the plan, then.'

34

Monday 31 October 1949

It was 5am and Montgomery's team were in position. Both the front and rear doors were covered. Ivor Montgomery and his sergeant, Vernon Peters, had spent the last two hours in the OP with Ian Mills and Patrick Walsh. A mist had come down over-night, which gave the fields and the gardens a ghostly hue. It was just before the dawn broke that Ivor and Vernon left the OP and walked out of the farmyard gate. Their movement towards the house was reported to Cooper by Ian Mills, using the farm telephone. Ivor and his sidekick entered the garden through a small gap in the hedge and they made their way slowly to the coal-chute, which was positioned along the rear wall, to one side of the kitchen window. Ian and Patrick could just see the outline of their bodies as they sat down with their backs against the rear wall. They sat and waited for the light.

At first light, using the key, Ivor and Vernon, opened the doors to the coal-chute and they quietly slid down the shaft to the mound of coal at the bottom. They made their way into the adjoining room. As they did so they shone their torch around the walls, located the switch and turned on the light. They were met with the tragic sight of an elderly woman lying dead on a sofa. She looked for all the world like an Egyptian mummy. Ivor checked her pulse but found that she was cold and had obviously long since departed. This upped the stakes somewhat and, if they hadn't realised before, they now knew for certain that they were dealing with a life--threatening situation. Unfortunately they were unable to convey this fact to their colleagues outside. They had to press on alone.

◈

Angela was exhausted as she had been lying for some hours without sleep, due to a combination of terror and Konrad's incessant snoring. The curtains had not been drawn so as she lay on her back, staring at the ceiling, she became aware that daylight was beginning to enter the room. Had she not been the victim of Konrad's attention she might have found the situation restful and even therapeutic. But she had this monster lying next to her and she wondered what the new day would bring. Would he lose interest in her and bring her life to an end?

As Angela lay looking about her, she examined her right wrist. She couldn't believe her eyes. Yes, she was manacled. But the key had been left in the lock. In his drunkenness Konrad had chained her to the bed and he had failed to remove it.

Thank God for Scotch whisky, thought Angela, not believing her luck. She reached across, carefully unlocked the cuff surrounding her wrist and removed the key. This she accomplished with the utmost stealth. She looked across at Konrad, whose hands were in the prayer position across his chest. Angela hoped that he would raise his arms within reach of the handcuffs and so she slid them gently along the bar of the bedhead in his direction. Her immediate thought was that she would wait until he placed a wrist within range and then cuff him, but she soon realised that that was just too ambitious. Angela then remembered the handgun.

The imperative was to check on her mother as, after all, Konrad may have been lying about her demise. So, she slid out of bed and tiptoed quietly around to the chair where he had earlier placed his coat. She searched the pockets and found the handgun. Angela had served in the ATS during the war and she had a basic knowledge of firearms. She was going to make damned sure that he wasn't going to be able to use it on her. She examined the breech and saw that it was fully loaded, but the noise that she made whilst doing so, woke Konrad from his slumber.

'What are you doing, baby?'

'Don't you call me baby, you arsehole. What have you done to my mother? I want the truth.'

'I haven't done anything to her.'

Konrad was lying on the bed. He was stark naked.

'The truth!'

Angela was holding the weapon, but the barrel was pointing to the floor. Suddenly, he leapt towards her and whilst gripping her throat with his left hand he attempted to grab the weapon from her.

Angela was in shock and feared for her life. She pulled the trigger. Konrad leapt as the bullet made contact with his groin. He screamed at the top of his voice, fell back on the bed and began to convulse in a violent manner, his blood flowing freely.

'You bitch. You, fuckin' bitch!'

Angela experienced an overwhelming urge to empty the gun into him but, despite everything that had gone before, she couldn't bring herself to do so. Blood was spurting from a very sensitive area of his body. Somehow that seemed to be enough to satisfy her. She left him screaming and whimpering on the bed and, in an almost trance-like state, Angela wandered out onto the landing.

◈

Ivor and Vernon, still in the cellar, moved to the stairs and slowly they climbed towards the ground floor. Then they heard a shot and a scream. They were stunned momentarily but gathered themselves and Ivor led the way up the stairs. He gingerly opened the door and peered out into the downstairs hall. He checked both right and left, finding that all was clear. They made their way out into the hall and "cleared" the kitchen. They moved carefully along the corridor to the dining room and then on to the living room, finding them both empty. The screaming and shouting continued. It was a male voice and this confused them somewhat.

Ivor opened the front door and quietly beckoned the two officers, whom he had detailed to cover the front of the house, to enter the porch. The next obstacle was the staircase leading to the first floor. As they were about to ascend, they were confronted with the sight of a naked woman, who appeared on the landing holding a handgun. Ivor and his colleagues presented their weapons and challenged her.

'Armed police! Stand still and put the gun down!'

Angela complied. She then collapsed to the floor. Ivor could hear screams and sobs coming from the bedroom. He left his colleagues to deal with Angela and moved on toward the sound of distress. Ivor found Konrad writhing on the bed. He made sure that he was unarmed and approached him. He was bleeding profusely. Tearing some cloth from the sheets Ivor rolled it into a ball and placed it against Konrad's groin.

'Right. I need you to hold this tightly against the wound. I'm going to call an ambulance.' Ivor called Vernon from the landing into the bedroom.

'Stay with him, Vernon. The DI is going to have to arrest him for murder. I'm going to call an ambulance.'

Ivor ran out into the back garden and waved his arms towards the OP, beckoning the occupants to join him. Ian Mills left the OP and ran out to the garden.

'Ian, can you call an ambulance? Lukas has a gunshot wound and is bleeding heavily, and let Mr Cooper know that he was shot by Angela Dickson. Her mother also appears to have been murdered. We found her in the cellar.'

Ian Mills turned on his heel and returned to the farm office, where he made the necessary phone calls. A short time later Cooper and Brown arrived on scene, where they found Ivor in the living room with Angela, who by now had acquired a dressing gown and some underwear. She was crying bitterly, having had the death of her mother confirmed.

Cooper and Tom Rogers remained with Angela whilst Arthur Brown went upstairs to deal with Lukas. They had to wait for a few minutes before speaking to Angela, as she needed to regain some composure.

'Angela, you have met my colleague, Tom, before, haven't you?'

'Yes. Yes, I have,' she said, wiping away her tears.

'And my name is Albert Cooper. I'm the head of Colchester CID and I'm dealing with Konrad Lukas's case. Can you tell me what happened here?'

'On Saturday morning I went out to the shop in the village to pick up some bits. Mum was downstairs in the living room. When I came back, I found him sitting in Mum's chair. I asked him where Mum was, and he said that she'd gone down the cellar. I knew that was a lie because she's not able to walk very well and she'd never go down there, the stairs are too dangerous. I checked the cellar and the lights weren't even on, so I didn't go down there to look for her. Then he said that she might have gone out into the garden, so we went outside, but I couldn't see her. I looked upstairs in the bedrooms. It was then that he told me that she had fallen down the cellar stairs and he found her at the bottom already dead. He said he'd laid her on the settee down there.'

'What happened after that?'

'I asked him to call the police and an ambulance. But he wouldn't. I tried to get away from him and ran out into the garden, but he caught me and dragged me back indoors by my hair. Then he forced me upstairs and handcuffed me to the bed. Since then he's raped me several times, front and back.'

'And he had a gun, I believe.'

'Yes. I first saw it when it dropped out of his coat pocket in the bedroom.'

'So, how did he get shot?'

'When I managed to get free from the handcuffs, I was desperate to find out what he'd done to Mum. I didn't want him coming after me with the gun, so I searched his coat pockets and took it. I checked it and I was about to empty the bullets out of it, when he jumped up from the bed and tried to strangle me. He's an animal.'

'How did you get free of him?'

'I was lucky because he stumbled, and I was able to break free. The gun went off. I didn't mean to shoot him. It was an accident. But the bastard deserved it.'

'OK Angela. We'll talk more about that later, but first I want to get you examined by a doctor.'

'But what about Mum? Is she really dead, like he said?'

'I'm sorry, Angela, but she is. She's lying on a sofa downstairs in the cellar. There's no obvious cause of death. I'm sure we'll find out what happened, though.'

Angela began to sob loudly.

'Mum. I want my mum.'

Cooper was joined by Jane Stewart, who had come across from Colchester and had been dropped off by the area car. They had to wait for some minutes before they could calm Angela down.

'Angela, this is Jane Stewart, who is one of my detectives. She is going to go with you by ambulance to Broomfield Hospital in Chelmsford, where we are going to have you examined, and she'll stay with you. Are you OK with that?'

'Yes, of course. But please look after Mum.'

'We will, don't worry,' said Jane, who placed her arm around Angela's shoulder.

'I don't want her lying down there all on her own.'

'Don't worry. We'll take care of her and treat her with the utmost respect and dignity,' said Cooper.

Cooper and Tom Rogers then made their way to the kitchen, to hold a conversation, out of Angela's hearing, during which they collaborated in the making of notes in Rogers' pocket note book as an early record of what Angela Dickson had said to them.

Cooper knew that when the time was right, they might have to arrest Angela for shooting Konrad. However, given that it was likely she would be in hospital for a few days, they recognised that they could delay any arrest. Whether or not she would ever be charged with an offence, would depend on the lawyers. Angela had been through great trauma. It was by no means certain that they would consider it to be in the public interest to prosecute her, but Cooper was in no position to predict the outcome, had to cover the possibility, and be seen to be taking the correct course of action.

An ambulance soon arrived on the scene and, given the fact that Konrad had life-threatening injuries, the crew were shepherded up the stairs to the bedroom. Guidance was really quite unnecessary since they only had to follow the howls of pain emanating from above to locate their casualty. They soon realised that Konrad had already lost a high volume of blood and needed to be taken to hospital rapidly. He was handcuffed to a stretcher by Arthur Brown, taken downstairs and placed into the back of the ambulance, which soon left to take Konrad to the Essex County Hospital in Colchester, escorted by Ian Mills and Tom Rogers.

After the ambulance had departed Arthur and Cooper got their heads together.

'Have Scenes of Crime been called yet, Alby?'

'Yes. Ian Mills put a call in to the information room at headquarters. They should be here shortly.'

'How are we going to do this, then? I don't want to get in your way. Shall I supervise the scene here, then you can concentrate on the prisoner?'

'Sounds like a good plan, Arthur. I have also suggested that we have Angela taken to a different hospital, at Broomfield.'

'Yes, that makes sense.'

'I'll get Scenes of Crime to send somebody to Broomfield to support Jane and to collect any samples taken from Angela by the doctor. They can then take them back to head quarters for analysis.'

'Good idea,' said Arthur. One thing is for certain, though.'

'Really? What's that?'

'We won't have to worry too much about taking a blood sample from Lukas. There's gallons of the stuff upstairs.'

'I see what you mean,' laughed Cooper. 'Serves the bugger right. I don't think he'll be having any more kids.'

'Poetic justice with a capital P,' laughed Arthur.

'Yes indeed,' said Cooper. 'One other thing does occur to me, though. Have you been down to the cellar to see Angela's mum?'

'No, I haven't. The firearms officers told me that, apparently, she's dead and laid out on a settee.

'Yes, that's right. Well, as I haven't had direct dealings with Lukas, it would make sense, from a forensic point of view, for me to deal with Mrs Dickson in the cellar when Scenes of Crime arrive. It may be that you have blood traces on you from Lukas and if you go down the cellar that could confuse matters and contaminate the scene.'

'Good point.'

'Shall we wait to see what Scenes of Crime say before we assess the need for a forensic pathologist to be called out?'

'Yes. There's no indication as to how she died, whether she fell down the stairs or something more sinister happened.'

A short time later Brendan Withers arrived at the house, together with a young colleague. After receiving a short briefing from Cooper, Brendan gingerly made his way down the steps to the cellar, leaving his colleague to concentrate on Angela's bedroom. After twenty minutes or so Brendan re-emerged.

'Not much to go on down there, Alby. She appears to have been laid on the settee after death. It almost looks as though she died in her sleep. I say almost, because there's some small scratches and scuff marks on her left cheek and her neck. No obvious signs of a struggle in the basement. No signs of blood. I don't think that there's anything that requires us to call out the pathologist at this stage. I suggest that we get her to the mortuary and see what the post-mortem tells us.'

While Arthur Brown remained in the house to supervise the forensic search and removal of the body, Cooper returned to Colchester.

◈

It was 9.20am before Cooper arrived back at Colchester Police Station. It had been a long night and he was knackered. As he entered his office, he found Superintendent Stockwell sitting in his chair, using the telephone. He acknowledged Cooper with a "thumbs up" as he sat down in front of him.

Stockwell carried on talking for a few more minutes and then thanked the person at the other end of the phone.

Stockwell stood up and walked around the desk. He offered Cooper his hand and they shook hands vigorously.

'Well done, Albert. You and the team did brilliantly last night.'

'Thank you, sir. It was a long night. Have you been fully updated on the outcome?'

'Yes. I'm aware that Mrs Dickson has been found in the cellar, dead, and her daughter was raped by Lukas and that she later shot him with his own gun. Taken together with the two other murders I believe that we should consult the County Prosecuting Solicitor's office and seek guidance before you interview either of them. It's a huge task, Albert.'

'I agree, sir. That makes a lot of sense. It should provide us with an interview strategy.'

'Good. I'll get on to them and arrange a case conference,' said Stockwell.

'Who was that on the phone, sir?'

'That was Sergeant Mills. Apparently, they have stemmed the blood flow and given Lukas a transfusion. He's now stable.'

'Good,' said Cooper. 'We don't want the evil bugger dying on us. Can I take it, sir, that we haven't heard anything from the Americans?'

'No. We haven't heard from them at all. Not since they informed us about the gun, anyway. Do you think you should give them a call and bring them up to date?'

'Yes. I think I ought to, sir.'

'Then after that, Albert, I think you had better go home and get some sleep. Lukas won't be available for interview for some time yet and Sergeant Pratt is in the office. He can take over for a while.'

'Thank you, sir.'

Stockwell left the office.

Cooper picked up the telephone to call Wilson Rudrow.

'Master Sergeant Rudrow speaking.'

'Wilson. It's Alby Cooper at Colchester CID. How are you?'

'OK Alby. But I'll be a lot happier when our man Lukas turns up.'

'Well, you're in luck, Wilson. We have him in custody.'

'Great! Where was he?'

'At his mother-in-law's house near Braintree.'

'I didn't know his mother-in-law was in this area.'

'Yes. We only found out recently,' lied Cooper. 'He has a sister-in-law living at the same address.'

'What was he doing there?'

'Hiding out. The thing is, it looks like he murdered his mother-in-law and raped his sister-in-law while he was there.'

'Holy shit. No!'

'Afraid so. There is one other good piece of news, though.'

'Oh yeah, what's that?'

'Angela, the sister-in-law, grabbed his gun and shot him in the balls.'

'Great. It serves the asshole right. Where is he now?'

'Hospital, under guard, having been arrested for murder. He's not going anywhere yet, but at least he's stable and we'll be able to interview him at some stage. There's no rush, it'll give us a chance to get our act together.'

'Death would have been too good for him,' said Rudrow. 'Is there anything we can do for you at this end, Alby?'

'We need to search his room for any documentary evidence that might relate to our two murders. If I send a couple of officers over to Lakenheath, could you allow them access to carry it out?'

'No problem. I'll be here for the rest of the day, if they ask for me at the gate. Now I'm going to have to inform the general. He's not going to be pleased.'

'Thanks, Wilson. I've been up all night so I'm going home to get some shut-eye. I'll be back in the office around six o'clock.'

Cooper replaced the phone and walked through to the main office, where he found Brian Pratt.

'Morning, governor. Had a busy night, I hear.'

'Yes, Brian, you could say that. You probably also heard that Mr Lukas was shot in the bollocks by Angela Dickson.'

'Yes,' said Pratt, 'can't say I'm sorry. No more than he deserved. Shall I tell Cecily's father that we've got our man?'

'We will in due course, Brian. It will be best to do it when we've charged Lukas with Cecily's murder and I'll come with you. Now, I'm going home to get my head down for a few hours. Can you hold the fort for me?'

'Yes, governor. I know what's happening at the two hospitals.'

'I know I don't need to remind you but, I'm going to anyway. I don't want you to leave the office, unless in an emergency, or go anywhere near Lukas.'

'Understood, governor.'

'One thing you could do is check on Jane Stewart and find out how she's getting on with Angela Dickson at hospital. We also need to start thinking about relieving Ian Mills and Tom Rogers. Oh, and another thing. Can you brief up two of the guys to go across to Lakenheath to search Lukas's room? We need to see if there is anything that might connect him to Cecily and Maggie, such as letters, address book, that kind of thing. They'll need to liaise with Wilson Rudrow on the base.'

'Yes, will do.'

'Anyway, I'm off. I'll be back about six.'

'Yes, governor. Leave it with me.'

Cooper got into his car and drove home. He fell asleep as soon as his head hit the pillow.

⊗

Cooper woke to the sound of his alarm, which had been set for five o'clock. He'd had a good six hours of deep sleep and on recalling the achievements of that morning he felt invigorated. He had a quick bath and shave and after getting dressed he went downstairs to the kitchen, where he set about making his "signature dish," beans on toast. He was just finishing his meal when he heard the front door open and in stepped Linda.

'Hello, darling. How are you? I understand that you got your man and that congratulations are in order.' She approached the table and Cooper stood up. They embraced and she kissed him tenderly on the lips.

'I'm so glad that you're alright and you didn't get shot.'

'Oh, thanks very much. So am I,' he laughed. 'I must

admit I was a bit worried when we learned that he had a gun in his possession.'

'Yes, so was I. You worry me, you know. Anyway, are you going back to work?'

'Yes. I need to catch up on a few issues to do with Jane and the search of Lukas's room at the base.'

'Why? What's happened to Jane?'

'Nothing. She's at hospital with Lukas's sister-in-law. He raped her while he was in the house.'

'On the basis of his usual method, she was lucky he didn't kill her as well.' Said Linda.

'Yes. She was lucky alright, but not only that, she grabbed his gun and shot him right in the goolies. That'll stop his "farting in church," for a while.'

'Nasty!' Linda winced. 'When are you going to speak to him?'

'I don't think that we'll be able to interview him quite yet. He's in hospital undergoing treatment. It'll be a day or two, at least, before he's well enough and we can get access, which is good in a way, because it will give us a chance to get all our ducks in a row.'

'Do you want me to stay tonight?'

'No, not tonight, darling,' said Cooper. 'I don't know what time I'll be in and anyway, my body clock is all askew. I probably won't be able to sleep at all tonight.'

'OK. I'll stay at mine.'

'If you drop me off, you can have the car and I'll get a lift home,' said Cooper.

◆

Cooper arrived in the office about 6pm and immediately called a meeting. Brian Pratt rustled up the troops.

'Right, Jane. We'll start with you. How is Miss Dickson?'

'She appears to be in a state of shock, governor. She's been put under sedation, and there's a uniform officer sitting with her. The doctor examined her and found traces of semen in both her vagina and anus, which has fissures that have been bleeding. He took samples from both areas. I don't think we'll be able interview her today, governor. She will probably be under for the rest of the night.'

'No, I don't suppose we will. Though, at some point, she'll have to be interviewed under caution because of the shooting.It would be a good idea to get her into a single room and we could do it there.No need to arrest her and bring her to the station.The poor woman's been through enough trauma, already.'

'She is in a single room, governor.'

'Good. We need to let the medical staff know what we intend to do, and she'll also need a solicitor. Can I leave you to contact one, please, Brian?'

'Yes, governor.'

'We'll see how she is tomorrow. Obviously, a uniform officer will have to stay with her, at all times, and if she gets up to leave,they'll have to stop her and even arrest her for the shooting if she doesn't cooperate.'

'I'll make sure that they're briefed accordingly, governor,' said Brian.

'What about Lukas, Ian?'

'There are two uniform officers with him, governor. He had an exploratory operation and apparently, they found no bullet in him, but they did find an entry and exit wound at the top of his thigh. Apparently, he was quite lucky. It was not far below the surface of the skin and just below his testicles.'

'So, his wedding tackle's in order, then?'

'Yes, governor. She missed, more's the pity.'

'Is he fit enough to interview?'

'Not today, governor.'

'OK. Well, technically he's in custody. Ian, can you make sure that we keep two officers on him. It will give us all time to get some rest and we'll be fresh when we do interview him. It'll be interesting to see if he has anything to say, but I'm not going to hold my breath. Where is Mrs Dickson, Angela's mum?'

'She's in the mortuary at Broomfield Hospital,' said Pratt.

'It'll be interesting to learn the exact cause of death when we have the post-mortem. Whatever the outcome that'll be the first thing we interview him about.'

'Who will be with you in the interview, governor?' asked Ian.

'Brian can't do it for obvious reasons, you're the only other one on the team who is experienced enough. I'll need you to help me interview Miss Dickson, as well. Jane can take the notes.'

'Right you are, boss.'

'Have we heard anything from the lads who carried out the search of Lukas's room on the base?'

'Yes, governor. We had nobody to send so Braintree covered the search for us. Apparently, his room was as clean as a whistle. Nothing was found other than his uniforms and some civilian clothes. He was obviously expecting to be arrested, at some point.'

'Well yes, he probably was, that's why he had it away on his toes,' said Cooper. 'And what about his passport? Any sign of it?'

'Yes, governor. It was found in his coat pocket at the Dickson house.'

'He was obviously going to try and leave the country, somehow, or other.'

'God knows where he thought he was going to go,' said Ian.

'It wouldn't have been Germany or America. That would have been far too dangerous. But it could have been Ireland, I suppose,' said Cooper.

'He'll be leaving the country via the gallows now, governor,' said Tom Rogers, stating the obvious.

35

Wednesday 2 November 1949

It was 4.30pm and Cooper was sitting in the waiting room outside the offices of the County Prosecuting Solicitor at County Hall, Chelmsford. Ian Mills was also in attendance. After twenty minutes or so they were joined by Herbert McIntyre, the Deputy Chief Prosecutor, who appeared to be somewhat flustered. He was a tall, spare-looking individual in his fifties, with half-moon spectacles and an ill-fitting three-piece suit. McIntyre was balding and what little hair he did have had been grown long and teased across his head in a "comb over." He was clutching a bundle of papers under one arm and a thick volume of *Archbold Criminal Pleading* under the other.

'I'm so sorry to keep you waiting, gentlemen. I've only just managed to escape from the Magistrates Court. The members of the bench don't seem to be able to think on their feet these days and want to adjourn to discuss every blessed decision. Anyway, enough of my troubles. If you'd like to follow me.'

McIntyre led them past reception and along a corridor to a meeting room. Cooper, who had met McIntyre before on several occasions, introduced Ian Mills.

'I received your covering report this morning, Inspector, and I was able to read it over lunch. Quite a sequence of events, I must say.'

'I do take your point about Miss Angela Dickson's culpability over the shooting of the prisoner and that this is at odds with the fact that she would be a valuable prosecution witness. However, unless there is anything else that you wish to add, what I would propose you do, is this. Obtain a detailed witness statement from Angela Dickson explaining the relationship of the Dickson family to Konrad Lukas; continue by explaining how she left the house to go to the shops on the day that she later found that Lukas had arrived, the fact that when she left, her mother was seated in the living room and that when she returned, she was nowhere to be seen. Have her reiterate what Lukas told her about her mother being in the cellar. I know from your report that you and DC Rogers made notes of what she told you. We can get that admitted as evidence of early complaint in relation to her rape. Take her account of the sexual offences committed upon her and then conclude the statement and get her to sign it. This statement, taken together with your notes and the forensic evidence, if it proves to be positive, will be enough to proceed against Lukas on the rape and buggery. That, in my considered opinion, gives you a good start. I would also suggest that, at some point, you take a fresh set of fingerprints from Mr Lukas and check them against the various marks found at the murder scenes.'

'And the shooting?' asked Cooper.

'If her account is consistent with what she told you so soon after the event, I would say that the discharge of the firearm could be construed as accidental. The weapon was his.

Why did he have it with him? The poor woman must have been terrified, not only for herself but for her mother as well. I will consult counsel on this point, but I am confident that, ultimately, she is unlikely to face charges. If she starts to speak about the shooting you will have to caution her, hear what she has to say about it and then report her for a decision.'

'And the mother?'

'I haven't seen the pathologist's report yet. Tell me, Mr Cooper, what was the result of the post-mortem?'

'She had suffered a heart attack, which in itself is not conclusive in terms of proving criminality on the part of Lukas, but given the fact that she was found in the cellar, an area where, due to her lack of mobility, she apparently never went, it does beg the question as to how and why she got there.'

'Were there any other marks found on her body?' interrupted McIntyre.

'Some contusions around the face and neck,' said Cooper.

'Well then, we need to get another statement from Miss Dickson stating that they were not present on her body when she left her; furthermore, that to her knowledge, she could not have managed the walk down to the cellar. I need to see the report from the pathologist before I make any recommendations on any appropriate charges in relation to the mother.'

'Can I take it then, sir, that you will provide me with written advice in due course?'

'Yes, Mr Cooper. Once I have spoken to counsel.'

After discussing a few more procedural matters with McIntyre, Cooper thanked the lawyer and the meeting was concluded.

36

Thursday 3 November 1949

It was some four days since Angela had suffered at the hands of Konrad Lukas and she had been admitted to hospital in Chelmsford. As if Konrad's invasion of her private parts was not enough she had been subjected to intimate examinations by the medical staff. Samples of blood and semen had been taken from her and where her nether regions had been split due to violent penetration, the fissures had been sutured. In addition, she was diagnosed as suffering from trauma and shock.

Alby Cooper and Jane Stewart were now present in Angela's hospital room, ready to carry out an interview with her, having, first, gained permission from the doctor in charge. Also present in the room was her solicitor, Mr Terence Gerald.

'Are you well enough for us to proceed, Angela?' asked Jane.

'As well as I'll ever be.'

Jane introduced Cooper.

'Yes. We spoke at the house,' said Angela.

'We did,' said Cooper.

'And for the benefit of your solicitor, you know me,' said Jane. 'We've spent a lot of time together in recent days, although you've been asleep for much of that time. Mr Cooper and I want to take a witness statement from you regarding the Dickson family's relationship to Konrad Lukas and what happened between you and Lukas at your home in Bocking. We'll take it slowly and if you feel that you need a break, just let us know.'

'OK. I understand. Thank you.'

'First, Angela, I need to just establish a few facts, before Jane puts pen to paper,' said Cooper. 'Konrad Lukas is your brother-in-law, is that right?'

'Yes. He's married to my sister, Daisy. She's living with their two children in Arizona.'

'And I understand he's a serving airman with the US Air Force stationed at Lakenheath. Is that correct?'

'Yes, that's right. He's a sergeant.'

'Until a few days ago, you lived with your mother, Ruth, at the house in Bocking?'

'Yes.'

Angela began to weep. On seeing this Cooper and Jane ceased their questioning in order to give her a chance to regain her composure.

After ten minutes or so they continued and Jane wrote the statement in long-hand. The account given by Angela was almost word verbatim to that told by her to Cooper and Tom Rogers when they were at the house. The fact that Lukas was not welcome at the house, had been loathed by her and her mother because of his violence towards Daisy, and, that he had raped and sodomised Angela. When it came to speaking about the shooting Angela was adamant that the discharge of the firearm was accidental and had come about when Lukas had leapt at her from the bed and tried to strangle her. Prosecution counsel had advised on this point and Cooper had no reason to doubt her.

37

Friday 4 November 1949

Today was the day that Cooper would finally get to confront Konrad Lukas with the consequences of the bestial crimes committed against his in-laws. The murders of Cecily and Maggie he would cover at a later date. Lukas had been finally deemed fit enough to be interviewed after his time spent in recovery at the Essex County Hospital.

All the while Cooper and his team had been tidying up the outstanding enquiries into what was now a complex sequence of events. Ruth Dickson's post-mortem had been conducted by Professor Westlake, and he had concluded that the cause of death had been due to hypoxia caused by suffocation and a heart attack.

Although in hospital, Lukas had been technically in custody, having been already arrested for Ruth's murder. Understanding that Lukas was a cunning and dangerous individual, who might try to engineer his escape, Cooper was taking no chances. The journey between the hospital and the police station, was a mere half-mile but he sent a team of four officers, with a 'Black Maria,' to transfer the prisoner.

While awaiting the arrival of Lukas, Cooper sat in his office with Ian Mills. He once again went over the interview plan. As for Brian Pratt. He had been given the day off to keep him out of the way.

'So Ian, I think it best that we start with the murder of Ruth Dickson. We've got the results of the post-mortem and the statement from Angela. You've seen those,' said Cooper, thinking aloud. 'We've got one from the family GP, speaking to her immobility and the fact that it would be extremely unlikely for her to be either willing or capable of going down to the cellar under her own steam.'

'Who's going to represent him?'

'Ivan Powis. A good solicitor and, unusually, quite fair and straight-forward. He was suggested by the County Prosecuting Solicitor.'

'Can't say that I've come across him before,' said Ian.

'Anyway, no doubt he'll want to speak to his client before we start. But before we touch on the murder of the old girl, I want to try to get him to talk about his relationship with the Dickson family. Why he was in the house, and to see if he'll give us his account as to what happened. I don't want us to touch on the murders of Cecily, Maggie or the two in Berlin otherwise he'll most likely just clam up. We'll interview him about those matters later. I want us to do this in stages.'

'Yes, governor. I'll leave most of the talking to you.'

'Yes. Anyway, you'll be taking notes.'

The telephone rang and Cooper answered the call. After a brief, one-sided conversation he thanked the caller and replaced the receiver.

'That was Ted Glover. Our man has arrived.'

Cooper and Ian both walked downstairs to the charge room, where they found one of the escorting officers unlocking the handcuffs that bound him to the prisoner. Lukas appeared quite out of place in his pyjamas, dressing gown and slippers.

Cooper and his colleague acknowledged Lukas with a nod and then stood to one side and waited before speaking to him, allowing Sergeant Glover to go through the formalities of arranging for a physical search and booking him in on a custody sheet.

'Is Mr Lukas having a solicitor, sir?' asked Glover.

'Yes, sarge. A Mr Ivan Powis, who was arranged by the County Prosecuting Solicitor's office. I think we ought to let him see his client before we go to interview. I believe he's due to arrive about ten o'clock.'

Cooper and Ian left the charge room and returned to the office.

❖

Later that morning Konrad Lukas was taken from his cell to an interview room, which was contained within the cell block. Already in the room were Cooper, Ian Mills and Ivan Powis, who had earlier spent a short time with Lukas in consultation. Lukas had related his account of the events that had taken place at the house but he kept it short, with little detail.

He didn't know Ivan from Adam and he wasn't prepared to trust or confide in him.

As he entered the room Lukas took a seat at the table.

'Good morning, Mr Lukas. I am Detective Inspector Cooper and this is my colleague, Detective Sergeant Mills. You have already met your solicitor, Mr Ivan Powis. You were arrested on Monday of this week at the Dickson house, which is located in Bocking. That was on suspicion of murdering Mrs Ruth Dickson and we want to interview you about that matter now.' Cooper cautioned him.

'I didn't kill her. She fell down the stairs into the cellar.'

'She was your mother-in-law, wasn't she?' said Cooper.

'Yeah, she was. I am married to her daughter, Daisy.'

'Who, as I understand it, is still in the US. Is that right?'

'Yeah. She's there with the kids. I was posted to Berlin for a while on the airlift. They weren't permitted to come with me.'

'And then you were posted to Lakenheath, I believe?'

'Yeah. But I haven't been there long.'

'And since you've been at Lakenheath you've been visiting Daisy's mother and sister, haven't you?'

'Yeah. I've been to the house a few times.'

'I see. Did you get on with them?'

'Yeah, I did. Ruth was a lovely lady.'

'I saw a photograph of some children with a lady on the mantelpiece in the living room. Is that a picture of your family?'

'Yeah, it is. There's my daughter Mandy, she's six, and my son Mitch. He's four. They're good kids.'

'And your wife Daisy.'

'Yeah. She won't be my wife for much longer when she finds out what I've done.'

'What have you done, then?'

'Had sex with her sister.'

'Did you give the photograph to Ruth and Angela?'

'No. It was sent by mail from the States.'

'So. You went to the house on Saturday?'

'Yeah. And I stayed for the weekend.'

'Were you expected?'

'By Angela, yes. At some time anyway. But Ruth didn't know that I was coming.'

'Where were Ruth and Angela when you arrived?'

'Angela was out shopping but Ruth was downstairs and she opened the front door to me.'

'Where did you go when she let you into the house?'

'We went into the lounge and she made me a cup of tea. She brought it in to me. A bit later she said she had something for me. A surprise. She left the room and seemed to be gone for ages. I went to look for her and I found the door to the cellar open. I saw her lying at the bottom of the stairs.'

'Did you try and help her?'

'Of course, but it was too late. She was dead.'

'So, what did you do?'

'Mouth to mouth. But that didn't work.'

'And then?'

'I saw there was a sofa nearby. So I picked her up and laid her on that.'

'You didn't think of calling an ambulance?'

'To be honest, I'm absent without leave, so I didn't want to chance calling anybody official and drawing attention to myself. She was dead, anyway. That was obvious.'

'The post-mortem showed that Ruth died of suffocation, which is at odds with your account, Konrad.'

'I don't know how that could have happened. She was fine when she left me.'

'Apparently, you told Angela, when she came back from her shopping, that her mother might be out in the garden. Why was that?'

'Garbage! That's not true.'

'You also told her that her mother had fallen down the steps of the cellar.'

'Yeah, I did.'

'You went downstairs with Angela, ostensibly to look for her mother, and you were walking down the cellar steps when she ran off out of the house. You gave chase, caught her in the garden, and dragged her back.'

'She's making it up.'

'Why would she do that?'

'I don't know. You'll have to ask her.'

'She also says that you forced her from the garden up to the bedroom, where you handcuffed her to the bed frame, raped her and subjected her to anal sex. Is that true?'

'She had sex with me, that's true. We were having an affair. Angela likes to be chained up and treated roughly. It's what she gets off on. That's her thing, you see.'

'Did Ruth know you were having an affair?'

'No, she wouldn't have approved. But we arranged to meet two or three times in Braintree for drinks.'

'How did you get there from Lakenheath?'

'I've got a guy I know who's in charge of the motor pool. He let me borrow a jeep a few times.'

'You get on well with her?'

'Yeah, very. She would do anything for me.'

'And she let you have, penetrative anal sex with her?'

'Yeah. All part of the treatment. She likes it. One foxy chick, I can tell you.'

'She's spent the last few days in hospital and during that time she was examined by a doctor, who took samples of semen from her anus and vagina. This was checked by our forensic team and found to be of the same blood group as yours.'

'Of course.'

'You know, in this country to have anal sex is against the law. It is known as sodomy or buggery.'

'Is that right? I didn't know. Well, she wanted me to do it to her and she enjoyed it. What's wrong with that?'

'In this country, ignorance of the law is no excuse.'

Konrad made no reply.

'You see. Angela says that you forced her to have sex and that she didn't consent at all. When examined by the doctor, she was found to have fissures or cuts to her anus. She said that it was where you forced your way into her.'

'No. She enjoyed it. She didn't complain.'

'So, are you telling me that Angela, knowing that her mother was lying downstairs in the cellar either dead or injured, chose to have sex with you rather than check on her?'

'No. Who knows what was going on in her mind?'

'She told us that you brought a gun with you, to the house, which was in your coat pocket in the bedroom. She managed to free herself from the handcuffs when you were asleep and she took the gun out and was trying to unload it when you leapt on her and tried to strangle her. She shot you in the leg. Why would that happen if she was consenting?'

'I don't know. She shot me alright. But it was an accident.'

'Why was it in your pocket?'

'It wasn't. It's not my gun. It must be hers.'

'If what you say is true, why would she take a gun to you?'

'I suppose it must be part of her role play.'

'I'm going to show you a witness statement taken from one of your colleagues called Jake Cassidy. I want you to read it. He states that you own a Walther pistol and ammunition. It is of the same type as that used by Angela when she shot you.'

Cooper slid the statement across the table. Konrad and his solicitor read it together. After they had done so, Ivan Powis spoke to the officers.

'I need to have a further consultation with my client, Inspector. If we could have a break for a short while, please.'

Cooper and Ian stood up and withdrew from the interview room, leaving Lukas and his solicitor alone. They informed Ted Glover and the gaoler of what was happening and went to the canteen for tea.

'Lying, smug bastard, isn't he, governor?'

'Yes. But it won't do him any good. He hasn't seen Angela's statement yet. I'm surprised that he's said as much as he has. As it stands we've probably got enough to charge him with rape, buggery and firearms offences, let alone murder or manslaughter in respect of the old girl.' After fifteen minutes they were called back down to the interview room.

'I'll remind you, Konrad, that you are still under caution and you're not obliged to say anything. After your consultation with your solicitor, is there anything further that you wish to add?'

'No comment.'

Ivan Powis interceded.

'As you rightly say, Inspector, I have consulted with my client and I believe that he has answered your questions. I believe that now you should either charge him or release him.'

'As you know, Mr Powis, we are putting questions to your client about serious offences that I am duty bound to investigate to the best of my ability.'

'Carry on, Inspector,' said Powis, 'but I think that you'll find that my client wishes to make no further comment.'

Cooper carried on for a while, but the outcome was as predicted.

At 5.15pm later that afternoon Konrad Lukas was charged with the murder of Ruth Dickson, rape and buggery of Angela Dickson and possession of a firearm whilst committing an indictable offence. He made no comment after caution.

Immediately after being charged Lukas was taken by Ian Mills and Brendan Withers to the medical room where he was photographed, and with his consent he was fingerprinted. He was then returned to the charge room where he was met by Cooper and the late shift custody sergeant, Terry Robson.

'Right, Mr Lukas. I want you to listen to what DI Cooper has to say to you,' said Robson.

'Konrad Lukas, I am arresting you on suspicion of the murder of Cecily White on or about Sunday the second of October of this year in Colchester, Essex.' He cautioned Lukas, who said nothing in reply but appeared to be shaken to the core.

He was returned to his cell and in the light of this latest revelation the custody sergeant was at pains to ensure that Konrad Lukas had his belt and laces taken from him lest he make a desperate attempt to take his own life.

It had been a long day and by the time Cooper and Ian had finished their notes it was approaching 7pm.

'I think it best that we jack it in now, Ian, so that we're fresh tomorrow morning to continue interviewing our man about Cecily and Maggie. But good work today, mate.'

'Thanks, governor. But what are we going to do if he continues to make no comment?'

'We'll still have to put all of the questions to him to give him the opportunity to answer them.Given all of the forensic and circumstantial evidence we have,even if he continues to make no comment, all he'll do is dig an even bigger hole for himself. Besides, I've got an idea that I want to put to our prosecutor's and counsel which,if they agree, would be clincher.'

'What's that then, governor?'

Cooper explained it to him.

38

Saturday 5 November 1949

Cooper was in bed, thinking about getting up, when a knock came on the front door. It had just gone 7.30am.

Who the bloody hell's that at this time of the morning? Cooper usually slept *au naturel* so he had to pull "yesterday's trousers" on with a jumper. He stumbled down the stairs and opened the door to find Linda smiling at him.

'Oh darling, did I wake you up from your bo bo's?'

'No, that's alright, Linda. I was just getting up anyway.'

'I thought I'd come around to see you and make you a nice breakfast.'

Linda brushed past Cooper and walked into the front room. He shut the door and then pulled her to him. Conscious that he hadn't yet cleaned his teeth, he made do with giving Linda a peck on the cheek. She opened her shopping bag and began unloading groceries onto the kitchen table.

'What do you fancy then, darling?' asked Linda.

'What a question,' said Cooper, 'I'll leave that entirely up to you.'

'Bacon and eggs it is, then,' she laughed. 'Anyway, how are you getting on with our friend Mr Lukas?'

'Cunning bastard. We interviewed him about the Dickson's yesterday. First off he said that the old girl fell down the stairs by accident. Then he told us that he was having an affair with Angela and that she consented to everything done to her because she's a bit kinky.'

'Really? He won't get away with that, surely?'

'No. He's even tried to say that the gun was hers. "All part of the role play," he said.'

When we showed him the statement from his colleague, who informed us about the gun in the first place, his solicitor intervened and we had a break so that he could speak to his client. When we restarted he went all "no comment". Anyway, we charged him with the murder of Ruth Dickson, sexual offences against Angela and a firearms offence.'

'Quite right too. Rotten swine,' said Linda, 'he should swing for what he's done.'

'Immediately after charging him, we managed to get a good full set of prints from him. I got Brendan Withers to do that, so we got a good copy with no smudges.'

'Didn't he protest?'

'No. He gave them willingly, which was most unexpected. The solicitor had left by that time. Had he still been present, I'm sure he would have found a reason to resist it.'

'So, what's on the agenda for today?'

'We arrested him for the murder of Cecily White last thing. He obviously wasn't expecting that and looked very shocked. So we have to interview him about that and the murder of Maggie McGee.'

'That will be more "no comments" then?'

'I'm sure that he'll stick to his solicitor's advice. We'll just have to go the long way round, that's all.'

'Do you think that you'll have enough to charge him without a confession or any admissions?'

'We'll need to hold an ID parade to prove that he was at the after-hockey match party, and we have his finger-prints at both murder scenes. He admitted that he had access to a jeep, which corresponds with what Levi Loveridge told us. The murderer mutilated both Cecily and Maggie in the same way.'

'I'm convinced,' said Linda, 'but then I'm biased.'

'Besides, there's a bit more evidence that I want to get in if I can, but I need to consult our counsel about that?'

'What's that?'

Cooper explained to Linda what he had in mind. She was impressed.

❖

Later that day the interview of Konrad Lukas was reconvened. Once again, solicitor Ivan Powis was present, having first had a consultation with his client. After the formalities Cooper thought that he would try a few questions around simple basic facts that might at least get Konrad to start talking again.

'Konrad, let's talk about your service in the US Air Force. How long have you been in?'

Lukas looked at his solicitor, who nodded.

'Seven years. I joined in 1942.'

'So when were you posted to England?'

'In 1944. I was posted to RAF Bentwaters.'

'It must have been quite soon after you came here that you met your wife Daisy, then.'

'Yeah. Almost straight away. We went out for about six months and then she fell pregnant, so we had to get married. We had a married quarter on the base and after a while we were posted back to the States.'

'After that you were posted to Berlin for a while, is that right?'

'Yeah, for the Berlin Airlift. I was there for three months.'

'In barracks?'

'Not on the base, no. A few of us were in an accommodation hostel in the city centre.'

'And then you moved on to Lakenheath after that?'

'Yeah.'

'Do you go to the BX club on the base?'

'Sometimes, but I'm not much of a drinker.'

'What alcohol do you drink?'

'I get a beer but mostly Coca Cola.'

'And scotch?'

'Yeah. Occasionally.'

'Do you remember being in the BX a few weeks ago when a ladies hockey team from Colchester came to play the Lakenheath ladies and stayed for drinks?'

Lukas looked at his solicitor who shook his head.

'No comment.'

'Have you ever met any ladies from Colchester and taken them out in your jeep?'

'No comment.'

'Anyone called Cecily White?'

'No comment.'

'Anyone called Maggie McGee?'

'No comment.'

'Both of these ladies were with the Colchester hockey team at Lakenheath. Did you dance with either of them?'

'No comment.'

'Both of these ladies were murdered separately in the days after their visit to Lakenheath.

Were you responsible for their murders?'

'No.'

'Are you prepared to take part in an identification parade?'

'No.'

'Are you prepared to let one of our forensic officers take a mould of your teeth?'

'No.'

'Who is the colleague who lets you borrow jeeps from the motor pool?'

'No comment.'

'Why are you absent without leave, Konrad?'

'No comment.'

'Is it because you found out that we were making enquiries about you?'

'No comment.'

'OK. I have further enquiries to make in relation to the murders of Miss White and Miss McGee. We will speak to you again at a later date about those matters.Later today you will be taken before a special hearing of the Magistrates Court, where we'll be applying for you to be remanded in custody to return next Friday.'

Konrad Lukas was taken back to his cell.

39

Sunday 6 November 1949

Rest Day

40

Thursday 17 November 1949

Ian Mills and Alby Cooper were sitting in the waiting room of Albany Chambers in the Middle Temple, which was located just off Fleet Street. There for a pre-trial conference with prosecution counsel, they were shown into the office, where they took their seats.

'Good morning, gentlemen,' said barrister Mr David Mirvis-Lock, QC. 'First thing. Just to be sure, am I correct in thinking that Mr Lukas reappeared before Colchester Magistrates court on Friday last?'

'Yes, sir. He was remanded in custody for a further two weeks until Friday of next week, the twenty-fifth.'

'I see. Thank you, Mr Cooper. Well, on the basis of the evidence that I have seen in relation to the Dicksons I would say that you have a strong case on all charges. In respect of Miss White and Miss McGee, the fingerprint evidence is strong connecting Lukas to both of the murders. The fact that they were both in the same hockey team and that they attended the match at Lakenheath is good circumstantial evidence, as is Mr Loveridge's assertion that the vehicle at the reservoir was a jeep.'

'And the fact that Lukas made no admissions or comment regarding their murders?'

'No great problem.'

'So we have a case?'

'Oh yes. But in respect of these two matters I would take an altogether different approach to that of Ruth Dickson. The *modus operandi* employed in both cases is so strikingly similar, the cause of death, and the fact that the killer bit off their left nipple and took it with them from the scene. This is "similar fact evidence," and it strengthens our case considerably.'

'That being the case, sir, there is a matter I wish to put to you. You might think it irregular but I believe it could be of considerable help in strengthening our case even further.'

Cooper explained his proposition.

41

Friday 18 November 1949

Alby Cooper and Ian Mills were sitting in the canteen awaiting the arrival of Johann Weber at the front counter of the police station. Cooper had telephoned Johann's place of work earlier and had spoken to the farmer. He only hoped that the message had been passed.

'What time's he due to arrive then, governor?'

'In about ten minutes or so.'

'Good meeting with counsel yesterday, I thought.'

'Yes, he seemed pretty positive, didn't he? If all goes according to plan, we should get a result,' said Cooper.

'I'm not so sure, boss."Best laid plans," and all that. I mean, in relation to these murders he stayed "no comment" all the way through the interview.'

'Don't be so bloody negative. You were there and you heard what counsel said, Ian. The lack of a confession presents "no great problem".'

'Hope he's right,' said Ian.

'Don't worry, mate. He's a very eminent chap, is our Mister Mirvis-Lock. He knows his onions alright. He's going to base the case on the doctrine of "similar fact evidence", and now we know for sure that young Johann is not responsible for the murders, he could make a very useful contribution to the enquiry.'

'In what way, guv?'

'Well, you know the Berlin police sent us a copy of the fingerprint lifts from their two murder scenes?'

'Yes.'

'And Brendan Withers came up with a positive match when he checked them against those found at our two scenes?'

'Yes.'

'If we can get that evidence in as well, he'll be linked to four different murders where the victim has had their left nipple chewed off. Game over, I'd say.'

'And what would Johann be able to do for us?'

'Well, now we need to do the same thing in reverse to be absolutely sure. That being the case, we need to liaise with the Berlin police to get them to check our prints against their marks. Also, Mister Mirvis-Lock believes that by us getting the German investigator to give evidence about their offences, it would strengthen our case considerably. To do that we need an interpreter to sit alongside us when we ring him up.'

'Couldn't we go back to the garrison though, guv? After all, they were good enough to help us out before.'

'Yes, they did. But they had to tell a lie about who they were. We don't want the Berlin police to find out that we were using the military as a point of contact, particularly a POW camp. They might be offended and refuse to cooperate.'

'What about just hiring a professional interpreter?'

'I'm told by Mr Stockwell that we haven't got the budget for it, Ian. Anyway, as Johann was in a relationship with Cecily, I'm pretty sure that he'll have the necessary motivation to do a good job for us.'

'And the Germans get to clear up their own cases as well.'

'Precisely. The only thing is that, as Lukas is a foreign national, they couldn't bring their own charges in an English court of law and we have no extradition arrangements, but at least it will give them closure. After all, if Lukas hangs for our case, which he should, he can only hang once, can't he?'

'How will the Yanks feel about that, do you think?'

'They've helped us so far. But we'll need them to provide evidence of Lukas's dates of service in Berlin to tie in with the murders.'

'No, governor, I meant, how would the Yanks feel about one their own servicemen being hanged in this country?'

'I don't suppose that they would want to advertise the fact, but they wouldn't want a serial killer in their air force any more than we would. Wilson Rudrow told us as much.

And, the plain fact is, he's in our jurisdiction. If they don't like it, they'll have to lump it.'

On the arrival of Johann Weber, Cooper and Ian greeted him at the front counter. They took him to a side room, where they explained the proposition. Johann was more than happy to oblige, so over a cup of coffee in the canteen Cooper explained, in more detail, what was needed. He appeared completely unfazed by their requirements, so, wishing to make immediate progress, they drove him to the Colchester Telephone Exchange, where arrangements had already been set in train by the management to facilitate their call to Klaus Walter in Berlin. They were in luck and found Walter at his desk. After a valuable sharing of information, Herr Walter pledged that, if it were necessary, he and his Scenes of Crime officer would come to London to give evidence at the trial, on the proviso that all costs were covered by the UK authorities.

42

Court 1 Essex Assizes, Chelmsford

Monday 9 January 1950

The court was packed to the gunwales with journalists and interested parties who were sitting in the public gallery, waiting, with eager anticipation, for their first opportunity of seeing the "Beast of Bocking". This was a nickname that had been projected onto Konrad Lukas by the *East Anglian Recorder*, in their coverage of the case. It had stirred the imagination of their readership and had been taken into common use.

All stood as Lord Justice Algernon Stevens entered the room and took his place on the bench. There was a delay of a few seconds whilst the court awaited the arrival of the "Beast", who would be brought up from the cells. As Lukas mounted the stairs and arrived in the dock, there was an audible gasp from the ladies in the gallery as, on taking their first glimpse, they were confronted with a handsome young man rather than the ugly monster they had imagined him to be.

After the selection and swearing-in of the jury, the clerk of the court wasted no time, and from his position in front of, but beneath, the bench, he opened the proceedings.

'Are you Konrad Lukas of the United States Air Force, Lakenheath?'

'Yes, sir.' The clerk read out the charges in chronological order: the murder of Cecily White; the murder of Margaret McGee; the murder of Ruth Dickson; possession of a firearm at the time of committing an indictable offence; the rape and buggery of Angela Dickson.

After the reading of each individual count on the indictment Lukas entered a plea of 'not guilty.'

The judge turned to the lead prosecuting counsel.

'Very well. Mister Mirvis-Lock, you may open.'

'Thank you, my lord.'

'Ladies and gentlemen of the jury, as you have heard from the reading of the charges on the indictment, this case relates to a sequence of events involving the murders of three women and serious sexual offences committed against another. The last murder victim was Ruth Dickson, mother-in-law of the accused. Her body was found in the basement of her home near Braintree when the accused was arrested at that address. The victim of the sexual offences, her daughter Angela, was also located at the address, she being sister-in-law to the accused. The earlier murders of Cecily White and Margaret McGee were committed in other parts of North Essex. They had both been mutilated, in a manner, similar to each other. During the trial you will be hearing from forensic witnesses who will give specific detail of this mutilation. We shall also be calling evidence which will be provided by various police officers…'

Gideon Trevalyon, QC, the lead defence counsel, got to his feet.

'Before my learned friend goes any further with his opening speech, my lord, I wish to make an application which, I submit, should be made *in camera.*'

'Can you be more specific about the nature of the application, Mr Trevalyon?'

'The application speaks to the question of whether certain witnesses should be called and the admissibility of their evidence, my lord.'

The judge turned to the jury and he explained that a legal point was to be discussed. He asked the members of the jury to retire to the jury room. He also ordered that the court be cleared of journalists and members of the public. This having been achieved he turned to defence counsel.

'Go ahead, Mr Trevalyon.'

'Thank you, my lord. My friend mentioned in his opening address that various police officers are to be called. I am given to understand that this would include German police officers. There are two aspects at the root of my objection to this, Firstly, I fail to see how their evidence could relate to the points in issue, Secondly, given the fact that five years ago we were at war with Germany, one seriously doubts whether they can be trusted or could be regarded as witnesses of the truth.'

The judge turned to prosecution counsel.

'Mr Mirvis-Lock, can you assist the court on this matter? What does the German evidence relate to?'

'Yes, my lord. The nature of the evidence is that of similar facts, that is to say, that, two murders committed in Berlin at the time of the airlift were strikingly similar to those committed against Cecily White and Margaret McGee. The mutilation of those victims is the same. Furthermore, there is fingerprint evidence at all four scenes connecting them to the accused. We will call a witness from the United States Air Force who will prove that at the time of the airlift the accused was stationed in Berlin. It will be our assertion that Konrad Lukas is a serial killer. The German witnesses will be the investigating officer and a forensic officer and it is my assertion that they can provide sound corroboration of their evidence.'

'On the face of it that sounds fair and reasonable to me, Mr Trevalyon. To be sure, I will retire and consider their witness statements.'

The judge retired to his rooms. After a period of thirty minutes he returned.

'I have read their evidence. Mr Mirvis-Lock, can I take it that you have an interpreter on call to assist the court?'

'Yes, my lord.'

'Then we will call the German witnesses.'

Trevalyon respectfully nodded to the judge and sat down. He was disappointed but not surprised by the outcome of his application.

The judge asked the clerk of the court to recall the members of the jury to the courtroom, whereupon he explained the doctrine of "similar fact evidence" to those assembled.

'That is the legal position and you may or may not consider it relevant in the trial of this accused. You will hear from two German witnesses, one a police officer and the other a forensic expert. You may be surprised that witnesses from the Berlin police should be called to give evidence at this court, particularly since there are no German counts on the indictment. However, their relevance will be a matter for discussion.

You do not need me to remind you that until five years ago this country was at war with Germany, but I must caution you. Whatever your experiences, that is no longer the case.

The witnesses are professional persons and their evidence should be treated the same as any other.' The judge turned his attention to the prosecution.

'Carry on please, Mr Mirvis-Lock. Call your first witness.'

❖

The trial lasted for nine days. Cooper was delighted to see that the German witnesses, Klaus Walter and Siegfried Kessler, attended the court as promised, and he had ensured that Johann Weber was on hand to welcome them and remain with them in their accommodation throughout their stay. Defence counsel, Gideon Trevalyon, QC, did his best to discredit them during cross-examination; however, their evidence was so well corroborated by the British forensic witnesses, he could make little headway.

Following the judge's summing-up, the jury were sent away to consider their verdict. It was clear that the members of the jury had found the prosecution evidence compelling, as they returned, early the next afternoon, with the foreman declaring a unanimous verdict of guilty on all counts.

The judge was quick to sentence.

'Have the prisoner stand up. Konrad Lukas, the jury have found you guilty on all counts.

The evidence shows that you are a highly dangerous

individual and, in essence, a serial killer, for whom it is an imperative to mutilate victims and consume human flesh. You will know by now that the mandatory sentence for murder is death. You will, therefore, be taken to a place of execution where you will be hanged by the neck until you are dead. And may God have mercy on your soul. Take him away.'

Lukas descended the stairs to the cells without a murmur. There was, however, some sobbing to be heard from the gallery.

Epilogue

The verdict of guilty came as no great surprise to Konrad, as he knew that the evidence against him was strong, although he had hoped that, during the interviews, he had given a plausible explanation to cover the events at the Dickson house. Furthermore, given the fact that he had spoken to both Cecily and Maggie at the BX club, the fingerprints found on their bags could be explained away by his having made innocent contact with the relevant items. It was the German evidence that had made the crucial difference.

Konrad's barrister, Trevalyon, despite his own misgivings and representing his client on the basis that he was an innocent man, had told him that he should be honest and open with those representing him and that anything other than total frankness would not help them to mount a defence to the charges. But Konrad was a victim of his own arrogance. It transpired that he would provide his barrister with only limited information and he would suffer the consequences.

The sentence for murder was fixed by law and he had no grounds for appeal against his conviction. The authorities wasted no time in despatching him.

Two months later, Alby and Linda celebrated their engagement with a party that was held in the barn at the Cooper family home on Mersea Island. It was a lively event which was attended by both family and friends, including members of the CID and the Women's team and their partners. Young Tom Rogers had managed to persuade Enid Johnson to accompany him on what would be their first date. Anticipating that there would be a fair amount of alcohol on offer, the two teams pooled their resources and wisely arranged for a coach to take them to and from the Island. During the evening, while the guests were still sober enough to receive it, Tom Stockwell gave a rousing speech in which, to the embarrassment of Alby and Linda, he praised them for their efforts and listed their qualities. He then proposed a toast to the happy couple.

The officers involved in the investigation and ultimate arrest of the "Beast of Bocking," received a Chief Constable's Commendation for their devotion to duty and detective ability. They were already elated without this, but it put an extra spring in the step of the members of both teams, whose morale was at an all-time high. They were ready for their next challenge.

Matador

For exclusive discounts on Matador titles,
sign up to our occasional newsletter at
troubador.co.uk/bookshop